S0-ADB-797

THE BELOVED SON

THE BELOVED SON

A NOVEL

JAY QUINN

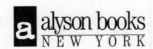

alyson books
NEW YORK

© 2007 BY JAY QUINN.
ALL RIGHTS RESERVED.

MANUFACTURED IN THE UNITED STATES OF AMERICA

THIS TRADE PAPERBACK ORIGINAL IS PUBLISHED BY
ALYSON BOOKS
245 WEST 17TH STREET
NEW YORK, NEW YORK 10011

DISTRIBUTION IN THE UNITED KINGDOM BY
TURNAROUND PUBLISHER SERVICES LTD.
UNIT 3, OLYMPIA TRADING ESTATE
COBURG ROAD, WOOD GREEN
LONDON N22 6TZ ENGLAND

FIRST HARDCOVER EDITION: JUNE 2007
FIRST PAPERBACK EDITION: MAY 2008

08 09 10 11 12 a 10 9 8 7 6 5 4 3 2 1

ISBN-10: 1-59350-054-8
ISBN-13: 978-1-59350-054-2

LIBRARY OF CONGRESS CATALOGING-IN-PUBLICATION DATA ARE ON FILE

COVER DESIGN BY VICTOR MINGOVITS

Dedication

For Jeffrey Auchter, the love and light of my life.

Acknowledgments

I'd like to thank my editor at Alyson Books, Joe Pittman, for his insight, commitment, and phenomenal patience.

As always, this book could not have been finished without the comments and encouragement of my first readers, Susan Highsmith and Joe Riddick. I must also thank Harold and Mary Parks, the Auchter family, Nathaniel Keller, M.D., and my constant companions: Patsy and Hailey.

THURSDAY

THURSDAY

FOR CONCRETE PROBLEMS, Karl Preston always had an elegant solution. He often woke, as he did this morning, with an idea or a theoretical answer presented as a clear gift from his subconscious. The clock at his beside read just after four, nearly thirty minutes ahead of the alarm and a full hour and a half earlier than usual. But today, Thursday, was not a typical day. His second thoughts veered toward the morning's itinerary, but he didn't want to lose the thread of the clever idea he'd had initially. There was nothing to do but rise quietly and find a way to hold that idea, to seal it against the demands that would come with today's trip. It was Karl's belief, based on experience, that the golden moments of inspiration shouldn't be set behind the quotidian aspects of forging ahead through the day.

He reached from under the warm covers and shut off the clock's alarm before it would chime and disturb Caroline, asleep beside him. Karl shifted and rose as gently as he could, though he was still beset by a spinning head rush on rising. He swayed unsteadily on his feet for only a few seconds before his view of the darkened room stopped spinning. He paid it no mind, assigning it to that list of middle-age tics to which he'd fallen heir. Once he was solid on his feet, he spared a lingering look at his beloved Caro to make sure she was still safely cocooned in sleep. Satisfied she was sleeping peacefully, he walked the length of the bedroom, pulled back the shutters from the windows, and looked out onto the street below. In the unnatural yellow of the streetlights' glow, he found his glasses on the desk between the windows. Conveniently, they rested on a legal pad with a mechanical pencil nearby. Karl was intimate with the experience of rising, being fully awakened by some bright possibility. It happened so frequently that he kept the pad and pencil safely near the window's meager light, ever ready for him to don his glasses and scribble away until he was satisfied he'd captured the essence of the answer that had eluded him during the business of the day.

He slipped on his glasses, quickly dashed off some notes, then made an effortless sketch of the idea. It was not particularly artful, but Karl was not an artist. Nor was it elaborate. Long ago, one of his favorite seniors at the engineering firm he'd started with had cautioned him to remember the difference between building a watch and a winch. Sometimes the brute efficiency of a winch worked perfectly well where the tiny, intricate details of watchmaking were overwrought and obfuscating. Now, whether his thoughts were captivated by a bridge design or roadway routes, he recalled the metaphor. Karl felt so much time and effort was wasted by the inefficiencies of Baroque design solutions when something gestural and economic in thought would work twice as well.

Now a senior partner himself, Karl had deservedly earned a reputation as somewhat of a creative genius by designing practical, beautiful structures. It was a talent much admired by both the other partners and the bean counters at his firm, especially when the crudity and quick, unsubtle excesses of the CADCAM designers cost time and money. To Karl's mind, the computer-aided drafting systems of his juniors allowed them either to wallow in excess or to settle too quickly for a poorly thought out solution. In all things, Karl was studied and thoughtful.

Karl glanced at his thoughts committed to paper. He was certain now that he could refine the sketch after he'd had some coffee, then quickly scan and email it to his office before he left for the airport. Replacing the pencil and pad on the desk, he looked again out the window, and the view pleased him. His home, a new four-story town house, sat at the end of the block, the last of a row of town houses to his left. Across the street, its mirror image rested serenely in the predawn stillness of Cary, North Carolina. The intersection to his right was a clean break before the march of identical, fine town houses began again on the other side.

It was a safe, prosperous setting. Karl's neighborhood had been conceived, designed, and built so. This newer part of Cary's unending sprawl had the sheen of newness still on it, though it was nearly a year since its completion. The neo-Georgian street façade harbored behind it a community of quiet professionals who, contrary to the popular myth of the southern city, were neither effusive nor loudly friendly. It was a very reserved place, and for what it cost it should be so, in Karl's opinion. He and Caroline had happily agreed to invest here for convenience and privacy, as their old home had maxed out its value potential, and simultaneously the neighborhood had begun to sprout bright plastic toys and SUVs that filled drives and spilled onto lawns.

Karl and Caroline were well beyond that stage in their lives. Their daughter, Melanie, had completed her master's degree in art history and was with them now only as a short-term arrangement. Inevitably, her life would continue on somewhere else at the end of her stopgap job teaching an art history seminar at a local women's college. That was her whole purpose in accepting the lectureship, actually: it was meant to give her the time and income to find something more permanent and challenging.

Karl and Caroline didn't think they could bear, as they entered their golden years, living through another generation of toddlers and elementary school kids growing to become obstreperous teenagers. There was no question they'd remain in North Carolina's Research Triangle area, as neither one of them had any intention of retiring early or moving to a more elder-friendly region or city. The thought of joining his parents and brother in southern Florida was not appealing to Karl, and Caroline had no intention of moving to the desolate eastern North Carolina town of her childhood. Affluent, dignified, and convenient, Cary suited them quite well.

As Karl admired the regularity and symmetry of his view, a young woman walking a very large dog made her way hurriedly down the street on the other side of the intersection. While the animal more pulled her along than allowed her to stroll, Karl noticed she kept glancing over her shoulder and then quickened her pace as she came his way. She was dressed oddly. She had thrown a long coat over what appeared to be an oversized T-shirt or a short nightgown, without the benefit of either belting or buttoning the coat. Her legs flashed somewhat obscenely as she half walked, half stumbled along. Even in the chill, she was barefooted on the sidewalk.

As Karl watched her dispassionately and considered the inappropriateness of her dress, a younger man came into view, jogging determinedly toward the young woman. As he gained on her, Karl noted that he wore a pair of jeans, no shirt, and a pair of sneakers. He saw rather than heard the young man call out to her. She'd crossed the street and was directly below Karl's window on the opposite side of the street when she stopped, reined in her dog, then turned and gave the young man following her an eloquent middle finger. The young man replied something, and though his words were unintelligible, Karl could hear his pleading tone. Promptly, the young woman replied, "Get the hell away from me," quite loudly.

Karl stepped back from the window, suddenly aware he was dressed only in a pair of flannel boxer shorts. He was certain the young woman wasn't in any danger; she had a forbidding mouth and the dog, after all, but he was reluctant to turn away and head into the bath for his shower until he witnessed the completion of the little scene that had seriously compromised his morning's satisfaction with his view and neighborhood.

The young man stumbled on the curb as he neared the woman, who was waiting for him now, and she lifted her face and laughed.

In the harsh yellow streetlight, Karl realized she wasn't as young as he'd supposed; in fact, she was nearer to his age than to the young man's. As the guy, not really much older than a teenager, collected himself, the woman shouted, "I'm sick of you, Sean. You need to go home, pack your shit, and get out. You've been my responsibility long enough and I've had it. *Grow up!*"

"Aw, Mom . . . can't we talk about this back home? Look at us. We look like an episode of *COPS* out here. I said I was sorry. Jeez."

For a moment, the woman paused and looked around. Suddenly aware of her deshabille, she used her free hand to gather her coat tighter around her and shook her head in disgust. Without another word, she steered the hulk of a dog around and walked with renewed dignity back in the direction she had come. The hapless Sean followed along well behind.

Karl was amused but also somewhat wearied by the exchange. He was very uncomfortable with unseemly emotional outbursts—a gift of his Swedish mother's restraint.

"What was that all about?" Caroline asked distinctly in the room's quiet.

"Did they wake you?" Karl answered gently.

"No, actually it was your burst of imagination. I've been awake for a while now," she replied as she threw back the covers and stretched.

"I'm sorry, Caro. Was I very noisy?"

Caroline chuckled. "Not at all. After all these years I know the morning muse won't be denied. I was just on my way back to the most wonderful dream, and then I heard all that noise outside. Who on earth was it?"

It was Karl's turn to chuckle. "I believe the correct term is 'white trash.'"

Caroline drew up into a fetal position and yawned. "White trash? On Belgravia Street?"

Karl made his way to her side of the bed and stroked her hair. "Ah, just remember this is Cary, not London. I believe the quote goes something like, 'The white trash you shall have with you always.'"

Caroline reached to take his hand and squeezed it. "I think the quote actually goes, 'The *poor* ye shall have with you always.' What time is it?"

"Only half past four. Nowhere near time for you to get up."

"I could make you coffee."

Karl leaned down to kiss her and said, "No, you rest a little longer. I'll start coffee. Then I'll email this idea off to Barry at the office and take a shower. When I'm done, we'll go down together." The smell of her, still sweet from the day before, was undercut by the scent of a night of sweat that was particularly feminine and appealing. Caroline was menopausal, and Karl sympathetically believed her body's internal thermometer was as erratic as the stock market.

"Please. I want to spend some time with you before you take off this morning," Caroline mumbled.

"Sleep some more, darling. There's plenty of time."

In reply, Caroline smiled with her eyes already closed.

Feeling the chill, Karl pulled on the sweatshirt he'd worn the night before, then drew the bedcovers over Caroline's drowsy form before he stepped into the bathroom and closed the door quietly behind him. He was amused to find himself definitely, but not committedly, aroused. Rather than fight the hesitation and false starts his prostate and semierection would impose on a good, long pee, he simply sat down on the toilet to relieve himself, telling himself vainly that it was only to keep from interfering with Caroline's sleep once again.

Postponing the trip downstairs to make coffee, he regarded himself in the mirror after he finished. Though he had his father's dark hair, his facial hair's growth patterns displayed his mother's genes: his day-old beard was darkest over his upper lip, beside his mouth, and over his chin. This gave him the look of a dog with a dark, friendly muzzle. For a moment he contemplated just letting it go for a couple of days, for God's sake. Facial hair styles were all the rage with the young men in his office.

At fifty-two, he was well beyond trendy facial hair, but the thought of it made him feel as manly and suddenly virile as his semi-erection and trim waist had done earlier. Karl remained a dedicated swimmer, even these days, when work tried its best to intrude and the will to make his way to the health club flagged. Still, it was a sense of ingrained duty rather than vanity that kept him from giving up and letting himself go long after his contemporaries had resigned themselves to respectable guts and prosperous jowls. At his mother's insistence, and with his father's stern support, Karl had been swimming daily since he was four years old. Forty-eight years later, he could not erase that parental programming.

He gave himself a smile in the mirror and suppressed his urge to go out scruffy with a proper shave from his electric razor. The rest of his ablutions he decided to leave until after he sent his marvelous idea off to Barry and had some good, strong coffee.

As quietly as he could, he retrieved his pencil and legal pad from the bedroom, and then found his way in the dark to the kitchen on the floor below. On his way down he noted the staircase already had a signature squeak, and he smiled to himself when he heard it. Though he and Caroline had been in residence for not quite a year, he was pleased that his familiarity with their new home had grown to the point that he could navigate it in the dark, with its peculiar sounds guiding him along.

In the kitchen, Karl turned on the lights first and the radio second, beginning the morning routine that he loved. He listened to the last of public radio's late-night programming give way to the morning's NPR news while he fed water and ground coffee to the expensive coffeemaker Melanie had presented to her parents on her return home from Europe the summer before. Fresh from her immersion in French and Italian culture, she'd insisted Karl and Caroline needed a decent cup of coffee in the mornings and throughout the day as they wished. The efficient machine boasted a stainless-steel carafe for pots of coffee as well as separate espresso and milk-steaming tubes, nozzles, and attachments. The gift and the thought pleased Karl immensely.

With the coffeemaker wheezing and steaming, Karl settled himself at the table with his pad and pencil before him. Reaching a hand under his glasses, he lifted the frames from the bridge of his nose with one finger and rubbed the sleep from his eyes with another. Unbidden, the sight of the improbable mother and son's little drama out on the sidewalk came to mind. Karl supposed other people took such family dramas in stride, but to him they seemed untidy and unseemly. He could no more imagine himself and Melanie half dressed and loudly yelling out in the predawn street than he could picture himself wandering around with a trendy unshaven face.

Karl didn't like problems without rational, solid solutions. Emotional problems were exactly that. He didn't come from a family that loudly argued, or left festering things unsaid only to erupt with ugly recriminations later on. Karl dropped his hand from his face and stared with newly clear eyes through his kitchen window to the still-sleeping backs of the town houses across the narrow yards. He had to admit that his aversion to family woes was exactly why he felt a thin skin of dread spread over this trip south to see his parents and his brother.

There had been something unexpectedly needy in his father's usually imperious tone when he had called the previous week. His father hadn't wheedled or tried to make him feel guilty about not visiting over Christmas—that wasn't it. On the whole, he had been his usual self, firmly suggesting that Karl, along with Caroline and Melanie, needed to come for a visit as soon as possible.

It was the taut "as soon as possible" that needled Karl. His father didn't elaborate on his reasons for the urgent request for a visit, and

Karl didn't ask. The inference was as evocative as the sketch Karl had done of his waking idea, now lying before him on the kitchen table. Karl sensed with dread that there was something much less concrete, more *emotional* behind this visit.

In that understanding, Karl was much like his father. There had never been a need for anything unsaid, but fraught with meaning, between the two of them. Both engineers, neither of them were inclined toward large pronouncements when it came to things closest to their hearts. They understood each other implicitly.

With his morning coffee streaming into its efficient carafe, Karl neatly put his unspoken fears aside. He filed them one by one as he considered all the awful things that might have raised his father's request for this visit. There were few things that weren't possible, as both of his parents were nearly eighty. Then there was his brother, Sven. Karl wouldn't allow himself any conjecture of problems that might have anything to do with Sven. Though his brother seemed fairly steady, Karl knew he was gay, and that context was terra incognita as far as Karl was concerned. Guiltily, he admitted to himself that he didn't know Sven, who was twelve years younger, all that well. He had lost interest in Sven at roughly the same time he himself had left for college, and that certainly was a long time ago. Though he had no reason to suspect Sven was anything other than the stolid, blond Swede he appeared to be, still Karl equated "gay" with emotionalism, and a certain louche emotionalism at that. As for the state of his brother's emotional life, he didn't know and he didn't really want to know. There was a partner of some years named Rob attached to Sven, but Karl's dealings with that man were limited to pleasant, infrequent holiday dinners. Karl assumed that Rob and Sven were happy and stable. His relationship with his brother didn't include the ease or intimacy that would allow any confidences to the contrary. Still, Karl dreaded the time when Sven might burden him with details of his emotional life and the peculiarities of his relationship, which Karl projected out of his cursory knowledge of gay life.

Despite his indefinable qualms, Karl had heard his father's barely spoken urgency and had acted on it immediately. He proposed the trip to Caroline and Melanie. Not used to such demands from either Karl or his father, both hastily arranged their schedules to fly out the following weekend, as had Karl. There were problems getting a flight together, so Karl volunteered to go on Thursday, leaving Melanie and Caroline to travel the next day. His wife and daughter were treating it as something of a lark, an unexpected pleasure and anticipation of warmth in the late winter. In fact, both of them seemed to be looking forward to the trip to Boca Raton a great deal. Karl kept his reservations to himself. When he'd called his father back two days later to give him the news that they all three would be down the following week, Karl had been surprised to hear both relief and gratitude in his father's voice.

"Coffee smells good," Melanie said as she broke her father's reverie at the kitchen table.

Karl offered her a genuine smile in return, then said, "What are you doing up so early?" He took in her fresh face and trim form dressed in a sweatshirt identical to his own over a pair of outsized boxer shorts. The boxer shorts called to mind Melanie's boyfriend, whom he didn't really want to think about just now.

"I have tests to grade before I can take off tomorrow," Melanie replied as she walked to the coffeemaker. She peered into the spout to make sure the coffee wasn't still running into the carafe. "I should have my head examined for giving them an essay question after the slide identification part of the test."

Karl watched as she took a pair of mugs from the cabinet over the coffeemaker and then retrieved the carton of half-and-half from the refrigerator. "What was the essay question?"

Melanie poured coffee for each of them, doctoring it with cream and packets of calorie-free sweetener. She took a sip of her own and turned back to face her father. "Mmmmm, that's good." Sleepily, she regarded her father's questioning gaze and nodded. "Oh, the question." Taking the other mug, she walked to the table, carefully placed Karl's coffee by his right hand, and sat opposite him. "Discuss the role of light in art between the Sumerian era and the Roman Empire." She smoothed her honey-colored hair back from her forehead, shook it, and gave her father a smile. "That probably threw them for a loop."

Karl laughed. He had always admired his daughter, never more than when her self-assurance and intelligence trumped her good looks.

"Seriously, Dad, the girls in the class need to know the course is about more than memorizing slides of the Venus of Willendorf or the Pyramid of Cheops. Though they resist it, they have to learn to think."

"No doubt they know now," Karl replied dryly, and took a sip of his own coffee. He smiled in satisfaction; she had made it exactly the way he liked. "You sound like your mother in the way you challenge your students." Caroline had retired early from an academic career, tired of university departmental politics and the relentless call to publish. Now she worked part-time as an English instructor for senior students at an affluent local private school, where she was improbably and wildly popular for her insistence that students read contemporary novels along with the typical high school canon.

"I should hope to be as good as she is, though I don't really love the teaching. So are you working this early?" Melanie asked as she turned the sketch on his legal pad to face her.

"Always."

Melanie studied the sketch and read the notes, then slid the pad back to face her father. "It never ceases to amaze me how you can make so little say so much."

"Do you know what you're looking at?" Karl asked with a smile.

"Not really. But I get the gist of it. Besides, the sketch is really for you, isn't it?" Melanie replied as she took up her own mug once more.

"Well, it will be for my drafter as well, so I'd better polish it up some before I shoot it off to him." Something in the sketch caught his eye. He added a few strokes to the drawing, then a few words to the notes. Satisfied, he allowed himself another sip of coffee.

"Dad, do you have any idea why Grandpa Frank wants us to tear down there to see them in such a hurry?"

Karl raised his eyes to meet his daughter's question. His earlier concentration was scattered now, and the sketch would have to wait until he could take it into his office to refine. "I don't think it's anything dire or he would have said so," he answered.

"I suppose you're right," Melanie said. "I thought he might just be feeling particularly dictatorial since we couldn't make it down for Christmas this year."

Karl hesitated before replying. "I don't think so, Mel."

"Well, I really couldn't help it. I had to get Drew settled in Manhattan, and if I'd left the details up to him, we'd be living in either a place we totally couldn't afford or a place I'd skeeve in when I move up there."

This was not a happy topic for Karl. He knew Melanie had job applications in for several positions at museums and auction houses all over Manhattan, but he didn't relish the thought of her living with Andrew Rigg, her boyfriend of five years. It wasn't that he disliked Drew, who was nice enough for the most part, though Karl suspected he was a bit too rich for his own good. Things seemed to come very easily to Drew, without the benefit of any real work on his part. Though that rankled Karl, he was loath to admit he still had some trouble with the thought of Melanie as an adult, especially in Manhattan.

"And, for once, it was nice for you and Mom to have the holiday to yourselves at home, without spending it in an airport," Melanie concluded.

"I don't disagree, sweetheart. But I don't think that's what's got into your grandfather," Karl answered sincerely.

"I don't know, then. I think he and Grandmere must just be lonely. In any event, I'm glad we're going. I've missed Uncle Sven."

Karl smiled. "You think your Uncle Sven will take you shopping."

Melanie gave him a sly smile in reply.

"Come now, Mel. Aren't you a little old to be so spoiled?"

Melanie laughed. "Never. Besides, if he doesn't take me shopping, I'll have just as much fun staying at his place."

Karl gave her a puzzled look.

"That's right . . . you've never been to his house, have you? Shame on you. He's lived there for nearly eight years."

"There's just never been time. Our trips down have been so quick. It's on the beach, right?" Karl answered defensively.

"No, not on the beach, but it is just a short walk away. It's heaven. It'll be good to see Uncle Rob, too . . ." Melanie suddenly stood and cocked her head. When Karl started to speak, she held up a hand and then pointed it toward the radio.

Karl listened as the news from Iraq was intoned with a brisk efficiency that belied the story of another car bomb and the number of dead.

As the report concluded, Melanie gave him a pointed look. "I wonder if your president or his sainted mother cares to have this news presented to their 'beautiful mind' today. After all, body counts are sort of beside the point in this little war, aren't they?"

Karl sighed. In a way, he welcomed the idea of Melanie moving to Manhattan if it meant he wouldn't need to continually defend his vote in the last election for the next three years. He held up his hands in surrender, though his pride demanded he respond. "It is hard to continue either an unwinnable war or argument, Mel. It's too early in the morning to have this discussion again. I suggest you take your views on the president and this war to your grandfather. I'm sure he can give you a run for your money, but I'm worn out by it, okay?"

Melanie visibly relaxed. "I'm sorry, Dad. It's just very real to me. I have a visceral disgust for the man and his sycophants. He doesn't even read, for God's sake; he relies on *them* to give him his news. He's like a child; he wants to be told only what he wants to hear." She shook her head as if to rid herself of an extremely unpleasant thought, then smiled. "Are you first in line for shower time?"

"Does it matter? You have your own bath," Karl replied evenly, again refusing to rise to the bait.

"I know. It just runs cold if two people are showering at once," Melanie said as she took both their mugs to the counter for a heat-up.

"You go ahead. I have to get this sketch off and then I'll get ready for the day," Karl answered.

"What time is your flight?" Melanie asked agreeably.

"Not until nine, but I want to be at the airport by seven-thirty. I have no idea how long it will take to get through security," Karl said.

Melanie nodded. He watched as she freshened their coffee, but his eyes were already back on his sketch, with his pencil in hand by the time she returned to the table, set his mug within reach, and kissed the top of his head. Absently, he patted her hand as she left to go to her room downstairs. Karl studied the sketch and notes for a few minutes more, then tore the sheet from the pad. His pencil raced on a clean sheet as he refined the sketch and his notes, ignoring his coffee.

At last satisfied, he left the table and walked into his office. The sky was gray now, betraying dawn and emphasizing the need for him to move along with his day. He quickly scanned the sheet of paper into a digital format, then attached it to an email to Barry, who would absorb and disseminate it. When the email was launched, he allowed himself a small smile. This one sketch, which had come to him so effortlessly, would see out his two days away from the office as his staff incorporated the ideas into the bits and bytes of a proper drawing on their computers. By the time he arrived back in the office on Monday morning, he knew, some meaningful progress would have been made on the project.

Karl checked his email and deleted messages he didn't recognize by subject or sender, and then he switched to the airline's Web site to check his flight and print his boarding pass. That chore accomplished, he gave himself a moment to relax and look out his office window. The morning light had begun to seep into his street, leaving it no less beautiful but somehow more impersonal than it had been under the lambent streetlights' glow. He missed the privacy of the predawn morning. Even Melanie, in a familiar loving way, had been an intrusion.

Karl allowed himself a smile at her eagerness to see his brother. Sven had never let the polite distance from his brother come between him and Melanie. During the time she was growing up, there were gifts and cards on all the great events of the child's calendar. At Caroline's insistence, Melanie had been allowed to fly down to visit her Uncle Sven for entire weeks during the summer or for spring break. Visits with her grandparents were entirely tangential. Karl marveled at their closeness and happily accepted it as the child's due. After all, she was the only niece and the only grandchild, and her fan club in southern Florida was a reflection on Karl himself, at least as far as he was concerned. He and Caroline had never been selfish with their child. She functioned as a presence in his family's lives by her own right and not merely in loco parentis.

Now that Melanie was a grown woman, he was pleased she had

a sense of family and continuity. His brother and mother spoke to her in Swedish in the same way one speaks to a small child, and Melanie obliged with a small child's command of Swedish. As she grew older and her education expanded, she conversed with her grandmother in French, which delighted her French-educated grandmother to no end. In the midst of so much open admiration, Melanie was not spoiled. Again, that must have been a gift of the family's natural reserve.

Caroline's family was much different. They had a familiarity with each other that bordered on intrusiveness, in Karl's opinion. They were, as he put it, "wooly"—they concerned themselves with each other's business in a way that Karl felt was entirely inappropriate. Caroline was indulgent with them but always seemed to be more comfortable with the way Karl related to family. Melanie saw family relationships in much the same way her parents did: close enough for comfort but far enough not to encourage overinvolvement in petty details.

From the kitchen, the soft clatter of dishes and the scent of sausage and eggs stole into his office. Karl looked at the clock on his computer; it was nearing six o'clock, and he had only an hour to go before he had to leave for the airport. He reluctantly shut down his computer. Now, with leaving so close and the inevitable hassles at airport check-in and security to go, he wished he could simply stay home. More than anything, he'd prefer to spend the weekend alone with his own family here in this town house in Cary. Caroline often teasingly mocked him for being such a creature of habit, but it was a quirk she shared as well. As a couple, they had long fell into their domestic rewards and rituals. Weekends were as orderly in their eagerly anticipated pleasures as their lives were regular and satisfying. It was not in their natures to blast away for the weekend. The rest of the world held little allure for them. Now, with the trip upon him, Karl resigned himself to it and made his way back to the kitchen.

Caroline stood at the counter, fishing two croissants from a plastic bag. Dressed in a white sweater with a pattern Karl always associated with L.L.Bean and a pair of jeans tight on her small hips, and with her short hair tousled from sleep, she reminded him of a young boy. The thought of it didn't give Karl any pause. Caroline had never been a voluptuous woman, but she had all her curves where Karl loved them most. He sidled up to her and, putting his arm around her waist, gave her neck a companionable nuzzle. Caroline rewarded him with a smile and an unembarrassed giggle when he allowed his hand to slide from her waist to give her ass a tentative squeeze.

"If you don't watch yourself, buster, you'll miss your flight," she said.

"That might not be such a bad thing," he said, and reluctantly left her to take his place at the table.

"Oh? And why is that?" she asked as she made her way to the table with their breakfast and an orange to share.

Karl took his plate as she sat down and sighed. "Oh, no reason, really. It's just that I can't shake the feeling there's some larger reason for us to drop everything and fly down so suddenly," Karl said and reached for the butter.

Caroline broke her croissant in two and took a tentative bite of a half without butter or jam. She chewed thoughtfully for a moment and then said, "Don't assume there's trouble, Karl. Older people get more demanding and petulant as they age."

Karl gave her a look as he wolfed down his croissant and wiped his hands on his napkin. Satisfied for the moment, he left his sausage and eggs for a bit. "I know that neither my father nor I can ever imagine him being 'petulant.'"

Caroline took a sip of her coffee and then said, "Do you think it's something grave?"

Karl shook his head. "It's just this notion of stepping into something I'm not ready for . . . having something sprung on me and not knowing how to react."

"I see." Caroline picked up the orange and scored it carefully with a sharp knife. "You shouldn't be so anxious. You're just afraid it will be something *untidy*."

Karl gave her a sharp look in reply.

Exasperated, Caroline said, "Oh, Karl, for God's sake, don't be so fastidious or act so affronted. You and I both know that what you're really saying is you're happy with the status quo and you don't really relish the thought of your father or mother being particularly needy."

Karl watched as she peeled away the skin of the orange in neat segments. "I don't do needy very well—I admit it," he said.

Caroline smiled forgivingly and presented him with half of the orange. "Eat your eggs; they'll be stone-cold in another minute or two."

Eager to leave the uncomfortable tack the conversation was taking, Karl obeyed, eating the sausage and eggs with a real appetite. Caroline placed the uneaten half of her croissant on his plate and left the table momentarily. She returned with an opened bar of dark chocolate and the carafe of coffee. Once she'd reclaimed her seat, she poured hot coffee in both their cups and broke off three squares of her treat.

"Chocolate for breakfast?" Karl scolded.

"It's heavenly with the orange. You should try it sometime," Caroline responded, nonplussed. It was a taste she'd acquired when they'd visited Melanie in Tuscany the summer before. The friendly smell of the orange brought the trip back to Karl in a flood of happy memories.

Despite the happy association of oranges and chocolate, Karl grunted. "If I did, I'd be eating antacids all morning."

"It's a menopause thing," Caroline admitted.

Karl noted the dampness across her forehead and over her upper lip. Wordlessly, he folded his napkin to the clean side and, reaching across the table, gently wiped his wife's brow.

"Thank you," Caroline murmured. "It's hot as four hells in here this morning."

Karl gave her a sympathetic smile and said, "Melanie is certainly looking forward to the trip. I hope Sven is ready for the niece from hell."

"I'm looking forward to seeing Sven myself," Caroline admitted. "I'd love to go rummaging in that shop of his. I'd really like something striking and Swedish for my office."

Karl had to stop himself from rolling his eyes. After nearly a year, the spare bedroom Caroline had designated as her office was still a collection of boxes on the hardwood floor in a room painted builder's white. Meanwhile, her papers and books cluttered the dining room, with its table doubling as her desk. Actually, he dreaded the time when she would commit herself to a "look," knowing full well it would mean a weekend of painting and an unexpected drain on their checking account, ultimately to no avail. As orderly as her mind was, Caroline was an inveterate slob when it came to her professional bits and bobs.

"I'd love some of your mother's things," Caroline said wistfully. "If I only had that lovely modern desk of hers, I'd be so much more organized."

"You mean like she is?" Karl countered.

Caroline sighed. "Yes. She always has things so together."

"That's the benefit of six years of being knocked about by French nuns," Karl said dryly.

Caroline took a small bite of a square of chocolate, obviously enjoying it a great deal. "Maybe that's my problem." She sighed. "I'm a product of the public schools."

Karl laughed as he stood and collected Caroline's plate along

with his own. He took them to the sink and rinsed them before placing them in the dishwasher. "I need to get showered and dressed,"
he said, interrupting Caroline's apparent reverie of convent-inspired
spare organization and efficiency.

"You're all packed, right?" she replied.

"I'll just need to drop in my dop kit once I'm dressed," Karl
said.

"I hope you remembered to pack your Tevas. There's nothing more
absurd than a middle-aged man dressed in a bathing suit with black
socks and dress shoes," Caroline said as she carefully folded the foil
cover over the remains of her chocolate bar.

"Oh, for God's sake, Caro. Give me some credit. I lived in Florida
for years. I'm not such a dweeb, am I?" Karl responded irritably.

Caroline walked to him with a smile. She placed her chocolate
on the counter and put her arms over his shoulders. "Did you pack
your bathing suit?"

Karl sighed. "Yes. But only because I knew you'd badger me if
I didn't." He shuddered. "Mom and Dad's pool must be only fifty
degrees this time of year. It's hardly August, even if it is forty degrees
warmer down there."

Caroline leaned back to get a look at his face. "Still, after all these
years, I like the look of you in a bathing suit, you know that?"

Karl chuckled. "Any excuse then, right?"

Caroline gave him a brief hug, and he awkwardly returned the
embrace with a single arm across her shoulders. "Karl?" she asked,
and stepped away.

"Yes?" he said, letting her go reluctantly.

"You'll try not to be so 'at arm's length' with them, right? I mean,
they are getting older, and we have no idea what their needs are,"
Caroline said thoughtfully. "Your parents aren't exactly forthcoming, but they must miss you. I'm sure they need you in a greater way
these days."

Karl sighed. "Look. I promise I'll let you be the intuitive one. If you pick up on something I'm missing, stomp my foot under the table or something. I'll admit I'm not very good with the *feelings* stuff, but I don't want to appear to be uncaring."

Caroline smiled and nodded. "Now, what are you planning to wear? The radio just said it's twenty-eight degrees outside, but it'll be a lot warmer once you get there."

"Woman, I'm not five. I think I can dress myself," Karl huffed.

Caroline laughed lovingly as he made his way out of the kitchen and on upstairs.

2

LATER, DRESSED ONLY in a bulky cotton sweater over a polo shirt, jeans, and sneakers in anticipation of the southern Florida warmth waiting to greet him, a chilly Karl watched Caroline drive away from the departure curb at RDU. Karl fought off a sense of wistfulness at their hurried good-bye. Exaggerated farewells were hardly his style, but the memory of 9/11 tinged his thoughts with foreboding, especially now, with his wife and daughter taking a separate flight. Determinedly, he left off gazing at the car making its way through traffic away from him and headed inside to experience for himself that other result of 9/11: the line through security. With his boarding pass in hand, he tugged at his rolling carry-on suitcase and made his way inside.

The cattle stalls through security were crowded, even at the beginning of this business day. His fellow passengers included no small number of parents with children and young people among the business travelers. Karl fished his passport from his back pocket and patiently took his place in line. Try as he might, he couldn't screen out the fragments of conversation and annoying cell phone calls all around him. Karl despised talking on his cell phone in public. He already felt soiled by the minutiae of strangers' lives sharply shouted into the little gizmos: someone was late and forgot the toaster oven was on; someone wanted Eric to email a file; someone decided Keisha was a bitch, while someone else pronounced Latrell a motherfucking dog. Karl hated adding the details of his own life to the miasma, though he knew he'd need to call Sven from the gate.

At last, he was next. He handed his passport and boarding pass to a disinterested overweight woman in a TSA uniform. With barely a glance, she scribbled something unintelligible on his boarding pass and curtly nodded for him to proceed to the tables and tubs before the x-ray machines. Karl hoisted his suitcase onto the table, pulled a gray tub from the stack, and placed it behind his suitcase. He quickly emptied his pockets into the tub and kicked off his shoes, placing them on top of his wallet, keys, and loose change. As the conveyor belt pulled the suitcase and tub into the maw of the x-ray machine, Karl stepped up to the metal-detecting gate and obediently waited for permission to pass.

The TSA man on the other side smiled at him genuinely and waved him through. When Karl successfully passed without a beep, the man reached for his passport and boarding pass and wished him a good morning.

"You're very cheerful today," Karl said amiably.

"Payday here and weekend's coming," the man answered with a smile.

His geniality was contagious. Karl found himself smiling in return.

"You go safe now, sir," the man said sincerely as he handed Karl his passport and boarding pass.

"You've actually made this pleasant," Karl commented.

The man laughed. "Just another service I offer. Bad enough to wait in line; might as well send you folks off with a smile."

"Thanks for that," Karl said genuinely.

The man nodded and moved to allow Karl to pass beyond him to the suitcase and tub waiting for him. Karl felt warmed by this touch of the personal as he plucked his shoes from the tub and dropped them to the floor. He awkwardly tried to step into them, but he succeeded only in squashing the heels under his half-inserted feet. Aware of the press behind him, he gathered his change and wallet, placed his suitcase back on the floor, and hobbled off to wait in line once more for a place to sit and comfortably fit his sneakers to his feet. Finally, a seat became available and Karl clumsily stepped to it and sat down.

"Ain't this a bitch?" an older woman examining a small run in her stockings said to Karl as he perched beside her.

Karl leaned forward to run a finger under his sneakers' bent backs and let out a small reserved laugh. "I suppose it's better to go through this than through a skyscraper."

The woman sighed and leaned forward to slip an uncomfortable-looking pair of heels over her stockinged feet. "Remember when it was a privilege and an event to fly? Remember when it was something you looked forward to?"

"Not so long ago, was it?" Karl answered carefully.

"Honey, I'm Advantage Platinum. One hundred and thirty thousand miles last year. I've seen the inside of enough planes to last the rest of my life, but there's three more years of this until I can cash out. How about you?" the woman asked briskly.

"I don't know if I'm going to ever get to cash out, but fortunately I love my job," Karl said and stood.

"Hartford," the woman said as she stood as well and stuck out her hand.

"West Palm," Karl replied and clasped her hand in a firm shake.

"Lucky," she replied, and let Karl's hand go. "Vacation?"

"Family."

"Think of me in the snow, will you?"

Karl smiled, and the woman smiled in return, then said, "Well . . . another day, another PowerPoint presentation." With that, she clasped the handle of her carry-on and turned resolutely toward her gate. As Karl watched her walk away, he thought about the companionability of the business world. From his looks, his age, and his studied air of nonchalance with the whole ordeal, the older woman had recognized in Karl a fellow air veteran—a fellow traveler heading for the gate of some reward that was approachable but still somehow out of reach. Karl felt more middle-aged than he had in a long time. It was not a particularly happy feeling. Most days he saw himself as he was at perhaps forty or so. Vital, loved, and respected, he never stopped to think of the air miles, the days that passed below as he soared from project to project, each a legitimate success bought by hard work and some inspiration.

The woman disappeared into the crowd and Karl turned himself toward his gate in the opposite direction. For a moment, he felt the sharp sting of the loss of all his individuality. He was just another traveler with a wait at the gate before him. It was an oddly depressing thought. As he made his way into the crowd and found a place in the flow of other travelers, he weaved through the baby strollers and rolling suitcases with the cold comfort that at least he was traveling to someplace warm, someplace where he would be welcomed with few expectations of him other than that he care about the people waiting for him there. He scolded himself for resenting his family for this trip out of his routine, for the demands they would subtly but undeniably make on his heart.

This resentment of his family was nothing new. Karl's sudden sensation of letdown at being recognized as one more anonymous middle-aged businessman in a crowd of other strangers in the airport was sharpened by the realization that it was, in some ways, exactly what he had always striven to be. The facts of his individuality among them wasn't anything he'd ever viewed with any pride, because those facts rested in his family's unique composition. While Karl's father was solidly American and middle-class, his mother was the daughter of a Swedish diplomat. After a childhood in Sweden, she had been educated from age twelve in a French convent school just outside Paris. She was a beautiful woman, but her ideas of child rearing and her exoticism in southern New Jersey and southern Florida had been an embarrassment to Karl while he was growing up. By the time his family moved to Boca Raton when he was twelve, he'd refused to speak either Swedish or French and had urged his mother to limit her cooking to things purely American. His mother had only laughed at the menu suggestions, but she had allowed him to slip away from the languages she'd spoken to him since infancy and from her rather strict form of Catholicism. She took his embarrassment over both her beauty and her strangeness in stride, allowing him the freedom to become as blandly American as apple pie and baseball. She was not so eager to surrender his brother, Sven, however, and as a result Karl tended to see Sven as an embarrassment as well. While these strains were never really discussed, what was not said was clearly understood. Karl ultimately moved away from his family and lived his life far away in North Carolina's Research Triangle area, a place eager to shed the distinctiveness of its past to embrace the modern and new.

At the gate, Karl noted with irritation that all the seats were taken exept those facing away from the door to the jetway. The crowd at the gate sprawled under the imposing overhead screens loudly tuned to CNN. Happily, there was no one waiting at the gate's ticket area but two agents working at their mysterious tasks with an animated air of authority. Impulsively, Karl decided he needed a treat. With some polite finagling and a little luck, he was able to purchase an upgrade to first class.

With professional warmth, the agent informed him they'd begin boarding in ten minutes. While Karl was grateful for the short wait-ing time, he also realized the immediate need to use his cell phone to check in with his brother. He made his way to the relative privacy of the concourse's edge, away from the waiting passengers. After he found his cell phone in the upper zippered pocket of his carry-on, he consulted his boarding pass for Sven's phone number, which he'd carefully copied in his office.

Sven answered cheerfully after only two rings.

"Good morning, Sven. Are you ready to pick up your old brother?" Karl asked jocularly, with a heartiness he'd had to search to find.

Sven laughed. "I'm looking forward to it! Is your flight on time?"

"Looks that way . . ." Karl hesitated, searching for something else to say. "I upgraded to first." He laughed. "This is starting to look like a vacation."

"You deserve it," Sven answered. "It's like a Trailways bus in the sky back in steerage." Silence hung heavily between them for a moment before Sven broke the quiet stretching in long radio waves between towers. "We're really looking forward to having you come home, Karl. Mom and Dad are really excited, and I'm just glad to have some time to visit with you."

Karl was taken aback by the genuine affection he heard in his brother's voice. "It . . . it'll be good to be home," he replied. "Will we get to see much of you?"

"I think so, Karl," Sven said and hesitated. "Mom isn't at her best; Dad thinks it would be better if you all stayed with me once Caroline and Melanie get here."

Karl noted the hesitation and a bit of anxiety in Sven's voice. "Is anything wrong with Mom? You say she's not at her best—what's wrong?"

"Nothing," Sven replied quickly. "She's, well, it's just that she gets all excited with a houseful of company and overdoes it. I think she'll enjoy the weekend a lot more if she doesn't have to worry about towels and linens and stuff like that. You see?"

"What about Dad?" Karl asked, not really put at ease by Sven's breezy reasoning.

"Oh, Dad's . . . well, Dad's the same. I mean, he feels great, good health, no need to worry about *him*. In fact, he's looking forward to having you all to himself tonight. He's made that really clear."

Karl winced. He knew his father had no compunctions about batting Sven away like a worrisome fly. He felt the sting of it on Sven's behalf. "Same old Dad, then."

Sven chuckled. "That and more. The irritable old bastard."

Karl laughed, relieved. "So you want to just pick me up downstairs by baggage claim?"

"Sounds good. About five after eleven then?"

"Yes. That ought to be just about perfect timing. I've only got a carry-on bag. I'm wearing a gray sweater and jeans," Karl said.

"Oh, I'll recognize you, big brother. It hasn't been that long. See you then."

"Alright."

"Fly safe, Karl. I love you," Sven answered happily.

Taken aback, Karl looked around him warily. "Ummm, yeah. That's back at you, as the kids say."

"Cool," he responded. "Bye," and he hung up.

Karl sighed and folded his phone and placed it back in the pocket of his carry-on. Zipping it shut, he glanced around. There was nothing to do now but get there.

On the plane, Karl accepted a drink—a screwdriver—something he almost never did in the morning. From his comfortable seat by a window in first class, he idly watched the unremarkable passing of clouds and soon drowsed into a satisfying sleep, only to wake with a start at some subconscious cue. Outside the window by his head, a USAir plane traveling north hurtled past close enough to register alarm. In all his years of flying, Karl couldn't remember seeing another plane pass so nearby. On the flight back from Italy earlier that year, there had been a companionable British Air 747 that had flown slightly below and at a measured distance from their wing for the entire trip over the Atlantic. It had been comforting having the other plane as a neighbor for the long trans-Atlantic trip. But seeing this plane so close by was wholly disconcerting.

Typically, there are few ways for passengers to gauge exactly how fast they are traveling in the air. The clouds, the crazy quilt of fields and roadways on the ground moved leisurely as you watched them. Karl knew the plane had to be doing nearly four hundred miles per hour, if not more. The distance covered and the rate calculated in his typically left-brain thinking assured him of the fact, but there was no sensation of speed, no sound other than the steady white noise of flight. There was no visceral *proof*, no gut feeling to warn you of the reality of blasting through the thin air thirty-three thousand feet above the ground. With the passing of the USAir flight in the opposite direction, Karl was, for the first time, aware of the speed he was traveling.

Earlier, in the airport, Karl had been startled by the ordinariness of his age and station in life. The experience of making his way through security, and the possibility of disaster it implied, had been a grim reminder that it all could suddenly end, violently suspended by a set of circumstances over which he had no control. Karl signaled the flight attendant and lifted his empty glass. The USAir flight's passing was a marvelous sensation, at once nauseating and thrilling, making the speed so vividly real to him. His life was moving faster than he had any sensation of or any real control over.

Karl accepted the new drink with a grateful smile and a slightly unsteady hand. It didn't occur to him then that everyone else's lives were traveling at the same unimaginable speed.

3

THE WARM BREEZE and the rough trunks of palm trees welcomed him home as he stepped onto the sidewalk outside the baggage claim doors. The Florida sun and the waving fronds overhead were hidden by the departure ramp above, but he felt his body relax with remembered fondness. Karl had not quite been a teenager when his father had decided to move south from New Jersey to Boca Raton. It had been a prescient move on his father's part: he would be in place and ready when IBM moved to Boca Raton years later, and would begin work that would ultimately take him from being an ordinary electrical engineer to being one of the men who midwifed the birth of the computer age.

Karl was nearly thirteen then and unaware of anything other than the fact that he found himself with a new life in the sun and a new baby brother. It was a memorable year and a memorable time as he found his feet on the unfamiliar shores of adolescence and brotherhood, all wrapped into one. Each was as strange and new to him as the orange trees growing in the backyard.

The warm, sleepy lump he'd held in his arms had become Sven, and his new life in Florida took him places he never dreamed he'd go. For years he experienced the kind of adolescence that the media portrayed as idyllic. While the Vietnam War raged on, Karl grew tanned and strong, swimming in the warm Atlantic and feeding his mind on the miracles of NASA. He never failed to reconnect with that notion of himself, that sense of life's exhilarating promise, when he returned to southern Florida. A sensation of raw newness washed over him every time he found himself back in Boca Raton.

Enjoying himself already, Karl scanned the oncoming cars, realizing he had neglected to ask Sven what he was driving these days. As swedephilic as Sven was, Karl imagined a SAAB or a Volvo, so he was surprised when a massive Ford Excursion stopped opposite him and Sven waved from inside before hopping out and racing around to greet him.

Sturdy and several inches shorter than Karl's six-two height, Sven hurtled toward him with the affectionate charge of a Labrador retriever puppy. His straight, ash-blond hair was choppily cut in an unfashionably long surfer style that looked as if he'd neglected the barber for over a year. It had natural highlights that alternated nearly white streaks with the darker blond below. With some surprise, it occurred to Karl that Caroline strove for the exact same hair color with expensive trips to the salon, with far less successful results. Sven grabbed Karl in an emphatic hug and looked up, beaming into his face. Effortlessly, Karl found himself returning the hug with enthusiasm. "Hey, kiddo," he said, a bit surprised by the catch in his throat.

"Hey bruvver," Sven mugged. "Let me get your bag."

"I'll get it," Karl insisted, so Sven shrugged and opened the back gate of the huge SUV. "My God. What on earth do you need such a beast of a vehicle for?" Karl demanded as he loaded his suitcase.

Sven heaved the back closed and watched as it settled into place with a satisfied whumph. "I have to haul furniture and stuff. All those Muffys and Biffs I work for like to see me drive up in something extravagant. If I showed up in Palm Beach with a panel truck, they'd be embarrassed for themselves and for me." Motioning Karl toward the passenger door, Sven said, "We've got to run a by the shop on the way to Mom and Dad's. It's out of the way, but I have to drop off some sample books I borrowed from Rob." With that, he bounded, heedless of traffic, around to the driver's side.

Once in the passenger's seat, Karl whistled. "This is a lot of leather for a delivery truck."

Sven shrugged, and hardly glancing over his shoulder, he merged the colossal SUV into the flow of traffic.

"You look good," Karl said approvingly, though he noted bluish circles under his brother's eyes.

"Thanks, so do you," Sven countered with a happy smile.

Karl wanted to take him into his lap and squeeze him. Sven was rare company. Karl had grudgingly changed his diapers and held on to his hand as he took toddler's steps. There was no one else on earth he had such a long and purely affectionate relationship with. While Karl cherished it, he also felt it was something of an artifact. Here was Sven, forty years old, and Karl wanted to hug him so tight he'd squirm and struggle to get down and toddle off.

Karl gave him a good, long look. Dressed in a navy long-sleeved T-shirt, cargo shorts, and leather flip-flops, he looked like an over-grown child. His haircut, slightly pug nose, and bright blue eyes did nothing to help. For a moment, Karl found himself disapproving of his brother. He also found himself disapproving of his own response to him. Surely it was nonsense that he'd want to pick up his forty-year-old brother and squeeze him.

"You could use a haircut," Karl offered as an expression of his sudden welling of affection for his brother and its companionable sense of disapproval.

Sven laughed and shook his hair, which caught the sunlight streaming in from the open sunroof. "Every other middle-aged gay man I know has his head nearly shaved these days. They say it takes attention away from the receding hairline. Well, I've still got a head full of hair, so I'm going to enjoy it while it lasts."

Karl pulled down the visor in front of him and glanced at his own short hair in the vanity mirror. Satisfied, he flicked the flap back up. "I think it looks distinguished," he said, of his own stylish short cut. "Besides, who said *you* were middle-aged? *I'm* middle-aged."

Sven spared a glance from the road. "You do look distinguished,

I have to say, big brother. But I'm afraid I am middle-aged. I turned forty last month. Dad's eighty in a couple of months, and believe me, Dad is getting old."

Mentally, Karl tried to remember if he'd sent Sven any birthday greetings. He hoped Caroline had thought to send at least a card. Sven unfailingly remembered to send him something for his birthday. Karl was somewhat less conscientious. He decided to let it pass.

To distract himself and Sven, he reached across the dash and turned up the volume to hear what was murmuring in the background. A woman's singsong voice spoke deliberately, followed by a male voice commanding, "Repeat." It was a conversational Swedish CD. Annoyed, Karl said, "Really, Sven. Is this an affectation or a necessity?"

Sven's smile faded and he looked across the generous span of the front seats with no small measure of hurt, then quickly shifted his gaze back to the road. "Do you remember, one time when I was little, you smacked the shit out of me when I spoke to you in Swedish in front of your friends?"

Karl did remember. At the time, Sven had been about five and Karl seventeen. He was embarrassed by having to explain to his friends why his brother spoke in such an odd way, and by the fact that he could, if he were willing, talk back to him in the same foreign language. It definitely set Karl apart, made him different at a time in his life when being different was unwanted. The other, darker, reason for the slap was a burst of resentment of their mother's insistence on speaking to Sven almost exclusively in Swedish, something that she had long since abandoned with Karl. Now, he was ashamed of the slap and saddened by Sven's long memory of it. He said nothing in reply, and his silence filled the car more loudly than the bland repetition on Swedish from the speakers.

After a while, Sven turned down the volume and broke the silence between them. "This 'affectation' earns me my living, Karl. I go on buying trips to Sweden on a regular basis."

Karl nodded, feeling somewhat chastened. Karl knew Sven's job took him to Sweden frequently. He guiltily reminded himself his brother would need the language at a more sophisticated level than his own childish command of it.

"As for being a necessity, well . . . I guess you'll see for yourself," Sven continued.

"What do you mean?" Karl asked guardedly.

Sven sighed and shook his head.

"C'mon Sven. Own up."

His brother spared a glance from the approach to I-95 and said, "It's Mom. She forgets sometimes. There are times when she only speaks Swedish. Other times she lapses into French."

Karl was startled by this information. "How long has this been going on?"

Sven shrugged, then his shoulders sagged. "Awhile now. Look, Dad will fill you in. I don't want to talk to you about it."

"I thought you said she was doing fine," Karl said accusingly.

"Healthwise, she is," Sven said. Beyond that, he would say nothing.

Somewhat taken aback by Sven's reluctance to discuss their mother's curious lapses into the languages of her youth, Karl felt the return of the dread he'd been feeling since his father's phone call. Still, he decided not to push Sven for further information on the topic. Instead, he sat quietly and tried to think of some amicable change of conversation. "How's Rob?" he finally asked.

Sven, concentrating on the I-95 traffic, spared him a quick glance and turned his eyes to the road once more. He sighed, then said, "Rob's good. But I guess I need to let you know that we're taking some time apart."

Karl nodded calmly. He was surprised at the news but braced himself for the kind of revelation he didn't particularly relish. There was a definite need to ask for details; after all, Rob and Sven had shared a relationship that had been almost disturbingly intimate since they were teenagers. It had always been as clear as glass that they were lovers starting at an early age. This had provoked their father's rage, until he grudgingly came to accept the relationship in the long years that followed. Cautiously, Karl said, "I'm sorry, Sven. I had no idea. You never said anything . . ."

"Well, there really wasn't much to say, Karl," Sven interrupted. He turned and gave his big brother a wan smile. "We found that we're growing apart in some important ways. For all that we worked together, and never spent more than a couple of days apart in nearly twenty-six years, we just woke up one day and realized we were living different lives. We're not split up, we're just taking some time to figure things out."

Karl reached across the seat and patted his brother awkwardly on the shoulder. "I'm sorry, Sven. I've always liked Rob. I mean, I don't really know him, but he seemed to be good for you, and I guess I'm sorry to hear that's over."

Sven nodded and reached up to pat his brother's hand on his shoulder. "Thanks, Karl. But it's not really over in any formal way."

Karl moved his hand from under his bother's touch and rested his arm on the console between the seats. "How do you mean?"

Sven laughed. "Well, the business we started has grown and is doing really well. Rob handles most of the interior design end of the business, and I run the store. It's called Tynnigo. Do you remember?"

Karl thought briefly, then the lovely little island in the archipelago near Stockholm bloomed in his memory. Their mother's parents had retired to a cottage there. Though the family had not visited there often, and not since Karl was young, each and every visit shone in his memory. It was a magical place full of the joy of a child's experiences.

"Of course I remember it! You named your store after it?"

Sven, concentrating on merging toward the exit to downtown

West Palm Beach, laughed and nodded. "I've been back there, Karl. Many times. It's much the same as it was when we were kids. I've made friends with the couple who bought the place after Grandmere passed away. They're a gay couple, believe it or not, and they've put a lot of work into the old place. They have a small apartment in Stockholm, but they basically live on Tynnigo year-round."

"So, the same ferry still goes there?" Karl asked incredulously.

Sven smiled. "Well, it's a new ferry now—but yes, there is a twice-daily ferry." Guiding the SUV onto the exit ramp, he continued. "Anyway, Rob and I still have the business together, and so we see each other every day. We're still very much involved in each other's lives, but he moved out about eight months ago."

"Are you guys seeing anyone else?" Karl asked cautiously.

"Rob's been going out some, but then he always was a lot more social than I am. I'm not seeing anyone, and to tell you the truth, I really don't have the energy or the time, between work and taking care of Mom and Dad."

Karl raised his eyebrows and turned in his seat to get a better read on his brother's face as he spoke. While Sven seemed perfectly at ease with what he was saying, it was what he wasn't saying that disturbed Karl. "Well, you seem to be handling it very well, but I had no idea Mom and Dad took so much looking after."

Sven's brow creased and his grasp on the steering wheel tightened noticeably. Choosing his words very carefully, he said, "They are getting old, Karl. Small things are sometimes very difficult for them. I'm happy to be close enough to be able to take care of them."

Karl merely nodded, taking in the casual explanation and weighing it against his brother's body language. He thought for a moment before he said, "No one has said anything to me about all this . . . all this *shit* going on with you guys. Is there anything else I need to know that I don't?"

"Nothing that affects you directly," Sven responded a little abruptly.

"Sven, look . . . I know I live eight hundred miles away, but it doesn't mean I don't care about you guys. I mean, you and Rob considering splitting up . . . I had no idea, and to tell you the truth, Dad's call out of the blue summoning my family on short notice came as sort of a surprise. What's going on down here?"

"Just life, Karl," Sven responded with a sigh. "Life just gets to be a bitch sometimes. We're not a particularly close family. That's not the kind of people we are. I wasn't about to call you and whine and cry because Rob decided to move into a condo he inherited. He's busy fixing it up with an eye toward resale. The whole condo thing dropped in his lap at a time when we needed a break. It is what it is. I'm okay."

"Fine," Karl responded, a bit hurt. "I'll admit to being a little distant, but that doesn't mean I don't give a damn," he repeated emphatically once more, as much to convince himself as Sven.

Sven glanced over and made eye contact with his brother. "I know that, Karl. But I also know that you don't particularly like being bothered with the details. It's not a problem, don't worry about it."

Karl met his brother's gaze, stung, and felt dismissed when his brother had to return his attention to his driving. "What's up with Mom and Dad, Sven? What are the details you think I don't care to be bothered with?"

Sven slowed the car and turned down an alley behind a row of pretty shops on a busy downtown street. "Look," he said as he pulled into a parking space beside a dumpster. "Dad's come to some decisions he wants to discuss with you. Tonight, over some excellent single-malt scotch—which is his latest obsession—I'm sure he'll fill you in. Meanwhile, we're here. Welcome to Tynnigo in West Palm Beach."

With that, Sven turned off the engine, unbuckled his seat belt, and nimbly twisted to retrieve a handful of fabric swatch books from the floor behind Karl's seat. With the bulky things in hand, he opened his car door and got out. There was nothing for Karl to do but follow. Sven strode to the shop's steel back door and unlocked its three locks in a swift maneuver of three different keys. He opened the door and stood aside so Karl could enter first. With a small smile for his brother, Karl stepped inside the shop's storage room. It was surprisingly well organized, with its boxes and assorted pieces of furniture tidily regimented into rows. Behind him, Karl heard Sven rebolt all the locks before he stepped ahead and motioned around the room. "It's a little sparse in here right now," Sven explained earnestly, "but I'm expecting a new container in a couple of weeks."

Karl nodded sagely, out of his element though he was. "This container . . . exactly what is it?"

"A shipping container," Sven said excitedly, "just like you see them loading on ships. It comes into the port, they load it onto a tractor-trailer rig, and deliver it here, all the way from Stockholm. I was there the first week of January and managed to find some nice things."

Karl raised his eyebrows in admiration "You *did* do some shopping, world class."

Sven chuckled. "You've never been to my shop before, have you?"

Karl shook his head. "I actually have no idea what you sell, other than antiques, which is a fairly broad category, isn't it?"

"C'mon," Sven said, and turned to stride toward the front of the building. "There's a lot more here than a bunch of old junk, I promise you."

Karl followed along behind him until they passed through an open door into the store itself. Light streamed in through the generous glass facing the street and illuminated the large space cheerily. The walls were painted a pale shade of grayish blue that gave the store a cool feel despite the sunniness of the setting. Pots of red geraniums bloomed in the cool brightness, punctuating the vignettes of furniture and wares with vivid points of red. Their grandmother had grown geraniums and nurtured their bright blooms as a source of cheer against the long Swedish winters. Their mother had continued the habit even in southern Florida's seasonal ambience, so geraniums had also punctuated Karl's life as a kid. Immediately, he felt a sense of nostalgia tug at the edges of his consciousness.

The store was empty of people but for a young man who stood several paces away, folding some heavy-looking wool blankets. He looked up and gave Karl a nod and Sven a more open smile.

"Johann, come meet my brother," Sven said.

The young man responded by placing the blanket on top of a stack on a table and walking toward them purposefully. Karl noted he was exceptionally good-looking. He was Karl's height, with a head full of black curls and honey-colored skin. The muscles in his shoulders and upper arms impressively filled the tight black sweater he wore, and Karl was struck by his animal sleekness as he joined them with his hand extended. Karl took the hand offered him and returned its firm grasp briefly before letting go. "Good morning, I'm Karl Preston."

"Johann Vidal," the young man responded. "I hope you had a nice flight. Sven has been looking forward to your visit."

Karl smiled in return and tried to place Johann's accent. His inflections told him English wasn't his first language. "Where are you from?" Karl asked bluntly.

"Johann is from Venezuela," Sven interrupted.

The young man smiled shyly, then said, "I have been in the United States since I was a child, but I still live with my parents and we speak Spanish at home. I forget I have an accent, but so do you. You sound more southern than Sven."

Karl was taken aback a bit. He didn't think he sounded particularly southern at all, but living with Caroline's flat eastern North

Carolina drawl and his many years in the Raleigh area had left their mark. "I'm like you," he said easily. "We speak southern—another language—at home." Sven and Johann both laughed, and Karl felt pleased with himself.

"My mother's father is from Germany," Johann replied, "so even in Venezuela I had an accent."

"Ah," Karl said. "That just makes you a citizen of the whole world."

"Would you like an espresso, or some Fiji water?" Johann offered.

"Go ahead, if you like," Sven encouraged him. "I have to go upstairs to drop these swatches off in Rob's office and check in with him. You can look around down here for a few minutes and see what the shop is all about."

Karl thought of his two drinks on the plane and felt their lingering languor. "An espresso would be great, if it's not an imposition," he said to Johann.

"It is no problem," Johann said. "We like to treat our customers as guests. A little espresso or cappuccino encourages them to linger and look around. If you'll excuse me, I'll fix you right up."

"In that case, thanks," Karl responded. With that, Johann nodded and strode toward the rear of the store, where Karl could see stools and a small bar, and behind that, an elaborate-looking espresso machine. Brass, with an old-world patina, it looked as if it could make more than a serviceable cup of coffee.

"Impressive," Karl said to Sven, who had lingered after. He had introduced his brother to Johann, enjoying their banter.

"Johann or the espresso maker?" Sven laughed.

"Well, both, I suppose," Karl retorted.

"Both would be correct," Sven said as he switched the heavy fabric sample books from one hand to the other. "Johann has been with us for two years and really runs the shop. It frees me up to do a lot of the installations and to go on buying trips."

"He's a good-looking kid," Karl said offhandedly.

"Venezuelans are beautiful people," Sven said, and spared a casual look in Johann's direction as the young man busied himself at the espresso maker. "They are like hybrid orchids."

"Gay?" Karl asked, sotto voce.

"Actually, no," Sven replied dryly. "He's had a run of quite beautiful girlfriends, but he's enjoying himself rather than being tied down. At home he's a little prince. He's very Latin in that way. He's told me he will most likely live at home until he gets married."

"Good for him," Karl said. "He should enjoy himself with those looks."

"He's certainly good for business," Sven said, and started away. "These damn samples are getting heavy. Look around. I'll bring Rob down to say hello in a few minutes."

Karl watched him turn and walk toward a door at the rear of the store, opposite the espresso bar. Sven opened the door with his free hand, revealing a staircase, and the door closed behind him as he made his way up the stairs to what Karl assumed was Rob's domain. Karl looked again toward Johann, working on his cup of espresso, which was starting to send its fragrance throughout the store.

Karl felt momentarily stranded in the store's large interior. He was no aficionado of antiques or housewares, but he knew what he liked and what interested him, so to begin he stepped toward the table where Johann had been folding blankets. There were several stacks of them on the old table, which featured chipped and flaking white paint. The table was almost a ruin, really, at least as far as its finish was concerned, but its lines were Gustavian, and there was no doubt it was one of Sven's finds from Sweden.

The blankets were made of dense, soft wool in solid, muted tones of saffron, paler yellow, jade, and soft worn blues. They boasted almost absurdly large fringes, with each strand twice as long and thick as his index finger. Idly flicking through the folds of one, he found a handwritten tag explaining the blanket's provenance as Finnish and boasting a price that made him raise his eyebrows. From the blankets he proceeded to examine the mix of the furniture. Among the antiques were also pieces he recognized as being mid-century modern Scandinavian designs, some Swedish, some Danish, and even Finnish. He stopped before a tiny settee of the Gustavian period that had been reupholstered in a pale pink check and sported an enormously plumped down seat cushion. The thing was precious. It was something he could see Caroline wistfully eyeing for her office in the town house. Interested, he bent to examine its tag and found the price to be sufficient for the down payment on a midsized car.

Stunned, he looked around and saw an old hutch holding a display of boxed and unboxed candles. He made his way over and examined the candles on the shelves. Their white wax and wicks were set in plain, clear-glass containers the size of smallish highball glasses. The label looked like vellum and was printed simply in blue ink stating: "Tynnigo, bougie parfumee, e 190g–6.5 oz. Made in France." Curious, he lifted one and brought it to his nose. Sniffing tentatively at first, he found himself inhaling deeply the candle's scent. Immediately, his mind was flooded with images of green firs towering over dark blue waters, the scent of wooden decking under a bright sun, and a slight salt breeze. There was a trace of wildflowers, grass, and even geranium in the complex scent. It was the smell of Tynnigo, the island of his childhood, his grandmere, and her home there.

So completely was he transported to another time and place that he didn't even notice Johann approach with his cup of espresso. It was the intrusion of the rich smell of coffee overwhelming the other, softer scent that caused him to look up.

"It is very nice, yes?" Johann asked.

Karl nodded and smiled. Carefully he placed the candle back on its shelf and reached with both hands to receive his cup of espresso.

"Sven worked for many months with a candle maker outside Paris to get the scent right," Johann explained. "We import them for sale only here. You would be surprised how many grand houses on the beach and other places smell of Tynnigo. We have people from New York who call and order half a dozen at a time to be shipped to them there."

"I can understand why," Karl said, and took a tentative sip of his coffee. He was almost reluctant to let the delicious taste impinge on his memory of the scent. "It brought back many memories of the place itself."

"I have been there," Johann confided. "Last summer was slow, so Sven took me along on a buying trip to Stockholm and Paris."

Karl nodded. "That must have been fun. This coffee is wonderful. Thank you very much."

Johann made an elegant, masculine dismissal with his hand of Karl's compliment and thanks. "There are many wonderful things here in this shop. Not just from Sweden, but from other places as well. Your brother has been teaching me to shop the flea markets of Paris. Take a look around; you will be surprised by what you might find."

Karl smiled. "I might be surprised, but I doubt I could afford it. Tynnigo is not Target."

Johann laughed happily. "A good joke," he said. "But what is rare and beautiful is often expensive."

"True," Karl said evenly. "But I suppose nothing is expensive if you really want it." He placed his coffee cup on the hutch's counter and picked up a boxed Tynnigo candle. It was marked fifty-two dollars, he noted, but he decided he didn't care. He handed it to Johann and said, "Could you take this for me and hold it at the register? I'd like to buy one before I leave."

Johann took the candle and nodded. "Please let me know if I can help you with anything else." With that, he favored Karl with a brilliant smile and walked away.

Alone once more, Karl strolled along the aisles of precious articles he had no use for, but he did admire their loveliness and guessed at the people who could afford such indulgences of whim and taste. He sipped at his coffee as he wandered and finally came to stand by the front windows to take in the street scene outside. Downtown West Palm Beach had become enlivened once more, after a decade-long slump as businesses and shops moved to the suburbs. At least this cheerful pocket of it had. Strolling the streets with purposeful strides were men and women dressed for the subtropical Florida winter, stylishly casual. Across the street was a high-end kitchen design shop, flanked by an art gallery and a chic women's clothing store. Further down the street was an oriental rug dealer and a patisserie. The street was hardly the dreary place Karl had last visited a decade before. He watched the street scene and finished his espresso with genuine ease. It felt good to be off work and out in the middle of the day. And, if West Palm Beach was hardly Marrakech, it was much different than any place in Raleigh, Cary, or Chapel Hill. In the early March sunlight of southern Florida, it was as exotic to Karl as if he had flown much further away from his familiar home.

His cup empty, Karl turned and started back across the store to dispose of it properly. Scanning the store, he couldn't find Johann's curly head, so he made his way to the espresso bar. Halfway there, the rear door to the upstairs opened and Sven made his way onto the sales floor, followed by Rob. Karl stopped and raised his free hand. Sven and Rob saw him immediately, and Karl was surprised when Rob hurried over and gave him a quick hug.

The hug flustered Karl, who gave a brief pleased chuckle and stepped back. Rob looked fit and as solidly muscled as the much younger Johann. Karl quickly surmised that Rob had been spending some time in the gym since his separation from Sven. His hair, while predictably receding, was still thick and featured a brush-cut style favored by Marine officers and gym teachers of Karl's past. His large brown eyes wore a pair of severe architectural glasses, very linear and black-rimmed. Behind them, Rob's eyes crinkled becomingly with the slight wrinkles that came with his self-assured smile. "Snazzy glasses you got there, Rob. You look like a celebrity architect."

Rob laughed, and Sven smiled and shook his head. "I'll settle for being a celebrity designer," Rob answered confidently.

"One of Rob's projects is going to be featured in a spread in *Elle Decor* in a couple of months," Sven interjected. "Those new glasses were on his face just in time for the photo shoot."

"I take it *Elle Decor* is a good magazine?" Karl asked carefully.

"Very good," Sven answered, while Rob only rolled his eyes and looked away modestly. "I'm very proud of him."

"Proud of *us*," Rob said easily. "Your brother is a big part of it, whether he wants to give me all the credit or not."

"Things are going well, I see," Karl said, noting that Rob had taken pains to include Sven in his achievements. Obviously, whatever caused them to separate didn't have anything to do with work.

Rob looked around the store and shrugged. "You know business. It could always be better, even if you're swamped. But I can say some of our tough years are starting to pay off. Right, Sven?"

Karl watched as Sven gave Rob a furtive glance that spoke at once of love and hurt. He then looked at Karl with a quick smile. "We're lucky," he said simply.

"How have you been, Karl?" Rob asked smoothly. "It's really great to see you."

"Can't complain," Karl responded easily. "My work is busy and challenging. Caro is happy, and Melanie is looking forward to spreading her wings once she finds a job in Manhattan. Life's good."

"I recently put in a good word for Mel with a guy I know at an auction house on Madison Avenue," Rob offered. "I emailed Mel and told her to send him her résumé. You never know, right?"

"I appreciate that," Karl said sincerely. "It's difficult at her age to get a foot in the door."

"No problem," Rob insisted, and then looked at his watch. "I hate to just say hi and run, but I've got a lunch meeting."

"And I need to swing by the deli and pick up lunch for us and Mom and Dad," Sven added.

"Karl," Rob said, and reached to grasp his shoulder, "I'll see you and the family tomorrow night at Sven's for dinner." He gave Karl's shoulder a squeeze and then turned to Sven. For a moment it seemed to Karl that he hesitated, as if he wanted to touch him, but instead he simply said, "I'll be back midafternoon."

Sven nodded and gave him a smile. "See you then."

"Until tomorrow night, then, Rob," Karl said heartily. "I know Caro and Mel will be pleased to see you."

Rob nodded and turned to step easily around a display of long case clocks. Once he reached the front door, he turned and waved before heading on his way.

Sven watched Rob possessively as he moved past the windows on the street before he changed his expression to one of bland cheerfulness, turned to Karl, and asked, "Getting hungry?"

Karl nodded and replied, "Starved. Mom's not making lunch?"

"She doesn't cook much these days," Sven said carefully. "I promised I'd bring lunch when I brought you. I hope deli's okay?"

"Sounds good," Karl replied agreeably. He decided not to comment on Sven's revelation that their mother had stopped cooking. Something in Sven's tone and earlier reluctance to discuss her current state stopped him. He decided to wait and see for himself how she was doing. There was much unsaid that signaled to him some seismic shifts in the world of southern Florida, which he had taken as terra firma from the perspective of his world in Cary. If the currents between Rob and Sven were any indication, Karl felt he'd be better off going with the flow.

"Let's roll, then," Sven said, and took Karl's espresso cup as he turned toward the store's rear exit.

Remembering his candle, Karl said, "Hold up just a minute. I asked Johann to hold something for me at the cash register that I need to pay for."

Sven gave him a puzzled look, but didn't say anything. Instead, he led him to an island in the middle of the store with a counter on all four sides. He let himself inside the swinging waist-high door that led to the checkout area's interior and sat down the espresso cup. "What did you find you liked, Karl?" he asked at last.

Karl saw the boxed candle waiting beside the register. He strolled to that side of the island and reached across the counter to pick up the box. Showing it to Sven, he said, "This is pretty amazing."

Sven looked at him with an eagerness for approval that touched Karl deeply. "Do you really like it?" Sven asked, then, "You remember?"

"How could I not?" Karl replied. "I took one whiff of this and it was like I was standing on the dock in front of the house. How did you manage to duplicate the exact *smell* of the place?"

Sven laughed happily. "That is an entire story in itself. I worked back and forth with this little old French man who has an amazing lab. Come on, I'll tell you all about it on the way."

Karl set the candle down and reached for his wallet.

"No way," Sven said bluntly. "Bring the candle and let's go."

"I can't just take it," Karl said dismissively.

"Of course you can," Sven said and laughed. "I own the store and I want you to have it. What's more, once it's burned out, let me know and I'll ship you some more."

"It's a fifty-two-dollar candle, Sven. I don't expect you to just keep me stocked—that's too much. Please," Karl said, and reached for his wallet once more.

Sven picked the candle up and started toward the door. "Johann! We're heading out," he called. Johann emerged from the stockroom and strode to meet him. "C'mon, Karl. Johann needs to lock up and get lunch as well."

Reluctantly, Karl followed behind him and gave Johann a smile and nod as they passed in the aisle. Once they were in the stockroom, he said, "Really, Sven, I appreciate it, but you're too generous."

Sven stopped by the door leading to the alley and pulled his keys from his pocket. He turned and looked up at his older brother with a look of hurt mixed with exasperation. "Karl, the markup on those Tynnigo candles is something like five hundred percent." He extended the candle for his brother to take. "Your wanting it is worth much more than the cost to me. Just be a brother and let me have the pleasure of giving you something that makes you happy, okay?"

Abashed, Karl took the candle from his brother and gave him a long look that he hoped communicated more than his simple spoken thanks. Sven rewarded him with a happy smile and busied himself with the locks on the door, leaving Karl to allow himself to recognize the happy feeling of being loved.

· 4 ·

THE OLD NEIGHBORHOOD had aged extremely well, to Karl's eye. In 1965, when his father had bought the sprawling Florida Caribbean-style colonial in the raw subdivision not far from downtown Boca Raton, everything had been fresh and new. Then the trees had been saplings and the palms only bushy-headed toddlers compared to the venerable and lush landscaping that canopied the streets now. Back then the interstate didn't even exist, much less divide the old, real Boca Raton from the rococo excess of faux-Boca to the west. As he sat next to his brother, riding down streets he had long ago seen being carved from sand, scrub oak, and palmetto trees, Karl felt almost disoriented by the familiar surroundings.

"When we first moved here, none of this was finished," Karl said softly. "I used to ride my bike here before this street was even paved."

"It must have been a lot different," Sven said. "I was just a baby then. But Boca has really changed even more in the past twenty years. I can imagine how it must look to you after thirty-four years away. You can't really take it all in coming back only once a year at Christmas."

Karl chuckled. "I remember Dad worrying because he paid twenty-nine thousand dollars for the house. God only knows what it's worth now."

"He's got it listed for seven fifteen," Sven confided. "He'll probably get at least seven for it, with the market the way it is right now."

"Dad has their house on the market?" Karl asked, stunned.

"Oh, shit," Sven muttered. Then, "Dad wanted to tell you himself."

"Why, Sven?" Karl demanded. "Give me some idea of what I'm walking into here. All this mystery crap is really getting on my nerves."

Sven slowed the car and turned away from the direction of their parents' house. "Okay, look," he said. "Don't let Dad know I've said anything." Sven easily swerved to miss a lone bicyclist riding along their side of the road. "I'm just going to drive around for a minute so I can talk to you."

"Whatever, just tell me for God's sake," Karl answered irritably as he recognized the house where his first crush had lived. Her name was Kathleen Kerry, and she always sat three rows ahead of them at Sunday mass. He could still see her tossing her long hair and reaching back to adjust her ponytail. He suddenly felt claustrophobic. There was too much of the past here. There was where he took that nasty spill on his bike and cracked his wrist. There was where he and Tommy Dempsey used to build forts and later smoke joints. For a moment, the past lived so vividly alongside the present that there didn't seem to be enough air in the car.

"Dad has decided to sell the house and move them into one of those continuing-care retirement communities. It's not a bad place—it's out in West Boca and it's pretty nice. He'll explain it all to you, and I think he plans on taking you over there tomorrow to show it to you."

"Why is he doing this? I thought they were fine aging where they are. I mean, why do they have to move?" Karl asked, dreading the answer he might get.

Sven sighed. "Karl, look . . . you know Dad. He's got to feel like he's in charge. He's got to be the big dog. This is his decision. He's given it a lot of thought and consideration, I'll say that for him. But the main thing is he feels like he's in control, got it? That's very important for you to understand."

Karl snorted. He knew his father. He had never not been in charge as long as he felt it was his business. Not until after Karl had graduated from college and married did he ever feel like his father loosened the reins. Only when he saw Karl on what he considered to be the right path did he let go entirely. "What does Mom think about this sudden urge to rearrange their lives?" Karl demanded.

Sven straightened his back, squared his shoulders, and gripped the steering wheel more tightly. Without looking at his brother, he calmly said, "That's the worst of it, Karl. Mom has dementia. It's not Alzheimer's, it's just geriatric, age-related dementia, and it's not going to get anything but worse."

Shocked, Karl sagged in his seat and rubbed his eyes tiredly. "How do you know this? I mean, besides the language stuff you told me about. Has she been tested or what?"

Sven stared resolutely ahead. "I have been taking her to specialists. She has been thoroughly tested—everything from shrinks to MRIs." He sighed heavily and continued. "It's the one thing Dad can't control. And it's fucking killing him."

"How long has she got?" Karl asked awkwardly. "I mean, how long will she be herself?"

"That's the bitch of it, Karl. Physically, she's in great shape. She could live another fifteen years. But her mind will be gone long before she passes away."

"Does she know?" Karl demanded.

"Yes, of course," Sven said defensively. "You don't think we would keep something like that from her, do you?"

"No, I don't suppose you would," Karl answered gently. "This place—this care community—can they help Mom?"

For the first time, Sven turned to look at him. "Yes. She'll be able to stay with Dad as long as possible in their apartment. But when it goes past a certain point, when she can't . . . when she can't function anymore, she'll be just a building away. Dad will be able to see her every day."

Karl nodded and batted his hands against the air in small, futile gestures. "How long before that point?"

Sven slowed and came to a stop at a yield sign. "Just months, maybe a year if we're lucky."

"So soon," Karl managed to say.

Sven checked both ways, then cut the big SUV's wheels hard to the right and managed to turn the thing around in the intersection and head back in the direction of their parents' house. "Not a word, Karl," Sven said again. "Let Dad think he's the one breaking all this to you."

Karl nodded, and when Sven looked his way he said, "Yes, of course." They rode a little way in silence before he gathered the courage to ask, "How bad is Mom right now?"

Sven shook his head and smiled. "Pretty much okay. It's just that time is fluid for her. She's stopped living in a straight line. You can be talking to her and she's perfectly lucid one moment, and the next it could be an afternoon in 1984 or 1964. It's subtle. She's still pretty independent as long as she takes her meds. She's not looney or anything, but she might forget she's talking to you and start talking about you." He snickered. "For some reason, I remind her of her brother Andreas, and she'll start talking to him about me . . . about something I did when I was a kid. The best thing to do is go with it. She comes out of it herself."

"Oh, boy." Karl sighed.

"How's your Swedish?" Sven asked rather smugly.

"About as good as it was when I was seven," Karl responded bleakly.

"Just answer as best you can. Humor her, she'll come back out of it pretty quickly," Sven said. "*Ja, mama. Tala mig hur mer.*"

Karl understood this. Sven had said, "Yes, Mama. Tell me more." Sven looked at him anxiously, and Karl forced himself to fit his stiff tongue to bend to the sounds that curved oddly in his mouth. "*Ja, mama. Tala mig hur mer,*" he repeated.

"That's pretty good," Sven encouraged him. "Don't even try anything more complicated. What you just don't want to do is frustrate her. She can get feisty if she thinks you're playing dumb."

"Okay," Karl said miserably. "How does Dad deal with it? He hardly speaks Swedish at all."

"Mainly he ignores her," Sven said sullenly. "If it goes on too long, he calls me on my cell phone and asks me to calm her down. Once she thought he was just being difficult and told me she was going to spank him with the wooden spoon."

Despite himself, Karl laughed. When he was very small, that's how she disciplined him. She would grab a wooden spoon and swat the back of his thighs. He found the picture of his mother doing that to his father in their kitchen genuinely hilarious.

Sven laughed as well. "It's not funny," he said. "But it's really interesting sometimes."

"Oh, man," Karl said, and looked as their house came into view. It sat serenely on a lawn that showed the meticulous hand of his father's boredom in retirement. Every bush, shrub, and tree was manicured with the precision of a topiary garden. Beds of bright impatiens flowed serenely around the trees and along the hibiscus hedge bordering the driveway. It looked like a storybook home. "How in the hell do I deal with this?" he asked Sven.

Sven pulled into the drive behind their father's Buick and turned off the engine. He pushed down the emergency brake to hold the big beast of a vehicle in place on the slight incline of the drive and said, "Just be yourself, Karl. It'll all be okay."

Karl looked at his brother and shook his head before letting himself out of the SUV and into the sunshine. As he walked to the rear of the vehicle to retrieve his suitcase, he suddenly felt very warm. His cotton sweater seemed to cling to him annoyingly. He was glad he had a polo shirt on underneath the sweater. As Sven opened the back hatch of the Excursion and pulled out the suitcase, Karl pulled his sweater over his head. When he opened his eyes after he'd pulled the sweater over his head, he saw his mother and father standing on the porch waiting to greet him.

His father was dressed in a pair of khakis, a golf shirt, and sneakers. His mother was similarly dressed, right down to the sneakers. They gazed at him with obvious delight.

How long had it been since he'd last seen them? Only a little more than a year. He and Caro and Melanie had flown down for Christmas only fourteen months before, but the sight of his parents stunned him. They seemed so small, so doll-like, that he was taken aback. He simply stared at them, frozen, until Frank raised his hand and Annike started off the porch toward him, raising her arms as she made her way down the brick-paved walkway to the drive.

Karl quickly pulled his arms from the sleeves of his sweater and stepped toward Annike. He found himself bending forward to allow himself to be enclosed by her embrace. Awkwardly, he wrapped his arms around her in return and hugged her slender form to his chest. She felt soft and very frail, and he was suddenly afraid he would hurt her by holding her so tightly, as if her birdlike bones could snap like twigs in his clumsy embrace.

"*Min Karl,*" she said softly, the Swedish sweet in his ears, as she grasped his shoulders and pulled him down so his cheeks could receive her kisses. "*Min Karl har komma hem,*" she said. *My Karl has come home.*

Karl gently moved his hands to her shoulders and straightened up to look down into her moist eyes. Easily, he found the words waiting. "*JAG älska du Mom,*" he said softly. *I love you, Mom.*

"*Du er så vacker,*" she replied. *You are so handsome.* She touched his cheek. "*Min vacker pojke,*" she said lovingly. *My handsome boy.*

"Son," Frank said as he stepped up beside them and extended his hand.

Karl released his mother and, ignoring the hand, quickly hugged his father as well. At one time, he had been the same height as his father, but now he was amazed to see his father's eyes lower than his own as he looked down into the old man's face. His grin was the same, the bright flash of denture white in the tanned and freshly shaven face, but his eyes seemed to have lost a spark of some sort. As he looked at Karl lovingly, it seemed his gaze was shuttered somehow. There was an absence there, a withdrawal that Karl could not have anticipated. "Dad, you look great," Karl said as he let his father go.

Approvingly, Frank reached up and grasped Karl's shoulder. "You do, too, Son. Staying fit, I see. Are you swimming still?"

"Just about every day, Dad." Karl replied. "Old habits are hard to break."

Frank nodded and gave Karl a long once-over. "Keep it up. I'm almost eighty and my heart rate is the same as it was when I was forty. Swimming keeps you young."

"Hi, Mom. Hi, Dad," Sven said cheerfully.

To Karl, it seemed as if they ignored his brother, continuing to gaze at Karl's face.

"Are you ready for some lunch?" Sven asked, and held up the bags from the deli.

"Did you remember my coleslaw?" Frank demanded.

"Sure thing, Dad," Sven said, and took a step around them all. "I know Karl has got to be famished."

"I have the table all set," Annike said, and took Karl's hand. "Come. Let's go inside."

Karl looked around for his carry-on bag and found it already in Frank's clasp. The old man gently nudged his son along with one hand at the small of Karl's back, tugging the carry-on behind him.

With Sven leading the way, they went in the front door and on to the breakfast nook next to the kitchen. Karl breathed in deeply the familiar smell of his old home. He allowed himself to be steered and led as his parents asked him what he wanted to drink and apologized for the temperature of the house. Annike let go of his hand once she had him positioned at his traditional seat at the table, already set for lunch. As Karl watched her move to her chair, something seemed amiss.

When he looked down at the table, he saw what was out of place. On each linen napkin, placed carefully next to each plate, rested an array of kitchen utensils. On his napkin lay a pair of tongs and a spatula. The other napkins bore a manual can opener, an egg timer, a pizza cutter, a small grater, and a carving knife. Wordlessly, Sven placed the bags of deli fare in the middle of the table and quickly began to collect the odd assortment of kitchen implements from each napkin. Annike and Frank sat down as if nothing were amiss at all, while Sven moved around the counter and into the kitchen.

"How was your flight?" Frank asked.

Annike placed her napkin on her lap and gave Karl her rapt attention.

"I upgraded to first class," Karl began.

"Sven, bring me a beer when you come back," Frank interrupted.

"I'll just have water," Annike added.

"It was a smooth trip, no bumps," Karl continued and then said, "Sven, can I give you a hand?"

From the other side of the counter, Sven gave him a smile and shook his head. He pulled open a drawer and Karl watched as he pulled out the appropriate flatware and laid it on the counter. "Would you like a beer?" he asked Karl.

"Please," Karl replied emphatically, and then looked at his mother and father in turn. "Caro and Mel are sorry they couldn't get down today, but they'll be here tomorrow afternoon. They are excited about the visit."

"We've been counting the days," Annike replied and sighed. "It will be so good for us all to be together."

"Has Melanie still got her heart set on following that boy to New

York?" Frank asked. "I don't know why they just don't go ahead and get married."

Karl simply held up both hands in surrender. "I'll let her explain it herself to you, Dad. She's an adult, I'm sure she has her reasons."

Sven rounded the counter hugging three bottles of beer against his chest, with one hand carrying the flatware and the other balancing a small blue plastic box on top of a glass of milk. He sat the glass of milk before their mother and put down the flatware before passing out the beers. Sitting next to Annike, he took the pillbox off the top of the glass of milk. Karl watched as he snapped open one of the tiny lids and extracted two pills. Then he snapped the lid shut and popped open another. Digging another pair of pills from the shallow container, he said, "Annike Preston, what am I going to do with you? You didn't take your morning pills, and now you have lunch pills to take as well."

"Leave her alone, Sven," Frank said firmly.

Sven shot his father a tired look. "You are a big help, you know that, Frank?" Gently, he reached for his mother's hand and carefully laid the pills on her open palm. "*Moder, behaga. Ta din medicin nu. Du don't vilja till få sjuk*," he said. *Mother, please. Take your medicine now. You don't want to get sick.*

"I want to enjoy Karl," Annike said petulantly. Then, "*Den här förbanna pillren göra jag inte mig själv. I'll bli sömnig likaledes*," she added in vehement Swedish. *Those damn pills make me not myself. I'll be sleepy as well.*

"Goddamn it, Sven. Stop humoring her. She understands English and she needs to remember that," Frank said irritably.

Ignoring him, Sven closed mother's fingers over her pills and handed her the glass of milk.

Glaring at her son, Annike brought her hand to her mouth and slowly took a sip of her milk. Then she brought her napkin to her lips.

"Mother," Sven said and shook his head.

Defeated, Annike put her napkin back in her lap and, taking up her glass, took two long swallows of milk. "Satisfied?" she asked Sven lightly, then turned to Karl. "If you live long enough, your children treat you like a child."

"Mom," Karl said gently. "Don't skip your medicine because I'm here. You'll make me sorry I came if you get sick."

"If I have to take a nap, please forgive me. I so much want to spend time with you while you're here, but the medicine makes me drowsy. You'll understand, won't you?"

"Of course I will, Mom," Karl said, and took her hand. He smiled at her warmly, and Annike nodded and looked at Sven reproachfully.

"Let's eat," Frank said suddenly, and reached across the table for a bag. He opened it and pulled out a sandwich wrapped in paper. Opening it, he peered inside and declared, "Tuna salad," before unceremoniously tossing the sandwich in the direction of Sven's plate.

Karl watched as Sven picked the sandwich from the table and unwrapped it slowly. Karl reached for his beer and took a long pull. He hadn't been in the house more than fifteen minutes and he had already learned a great deal about how life had changed in his family. He was suddenly aware of how long he had been away. And how he wished he'd never come.

Throughout lunch, Karl mostly remained quiet, eating his Reuben sandwich and ignoring his cold french fries. Around him, his brother and parents ate quietly as well, proffering only an occasional question about his work, which Karl deftly answered with enough information to give them an idea of his projects, without taxing them with details.

After everyone was finished eating, Sven stood and quickly cleared away the remains of the meal. As he moved from the table to the kitchen, loading the dishwasher and disposing of the trash, Karl saw his father watching his brother with a look that seemed to contain both resentment and appreciation. When Sven returned to the table with a bowl of fresh strawberries and dessert plates holding slices of pound cake, Frank took a plate and said, "I would say you'd make somebody a good wife, but evidently that didn't work out so well for you, did it, boy?"

Karl looked at his brother with alarm, anticipating a sharp response. Instead, Sven chuckled and resumed his place at the table, where he took his mother's plate and began to serve her a portion of the fresh strawberries. "I'm good at a lot of things, Dad."

"Gay marriage." Frank snorted, then, looking at Karl, said, "Can you believe that son of a bitch left your brother after completely dominating his life for twenty-six years?"

Annike took up her fork and, before taking the bite, said, "Rob loves Sven. He'll come back, you mark my words."

"You're better off without him," Frank said to Sven, making his point with a jab of his fork. "For once in your life, you can think for yourself."

Sven merely shrugged and turned his attention to his own plate.

"I should have beat the crap out of him—or both of you—when you were teenagers," Frank said resignedly. "But I listened to your mother instead. Leave them alone, she said, they'll outgrow it, she said. Now you've wasted your whole life, and for what?" he demanded.

Sven looked up from his plate and met his father's eyes. "Frank, give it a rest. I've hardly wasted my life," he said evenly. "And it really doesn't concern you. I'm happy, okay?"

Frank turned to Karl and said, "He's happy. If he had kids of his own, he'd be too busy to show up here all the time and try to run my house."

"No, Frank," Annike said sharply. "Sven is a good son. He is a tremendous help. . ."

"Yeah," Frank retorted. "Well, not for very much longer."

Helplessly, Karl watched this little exchange as if it were a game. Extremely uncomfortable, he had nothing to add, so he simply finished his dessert and sat back in silence.

Sven finished his dessert and stood with his empty plate in his hand. He reached for Karl's plate and waited for his mother to finish the last bite of her own dessert before picking her plate up as well. He ignored his father as he walked around the counter and put the dishes in the dishwasher. Karl watched as he consulted his watch and said, "I need to get back to the store. Karl, I'll see you tomorrow. We thought you could take Mom's car and pick up Caro and Mel. We'll hook up before dinner so you can follow me to my place. Sound good?"

"Sounds good," Karl answered heartily. He pushed back his chair to stand, but Sven motioned for him to sit.

"We're going to the club for dinner," Annike said cheerfully.

"Mom, try to get a little rest this afternoon," Sven urged gently.

"She has no choice now that you've doped her up," Frank said, and without standing, he held up his plate toward Sven, who leaned across the counter to take it. He placed the plate in the dishwasher and walked around the counter to put his arm over his father's shoulders. He gave him a quick hug, and Karl watched as Frank awkwardly patted his arm in reply. Evidently, there were no hard feelings, despite Frank's irascibility.

"Call me if you need me," Sven said to no one in particular, and with that, he left.

Karl waited until he heard the front door close behind his brother, then said, "Aren't you a little hard on him, Dad?"

"Have to be," Frank said, and pushed back his chair. He stood up and said, "Can I get you another beer?"

Karl lifted his nearly empty bottle of Budweiser and said, "Sounds good. But why do you feel you have to be so hard on Sven?"

"He always has been," Annike interrupted.

"Forty was too old to have another child," Frank said from the refrigerator. "He came along when my life was at its height. I was working my ass off already, and then the opportunity to work for IBM came along and that consumed me." Offhandedly he added, "I've often wondered if he's really my kid."

Annike touched Karl's hand and rolled her eyes at that. Karl gave her a wink in reply. He understood his father's irritability, but he hadn't realized how badly he took out his frustrations on Sven.

Frank strode back to the table, twisted the caps off the beer bottles, and handed one to Karl. "In any event, Sven was your mother's toy. She's been entranced with him for forty years, much to his own detriment. I gave up a long time ago." Heavily, Frank sank back into his chair at the table.

"Frank, may I please have my cigarette?" Annike asked gently, then turned to Karl and said, "I am allowed three a day. I've lived long enough to rediscover my vices."

"I'm sorry, my dear," Frank said, and got to his feet once more. He stepped into the kitchen and reached high to the top shelf of one of the kitchen cabinets, retrieving a pack of Benson & Hedges 100s. Karl watched as he drew one from the pack and returned it to the top shelf.

"He's afraid I'll burn the house down," Annike explained to her son. "He keeps them where he thinks I can't reach them, but I'm not so crazy that I can't drag a chair over there and get one for myself if I like."

"You are not crazy," Frank said adamantly as he returned to the table and handed her the cigarette. He fished in his pants pocket and found a yellow Bic lighter. Annike placed the cigarette between her lips, and Frank lit the cigarette with a flourish and a slight bow.

Annike inhaled the cigarette with obvious pleasure and exhaled a long stream of smoke. Coyly, she looked at Frank and winked. In response, he tenderly placed his palm against her cheek and then returned to his chair to sit.

Karl noted his father's courtliness with a smile. Throughout his childhood, he had been aware that his father adored his mother. He had always treated her as a porcelain doll, opening doors for her, lighting her cigarettes, holding her chair out for her at the table. Though Karl had never thought much about it before, these were courtesies that he extended to his own wife. Frank had been a role model in a thousand effortless ways. Karl recognized this now, sitting in the company of his parents after lunch, and he found himself missing Caroline acutely.

"Frank finds it easy to blame all of Sven's shortcomings on me," Annike said as she delicately ran the burning end of her cigarette around the inside of the ashtray. "He thinks I spoiled him and made him the way he is."

"And how is he?" Karl asked bluntly. "He's successful, he's in good shape, and he seems devoted to the both of you. His personal life is his own business."

"I could stand a little less devotion," Frank told him dismissively. "And as for his personal life, I worry about him. He invested himself in another man, and now he and that man are thinking of calling it quits. Sven's middle-aged, and except for that stupid dog of his, he has no one. If he's devoted to us, who's going to be devoted to him when he gets to be our age?"

"I do not believe Rob is gone for good," Annike said once more. "He is just a *cette* age, all men go through it. Even you," she said to Frank and thumped her cigarette decisively against the rim of the ashtray.

"Let's not dig up ancient history, Annike," Frank said evenly. "I worry about Sven, and that's a fact. I'll admit he's made a real go of that store of his, but . . ."

"Sven will be okay, Dad," Karl said, and took a swig of his beer.

Frank grunted in reply and turned his attention to his own beer.

Karl looked at his mother. She sat with her back perfectly straight, inches away from the back of her chair. She held her cigarette elegantly and slowly turned to meet his eyes with a look that said she agreed with him totally. Karl was struck by how pretty she was still, despite the toll time had taken on what had been a very remarkable, self-contained beauty.

Annike lifted her free hand and placed it over Karl's forearm resting on the table. "You look tired, Son. Did you have to get up very early to make your flight?"

Karl set down his beer and laid his hand over his mother's. "Not so very early, Mom. How about you? Are you well? You still are very beautiful."

Annike laughed and withdrew her hand. She shook her hair, worn straight and cut in an abrupt line halfway between her shoulders and chin. He could see in her the shadow of a much younger woman's self-regard. "I am hardly beautiful, but you are sweet for thinking so," she said cheerfully

"Are you well?" Karl asked again, more urgently this time.

Annike looked away and took a studied drag off her cigarette.

Frank answered for her. "Your mother is having some problems, Son. But it isn't anything we can't handle, is it, sweetheart?"

Annike looked down and carefully put out her cigarette. She looked up at Karl through her lashes and said, "I'm fine now. I have to take some medicine, but my health is good—far better than many women I know who have to take all kinds of pills. It is just a fact of old age, isn't it, Frank?"

"That's right," he replied, and returned her look with a haunted smile.

With careful dignity, Annike stood and placed her hand on Karl's shoulder. "What time is it, dear?" she asked Frank.

Consulting his watch, Frank responded, "Two-twenty-five."

Annike squeezed Karl's shoulder and said to his upturned face, "Our dinner reservations are for six. We old people eat early, you know. Now I must excuse myself. I nap these days, like a fat cat in the sun."

Karl reached up to squeeze his mother's hand. "Sleep well, Mom. I'll be here when you get up. Then we'll have a nice evening at the club. I'm looking forward to it."

Annike nodded, then looked at Frank and said, "Wake me by four-thirty, please."

"Sure thing," Frank said and smiled at her.

Annike bent and kissed the top of Karl's head, then turned and left the breakfast nook.

Karl watched her walk away, as self-possessed as ever. When he turned to look at his father, he was surprised to find Frank had buried his face in his hands. As Karl watched, his father rubbed his eyes and lifted his head to look at his son.

Frank pushed back his chair and stood slowly. "Bring your beer and let's go outside," he said with a note of false cheer. "I have something new to show you."

Karl stood, clutching his beer, and waited for his father to make his way outside to the lanai. Following along behind him, he took in the familiar sight of the pool and scattered lawn furniture. Something seemed very wrong with the view. "The pool enclosure is gone!" he exclaimed.

His father looked overhead and then stepped around the pool, motioning for Karl to follow him. "The last hurricane took it. The homeowners' insurance didn't cover it, and the screen company wanted twenty-five thousand to replace it. I said to hell with it. I actually like it better open to the sky like this."

Karl stood in the bright afternoon sunshine and couldn't disagree. Without the screened pool enclosure, the entire yard looked bigger. "I think you're right, Dad," he said.

Frank continued to walk away, deeper into the yard. "I can't offer you any oranges," he said sadly. "It was a sorry crop this year, and they were mostly gone by February."

Karl looked at the gnarled trunks of the orange trees that had once been such a source of pleasure, especially when they had first moved down from up north. He could still taste the sun-warmed fruit in this familiar place.

"They're dying," Frank said as he stopped and lingered under one of the trees. "Their life expectancy is really only twenty-five years or so for bearing fruit." He ran his hand appreciatively over the trunk of the tree. "Our landscape guy's been at me to cut them down and get some more growing," Frank said tiredly. "But they're like old friends. I can't just kill them. Besides, I'm too old to wait for a new bunch of saplings to get established and start bearing fruit. Hell, I'd be too old to gum them by then."

Karl found he had nothing to say. He simply looked at his father, who smiled back at him. Karl nodded and took a swallow of his beer.

Frank turned and walked from under the orange tree to a smaller tree, really a large bush, growing in a well-groomed corner of the yard. It was hung all over with tangerines, ripe and deliciously sweet-smelling. Frank pulled a few branches back to show off its fruit. "Isn't she a beauty?"

Karl looked at the tree and nodded appreciatively.

"I planted this four years ago. My old buddy John Knight and his wife, Linda, gave it to us for Christmas." His father stooped and searched among the fruit before plucking two tangerines from a branch. "John died four months ago," he added bluntly. He extended a tangerine to Karl, then eagerly scored his own with his thumbnail. As he began to peel the ripe fruit, he said, "Your mother's sick, Son."

This, without preamble, took Karl off guard. Though he knew the essential facts, he wasn't quite ready for this. For lack of anything better to do, he looked at his father and watched him peel away at his tangerine.

"She's been through a whole bunch of tests. This specialist, that one, even one down in Miami. The long and short of it is, she's losing her mind. It's organic," he said helplessly, as if the word explained everything.

"What can they do?" Karl said evenly, aware of the weight of the fruit in his hand.

His father dropped the long curl of peel from the tangerine and kicked it under the tree carelessly. He split the tangerine in half and placed one half on the flat of his hand. He pointed carefully to an area of its surface and said, "Something's gone wrong in her brain, a piece is dying in this region right here," he said. "There isn't anything they can do. There are pills she takes, but that's just to keep her from slipping into these fugue states where she forgets what's what." Frank searched his son's eyes before he continued. "Like when she set the table for lunch—in her mind, she knows what she's supposed to be doing, but then it misfires and you end up with an egg timer and a spatula instead of a knife and fork. Right idea, wrong drawer."

Unable to offer anything, Karl gulped half his beer, then simply nodded and waited for him to continue.

"Son, it's going to get a lot worse, and it won't take long. All I have to tell you is that how she is right now. . .well, it's going to be as good as it gets. If you have anything to say to your mother, make sure you say it on this trip. You understand?" Frank added pleadingly.

"I understand, Dad," Karl said comfortingly. "How about you? How are you doing with this?"

Frank looked at him and then away. He scanned the yard and then looked at the tangerine half still resting in his palm. With surprising force, he threw both halves across the yard, one after the other. "I'm mad as hell, Son," Frank said angrily. "And there isn't a fucking thing I can do to make it right."

Karl put his own tangerine in his jeans pocket and reached out to touch his father's arm, but the old man turned and walked away.

Karl hesitated and then followed him to the opposite corner of the yard, where he had stopped and was now studying the ripening globes of coconut high in a tree. Karl stopped next to him and simply waited.

Frank sighed and looked at his son. "There are some things I can do. I'm going to need . . . your mom's going to need help. Sven . . . well, I give him a hard time, but he's been a big help. Pretty soon your mom's going to need a lot more help than he can give her."

"So what are you going to do, Dad?" Karl asked, careful lest he sound either condescending or contentious.

"Have you ever heard of a continuing-care retirement community?" Frank asked eagerly.

"I understand the concept of places like that, Dad, yes," Karl said carefully and then finished his beer. "But I'll admit, I don't know how they work. I just know you sort of have a buy-in fee, and then they agree to look after you until you die, right?"

Frank chuckled. "Well, that's pretty much it. There's a place called Palladian Gardens a few miles out west that I've checked out. It's not cheap, but they have a facility where your mom can be properly looked after if anything happens to me, for as long as she lives."

"Tell me about it," Karl urged his father.

"Well, it's going to eat the hell out of your inheritance," Frank said.

"Dad," Karl said patiently, "your money is there to take care of you and Mom as long as you live. I don't give a damn if you spend your last cent when you draw your last breath. What's yours wasn't ever mine to begin with."

"Do you really feel that way?" his father asked.

"Of course," Karl said adamantly. "You forget. I'm only about thirteen years from retiring myself. I've bought Caro and myself a town house we can grow old in. If the future holds any surprises like . . . like this thing with Mom, well, I have other plans that take that into consideration as well, but I never counted on anything from you to make that happen."

"Good boy," his father said, and began to stroll back toward the house.

"Do you have enough, Dad? Do you need any help?" Karl asked as he walked beside him.

Lifting his arm and gesturing around him, Frank replied, "All this is worth a lot more than you think, Son. Between my retirement, my investments in IBM and some other stock, and what this house will bring, there will be plenty. I won't be a burden on my children," Frank ended resolutely.

"You would never be a burden, Dad," Karl said genuinely.

Frank laughed. "You say that now. I've changed your shitty diapers, but I won't have you changing mine."

When they reached the far side of the pool, Frank eased himself into one of the chaise longues and motioned for Karl to do the same. Gratefully, Karl sank down onto a chaise and lifted his feet to rest, as his father had. The afternoon's warmth was comforting, not uncomfortable. He set his beer bottle on the pool deck, leaned back, and folded his arms over his head. "Dad, how soon do you plan to buy into this Palladian place?"

"Palladian Gardens," his father corrected. "They have a unit available in sixty days. A nice little one-bedroom that'll be plenty big for your mom and me for as long as she can stay with me. I'm taking you to lunch there tomorrow so you can see the place for yourself. I want you to understand what I'm doing and why I'm doing it."

"Do you think you'll be happy there?" Karl pressed his father.

"Happy is something you look for when you're young, Karl," Frank said easily. He waited and studied the clouds as they sailed overhead. "We'll be comfortable, and your mother will be safe. That's as good as it gets at eighty, Son."

Karl watched his father as Frank peered into the sky for many minutes and considered the resignation his father had revealed. "What does Sven think about this move, Dad?" Karl asked finally.

Frank snorted. "He's been trying to get me to sell out and move into one of these retirement communities for a couple of years. I didn't pay him any mind. It wasn't until your mom forgot how to speak English that I started thinking about it seriously." He yawned comfortably and stretched easily in the sunshine. "Once I realized your mom was going to need help beyond the cleaning lady, and beyond making sure she takes her medicine and doesn't get lost on the way home from the grocery store, well . . . I ran the numbers, Karl. It makes sense."

"Is it very expensive?" Karl asked, not sure how far he should pry.

"The longer you wait, the more expensive it gets," his father said. "To tell you the truth, when you take into account groceries, the maid, the lawn service, the pool guy, the taxes, it's a wash."

"Well, there's the social aspect of it as well, Dad. You'll be around a lot of other folks and not here all by yourselves," Karl offered encouragingly.

Frank chuckled. "When you get to be my age, boy, there are a lot more hens than roosters. I'm not the kind of man who enjoys sitting around gabbing with a bunch of old women."

Karl laughed. "Well, there's an upside to that. Think of all those lonely widows who'll want to keep you company when Mom's . . ."

Frank cut him off with a sharp glance and a sharply raised hand. "Don't even say it, Karl. I'll love that woman as long as I breathe. There'll never be another one for me."

"I'm sorry Dad," Karl replied, chastened. "I was just kidding around."

Frank sighed deeply and sat in silence for a long while. "I wouldn't wish it on a dog," he said finally.

"Wish what, Dad?" Frank asked gently.

"To lose her while she's still alive." Frank rubbed his eyes, and

Karl was surprised to see the wetness on his cheekbones shine in the westerning light. "You can't know how I hate the thought of that, boy."

"I'm sorry, Dad," Karl said again weakly. "I'm so sorry."

"I should have been dead first," Frank said apologetically. "I've outlived my life, Son."

Karl wondered how to respond. His father sounded so bleak and lost. He wondered if he should try and joke him out of it, but that had fallen flat shortly before. He wondered if he should tell him how much he still needed him, and then he realized he had cut his father out of being needed many long years ago. So Karl settled on taking his father's hand and squeezing it. He felt a deep peace when his father returned his grasp and didn't let go. Karl held his father's hand gratefully as they lay in their lounge chairs, watching the clouds chase themselves in the high, thin blue of the southern Florida winter sky.

5

"DINNER AT THE CLUB," as Karl's mother had so excitedly put it, had not been a part of Karl's childhood. His parents' country club membership hadn't begun until his father's retirement. At that time, golf had been a social activity Frank had enjoyed with his fellow ex-IBMers. While Annike never had taken up golf, or even tennis, she enjoyed having dinner at the country club a great deal. As they had grown older, it had become their cafeteria, in a way. It gave them something to look forward to at the end of the day and a place to entertain on the infrequent occasions when they did entertain.

Karl followed his parents into the dining room, dressed as formally as his suitcase could provide, with the addition of a sports jacket pressed on him from his father's closet. He felt distinctly out of place, though his mother seemed to be in her element, and his father proceeded to their table with magisterial nods at various acquaintances. They didn't deign to stop at anyone's table, Karl noted. He wasn't sure if it was because of his own odd attire, or if his parents had simply stopped feeling the need to glad-hand and politesse their way around a room.

The maître d' seated Annike first, then waited as Karl and Frank took their seats before handing them their menus.

"May I get you something from the bar? Or would you prefer to see a wine list?" the maître d' asked unctuously.

Karl saw his mother give his father a brief look, which he answered with a slight nod. "I'll have a Limoncello martini," she answered with reserved politeness.

"Dewar's on the rocks," Frank responded, then added, "Make it a double."

Karl thought for a moment as the maître d' turned his attention to him. Obviously, his father was going to be well lubricated, considering he'd had two scotches while waiting for Annike to finish dressing. He thought it possible he would have to drive the unfamiliar streets back home if his father got drunk. Finally, he said, "Do you have Stoli orange?"

The maître d' smiled ruefully and shook his head. "I'm sorry, no," he said. "May I suggest a Smirnoff with a shot of Cointreau?"

Karl smiled, but shook his head. "I think I'll settle for a nice glass of your house red," he told the gentleman. Karl wasn't a big drinker, so he'd deliberately asked for something he considered obscure or specific enough to guarantee it wouldn't be available. A glass of red wine he could handle if he were called on to drive home.

"Excellent," the maître d' said with a slight bow. "Your server will bring your drinks shortly. Is there anything else I can get you?"

Everyone at the table demurred quietly, and the maître d' left them. Karl looked around the dining room and commented, "This is very nice. I take it you come often?"

Annike smiled and laid her warm hand over her son's as it rested at the table's edge. "Yes. Frank is very generous to bring me as often as he does. I simply can't cook for two people anymore. It's impossible. Your father hates leftovers."

"It's true," Frank concurred. "I can't stand heated-over food. Besides, they do a very good job here. I can recommend anything on the menu. I'm going to have the small sirloin with a baked potato. The ranch dressing is good. Homemade."

"I'm having the scampi," Annike told Karl as she pointed to his menu. "The secret to staying slim is to have only two bites of the pasta, no more. I try to fill up on salad," she confided.

Karl scanned the menu. He was a bit disappointed by its offerings; none were very adventurous. He surmised that the country club's membership was not culinarily sophisticated. For most of the men of his father's generation, the height of success and good eating was beefsteak, cooked rare and presented simply. "I think I'll have what you're having, Dad," he said, without much more than a glance at the menu.

"Good choice," his father said approvingly. "It's hard to screw up a good steak."

Karl had nothing to add to that, so he was relieved when the server brought them their drinks. He tasted his wine as his parents placed their dinner orders and found it to be quite good. Pleased, he ordered his own steak, medium rare. After the waitress took their orders with a kind of fond familiarity, she gave Karl an appreciative once-over before collecting their menus. Karl caught her complimenting look, but responded with a shy glance down at his bread plate.

As the waitress left, Frank followed her swinging gait appreciatively and said, "It seems our Nydia likes your looks, Son."

"You think?" Karl responded blandly. "I didn't really notice."

"Come now, Karl," his father teased. "You're just married, you didn't go blind."

"Frank," Annike said disapprovingly, "that's enough of that."

Frank responded by giving his son a rather obvious wink and changed the subject to golfing. "I'm giving up my cart," he finally announced. "In fact, your mother and I are giving up our membership here when we move to Palladian Gardens."

"I'm sorry to hear that, Dad," Karl responded automatically. "Are you giving up golf entirely, then?"

"Well, that remains to be seen," Frank replied. "Palladian Gardens has an arrangement with a couple of courses out west. I've never played either of them. I might have to check them out if I feel up to it."

"Will you miss the country club, Mom?" Karl asked.

Annike looked at him a bit blankly for a moment before she looked questioningly at Frank.

"Palladian Gardens," he prompted her.

She smiled sweetly for a moment, and Karl could almost see the concept of the place revealing itself behind her eyes as if clouds were parting there. Finally, she said, "Palladian Gardens has a lovely dining room. The food there is quite good as well."

Karl nodded, discerning he had gotten his answer, though not to the question he had really asked. He noted the level of the cocktail in his mother's martini glass. Though it was only half gone, she was disappearing along with the martini as she drank it.

"Are you looking forward to moving to Palladian Gardens, Mom?" he asked her gently.

She again returned his question with a blank smile before consulting Frank with her eyes once more. He nodded at her and smiled sadly. Encouraged, she told Karl, "Yes, my drink is very nice. How is your wine?"

"It's very good, Mom," Karl told her lovingly, yet she must have read the confusion on his face.

"Palladian Gardens is very nice," she told him, and then looked at Frank for approval.

"We're going to be very happy there, Karl," his father told him. "You'll see for yourself tomorrow."

"I'm looking forward to it," Karl replied, and took a sip of his wine. Suddenly, he found it sour and not as good as he recalled. He put his glass down and took a sip of water, praying that dinner would come soon. He suddenly felt very tired and certainly out of place. He thought of Caroline and glanced at his watch. She would be sitting at the dinner table, reading student work by now. Soon she'd make herself a cup of tea, sneak a bit of chocolate, and settle herself on her end of the sofa to watch TV. More than anything, he wanted to be home just then. Home, and far away from the funhouse mirror his parents inhabited now, where everything and nothing was just as it had always been.

At last, Karl found himself alone in his old bedroom. Any of the vestiges of the room he'd left thirty-four years earlier had, of course, long since disappeared. When he'd left at eighteen, the room had been a pale blue. Now it was a bruiselike mauve that bespoke his mother's last redecoration twenty years ago. It had been a guest room far longer than it had been his.

His evening ablutions were accomplished quickly after returning home from a long, mostly silent dinner at the country club. He offered no objections when his parents had declared they were ready to turn in just after nine. Quietly, he undressed to his boxers in the dim light of a bedside lamp and folded his clothes neatly to return to his suitcase. That task accomplished, he found his cell phone in his carry-on and powered it up. He was so wrapped up in the day's awful revelations that he had never even checked his voice mail for messages. Concerned he'd neglected any questions Barry might have had at work, he was relieved to find he had no messages save one from Caroline, who had called about the time he and his father had been lounging in the backyard sun. Her cheerful message let him know she was home after a good day and was just checking in, and that she wanted him to call her to say good night.

Karl sat on the edge of the bed and dialed his home number, eager to hear her voice. When she picked up he said, "Hello, sweetheart. What are you doing?"

"Watching *Project Runway* reruns," Caroline admitted guiltily. "And waiting for you to call," she added. "How are things going down there?"

"Oh, boy, where do I begin?" Karl said as he twisted and sat up against the headboard of the bed.

"Oh, no," Caro said with obvious concern.

"Well, the happiest news I have to report is that Sven and Rob are having some problems and may separate. Or not. They don't seem to know," Karl said evenly.

"That is bad news," Caroline said genuinely. "Is it a difficult situation?"

"No," Karl told her. "It's almost eerily congenial. Rob's having dinner with us tomorrow night, in fact."

"So they're not being hateful to each other," Caroline responded.

"Quite the opposite. Watching them together, you'd think nothing was wrong at all between them," Karl told her. "The bad news is Mom."

"Oh, Karl, what's wrong?" she asked anxiously.

Quickly, Karl outlined the facts, elaborating with the story of the misplaced kitchen utensils at lunch and her increasing vagueness over dinner.

"Damn," Caro said gently. "You know, in an odd way, I feel cheated by all this."

"What do you mean, hon?" Karl asked quietly.

"I just . . . I just enjoy your mother so much. We've always had a great relationship, and now it's like she's dying, but she's not. Do you understand what I'm trying to say? It would almost be easier if she was dying."

"I understand completely, Caro. I feel exactly the same way," Karl replied sadly.

"Have you talked about it with her?" Caroline asked gently.

"No," Karl said. "There really hasn't been an opportunity to speak with her alone. And the weird thing is, Dad and Sven know, but they don't talk about it in front of her. They just sort of overlook anything odd, and go on as if nothing is happening."

"Maybe it's easier for them that way," Caroline offered. "I mean, there's no need to dwell on it."

"Maybe you're right," Karl said. "I hadn't considered that."

"How are we supposed to act, Mel and I? I mean, do you even want me to tell anything to Melanie?"

"Of course, tell her," Karl said emphatically. "The only advice I can give you is what Sven told me. Just be yourself and everything will be fine."

"I wish I was there now," Caroline said solicitously. "For you."

Karl looked around the smartly appointed guest room and sighed. "So do I. But you'll be here soon. I'll pick you up in front of baggage claim. Be patient if I'm late. I-95 is still under construction and traffic is a bitch."

"Don't worry about it, love. We'll be there waiting for you," Caroline said.

"Travel safe," Karl asked wistfully.

"From your mouth to God's ears," Caroline replied easily. "I love you."

"I love you, too," Karl said. "Give Mel a hug for me."

"I will. Meanwhile, get a good night's sleep. You must be exhausted. You've been up since four or so." Caroline encouraged him, "Don't dwell on any of this. We'll get through it."

"I won't," Karl said, his wistfulness coming in clearly across the radio towers between them. "I miss you."

"And I miss you," Caroline said with love. "Sleep well."

"You, too," Karl told her and pressed his thumb on the end button. He powered down the phone and, checking the battery, decided it didn't need to be hooked to its charger. He laid the phone on the bedside table and got under the covers against the chill stirring of the ceiling fan. He switched off the light and allowed his eyes to adjust to the dimness of the room. Thanks to a streetlight, the room didn't become completely dark but rather achieved a kind of grainy dimness that revealed the edges of the room's furnishings.

Karl folded his hands behind his head and stared at the ceiling. He wondered at the funk of the six growing years and their secrets he had secured in this room. Here he had learned to dream, and to pleasure himself with certain dreams. Here he had studied for exams. Here he had rested from labors on the basketball court, and from the liquid resistance of many long laps in the pool. Now, with youthful energy mostly spent, he rested for the demands of the coming days and longed for the release of sleep. The man wistfully envisioned the boy he had been, and then his thoughts turned to the complexity of his new challenges.

Briefly, he recalled the little street scene he'd witnessed between the mother and her son early that morning. He'd been so quick to judge them and their loudly vocalized problems as just another lower-class vignette played out in his pretentious neighborhood. Now, far south, he was acutely aware of being a son and a brother rather than a husband and father with his own family. His own man, far from the little dramas of his own family. He suddenly felt ashamed of the earlier smugness he'd felt looking down from his high bedroom window in Cary. Now, lying in his old bedroom in his parents' home, he felt less in control and less self-assured. Karl wasn't certain how to assimilate his feelings about the day's news.

As a man who liked simple, elegant solutions to problems, Karl was deeply grateful to learn that his father had found a way to keep him away from the messiness and untidy facts of his mother's descent into limbo and helplessness. He knew he was lucky that his father had the resources to insulate his sons from the neediness that would accompany his own eventual decline. What Karl was left utterly unprepared for was finding a solution to the emotional need that came along with his parents' decline. Karl didn't know what to do with his feelings. He didn't know exactly how to approach the inevitability of saying good-bye to the people he had loved so easily from afar.

FRIDAY

6

KARL BROKE CLEANLY from sleep at the sound of a splash followed by the rhythmic chuffing of waters outside his window. Disoriented, he looked around the guest room and situated himself before searching for his watch on the bedside table. It was seven-fifteen. Abruptly, he tossed back the covers and stood up, as if to confront some unforeseen threat, and was rewarded with a spinning head rush as his blood pressure adjusted to being erect after lying prone for so long. He steadied himself for a moment, telling himself this annoying result of the rising was the fault of the rate at which he stood. He cautioned himself to remember to first sit on waking, and then stand. Dismissing the familiar physical routine, he then walked around the bed to the window looking out on the backyard.

Frank was in the pool, doing a slow breaststroke. Karl watched as he reached the opposite end of the lozenge-shaped pool and alternated with a backstroke for his return length. In nothing but his boxer shorts in the air-conditioned room, Karl shivered and marveled at his father's determination to brave the cold morning water of the pool outside. Frank reached the end of the pool nearest Karl's window and turned to breaststroke once more to the other end. Karl looked at the bulky expanse of his father's back shining in the meager sun rising overhead, and he marveled at the muscle still evident there. He hoped he looked as good as his father did when he got to be his age. Karl did his laps in the heated pool at the Y, and like Frank, he remained committed to the exercise and the peace that came with the repetitive motion in the pool's confines.

For a moment, Karl considered putting on his swim trunks and joining his father, but then decided he'd rather spend some time with his mother. Karl smiled to himself, happy just then to be "home" in a sense that was so distinct from the home he had made for himself as an adult. Despite the difficult new realties he'd discovered so far on this little pilgrimage home, he felt eager to begin the new day.

Karl headed to the bathroom, picking up his dop kit along the way. Within a few minutes he'd bathed from the sink and shaved himself satisfactorily in preparation for the day. He was anxious to see if his mother was up. He looked forward to spending some time alone with her before his father finished with his morning exercise and came in to dominate the conversation—and, Karl thought, to cover for any hint of unusual behavior from his mother. He dressed quickly in only a clean T-shirt and jeans, straightened the bedcovers, and padded out across the house to the breakfast nook.

Annike was sitting at the breakfast table with a pack of cigarettes, a lighter, and an ashtray next to her cup of coffee. When she saw Karl come in, she quickly tucked the cigarettes and lighter in the pocket of her robe and look at him pleadingly. "Don't tattle on me, Karl," she said by way of good morning.

Karl walked over to her and bent to wrap her in a hug. "Don't worry, Mom," he said assuringly. "Your secret's safe with me."

"Thank God," she said as she looked up at him and smiled. "Your father watches me like a hawk ever since I accidentally dropped a cigarette between the sofa and the side table in the living room and didn't recall doing it."

Karl walked around the counter and into the kitchen, and found the coffeepot nearly full. "I'm not so sure I approve of you smoking, either, but because of your health," Karl said as he found a mug in its familiar place in the cabinet over the coffeemaker.

His mother laughed. "I am seventy-seven years old. Smoking hasn't killed me yet and I haven't had as much as a cold in two years," she said as Karl poured his coffee. "It's one of the few pleasures I have left now that I have to forgo most of my cocktails."

"Why have you stopped drinking?" Karl asked as he made his way back to the table and sat down.

Annike chuckled. "It's this medicine I take these days. It's bad enough on its own, but if I have a scotch, or more than a glass of wine, I quickly become a vegetable."

Karl looked at her sharply, then masked his concern with a studied sip from his mug.

"Your father has spoken with you about me, I suppose," his mother said casually.

"He's told me you have some challenges right now, yes," Karl answered carefully.

Annike drew the cigarettes and lighter from her robe pocket and lit one, inhaling deeply. "In perspective," she said before blowing out the smoke, "this," she said, regarding the cigarette, "is not a real problem."

"True," Karl allowed grudgingly.

"*JAG er snart går till bli en spoke,*" Annike said happily. *I am soon going to be a ghost* "*JAG skal bli så mycket som av mig själv så JAG kanna framför då,*" she added confidently. *I am going to be as much of myself as I can before then.*

Karl looked at her with some perplexity. "Sorry, Mom, I only caught something about you being . . . *something,* and you trying to be . . ." He lifted his hands and opened them questioningly.

"I'm sorry, Son. I was only testing you. I know they say I drift in and out of my Swedish without thinking of it." She laughed cheerfully. "Sometimes it just seems easier to use it to say what I mean. I do it without thinking," she explained, then added with a sigh, "English is such a difficult language. It is clunky."

"But Dad and I can't keep up with you in Swedish," Karl said patiently.

"I wish I had been more encouraging with you when you were

small," Annike said, and reached across the table to pat his hand. She took a drag off her cigarette and played its tip around the rim of the ashtray. "But you were a very stubborn child. "I *Engelsk, Mama*," you used to say. "In English, Mama. By the time you were five, you were determined to speak English only."

"I'm sorry," Karl said awkwardly. "I . . . I couldn't think in Swedish."

"You could if you were being naughty, or if you didn't want your father to know what you were saying." Annike laughed.

Karl smiled and looked into his coffee cup as if those long-old memories were distilled there. Once when he was small, he had scratched his father's car rather badly with the edge of the handle-bars of his bike, the red rubber grip having come off and become lost long before. His father had noticed the scratch and was threatening to spank him. Karl quickly told his mother in Swedish what had happened, and just as quickly she told Frank that she had made the scratch with her keys as she was juggling bags of groceries. Karl avoided his spanking, and his mother never betrayed him.

"*Ja, Mama. Du er rätt och du er underbar*," Karl said neatly in Swedish and gave her a grin. *Yes, Mama. You are right and you are wonderful.*

"Very good," she complimented him. "But you really can't be blamed for not being able to keep up. It is different for you. You have no reason to use Swedish all the time, and if you don't use it it's like trying to grab at smoke when you need it. I feel that way about English more and more, Karl," she explained gently.

"Sven can understand you, though, right?" Karl asked her.

"Sven is my baby," Annike said. "Your father resents it when we speak Swedish. He feels left out. But I can't be concerned about that when I lose my English. Sven tries very hard to make things go easily for me. Of course," she said as she inhaled her cigarette once more, "Sven has a natural aptitude for the language. He has been going back and forth in English and Swedish since he was a baby."

"It's helpful now more than ever," Karl admitted, "isn't it?"

"For me, it is," his mother told him and sighed. "I get confused between . . ." She hesitated and searched Karl's eyes, begging to be understood. ". . . between now and other times, some long ago. They tell me the newer brain cells die more quickly. Soon, I will have only the past," she said resignedly.

"Are you frightened?" Karl asked with real concern.

Annike took another hit off her cigarette and then stubbed it out decisively in the ashtray. "No," she told him. "The past is very seductive. I have had a remarkable life, and I am not afraid to fall backwards down Alice's rabbit hole. When I am alone, it is very pleasant. I stand in my kitchen in New Jersey with you playing on the floor with your trucks. I go back to very ordinary things, really. But when I get lost in time, your father just can't go with me. I really wish he could live it all over again with me," she said wistfully. "The doctor says eventually I will lose my way back to the present altogether. But I am not frightened by that—believe me."

Karl once more reached across the table and took her hand. "Don't be in a hurry to leave us, Mom. We still need you."

Annike smiled wanly. "No. You no longer need me, my good son. But I need you to remember me as I was before I was . . . *erased.*" She cocked her head as if she heard something. "That is what I feel—as if I am being erased." She laughed then and stood. "Can I heat up your coffee?"

Karl handed his mug to her wordlessly and watched as she moved to the kitchen. "I wish I could do something," Karl said with a ring of frustration.

Annike freshened their mugs with coffee and cream and returned to the table. Standing over Karl, she handed him his cup and said, "Don't be silly."

Karl looked up at her searchingly as he took his mug in both hands. "What do you mean?"

"There is nothing anyone can do, dear. About being erased, or growing old, or dying. It's just life," Annike said as she sat down once more and took a sip of her coffee.

"You sound so okay with it," Karl told her. "Aren't you angry? Don't you feel cheated?"

"You don't go to mass anymore, do you, Karl?" Annike asked.

"No, not really. I go sometimes on holy days, but I stopped really believing years ago," Karl told her honestly.

"How sad for you," Annike told him gently.

"You can't sit there and be so sanguine about what's happening to you because you believe in heaven and all that, not really," Karl said defensively. "Why would God take your life from you before you stop living? What kind of God would do that?" he concluded angrily.

Annike calmly took a sip of her coffee, then thoughtfully drew her pack of cigarettes and lighter from her robe pocket. She lit one and smiled. "There is so much comfort in simply having coffee and a cigarette," she said, and looked Karl in the eye. "Why would you deny yourself the comfort of faith when it is so much richer?"

"I have no answer for that, Mother," Karl replied stiffly.

Annike smiled. "I have no answers left at all, Karl. That's where faith comes in. To be perfectly honest with you, I cannot explain it. But yes, I do believe in heaven and in that God you find so vindictive and uncaring."

"Let's talk about something else," Karl said, and defiantly concentrated on his coffee.

Annike nodded and took a drag off her cigarette. "Okay. You have asked me how I am. Now let me ask you how you are."

Karl gave her a surprised look and shrugged. "Never better. Work is going well. I'm healthy, Caro's healthy. My daughter has grown into an adult I find very easy to like and love. I'm a lucky average guy."

"So, you are happy?" Annike pressed him.

Karl thought of what his father had said about happiness the day before in the garden. He was safe, he was comfortable. Like his father had told him in *his* way, Karl honestly told his mother he was happy.

"That's a good thing," Annike said as she toyed with her cigarette. "A mother wants to see her sons happy and well. I have no reason to be anything other than very pleased with you."

"Well, that's good to hear," Karl answered, relieved.

"But I miss you," she said simply. "Simply sitting with you like we are now, just talking and being together. It is such a little thing, but it means a great deal."

"I wish I lived closer, Mom. It just didn't work out that way," Karl reasoned.

"Oh, I know that," Annike assured him. "And I certainly wouldn't grudge you your life up in North Carolina." She looked at him a long time and took his form in as he sat hunched over his coffee at the table. "You just don't understand the sense of closeness I miss. It's a mom thing," she said and laughed. "I made you. You never stop being amazed at that as a parent. You are a grown man, with an adult's life and responsibilities, but you are still . . ."

"Still your baby," Karl said and smiled.

"Yes," Annike said simply.

"I thought Sven is your baby," Karl teased her.

"Sven is more like me," Annike said with certainty. "You are so much like your father. It's as if he is distilled in you. I suppose it is a natural extension of my love for Frank to love you, his son, so. You look like him, you have his . . . his *distance* from me. I'm losing my words. I can't explain," she said finally.

Karl was taken aback. His mother had never spoken so intimately of her feelings for him before. In a thousand ways that were inarticulate, he knew she loved him, but she had never spoken to him this way.

As he considered this, she looked away and sat smoking in silence, absently taking sips of her coffee and gathering herself back into herself. He could almost feel the moment dissipating in the smoky room. He badly wanted to reconnect with what they had been sharing, but he couldn't find the words himself. Finally he took a sip of his coffee and said, "I'm going to miss you so much."

She looked at him and smiled. "Well, I'm not gone yet. Let's concentrate on having a wonderful weekend, yes?"

Karl leaned across the table and kissed her cheek. "*Ja Mama. Det er alt god,*" he said. *Yes, mama. It will be good.*

Her only reply was a loving look and a happy smile. "So, are you hungry?" she demanded.

Karl nodded, unwilling to admit that so much coffee and such deep conversation were turning his stomach a bit sour.

"Publix makes the most marvelous pastries," she said as she stubbed out her cigarette, then stood and picked up her ashtray. "I can offer you an excellent cheese or raspberry Danish, or some Danish pecan ring. I no longer cook in the mornings. If you would like something simpler, I have an oatmeal cereal your father eats each day for his cholesterol."

Karl grimaced at the final offer and said, "How about a small slice each of the cheese and raspberry Danish?"

"Good choice," Annike said and patted his shoulder as she passed behind him on her way to the kitchen.

"When is Dad coming in?" Karl asked as he peered out the back door.

Annike emptied her ashtray and then put it back in its place on the counter, under the cabinet where her official cigarettes were kept from her reach. "After he finishes his paper," she replied easily. "On pretty mornings like this, he likes to take out a Thermos of coffee and have his breakfast *en plein air.*" She laughed as she reached for two small plates and napkins. "He will be in once he has checked in with his friends George W. Bush and Donald Rumsfeld. Then we will get to hear all about how they are making America safe from the terrorists."

"He's really into it, then?" Karl asked, bemused.

"Oh, yes," Annike replied as she opened the pastry containers with a shriek of stiff plastic. "They cannot run the country without him. But Nancy Pelosi or Howard Dean will say something to infuriate him and he will come in very irritable. You mark my words," she said with an upraised finger wagging knowingly.

Karl watched as she cut pieces of pastry far too large for him and only slivers for herself.

"Or it will be the gay people, or the president of Venezuela, or the black people, or those poor migrants from Mexico. Your father is angered by many things beyond his control," she said as she returned to the table with the sweets. She set his plate and napkin before him and then sat down herself.

"No fork?" Karl asked carefully.

"You have no fingers?" his mother replied tartly.

Karl laughed as he picked up a piece of raspberry Danish and took a bite. The pastry was actually very good, and he found himself wolfing it down with relish. Then he ostentatiously licked his fingers before using his napkin. "Delicious," he said easily.

His mother took a small bite of her pastry and nodded. She chewed carefully and swallowed before she continued. "I tell him, 'Frank, your son is gay, our maid is from Colombia, our lawn man is Haitian, and I am an immigrant myself. Why must you pick on those people so?'"

"And what does Dad say to that?" Karl wondered with interest.

Annike rolled her eyes and took another bite of her pastry before she said, "He mostly says nothing to that. He just shakes his paper and gives me a dirty look."

Karl laughed.

"America should be more like Sweden," Annike said. "There are many taxes, but everyone has health care and it is a quiet, peaceful country where people take care of each other. When I tell him this, he says I am crazy and a socialist."

"And how do you answer that?" Karl asked once more.

"I tell him I am a mother and a very well-educated woman. It would be better if women ran the world and let the men play with their little armies only in the Arctic or someplace harmless," she said stubbornly.

"I bet he loves to hear that," Karl said evenly.

"He pays no attention to me," Annike said dismissively. "He thinks I am *une naïf*."

"You are not naïve or simple-minded," Karl told her. "I think much the way you do."

"Don't tell your father that." His mother chuckled. "He will become most difficult."

Karl gave her a complicit look and nod of his head before attacking his cheese Danish. When he finished it, he said, "Your granddaughter is looking forward to taking him on. She isn't afraid to argue about politics one bit."

Annike laughed delightedly. "Melanie is afraid of no one. And she is very intelligent. I will sit and cheer her from the sidelines." Then Annike grew silent and played a moment with her napkin, folding it prettily before placing it once more in her lap. "Karl," she asked, "do you approve of her living with this Andrew before she marries him? She is moving far away, with no guarantee he will look after her or be kind to her. I am concerned."

Karl scooted back from the breakfast table to allow himself room to cross his legs. He looked at his mother and shook his head. "Mom, I trust her instincts. She tells me she is only moving in with him for practical reasons. She wants time to become established in a new job, and to get used to living with Andrew before she goes ahead with the wedding. To tell you the truth, I think he would marry her now. It's obvious he is in love with her. Melanie is putting off the wedding."

Annike sighed. "Young women these days wait so long to have their babies. I was twenty-two when I had you, and you were a very busy little boy. You could be exhausting. Melanie is now twenty-four; when does she plan to have children?"

"I don't know, Mom," Karl said earnestly. "But remember, you were thirty-seven when you had Sven, and he's turned out well. I know I was almost thirteen, but you seemed to handle both him and me, for God's sake."

Annike made a dismissive wave of her hands and said, "I had Sven because I was bored. Your father believes Sven was an accident, but I wanted another child. Your father did not want me to work, and you were nearly a teenager. He worked long hours and was away a great deal. Back then he was in love with his job more than me. I had Sven to have someone I could play with," she admitted.

"Do you ever regret that?" Karl asked.

"Do you know what Sven means in Old Swedish?" Annike countered.

Karl shook his head.

"It means *beloved*," Annike answered gently.

"And what does Karl mean?" he asked out of curiosity.

"*Strong*," Annike told him. "I wanted to name you Andreas, after my brother, but your father didn't want you to have a Swedish name. He compromised on the spelling. I got the K, but he wanted you to be an American boy."

"You never told me this," Karl said, taken aback somewhat. "So I'm supposed to be the strong one."

"There is a lot of magic in names, Karl," Annike told him with assurance. "You are strong and independent and a man's man."

"And Sven is *beloved*," Karl said snidely.

"You're no less loved," Annike told him patiently. "But I told you I had Sven for myself."

Karl wasn't sure how this new information sat with him. It came from a line of reasoning he felt to be distinctly feminine, and thus alien to a certain extent. The fact that his mother could simply choose to create another child, and then do it, was on the other side of that no-man's-land between men and women that had always existed. That decision, made forty years ago, seemed very powerful to him at that moment. It was a part of his mother he had never considered.

"Have I made you sad?" Annike gently asked him.

Karl chuckled hesitantly, but gave her a smile. "No. Not sad, it's just something I've never given any thought to," he admitted honestly.

"Wait here," she said and stood suddenly. "I'll just be a moment."

Thinking she might have to go to the bathroom, Karl unfolded his legs and stood to let her pass behind him. "I'm going to heat up my coffee. Would you like another cup?"

"No, thank you," Annike said as she passed him and turned to go down the hall. "But please bring my ashtray back to the table," she said over her shoulder. "This is a holiday, yes? I can spoil myself."

Karl chuckled to himself as he went around the counter and into the kitchen. He made himself a fresh cup of coffee and tried to sort out his feelings regarding the difference between his mother's relationship with him and with his brother. It was unnerving to have his attention called to the very different ways she perceived each of their natures. He was surprised to find how they interlocked with his own perceptions of himself and Sven. He recalled the sudden urge he had felt the day before when Sven had picked him up at the airport. He had felt as if Sven were a child still, delightful and sunny, and he'd wanted to hug him and treat him with all the loving impulse given to an adored toddler. To Karl at twelve, Sven had been like a fascinating new toy. Karl was certain his mother didn't see Sven as a toy, considering her maternal instincts, but he was an object of entertainment, the same by her own admission. He tried to decide if thinking of Sven as a toy was a good thing for Sven as he resumed his seat at the table.

If Annike had tried to name them with any kind of prescience, she had done a good job. Karl did feel he was strong. He had confidently made decisions about his own life and acted on them with a great degree of success and accomplishment. What left him unsettled was the impact Sven's name may have had on Sven's life. In what way did being beloved mold him? To Karl, Sven had never appeared to be spoiled or self-centered. In fact, from the little interaction he'd had with him on this trip, Sven seemed to be quite the opposite of a spoiled, capricious man, which many beloved children become. His care for their parents was obvious. He was maintaining a civilized relationship with Rob, despite their problems. Then there was the whole business of the gift of the candle. It was a small gesture, but it said a great deal about Sven's openhanded nature.

Breaking into his reverie, Annike said, "I want to show you these." She pushed his plate away and set a large photo album on the table before him. Unaware of his musings, Annike sat down. "Where is my ashtray?" she asked politely.

Karl shook his head and stood quickly. "I completely forgot," he admitted as he went to the kitchen to retrieve it. By the time he returned to the table and sat down, his mother had lit a cigarette and opened the album. He looked at the old, square, black-and-white images of himself and his parents from when he was a baby.

The left-hand page was filled with an eight-by-ten studio portrait of Karl and his parents. Karl, at perhaps two years old, stolidly sat on a carpeted platform, dressed in a tiny suit and tie. His hair was nearly white and rather long, considering the styles of 1953. He was a grave-faced baby, looking at the camera without any fear.

Behind him stood Frank and Annike, so young and slender, fresh-faced, and earnest. His crew-cut-handsome father easily rested his arm across his mother's shoulders and held her possessively. He, like his son, peered at the camera soberly. Karl's mother had her hair, which was as bright as her son's, up in a French bun, and she held Karl protectively, her hand resting on his chubby tummy. The photographer's flash had caught her looking at her baby. Her eyes and soft smile betrayed both pride and love.

Annike reached across the table and gently tapped on the page holding the picture. "You were beloved, too."

Karl gave her an embarrassed smile and looked again at the picture. "Was I always so somber?"

Annike laughed. Forgetting she had a cigarette burning in the ashtray, she took her cigarettes and lighter out once more. After she lit another cigarette, she said, "You were very no-nonsense. Very quick and clever, but you weren't a jolly child."

Karl spared her a glance and shook his head. "I was busy being strong," he commented dryly. "Mom, are you going to smoke with both hands?" he asked and pointed to the ashtray.

Annike only chuckled and put out her earlier cigarette, then pointed to a picture of Karl on the opposite page. Annike held him on her hip, and both were bundled in coats behind blown snow caught forever in the wind's drift. She began a story about the photograph, which grew into more stories as she moved on to other pictures. Together they went through the pages of the album. By the time they reached its end, Karl realized that he was understanding only occasional words in Annike's running narrative. Long familiarity with the events behind the pictures, as well as the soothing voice of his mother, had kept him from noticing that she had slipped completely into Swedish far more complex than Karl could comprehend. She stopped and looked at him expectantly. Karl felt his eyes grow moist, and he searched for the phrases Sven had coached him on the day before.

"Ja Mama. Tala mig hur mer," he replied. *Yes, mama. Tell me more.*

Annike turned the page and continued with her story, happily unaware that Karl could no longer understand her, or that her cigarette had burned to a long cylindrical ash that threatened to fall as she gestured with her hand.

Karl tried as hard as he could to be casual as he wiped his eyes free of the tears that had collected and threatened to spill. She had slipped away from him in a matter of moments, and he hadn't even noticed. Now he felt being closed off from her even as she sat so fondly by his side. It was a fearful taste of the future in the sunny breakfast nook of the present. He wondered how long she would be gone, and if there were any gentle way he could bring her back to language they could both understand.

As he sat watching Annike's happily animated face, the door to the lanai opened and Frank stepped into the room with his Thermos, coffee mug, and newspaper. Karl looked up at him helplessly as his mother chattered on. Frank's eyes communicated a deep sadness to his son before he stepped behind Annike and gently kissed the top of her head. "Are you walking Karl down memory lane, darling?" he asked casually.

Annike turned her head and looked up at him with a radiant smile. For a moment she hesitated, and then something seemed to click behind her eyes. Karl almost heard the sound of the gears shifting in her mind. His mother's happy expression briefly shifted to one of confusion, then she nodded and said, "Karl is being very patient with his old mother, listening to these stories again." She looked down at the table and anxiously put her cigarette out in the ashtray. "Why don't you tell us what is going on in the world today," she said as she glanced up at her husband once more.

Relief surged through Karl and he almost slumped, so tensely had his whole body been focused on his mother. "Anything good happening, Dad?"

Frank moved from behind Annike and walked into the kitchen,

setting his thermos and paper on the counter as he passed. From the coffeepot he said, "Well, my son is home and my granddaughter and her mother are on their way. That's the best news I've had in a while." He filled his cup with coffee and then strode confidently to the table and sat down. "Other than that, the world has gone crazy."

7

AS THEY PASSED out of the hallway into the reception area of the main building, Karl felt as if he'd been let out of a maze. The ceiling in this part of the octagonal building was double-height and filled with sunshine streaming through the oversized Palladian windows, from which the company derived its name, that framed the entry. After the long hall of a residential wing, lined with anonymous apartment doors, Karl's spirits lifted in the large room. Tastefully furnished with leather wingback chairs and chintz-covered settees arranged in conversation-friendly groupings, the reception area was more country club than nursing home. Karl wondered if the architect had planned this spirit-lifting space in a calculated attempt to alleviate the sense of confinement that permeated the halls branching off the cheerful space.

"Our residents say Palladian Gardens is just like a cruise ship that never leaves port," the professionally gracious woman named Roberta said as she led Karl and his father to the dining room. "Many residents say they regret not making the move here when they were younger," she said as she stopped at the maître d's podium and looked at Karl with a bright smile.

Karl somehow managed to return Roberta's smile, though after nearly two hours in her soft-sell presence he felt the urge to slap her. While her conversation had been consistently upbeat, it also relentlessly addressed the facts of his parents' aging and eventual physical decline toward death. Searching for something innocuous to say, he looked at his father, who returned his look with an eagerness for approval that filled Karl with pity. "I am impressed," he said to his father carefully.

"I'm so glad Mr. Preston brought you to look us over," Roberta interrupted. "Now you're in for a real treat. We have a choice of roast beef or baked halibut today. We put a great deal of emphasis on the quality and presentation of our meals. Mealtime is something our residents really look forward to," she said earnestly. "Your mother and father can choose between two- or three-meal-a-day plans. We find that most of our residents choose the two-meal plan, preferring to eat breakfast in their homes or to have the freedom of being out and about during lunch."

Karl nodded his head approvingly and was relieved to see a tall, middle-aged African-American man dressed in a coat and tie step up to the podium at the dining room doors.

"This is Charles Lawson, our dining services manager," Roberta told them. "Mr. Lawson, this is Mr. Frank Preston and his son Karl. Frank and his wife, Annike, are going to become part of our family in June, and Karl is here to check us out. They're our guests for lunch, so make sure they feel at home, okay?"

Mr. Lawson extended his hand to Frank and Karl in turn. "It's a pleasure to meet you," he said to Karl. "I recall meeting your father and mother not long ago. Welcome back, Mr. Preston."

"Thank you, sir," Frank said confidently. "Now, which do you recommend, the roast or the halibut?"

Mr. Lawson leaned in conspiratorially toward Frank's ear and said, "I'm partial to the roast beef, myself."

"Good man," Frank replied heartily.

Roberta extended her hand to Karl and said, "I'll say good-bye here and let you and your father enjoy lunch."

Karl took her hand and found her surreptitiously leaving a business card in his palm. "Thanks for your time," he said genuinely.

Roberta looked directly in his eyes and said, "If you have any further questions or concerns, *whatsoever*, please don't hesitate to contact me."

Having been subjected to a tour of a one-bedroom apartment similar to the one his parents would be occupying, as well as a professionally produced sales presentation, Karl had no further questions except ones that had no real answers: questions about love, loss, and family that Roberta didn't address. Her topics ranged from fiscal to physical fitness, all presented with relentless optimism. Any practical questions Karl had in that regard were well answered. Palladian Gardens appeared to be exactly what the brochure presented: a place for well-heeled Republicans to be well cared for as they waited to die. "I will if anything comes to mind," Karl told her. "But you've been very informative. I think my parents have made an excellent choice," he said, looking at his father and smiling.

Roberta nodded, obviously pleased by his response, then said, "Mr. Preston, we'll be in touch with you about the final paperwork and details."

"Thank you, Roberta," Frank said sincerely.

"Gentlemen," Mr. Lawson interrupted, "right this way."

With that, Frank and Karl followed Mr. Lawson's broad back to the buffet line. He preceded them as they collected cloth napkins and flatware and placed them on trays, which they slid along a handy shelf in front of an array of foods in large, gleaming chafing dishes presented on white, linen-draped tables. There were staff interspersed along the line who placed their selected items on their plates, and at the end of the line was a teenaged boy who took Frank's tray for him and accompanied them to an empty table by one of the huge Palladian windows. Mr. Lawson seated Frank, then took the plates of salad, roast and vegetables, and dessert from the waiting teenager and set them on the table. The teenager waited while Karl divested his own tray of its food and took his tray when he'd finished. He then took their beverage orders and made his way back across the dining room.

"Gentlemen," Mr. Lawson said unctuously, "is there anything else we can get you?"

Karl and Frank glanced around the table and shook their heads.

"Please, let me remind you. We have a no-tipping policy in our dining room. Your server is Raul, and he'll bring along your bread and drinks shortly. Do you have any questions I can answer for you?"

"No, Mr. Lawson," Frank said assertively. "Everything is fine. Thank you for our lunch."

"Yes, thank you," Karl echoed.

"My pleasure," Mr. Lawson said and smiled. Once more, Karl found himself with a business card pressed into his palm. "Please remember we have facilities here for our residents' use, for everything from small, private dinners to family reunions. If you think of any special event I can help you with in the future, or questions I can answer, please let me know."

Karl placed the business card with Roberta's in his inside jacket pocket—a jacket his father had taken from his own closet and insisted he wear. Karl now understood why: Palladian Gardens was a rather formal place that tried to have both the atmosphere of a grand hotel and a family feel. Matching the formality of the place, Karl said politely, "Thank you, Mr. Lawson, I'm sure my parents will be well taken care of here."

Mr. Lawson responded with a dignified nod and said, "If you'll excuse me, then. Enjoy your lunch."

Before Karl could say anything to his father, Raul returned with their drinks and a basket of assorted breads and butter. He checked with Karl and Frank with only a look and a nod, and having suitably ascertained that they had no further need of him, he left them to their lunch.

"So, what do you think?" Frank asked his son as he eagerly attacked his slice of well-done roast.

"I don't know what to think," Karl admitted honestly. "It's a lot to take in." Karl looked around the dining room, which was only about half full. While there were a few solitary diners, most tables were occupied by sociable small groups of six or eight. To Karl, it reminded him of a posh country club. The sun shone through the large windows, but the air-conditioning held out any excessive warmth. The room itself was thickly carpeted, and expensive drapes hung at the mammoth windows. There were small vases of fresh-cut daisies and mums on each table. But for the presence of a few wheelchairs and portable oxygen tanks identifying some of the diners as particularly elderly, he might have been having lunch at the haunt of a bunch of bankers and lawyers.

Frank chewed on his roast, gesturing in small circles with his knife and fork as they hovered over his plate. "It's definitely not a nursing home," he said confidently.

"What does Mom think about all this?" Karl said as he cut into his own lunch.

"Oh, she thinks it's all rather grand," Frank said. "All I care about is that she'll be treated like a queen as long as she's aware of what's going on. Living here will be like being on permanent vacation."

"The apartment is kind of small, isn't it?" Karl asked honestly. Despite the grandeur of its public spaces, the actual living units were Spartan. Though each apartment boasted a balcony just large enough for a couple of chairs and a small table, the interior was less than generous, with a tiny kitchen, dining area, living room, bedroom, and bath. On the whole, they were rather like the apartments many of these people had begun their adult lives in.

"Karl, your mother and I don't need a lot of space. We live in the kitchen and breakfast nook now, except when we're asleep," Frank told him bluntly.

"Won't you miss your yard?" Karl asked.

"Not one bit," Frank said. "The grounds here are lovely, and the Olympic-sized pool is indoors and heated."

"Well, that's certainly something," Karl admitted.

"Once your mother goes into the full-time-care wing, I'll probably downgrade to a studio apartment," Frank added as he finished off his plate. For Frank, eating had always been a matter of utility, and evidently, now so had his requirements for living. While Karl thought the accommodations and the food rather bland, Frank seemed to appreciate all of it without any apparent concern. "I'm going to buy one of those big LCD televisions and have it installed on the wall as soon as we move in," his father said. "They have satellite TV here."

"Sounds nice," Karl said quietly. "What are you going to do with all of your furniture and things?"

Frank replaced his lunch plate with his dessert plate and took a bite of peach pie. "Tomorrow we're going to let you kids decide what pieces you want, and which of the china and knickknacks you'll want to keep for sentimental reasons. What you don't want, I'm giving to Saint Vincent de Paul for the tax deduction."

Karl was impressed by his father's equanimity. He seemed to have it all planned out thoughtfully. "Caro wants Mom's desk," he admitted.

Frank looked up from what was left of his pie and nodded. "Excellent. That desk means a lot to your mother. She'll be pleased Caro wants it."

"Where did that desk come from, anyway?" Karl asked suddenly. It was a remarkable piece of furniture, very efficient in its nooks and crannies, but also very elegant and obviously well designed. He couldn't remember it from his childhood, yet he associated it with his mother very strongly. Even now he could imagine her sitting at it, writing a letter in her beautiful cursive.

"We got it after you left home. Your mother found that desk in a very expensive shop in Stockholm and wanted it badly. It's by some famous designer. Don't ask me which one, just one of the modern Scandinavians. Anyway, she had the money, so I told her to go on and buy it. We had it shipped over." Frank thought for a moment before he continued. "When your grandmother died, she left her bank account in your mother's name in Stockholm. It was easier for us to convert everything to cash and just leave it in the bank in Kroners. We used the account whenever we went over to visit."

"I had no idea," Karl admitted. "I just know Mom is very fond of that desk."

"Sven says it's worth a fortune," Frank told him. "All that modernist crap is all the rage these days."

"Does Sven want it, then?" Karl asked.

Frank finished his pie and took a sip of his iced tea. He pushed his chair back from the table and crossed his legs as if he were already at home in the formal dining room. "Your brother has been curiously quiet when asked what he wants. I don't know if he wants everything for that shop of his—you know how much Swedish stuff we have—or if he's sick of it all and wants nothing to do with it."

"That seems odd," Karl admitted.

"Not really," Frank said easily. "You don't see all the old stuff in our house on a regular basis. Sven does. Anyway, as far as I'm concerned, it's all become a burden, like some big shell on my back. I'm really looking forward to taking just a few things and moving here. Life is going to be simpler, lighter," he said optimistically.

"You'll miss your trees and your flower beds and your study—I know you will," Karl countered.

Frank snorted and said, "No, I won't. I'm tired of being responsible for all of it, and don't even get me started on the property taxes." He snorted again, then looked Karl in the eye and said, "Somehow, the house seems like it belongs to another time and place. Like losing my orange trees to old age—it's too sad. As for my office, I bet I don't spend fifteen minutes a week in there. I pay every bill the day it comes in and I'm out of there."

"So moving to Palladian Gardens is like starting on a new, exciting phase of your life," Karl responded, his tone encouraging. Then he pressed further. "Do you think you'll find more things to do here? More people to interact with?"

Frank looked around the dining room and surveyed its occupants. Completing his survey at his son's face, he said, "There are probably some interesting old farts around here, but I imagine I'll do what I've been doing. Read my morning paper back to front, swim a little every day, and watch CNN and C-SPAN. Read a good Tom Clancy or Robert Ludlum or James Patterson novel once a month. Hell, Son, at eighty you're not looking for a lot of stimulation."

"You make it sound kind of boring to live to be eighty," Karl replied curiously.

"It is boring," Frank admitted. "I wouldn't have retired if they'd let me keep on working," he said sadly. "That's a man's life. Work til you die—that way you're useful."

Karl nodded. He himself had not even begun to comprehend retirement. He loved his job and felt no driving urge to give up the mental stimulation and routine he loved. That was one of the nice things about being a partner in the firm. He at least had a say about how he'd make his exit. IBM hadn't been so kind to his father in that regard.

"I guess if I'm going to be useless, I can at least enjoy it," Frank said and chuckled. "After all these years, I'm looking forward to having someone else be responsible for all the bullshit. Here I don't have to worry about even driving to mass. They have a chapel here, and a priest who comes in on Saturday night to hear confessions and say the mass."

"Won't they miss you at your church?" Karl asked evenly. "You've been a parishioner for forty years at that place."

"I won't miss paying for the refurbishment of the sanctuary," Frank said truculently. "Hell, I helped pay for the first church and the school. Now they're starting another building drive to completely update the sanctuary. They never stop with the funding drives. And then there was Sven's parochial school tuition for twelve years on top of that. I've had it."

"That's part of why I'm glad I don't belong to a parish," Karl admitted.

His father looked at him disapprovingly. "So you don't belong to any church up there in Cary?"

"No. We stopped going after Melanie was confirmed," Karl answered him carefully. "I promised you and Mom I'd raise her Catholic, even though Caro is—*was*—a Methodist. I kept my promise, now I'm done with it," Karl finished decisively.

"I felt that way when I was your age," Frank admitted. "But your mother insisted we still attend mass, and Sven was being schooled in the church, so I went along with her. But I'll be honest with you, Son. My faith has come to mean a lot to me as I've gotten older. One day you'll find your way back to the church. It happens when you get closer to the end," he added with authority.

"Why would I do that, Dad?" Karl replied sarcastically. "Fire insurance?"

Frank didn't laugh at the joke, but studied his son's face for a long moment and finally unfolded his legs and leaned in closer, his forearms resting on the table. "I'm not scared of hell, Karl. I just came to the realization that nothing in this world makes any kind of sense without something to believe in."

"I don't believe anymore, Dad," Karl told him gently. "I'm just not built to swallow all the rules and regulations, much less the willful ignorance it takes to be a believer. Yes, I believe there's a God, but I long ago stopped thinking he had any interest in me personally. Life is what you make it yourself. I'm content with believing that," Karl ended placidly.

"You haven't needed God for anything yet," Frank said with certainty.

"And you have?" Karl asked dismissively. "Your own hard work provided the wherewithal for you to spend your last years here, rather than in some nursing home that smells like pee and Pine-Sol. I don't see God or your church writing you any checks."

Frank peered at his son from under the long, wild hairs of his aged brow and said, "I can't tell you anything to convince you or change your mind, Karl. It's about faith. I still have it, and I think one day you'll find yours again. All I can tell you is the only thing that keeps me from putting a pistol in your mother's mouth and then in mine is faith that somehow everything is going to be alright and that there's a reason why things are the way they are right now. I can't go on living without believing that with all my heart. It's just too unbearable."

"Look, Dad, I don't grudge you your faith, and as for hell, maybe you're right—maybe someday I'll find myself looking for some answers in church again. I just want you to not worry about me, okay?"

"Oh, I don't worry about you," Frank said easily. "I've prayed for you every day of your life, and look at what you've become. I'm proud of you, you know that, right?"

"I know, Dad," Karl said, slightly embarrassed. "And I want you to know I appreciate your wisdom in taking care of yourself and Mom by moving into this place. You're still on top of everything. I'll say that for you," Karl said stiffly. "You're still looking out for all of us."

His father looked at him and nodded. "Thanks, Son. I do my best," he said gruffly. "Now eat your pie. We need to be getting back to the house to check on your mother. I don't like leaving her alone for so long."

Karl nodded and drew his dessert plate toward him, relieved at the chance to stop talking for a while. He was surprised to find that the pie was better than his lunch had been. As he ate, he was aware of his father watching him quietly. It made him self-conscious as he chewed and swallowed. Finally, he looked up and met his father's gaze, and he was surprised by the love he saw there. It was obvious his father missed him as much as his mother had been better able to explain, but the look Karl found spoke volumes.

"It's good?" his father asked him softly.

"It's *all* good," Karl said and smiled.

8

ON THE WAY back to his parents' house, Karl endured his father's driving, which alternated between being overly cautious and very aggressive. Even at midday, all of the streets were congested and the traffic was like the inside of a pinball machine, with other vehicles darting in and out of their lanes when his father deemed it necessary to drive the speed limit. When faced with anyone driving not to his liking, Frank would angrily switch lanes without warning and then cut other drivers off to get back into the familiar lanes he knew led him most easily home. Karl was a nervous wreck as a result by the time they drove onto the street his parents lived on.

"What the hell is he doing here?" Frank said as he pulled up behind Sven's Excursion parked in his drive. The big vehicle's back end loomed into the windshield's view and filled it with its broad-assed bulk, and Frank swerved the Buick hard to the left. Karl clung anxiously to his armrest as his father abruptly steered the car to the other side of the drive and came to a stop beside the SUV.

Karl didn't answer, but he felt a sense of unease grow steadily as he got out of the car and followed his father up the pathway to the front door. Though it was closed, Sven's set of keys dangled from the outside lock. Frank pulled them out angrily and let himself in the door as he called out "Annike! Sven!"

Karl followed his father into the foyer and shut the door quietly behind them. From the bedroom side of the house, he heard the sound of muffled song. As Frank strode toward the master bedroom, the song became recognizable: Sven and Annike were singing a lilting

Swedish tune about springtime. It was familiar to Karl from his childhood. His mother would sing it to him, and later to Sven, to calm them as they lay down for their afternoon naps.

Frank stormed through the bedroom and came to a sudden halt at the master bath's door. Karl nearly ran into him. From over the top of his father's head, Karl glimpsed his mother, nude in the tub with her knees drawn up to her chest, and Sven, kneeling by the tub's edge, gently squeezing water from a washcloth onto his mother's back. Sven stopped singing when he looked up and saw his father and brother, but Annike sang on, oblivious to their presence.

"Just what the hell do you think you're doing?" Frank bellowed.

Annike looked up at him and started to cry. "*Andreas, don't låta honom spännvidd jag! Den var en olycksfall!*" she cried in a small, high voice. *Andreas, don't let him spank me! It was an accident!* "*Behaga don't spännvidd jag. JAG won't gör den igen!*" she pleaded. *Please don't spank me. I won't do it again!*

"Ssssssh," Sven said soothingly, "*It's i orden, Annike. Han won't disciplin du.*" *It's alright, Annike. He won't discipline you.* Sven rubbed her back gently with the washcloth and looked his father in the eye. "Keep your voice down. You're scaring her," he said evenly.

"You'd better tell me what's going on," Frank said urgently, in a much lower volume that still managed to communicate his strong disapproval.

"I got a call from someone at Publix," Sven began with a disarmingly calm and even voice. "Mom was shopping and got disoriented. She'd wet herself and couldn't communicate with anyone. A nice lady at the front counter tried to calm her down, but she couldn't understand anything Mom was trying to tell her. So she and a manager took her into the lunchroom and looked through her purse. She found the emergency card we put in Mom's wallet and tried calling here. When she didn't get an answer, she called me."

"Is she alright?" Frank demanded.

"She's slipped back further than she ever has before. She's about four years old at the moment, and I'm just getting her calmed down," Sven said wearily.

"Do you know how inappropriate it is for you to be giving your mother a bath!" Frank seethed.

With that, Annike started to cry once more.

"What was I supposed to do?" Sven hissed. "Let her wander around in piss-wet clothes?"

"You could have waited for me," Frank said angrily.

"You're upsetting her again," Sven said, with barely contained anger. "Why don't you do something useful and go see if you can find the valet ticket in her purse? Karl and I have to go back and get her car once I get her dry and dressed."

Chagrined, Frank asked more softly, "Did you call the doctor?"

"I called Dr. Kleinberg. He told me how to dose her medicine to try and break this fugue," Sven told him evenly. "Dad, I checked her medicine box. She hasn't taken any pills since lunch yesterday. Can't I trust you to make sure she's medicated?"

"She told me she'd taken her medicine," Frank said helplessly. "She slept through the night."

Soothed by Sven's rhythmic strokes on her back, Annike ceased snuffling and started to sing softly to herself.

"Whatever," Sven said disgustedly. "Just please, go take care of the groceries in the kitchen. Once I get her in her nightgown and settled down for a nap, I'll come get you and you can sit with her. She's going to be pretty knocked out for the rest of the day."

"Fine, just take over," Frank fumed.

"Dad, I can deal with her or with you, but not both right now," Sven said tiredly. "You can chew me out later, just let me handle this. Okay?"

Without another word, Frank turned, and finding Karl still behind him, spared him a glare before striding toward the kitchen.

"Are you okay?" Karl asked his brother gently.

"Yeah," Sven said and nodded before looking at his mother pityingly. "Give me about ten minutes and I'll be out," he assured him.

Karl watched as he got stiffly off his knees and reached for a towel. Sven looked at him expectantly, and Karl got the point. He wanted to spare his mother's compromised modesty. "I'll go give Dad a hand," Karl told him helplessly.

"Thanks." Sven opened the towel and bent down, saying, "*Annike, it's tid till få torka och tråka i din nightdress. Er du klar?*" Annike, it's time to get dry and get into your nightdress. Are you ready?

"I'm *sömnig*," she responded, I'm *sleepy*, and she started to stand.

Karl turned away from the sight of his mother emerging from her bath and walked blindly out of the master bath and on to the kitchen. He found his father standing at the counter with an open fifth of scotch in one hand and a glass in the other.

Frank poured himself a generous slug from the bottle and drained the glass in two gulps. He looked at Karl and then gestured around the counter, taking in the plastic bags of assorted groceries lying there. "The little bastard didn't forget a thing, did he?"

Karl stepped around the counter and reached for a bag.

"Leave it!" Frank said instantly. "I'll take care of it. You don't know where all this shit goes anyway."

Karl stepped back and went to the breakfast table and sat down.

"There are limits," Frank told Karl angrily, but he didn't go on.

Karl only watched as his father poured a little less into his glass for the next round and tossed it back. As Karl sat in silence, Frank squared his shoulders and placed the glass in the dishwasher. He screwed the lid back on the bottle of scotch and returned it to the liquor cabinet. Then he concentrated on putting the groceries away, slowly and methodically. When he had finished, he picked up Annike's purse, brought it to the table, and sat down opposite Karl. For a moment he just sat, both hands clutching the purse in his lap as he looked at it tenderly. Finally, he opened the purse and slowly sifted through its contents until he found the valet ticket for her car. Wordlessly, he slid it across the table to Karl.

"Your Publix has gone upscale," Karl commented. "Valet parking at the grocery store?"

Frank gave a bitter chuckle. "Welcome to Boca Raton," he said snidely. "When we moved here forty years ago, I had no idea the Jews were going to turn it into Beverly Hills."

Ignoring the hateful comment, Karl sat in silence for a moment before saying, "It's a good thing Sven is so good with Mom. I couldn't handle it."

Frank rubbed his eyes tiredly and said, "I know. I shouldn't have flown off the handle, but sometimes I just want to wring his neck."

"Why, Dad?" Karl asked quietly.

"Jealousy," Frank said and laughed. "Resentment. Fear. You name it."

"Isn't that a little crazy, Dad?" Karl pleaded. "I mean, he's just taking care of her—and you."

"Did it ever occur to you that I might resent having to be taken care of?" Frank asked honestly. "Do you know how bad I feel for not making sure she'd taken those damn pills, and for letting her get into such a state?"

"Dad, don't be so hard on yourself. Mom told you she took her medicine, and she seemed pretty together all morning," Karl said soothingly. "Why *would* you doubt her?"

"Because she's not . . . because she's not in her proper mind, Karl. I should have checked for myself, but it's so hard to admit she's slipping away from me so fast," Frank said and slumped a little further down in his chair.

Karl looked at his father, so sad and defeated, and tried to think how to comfort him. He was confounded to find he needed some comforting himself. It was truly disturbing to feel so helpless at the hard evidence of his mother's precarious mental state. Knowing how unpredictably it could upset the even tone and steady routine of their days was not only frustrating, it was frightening.

Karl thought about the wing of Palladian Gardens that had been pointed out to him, but into which he hadn't been invited. Roberta had been very careful to explain that there was a separate wing just for Alzheimer's and dementia patients. It was set up to make sure they were safe and properly supervised, medicated, and controlled. He shuddered at the thought of his mother there, locked in a world where no one could understand her simplest requests, such as for water or warmth against the chill of the air-conditioning. When it got to the point that Swedish was the only language left available to her, she would be completely isolated and alone.

As he brooded along with his father in silence, the awful reality of his mother's condition pierced him. Karl had only been aware of his mother's condition for twenty-four hours. He wondered how his father and Sven had been dealing with this knowledge for months. He felt a deepening sense of shame for not being the kind of son or brother that his family could easily have called and told what was going on. He wondered why they had waited so long to make him aware of the situation, and he wondered what, if anything, he could have done had he known sooner.

At last Sven came into the room and stood opposite the table. Karl held up the valet ticket, and Sven nodded and checked his watch. "She's better," he said finally. "She's about to drift off to sleep. Dad, you might want to go on in and sit with her so she doesn't get scared."

Frank nodded miserably. "What am I supposed to say to her if she starts jabbering at me in Swedish?" he asked as he fished in his pocket for Sven's forgotten car keys.

Sven took his keys and said, "Just answer her calmly and gently in English. She calms down when you're sweet to her, even if you speak English. When she's like this, she usually responds to you no matter what. It's you she loves and trusts, Dad, just remember that," Sven told him gently.

"Can I call you if she gets bad?" Frank asked worriedly.

"Of course," Sven said, "but I gave her enough medicine that she should be out the rest of the day. At nine o'clock, give her a Risperdal, a Trazodone, and a Zoloft," Sven instructed him carefully. "Do you want me to write it down, or give you a call to remind you?"

"Could you call to remind me, Son?" Frank asked humbly.

Sven took two steps toward his father and patted his shoulder reassuringly. "Sure thing, Dad. Karl will help me remember. Right, Karl?"

Karl nodded. In some ways, he was as shaken by the last thirty minutes as his father was.

"Karl, we better get a move on," Sven said gently. "You have to meet Caro and Melanie at the airport in just a little over an hour."

Karl noted that his father's eyes had started to droop a little. The shots of scotch he'd thrown back were kicking in. "Will you be alright, Dad?" he asked uneasily.

Frank nodded and stood up carefully. "I'm a little tired myself. I think I'll just slip off my shoes and lie down with your mother for a little while. You boys go ahead and take off. We'll be fine," he said determinedly.

"Okay, Dad," Sven said as he stepped into the kitchen and switched on the fluorescent lights under the cabinets.

"See ya," Frank said as he shambled down the hall toward the master bedroom.

Sven waited and watched until Frank had gone in before nudging Karl toward the front of the house. In the foyer, he turned on a small lamp, then stepped into the living room and did the same. As he joined Karl back in the foyer, he said softly, "It'll be pitch-dark when he wakes up. I guess he got in the scotch?"

"Yes," Karl replied as he followed Sven out the front door. "He had a few shots."

"Best thing in the world for him," Sven said as he headed down the steps, then he stopped dead in his tracks, and Karl found himself once more almost running into someone. "Shit," Sven hissed, "we forgot your suitcase."

Karl groaned and rolled his eyes, remembering that he, Caro, and Melanie were to stay at Sven's place for the rest of the visit.

"C'mon," Sven said, unlocking the front door and opening it for Karl. "Just make it quick."

Karl made his way to the guest room as quietly as he could and retrieved his carry-on bag. It rolled along the carpeted floor noise-lessly. When he passed the master bedroom, he paused and looked in on his parents. His father lay on his side, his arm wrapped protec-tively across his mother's waist. Both of them appeared deeply asleep. The sun lit their room with a hazy gold glow as it passed through the sheers at the window, bathing them in soft, warm light. After the chaos of the past couple of hours, everything appeared serene and calm. Satisfied that they were alright, Karl grasped the handle of his carry-on and walked through sudden tears toward the front door and his brother.

That moment felt like the worst time to leave them, alone and help-less in the peaceful afternoon. Karl thought of his father waking with a slight headache in the dark, quiet house and making his solitary way into the kitchen, as Annike lay drugged and drowsy in the bedroom. Karl wondered how many of their days passed this way as he himself sat at his desk or made his way home in the Triangle's traffic. Before he got to the end of the hallway, he wiped his eyes with the heel of his free hand, hoping his brother wouldn't notice his guilty tears.

In the foyer, he pulled his suitcase out the front door. Sven had already opened the back door of his SUV and was pulling a torn grocery bag from the passenger seat as Karl made his way down the walk. Before Sven crumpled the bag into a ball, Karl noticed it held the damp impression of his mother's butt and thighs.

"The seat's dry," Sven said. "Throw your bag in the back, and I'll get rid of this and lock the front door."

"No problem," Karl said. As he lifted the suitcase into the back of the Excursion, he saw Sven disappear into the house. Karl closed the back door and got into the SUV. Glancing toward the house, he ran his hand over the seat to make sure of Sven's claim. The seat was dry, but as he settled into the Excursion he could smell the lingering scent of urine. The car had been locked up tight in the sunshine for too long.

Fortunately, Sven reappeared at the front door, locked it, and bounded down the path to the Excursion. He opened his door and swung into the big vehicle easily. Without comment, he started the car and immediately rolled down all the windows with the control on his armrest, then turned on the air-conditioning.

"Will they be alright?" Karl asked as Sven backed into the street.

"They'll be fine," Sven answered confidently. "There's some yogurt, cheese, and crackers if they get hungry later on. They don't eat much dinner as a rule."

Karl nodded and watched as the streets began to slip by. Sven was quiet as well. For a while, they rode in silence before Karl gathered the courage to ask, "Do things like this happen often?"

"No so much," Sven told him. "But now I think it's time to take Mom's car keys away. Up until now, she's never gotten disoriented so badly—at least not away from home. At least not that I know about," he admitted warily.

"You'd know if it happened, wouldn't you?" Karl asked, hoping for reassurance.

"Dad isn't always honest with me," Sven answered carefully. "He tends to cover for her, or underplay how bad it gets sometimes."

"I guess it's a good thing they're getting into Palladian Gardens sooner rather than later, then, right?"

Sven laughed without cheer. "Well, it'll be easier on me, that's for sure."

"Just how often are you over here?" Karl asked him.

Sven shrugged. "Every day for the past few months. It's become routine. I've started bringing Gretchen to work with me so she won't be locked in the house alone for so long."

"And Gretchen is . . . ?" Karl asked.

"My dog," Sven said.

"Oh, yeah, Dad said something about you having a dog. When did that happen?"

"About a year ago, a friend of mine and Rob's had AIDS. When he went into a hospice before he died, I said we'd keep her. She's sweet and good company."

"What kind of dog is she?" Karl pressed. He'd never thought of Sven as a pet person, as much as he traveled.

"She's a vizsla," Sven responded happily. "Do you have any idea what one looks like?"

"No," Karl admitted honestly. He'd never been a pet person himself.

"She's a kind of hunting dog. Not as slender as a greyhound but definitely more elegant than a Lab," Sven explained. "She has a short tail and hound-type ears, solid orangey-brown coat. She's actually a very pretty dog," he concluded with a smile. "Mom loves her."

"And Dad doesn't, I take it," Karl replied.

"Dad doesn't *get* dogs," Sven said and sighed. "For him it's just an unwanted responsibility. He has no empathy to spare."

"I don't know," Karl replied defensively. "You should have heard him talking about his orange trees. He seemed really sad that their best years are over. He won't let the landscaper take them out. He told me they were like old friends."

"He actually said that?" Sven seemed honestly surprised.

"Yes," Karl said emphatically. "We were out in the backyard yesterday, and he was talking about them. He also seemed to be particularly proud of his new tangerine bush—or tree, or whatever."

"Wow," Sven said and shook his head. "He must finally be mellowing. He sure confides more in you than he does in me. I don't get that side of him at all."

"He really doesn't like you taking care of Mom, or him, does he?" Karl asked, curious as to how Sven would respond.

"He does and he doesn't. I'm just an easy whipping boy for his frustration about how bad things have gotten. But he's never been particularly fond of me to begin with. I'm sort of the mistake that came along and fucked up his midlife plans," Sven said and laughed.

"You really think that?" Karl asked.

"Oh, hell, yes. He thinks I'm a lightweight mama's boy. He's never missed an opportunity to let me know that," Sven told his brother without any bitterness. "He loves Mom very much, and he doesn't like me for taking her attention away from him. He's always been like that." Sven stole a glance at his brother. "I'm surprised you haven't noticed."

"Well, I've never said anything, but I've suspected. Even when you were small, he wasn't all that enthusiastic about you," Karl admitted gently. "Does it ever get to you?"

"No," Sven answered. "Why would I let it? Fuck him."

"You say that, yet you go out of your way to look after Mom and Dad both," Karl noted.

"Well, he's my dad," Sven countered. "You make do with the hand you're dealt. No big deal."

"I know he's always given you a hard time about the gay thing," Karl admitted. "How do you deal with that?"

Sven sighed. "I used to hate him for making me miserable about it, but then, one day, I just decided it was counterproductive and wasn't making me any less miserable. I'm as stubborn as he is, so I figured the best way to make him miserable was to just be myself." Sven snorted. "Rob thinks we're all passive-aggressive as hell. He stopped taking Dad's bullshit about two years ago and told him exactly what he thought of him. That was a Sunday dinner to remember."

"I bet," Karl conceded. "What did Dad have to say to that?"

"Not a lot," Sven told him and laughed. "Dad's a bully. He backed right down when Rob reared up on his hind legs and showed him his teeth."

"Good for Rob," Karl said, and laughed as well.

Sven cast him a long sideways look. "Rob doesn't understand why I can't just tell him to back the fuck off. He knows I have Mom to consider, but he still resents it."

"Exactly what does he resent?" Karl asked in earnest.

"Rob has a very distant relationship with his parents and siblings. I'm his whole family, really." Sven sighed. "All my looking after Mom and Dad takes its toll on our relationship. Rob would prefer I be all about him. In an odd way, it's like I've married my father, the way they're both so possessive."

"I'm sorry," Karl told him. "I had no idea." As Sven pushed the hair back out of his eyes, Karl caught the unmistakable flash of gray mixed in with the darker blond at his temples. "Is there any chance you and Rob will get all this straightened out, now that Mom and Dad are going to a place where you won't have so much responsibility for them?"

Sven smiled slightly and shrugged. "These things have a way of working themselves out. But the wrangling back and forth takes something special out of the relationship."

"But you still love Rob, don't you?" Karl asked gently.

"Yes," Sven admitted easily. "But right now, I'm really tired of being the one responsible for making everything right for everybody, and trying to live up to everybody's expectations. I have a business and a payroll to make, clients to keep happy, a partner with very grand ideas, and parents who are becoming more and more like children. I'm just really, really tired."

Karl noticed that the bluish circles under Sven's eyes had grown darker since the day before. He did look tired, and there was a spark missing, a deadness in his eyes that Karl had never seen in his brother before. "You didn't have to carry this all on your own, Sven," Karl chided him gently. "Why didn't you call sooner and let me know what was going on? Your life is really a pile of shit right now, I can see that."

"What could you have done, Karl?" Sven replied without rancor.

"I don't know," Karl admitted. "I could have at least listened."

Sven turned to look at him, and Karl caught a glimpse of the loveliness that his mother possessed. Sven looked a lot like her. Both had an air of something that set them apart. It was a Nordic remoteness, a kind of self-possession. Though Karl also was self-possessed, he identified more strongly with his father. Karl had always somewhat casually lumped Sven in with his mother, and had given him the same sort of condescending affection he gave his mother. Karl realized it was an attitude people reserved for those blessed with good looks. It assumed they had no real depth or dimension beyond their surface attractiveness.

Now, looking at Sven, Karl realized his own self-absorption and family preconceptions had been seriously eroded, and very suddenly. Karl had wept for his mother's growing isolation, and her increasing inability to express her most basic needs in a way that could be understood. It struck him now that Sven was isolated in much the same way, though his mind was steady. Karl was newly aware of how far his own shortcomings had distanced him from his brother.

"Here's Publix," Sven declared. "We need to get you on your way to the airport." With that, he leaned across the center console and opened the glove box in front of Karl. Reaching inside, he picked out a folded sheet of paper and handed it to his brother. "Directions to my house," he said with a smile. "I'll be there waiting for you guys once you leave the airport, okay?"

"Thanks," Karl said as he unfolded the sheet and looked at the typed instructions on how to get from the airport to Sven's home in Singer Island's tiny town of Palm Beach Shores. Sven had obviously taken some care in preparing the directions for him. "Thanks for looking after me, too," he added awkwardly.

"Oh, you're easy," Sven said lightly as he pulled into a parking space and switched off the car.

"You don't need to go with me to the valet," Karl told him.

"No," Sven said and smiled. "I need to go in and pick up some stuff for our dinner. Is there anything special you or Caro or Mel need while I'm here?"

"No," Karl started, then said, "Wait—Caro is craving chocolate these days. She says it's a menopausal thing."

Sven laughed, and then unexpectedly reached across the console to grasp his brother's shoulder. "I'm glad you're here," he said earnestly.

"At long last," Karl said guiltily. "I feel badly about not being more help."

"Don't," Sven said and squeezed his shoulder firmly. "Don't beat yourself up that way. Everything's going to be just fine, okay?"

Karl nodded and smiled in reply, though he couldn't help but feel that he'd found his family irrevocably broken, and that nothing was ever going to be quite *fine* ever again.

9

SVEN LEFT HIM as they reached the generous portico at the front of the grocery store, and Karl easily found the valet's stand and prepared himself for an uncomfortable explanation of why he was claiming his mother's car. But the valet simply took his ticket, located Annike's keys, and took off at a trot to retrieve the car. As he reached into his pocket for a small bill to tip the valet, Karl tried to remember exactly what his mother drove. In the past, she had always driven the best car of the two his parents owned, while his father satisfied himself with the older vehicle. These days, his father drove a newer Buick, of which he seemed inordinately proud, evidenced by his boasts about its economy and stylishness during their drive to Palladian Gardens.

Karl watched as the valet finally backed out the champagne-colored Toyota Camry that Karl remembered his parents purchasing several years before. He had been surprised then that his father had bought a Japanese car, and had been amused when it had been replaced with a solid, American-made model. The valet pulled the Camry to the curb and accepted Karl's tip with a pleasant thanks. Karl got in awkwardly and adjusted the seat to accommodate his much longer legs, which reminded him how much his parents appeared to have shrunk in height.

Pondering this, Karl made his way out of the parking lot. He was relieved by the need to concentrate on where he was going. While the route was clear, the streetscape had changed so much that he had to read the street signs suspended over the intersections. Distances between once-familiar landmarks seemed to have either abruptly shortened or improbably lengthened in his mind during his fourteen-month absence from Boca Raton.

The congested traffic on the way to I-95 distracted him from an unwelcome, jarring image that kept returning unbidden to his mind. Over and over again he recalled the fleeting glimpse he'd had of his mother as she rose from her bath earlier in the afternoon. The sight of her sagging breasts, thickened waist, and gray blur of pubic hair at once repulsed and fascinated him. It was something he wished he'd never seen. He recalled averting his eyes as quickly as he could, yet the sight was burned into his brain.

Karl replaced that image with the sight of his father's aged body swimming in the pool that morning. Like his mother's thickened and humbled form, his father's had been a curt reminder of Karl's own aging. The inevitability of physical decline and aging were things he never gave much thought to. While he had never been vain, Karl was aware of his good looks and proud of keeping himself in shape even as he'd passed his fifty-second birthday. Caro's menopause was a constant reminder that he and his wife both were headed for the bodies of his parents, but before the sights and events of that day, it had been an abstract reality.

As he swung onto the on-ramp for northbound I-95, a chilling thought occurred to Karl. Neither his father nor Sven had mentioned whether or not his mother's dementia might be genetic. Karl wondered if somewhere deep in his own brain there were connections breaking down even now. Could it be possible that either he or Sven faced such a horrible decline? Was it something that might manifest in Melanie's future? It was a sobering thought. He made a mental note to ask Sven what the chances were and tried to shake the thought from his currently perfectly normal mind.

Suddenly, he longed to see his wife. With his view of his family's life so thoroughly shaken in the past two days, Caro's companionable constancy promised to right him and get him feeling stable once more.

Karl found himself falling into the traffic's rhythm with more than a sense of urgency. He pushed the uncomplaining Camry faster toward the airport with near desperation.

For the past two days, Karl had found himself heavily taxed by emotional concerns that were not part of his fundamental nature. There were no simple, elegant answers to the problems he'd found waiting for him in southern Florida. It was true that his father's timely decision to move into a continuing-care retirement community resolved some of the inconveniences of the years ahead, but it was no solution to what Karl was feeling. He found he simply couldn't separate the mass of emotional complexity presented by his father, mother, and brother into individual strands at the moment. *I'm not good with the feelings stuff*, he recalled telling Caroline smugly in their own kitchen the previous morning.

Karl considered Sven as he inched along in a knot of stop-and-go traffic. Sven was good with feelings. Karl marveled at how he deftly juggled caring for his mother and father along with the current situation with Rob. While Sven admitted to being fatigued by it all, he still seemed utterly in control of himself and what was going on around him. Karl recalled the curious mixture of love and hurt in the look Sven had given Rob in their store the day before. Yet Sven had never said anything unkind about Rob, nor did he discount any of the close ties that still bound them together. Karl found himself puzzled by his brother's equanimity. His father was condescending and resentful to Sven, by his own admission. His mother seemed to take Sven's care and devotion as her due, as she had selfishly created him for herself, by her own admission. Rob was gone yet still present in Sven's life. Karl wondered how Sven bore all these expectations and indignities yet remained so easygoing and unperturbed by them.

As Karl made his way into the airport, he found himself wishing Caroline alone was waiting for him. He thought she might somehow make sense of things for him. He longed for some time alone to talk with her. He wanted to hold her solidly against him, against all of the unknown inevitabilities that his parents had demonstrated would come.

Karl scanned the mill and spill of passengers outside baggage claim. He had run later than expected because of the traffic on I-95. For an instant, his practical side gave way to a heave of panic that he might not find Caroline and Melanie in the throng. At last he saw them waiting at the far end of the terminal. He eased the car into the lane closest to the curb and was able to stop only a few feet beyond them. He put the Camry in park and awkwardly let himself out of the low-slung car. "Caro!" he called out, and waved.

She heard him instantly and turned to him with a smile and a wave. Karl heaved a sigh of relief at the sight of his wife and daughter as they clasped their carry-on bags and began to walk toward him. He pulled the trunk release and strode to gather them in his arms. "Hey," he said simply, at a loss for anything more articulate at that moment. "Hey," he repeated, as he let his arm drop from Melanie's shoulder and wrapped Caroline in a hug.

Caroline hugged him in return, then grasped his upper arms and pushed him away gently, looking into his eyes with concern. "Hey yourself," she said, and gave him a private smile.

"Mom," Melanie interrupted as she reached for her mother's carry-on, "let me get that." Briskly, she had her own bag and her mother's in the trunk, then pushed it closed with a satisfying whump.

"Wow, thanks, Mel," Karl said. "You took care of that lickety-split."

Melanie laughed. "We're going to Uncle Sven's, right? I'm ready to get this party started. Why don't you let me drive? I know the way."

"It's okay, Sven gave me directions," Karl protested.

"Good, then we can use them if I get turned around," Mel insisted.

"Let her drive, Karl," Caroline urged. "You can ride shotgun; I'll get in the back."

Melanie walked passed her father and headed for the driver's door. "C'mon, the TSA guy is going to get nervous if we stand out here much longer blocking traffic."

Karl held up his hands in surrender and turned toward the passenger side of the car. He opened the rear door behind him for Caroline and made sure she was in before getting in the front with Melanie.

Melanie adjusted the driver's seat to her liking, buckled her seat belt, and moved the car into the stream of traffic leaving the airport. "Thanks, Dad," she said, then added, "Your driving in city traffic makes me crazy."

Recalling his own dismay at his father's driving earlier in the day, Karl wondered if he gave Melanie as extreme a feeling of impatience and discomfort. Having the tables turned on him by his own daughter was disconcerting. He felt Caroline reach across from the backseat and pat his shoulder comfortingly. "You're welcome," Karl said. "But I warn you, I-95 is a bitch. It was stop-and-go most of the way here."

"I can handle it," Melanie said confidently.

"How was your flight?" Karl asked, eager to leave the subject.

"Easy," Melanie commented.

"No bumps," Caroline offered from the back. "How are things down here?"

Karl hesitated before he spoke. There were some things, such as the details of his mother's episode earlier that day, that he wanted to tell Caroline privately. Melanie had all the self-assurance of a very young adult, and Karl knew she would look at the event from a too-clinical angle. The impact of his mother's fugue state and its graphic spectacle had wounded him and left him uncertain how he felt. He wanted to share the details within the safety of Caroline's empathy before facing Melanie's cooler reaction and her questions.

Finally, he said, "It's been a difficult day for Mom. She's not well and is resting."

"What exactly is wrong with her?" Melanie asked. "Mom said she has been having some emotional problems for the past few months."

"No, I didn't tell you that," Caroline said calmly from the backseat. "I said she was experiencing some age-related dementia."

"Well, a lot of seniors have severe depression," Melanie countered. "But there are so many forms of treatment for that. I'm not convinced Grandmere is losing her mind. I'm sure it's just a matter of finding the right combination of meds," she concluded brightly.

Karl sighed. It appeared that explaining was going to be more difficult than he wanted it to be. "Mel, it's not that simple. It's not just depression. Your grandmere has age-related dementia. She is losing her grasp on the here and now," Karl said and remembered his mother's analogy. "She says she feels as if she's being erased."

Melanie glanced at her father. "I think I understand," she said, her previously bright assessment obviously dulled by her father's unsparing words. "Is it really bad?"

Karl felt backed into a corner. Again, something said earlier came to him. "Let me put it this way, Melanie. Your grandfather told me that if there is anything special we want to say to her, now is the time to do it. Within a year, at the outside, she won't remember any of us anymore. Do you understand?"

"So we've come to say good-bye?" Melanie asked soberly.

"Essentially, yes."

"I'm so sorry, Karl," Caroline said from the backseat, again reaching to touch his shoulder.

Karl felt the warmth of her touch even under the ridiculous dress jacket his father had made him wear, which he had yet to remove since the morning's visit to Palladian Gardens.

"Why did they wait so long to tell us?" Melanie demanded. "I mean, it's so unfair to have this dumped on us. If we had known, we could have visited more often. We could have *done* something . . ."

"Mel," Karl interrupted gently, "I don't think they knew how swiftly she was going downhill mentally. Your grandfather and Uncle Sven have been so caught up in living it, they probably couldn't see the obvious. In any event, there's nothing we could have done any differently."

"I could have visited!" Mel insisted. "There are a thousand things I wanted to ask her about and get her to tell me. I don't even know how to make the Swedish Christmas cookies," she added despondently. "She was always promising to teach me. This really fucking sucks."

"Melanie," Caroline said sharply from the backseat.

Karl allowed himself a pitiable chuckle and said, "No, Caro. Melanie's right. This fucking sucks."

At that, the car fell silent. Karl pulled down the sun visor and opened the mirror to search for Caroline's face in the backseat. He found her staring out the window, her face lit by the strong sun hastening its descent into the west. In her highlighted profile, he saw a deep sadness untouched by pity. Like he had been doing earlier, she seemed to be scanning the future for the wreckage it promised.

As they passed downtown West Palm Beach and continued north toward Singer Island, the traffic thinned, and Karl checked the directions. "You'll want to take the Blue Heron Boulevard exit," he reminded Melanie carefully.

She nodded and immediately changed lanes. "Then I just continue straight on Blue Heron, through Riviera Beach, and cross the Intracoastal Waterway, right?"

Karl scanned the directions and agreed.

From the driver's seat, Melanie locked all the doors. Riviera Beach was a slum. Karl was glad they would make it through before dark. Though they probably were in no particular danger, it was not a place where he'd want to have the car break down.

As Melanie exited onto Blue Heron Boulevard and began to pass through the warehouse wasteland on the western edge of Riviera Beach, Karl thought of something to break the spell of gloom in the car. "Did you know your Uncle Sven got a dog?" he asked Melanie brightly. Of the entire family, Melanie was the one most fond of dogs. She had begged for one as a child until Caroline and Karl had relented and gotten her a springer spaniel. Melanie had adored the creature, and for a ten-year-old she had been very good about taking care of it. Unfortunately, the dog got cancer and died before she finished middle school. Melanie had been so bereft, there had never been any talk of another dog, much to Caroline and Karl's relief.

"Yes, Gretchen!" Melanie replied with enthusiasm, which took Karl by surprise. "Uncle Sven emails me pictures of her every once in a while. She's beautiful."

"What kind of dog?" Caroline asked from the backseat.

"A vizsla," Melanie answered before Karl could.

"Are they large?" Caroline asked with some concern.

"Well, not huge," Melanie countered. "But bigger than a springer spaniel."

"Who looks after it while Rob and Sven are away on buying trips?" Caroline asked practically.

"Johann house-sits," Melanie told her, explaining further. "Johann is this *god* that works for Uncle Sven in the shop. He's Venezuelan, straight, and gorgeous," Melanie elaborated.

"You seem on top of things," Karl commented dryly. "I had no idea you and your uncle had such a thorough correspondence."

"Oh, we email about once a week," Melanie answered breezily as she stopped at an intersection. The bridge that spanned the Intracoastal Waterway to Singer Island loomed in front of them.

Karl anxiously checked his side-view mirror, trying to discreetly look around. A young black man with a head full of dreadlocks, wearing a guinea-T and baggy shorts riding at least five inches below his hips, sauntered in front of them, swinging a twelve-pack of beer. On one corner, a group of young black women were laughing loudly and yelling across the street to a low-rider, thumping with seismic bass behind them. Though he knew his fear was probably irrational, Karl was hyperaware of his whiteness at that moment and was completely engulfed by a sense of displacement that jangled his raw nerves. "Why in the hell does Sven come this way?" he grumbled out loud. "There's a much better bridge north of here, and in a much better neighborhood."

The light turned green, and Melanie proceeded calmly through the intersection onto the bridge. "Because he lives in Palm Beach Shores, and it's just over there to the right," she said, and pointed to the southern end of the island. "It's a whole different world on the island."

Indeed it was, Karl noted as they drove onto the island itself. Sven's neighborhood was within walking distance of the beach, in an area of what had once been solidly middle-class three-bedroom, one-car-garage homes. From the looks of it, the community was the same age as his parents' neighborhood in Boca Raton but was a less affluent version.

Melanie steered the car to the road that ran closest to the beach and drove south. On the ocean side of the road stood high-rise condos and hotels of a recent vintage, while across the street stood the motor courts and small motels that once predominated on the island. Nearing the end of the street where it dead-ended at the inlet to the port of West Palm Beach, Melanie took a right and headed down a quiet street lined with small stucco houses set back on green lawns. She hadn't driven far when she turned into a drive that held both Sven's large Excursion and a new E-series black Mercedes. "Uncle Rob is here," Melanie exclaimed as she pulled the Camry behind Sven's SUV.

As they got out of the car, Karl stood a moment and took in

Sven's house. It was painted white with sun-bleached turquoise trim, including vignettes of a flamingo framed by palms, set in bas-relief into the stucco, over the garage door and by the front door. It was a quintessential 1960s Florida beach house, complete with clamshell metal awnings painted to match the trim and designed to swing down over the windows during hurricanes. The sight of it took Karl back in time. Though Sven had replaced the jalousie windows with new energy-efficient ones, it was very much a period house.

The sound of Melanie retrieving the luggage from the trunk brought Karl out of his reverie. He turned to find Caroline and Melanie pulling their carry-on bags up the drive. He grabbed his suitcase and joined his wife and daughter as Sven and Rob came out to the front porch to greet them.

"Welcome to Singer Island!" Sven called out, and he and Rob walked down to meet them.

Karl watched as hugs and murmurs of welcome enveloped his wife and daughter. Behind the screen door, Gretchen scratched and added her cautious welcome in a series of short, sharp barks.

Sven reached to hug Karl as well. "At last, I got you to see my place!"

"Yes, finally," Karl said, and Rob walked over to hug him as well.

"God, it's great to have all of you here together," Rob said as he released Karl and took in the sight of them with a genuinely happy grin. "Now, who needs a glass of wine?" he asked as he stepped back and took Caroline's bag from her.

"Sounds heavenly," Caroline admitted tiredly. "But first I want to see the house!"

"Well, c'mon!" Sven declared and led the group up the walk.

Karl hung back with Rob, and together they followed everyone into the house. Once inside, Karl took in the large combination living-dining room, which Sven had furnished simply with only an enormous, white leather Italian sofa, its matching ottoman, and a long rectangular antique wood table flanked by slouchy leather chairs, also of contemporary Italian design. The inside was painted a bluish shade of white and gave off an air of cool simplicity. Considering the access he had to accessories from exotic sources, the room was free of clutter—even art, save for one large color photo that hung on the wall behind the huge sofa, across from a large LCD TV mounted on the opposite wall.

While the others continued toward the other side of the house and their chatter receded, Karl stopped to study the photo closely. His father must have taken it, but it was one he'd never seen before. On a blanket in the sand lay a young, lithe Annike. Sven, perhaps six years old, rested on his knees by her side. His mother was lying on her stomach, her bathing suit top was undone, and she leaned on an elbow to look back over her shoulder at the camera. Her other arm held her bathing suit top close, covering her breasts. Her hair was pulled back in a loose knot at the back of her head and gleamed almost white against her tan.

Skinny Sven, his towhead in a bowl cut, looked at the camera warily, as if expecting to be scolded. Like his mother, his skin gleamed like honey. He wore a pair of red swim trunks and held a large piece of battered coral. The photo's color was faded, holding that particular day at the beach in diminished tones of recollection. That faded golden color suffused Karl's memories of the times—of the Kennedy assassinations and the broadcasts from Vietnam on the evening news. In Sven's contemporary décor, it brought the past into high relief. And it spoke volumes about Sven's relationship with his mother, as well as his father behind the camera.

"Sven had that old snapshot blown up to poster size and transferred to canvas," Rob commented from behind Karl's shoulder. "Your mother was very beautiful, wasn't she?"

Karl turned and looked at Rob. "Yes. She was almost glamorous.

I was always aware of how people stared at us. She was . . . she was something else," he willingly admitted.

Rob gestured at the photo. "Sven looks like her. He was a beautiful child."

"Why did you leave him?" Karl asked without thinking. Karl noted with surprise his unabashed desire to know.

Rob seemed taken aback by the question and took a moment to collect himself. Finally, he looked Karl in the eye and said, "Come with me while I pour some wine. I'll try to answer your question in the kitchen." With a glance toward the bedrooms down the hall, Rob strode through the dining room into the kitchen behind the garage.

Karl had found the kitchen had been updated and enlarged into the backyard. Here too, Sven had shown a spare hand in décor. He sat at a small old oak table with barley twist legs in one of the chairs and waited for Rob's response without another word.

Though they were not close, Rob had been a part of the family for a long time, so Karl felt justified in his question. The sufferance he had always allowed Rob was far greater than he imagined his father or even his mother bore him. Karl remembered that after the initial shock of Sven's relationship with Rob had worn off, Karl had simply relegated it to a place of fact in his dealings with Sven. He'd never even discussed with Sven the fact that he was gay. There had never been any confessions or entreaties on either of their parts. Because he had always accepted Rob for who he was, he felt entitled to some explanation about what was going on between his brother and his boyfriend.

Rob busied himself opening a bottle of red wine and shared it among five glasses waiting on the marble countertop. When he had finished, he took two glasses and joined Karl at the kitchen table. As he slid Karl's glass toward him, he patted Gretchen, who stood panting by his side. "I haven't really left Sven," he said carefully.

"But you're not living together anymore," Karl said bluntly and then added, "And Sven says you've been dating."

"You can't exactly call what I've been doing dating," Rob replied, "but I have had pleasant dinners with a few people, yes." Rob took a sip of his wine and looked at Karl openly. "As for us living apart, my great aunt died and left me a rather nice condo on Palm Beach. I wanted us to move there, but Sven volunteered to take Gretchen when our friend Tommy went into hospice. My place has a no-pets rule."

"So you've separated over the dog?" Karl asked doubtfully.

"Well, you can say the dog was the straw that broke my back," Rob said honestly. "The past two years haven't been easy. It appeared to me that Sven was putting many things ahead of our relationship. Your parents, work, even ol' Gretchen here," Rob said as he continued to stroke the happily panting dog. "I very badly wanted to take the place in Palm Beach and fix it up. Eventually I'll sell it, but I want Sven to sell this place, too, and for us to make a move somewhere else. We have an ongoing discussion about relocating the business to New York. I have a growing client list up there, and I think Sven could be a hit with Tynnigo somewhere in Manhattan. Hell, half of our clients here have a place in the city."

"But Sven won't make a move because of Mom and Dad, is that it?" Karl asked soberly.

"Yes, and frankly I resent it," Rob said with some heat.

"But soon Mom and Dad won't be putting such demands on him," Karl said hopefully.

Rob sighed. "That's why I haven't really left him, Karl. I want him in my future, but he has to want to be in it. For now, with me staying in Palm Beach, we're not arguing, we're waiting. I think they call it détente." Rob looked Karl in the eye and continued. "There's no anger between us. I love him more than I ever have, but some things need to change, for both of us."

Karl nodded and took a sip of his wine. Finding it surprisingly good, he took another sip and gave himself a moment to take in what Rob had told him. "Thanks for explaining this to me, Rob," he said gently. "I know it's none of my business, and you have to admit, I've never butted into your and Sven's affairs before. I just hope you'll give Sven time to deal with getting Mom and Dad settled in at Palladian Gardens."

Rob nodded and smiled. "I am giving him time. Do you think I don't know what kind of relationship he has with your mother and the responsibility he feels for her?"

"I heard you finally told Dad to back off," Karl said and chuckled.

"Look, I know he's your father, so I apologize, but he is a total bastard," Rob said candidly.

"He's never given you or Sven a break, I know," Karl told him. "I can imagine it must be hard for you to take him as part of the parent package deal."

"I have a completely different relationship with my family," Rob told him. "We exchange holiday cards, but we don't interact much beyond that." He sighed and took another sip of wine. "I have given up a lot to have Sven in my life. Do you think I'd give up on him easily after twenty-six years?"

"You two got together when you were fourteen, didn't you?" Karl asked even though he could do the math; the reality of it beggared his imagination.

Rob gave a small laugh. "The first time I ever saw him was at school in fourth-period math," Rob said. "I prayed to God that if he would just give me Sven, I'd never ask him for anything else."

"And have you ever asked him for anything else?" Karl laughed as he raised his wineglass.

Rob looked him in the eye and said, "You'd better be careful when you make deals with God. I should have talked with a lawyer first. I'd have added a part where he had to love me more than he did his mother."

Karl nodded and looked away. "Pretty soon, Mom won't even be able to recognize him. Maybe then he'll be able to let go."

"I don't know whether I want that or not," Rob said evenly. "I don't wish your mother's mental state to decline any more than it has. I'm not an asshole, Karl. I just want us to be able to move on with our lives."

"Rob, believe me when I tell you, I want the same thing, for both of you," Karl said genuinely.

Rob nodded and smiled. "So you're not going to beat me up for messing with your brother?"

Karl laughed easily. "I'm more likely to take Sven and shake some sense into him."

Rob stood up and walked over to the counter. He placed the other four glasses of wine on a tray. "Thanks, Karl," he said sincerely. "Now I better serve this wine and get everyone together."

"Thank you, Rob, for being so good to him." He was pleased when Rob smiled and grasped his shoulder affectionately before picking up the tray and walking out of the kitchen.

Gretchen followed Rob as far as the door, then stopped and looked back at Karl expectantly. When he didn't respond, she turned and walked back to his side and sat. She pushed his wrist up with her nose and waited for him to pet her. Karl responded by absently stroking her head a couple of times before returning his hand to the table. Once again, the dog nosed his wrist and urged him to pay attention to her.

"You're a pretty girl," Karl said as he stroked the dog's head and gently ran her long hound's ears between his fingers, enjoying their softness. Gretchen had odd, light-colored eyes, more yellow than green, and she regarded him somberly. Karl smiled. "You look like the kind of dog Sven would have," he remarked. Gretchen panted and yawned, curling her long tongue appreciatively.

Karl thought of Rob's dilemma. Sven did seem to take on responsibility as easily as others collected bric-a-brac. The dog seemed to know she was well placed here. Karl wondered what would have become of her had Sven not agreed to care for her when her master had become unable to provide for himself, much less a dog.

Karl looked around the spare, utilitarian kitchen that was giving off promising scents of the dinner to come. While its finishes were expensive, it was like the rest of the house he'd seen so far, stripped of any excess. It spoke of an owner-occupant who had streamlined himself in such a way that he expressed his character through the quality of materials in his home, which was otherwise devoid of pretty bits and bobs or any other assertion of self. Karl wondered if Sven was so busy taking care of others that he subsumed himself in their needs, or if he simply had become so diminished in himself that he no longer mattered. Was that what was keeping him from forging ahead with his life with Rob? Karl wondered. It was as if he didn't really know his brother at all. What he did for others gave the clearest picture of the man himself. Karl wondered what there was under the altruism.

Gretchen stood and barked at him sharply. Then she walked to the kitchen door and stood, looking back at him encouragingly. Amused, Karl stood and carried his wineglass to the counter. Finding there was still wine in the bottle, he poured what was left into his glass and walked to Gretchen at the door. Happily, she took off in a trot and he followed along behind her to join his family in the other room.

Karl saw everyone sprawled on the generous cushions of the large sofa, listening to Melanie regale them with what appeared to be a story about one of her students. Her voice seemed loud over the background of smooth jazz flowing from speakers he couldn't see. Karl noticed that Melanie and Caroline had shed the bulky sweaters they'd arrived in and had joined their hosts in removing their shoes. They all looked so comfortable. Karl became aware of how stuffily dressed he was, still clad in his father's jacket and his own dress shoes.

"Come sit, Karl," Sven encouraged him, shifting from Caroline's side to make room on the sofa.

"I think I want to get rid of this jacket and take off my shoes," Karl told him. "I feel like I've just gotten home from work to find a beach party going on."

"By all means," Rob told him. "Make yourself at home."

"Come with me," Caroline said as she unfolded her legs from under her and stood with quick grace. "I'll show you to the guest room."

Wordlessly, Karl gave her a small smile and followed her to a door midway down the hall. Caroline walked in, turned to face him, and took his wineglass as he stepped inside. She sat both their glasses on the nightstand as he took off the jacket. Taking it from him and laying it over a nearby chair, she asked, "Are you okay? You seem sorta lost."

Karl opened his arms and stepped toward her and enfolded her in a hug. "I'm so glad you're here," he whispered as he laid his cheek on the top of her head.

Caroline returned his hug and, taking his hand, led him to the edge of the bed, where they sat. "Has it been rough?" she asked as she searched his face.

Karl bent to undo his shoes and free his feet from his socks. Fortunately, he noted, his feet were relatively fresh. With his face hidden from view, he answered, "Mom had a very bad spell today. It was really unnerving."

As he sat up and looked at her, Caroline asked what happened. Briefly, Karl gave her the unvarnished facts and sighed. "I had a gut feeling that something was off before I left," he said. "You remember?"

Caroline nodded. "Still, when you come face-to-face with it—the ugliness of it—it's tough."

Karl took her hand and squeezed it. "I don't know. I just imagine

Dad and Sven dealing with this for the past several months, and I feel guilty. Even though I know there's nothing I could have done. It's just so horrible saying good-bye to her while she's still alive."

"Don't look at it that way, Karl. You can't. You'll make yourself crazy. You have to treat this as a really great opportunity to visit with your mother—and father—and let them know how much you care about them. That's what this is about," Caroline concluded confidently. "You hear me?"

Karl nodded and said, "I hear you." He smiled at her and said, "You know me, I want everything neat and solvable, with as little fuss as possible. I just find myself in a place where my usual detachment isn't working. And there's nothing really for me to solve. Dad's taking care of everything, and his plans are excellent."

"The place you said you were going to visit? Where your folks are moving into—did you go?" Caroline asked him.

"Yes. I got the grand tour today," Karl told her. "For what it is, it's the top of the line. I could even picture you and me living there if, you know, the situation warranted it."

"Well, that's good news, then," Caroline said, and nudged his shoulder. "But hopefully, that's a long time off in the future for us."

"Thank God," he said, honestly grateful to a god he claimed didn't have any personal regard for him.

"And how's Sven in all this?" Caroline pressed him carefully.

"To Mom and Dad, he's an angel. Patient as hell—I don't think I could do what he's doing. But I'm a little worried about him," Karl admitted as he lowered his voice and looked toward the door. "You know, Rob just told me they're not really splitting up. They're just taking some time apart. Sven's been so focused on looking after Mom and Dad, it's really interfered with his personal life."

Caroline nodded and stood. She pointed at something on the bed and said, "Sven is the most considerate person I know. Look at the box of chocolate truffles he left on the pillow."

Karl glanced at the elegant little box and smiled. "I told him you were craving chocolate these days. Looks like he listened."

"Well, I thank him, and I thank you for thinking of me," she told him with a slight bow of her head. Taking his free hand, she urged him up and off the bed to stand. "I think Sven and Rob are going to be alright," she whispered. "Now, you cheer up. Your Caroline's here now, and you don't have to deal with all the feelings stuff on your own."

Karl looked her in the eyes and nodded shyly, then turned to retrieve their wineglasses from the nightstand. He quickly checked the rims for lip gloss imprints and handed her the telltale glass. Together they returned to the living room to join in the conversation there.

"We have living wills," Rob was telling Melanie as Caroline and Karl settled themselves with the others on the sofa. "Sven knows how I feel about becoming a vegetable or being kept alive when it's no longer viable, and so he's got my power of attorney for health matters."

"Well, Drew knows where I stand on those things," Melanie responded. "After that dreadful Terri Schiavo case down here in Florida, we talked about it. But things are different for us because we'll be married. It's a shame you and Uncle Sven have to get all those special documents. It must have cost a fortune in legal fees."

"What are we talking about?" Caroline asked cheerfully.

"We're talking about what we'd do if we were faced with what Grandmere is going through," Melanie answered with a glance at her father. "I don't think I'd stick around for the inevitable. I'd just quietly find a way to end my life."

"Mom's faith won't allow that," Sven answered gently. "She's very firm in her resolve to deal with whatever comes. She's very devout. We've discussed it, and she feels she can't go against her religious beliefs."

"You're still a practicing Catholic, Uncle Sven—what would you do?" Melanie asked bluntly.

Sven took a sip of his wine and thought for a moment before he answered, "Well, having already reconciled myself to being gay and Catholic, it's not too big a step for me to reconcile my beliefs about ending my life. I think God deals with each of us individually. I don't have a problem bending the Church's rules a bit further to include suicide."

"You're good at that, Sven. But sooner or later you're going to bend that Catholic Church so far it'll snap." Rob laughed.

"Well, I can't justify bankrupting us just to buy a few more weeks or months of living in terrible pain, or not even knowing I'm in the world," Sven said evenly. "Science has gone far in the direction of prolonging life, and at a huge cost. I'd rather go ahead and check out, leaving you with the money," Sven told Rob.

"How do you feel about it, Dad?" Melanie asked her father.

"Is there any more wine?" Karl looked around the group. "Can I get anyone any more wine?"

Everyone laughed at his obvious ducking of the question, except Melanie. "Seriously, Dad," she insisted. "I hope it's not for ages, but one of these days I'll need to know how you feel about terminal illness and end-of-life questions. I'll be the one responsible for you and Mom."

Karl glanced at Caroline, who responded with a slight nod. Karl leaned back into the sofa's cushions and smiled at his daughter. "Your mother and I have living wills, Mel. Neither one of us wants to be kept alive past a reasonable point of no return. What that point is, we'll figure out when we get there. I mean, if either of us has the option for chemo or radiation with a reasonable expectation of living a decent life afterwards, we'd do that. Right, dear?"

"That's right, Mel. We would. But if we were to have a heart attack or a stroke, our living wills say let us go," Caroline told her daughter simply.

"Really?" Melanie asked, stunned. "I mean, I'm glad to hear you've taken care of this for me, but I didn't expect you to feel the same way I do."

"Well, we do, dear," Caroline assured her. "Now can we change the subject? This excellent wine your Uncle Rob is pouring is too good to waste on such a sad subject."

"I think that's my cue to open another bottle. Do we have time for another glass before dinner, Sven?" Rob asked as he stood.

"We're having lobster bisque and a salad," Sven told him. "It won't take long to finish up and serve. But I imagine you guys must be getting hungry. I'll get us something to nibble on while we have another glass of wine."

"Sounds good," Karl told him. "Can we give you a hand?"

"Nope," Sven said as he stood to join Rob. "You guys stay put and we'll be right back."

As Sven and Rob made their way to the kitchen, Gretchen climbed onto the sofa and settled in with a deep sigh. "Well, make yourself at home, missy," Melanie said as she leaned over to stroke the dog's neck.

"She's a beautiful animal, isn't she?" Caroline said approvingly.

"Yes she is," Karl said and grinned. "Who do you think she looks like, Sven or Rob?"

"You're terrible," Melanie said as she stroked the dog's side.

"I don't know, they say people look like their pets," Karl teased her.

"I think she looks like her own sweet self," Caroline said and yawned.

"Are you getting sleepy on us?" Karl asked lightly.

Caroline ran her fingers through her hair and stretched. "It's been a long day, but I think I'm good for another couple of hours. But I am glad Sven's bringing some nibbles. I'm starved."

"You better save room for the lobster bisque. It smells wonderful," Karl told her.

"Mom? Dad?" Melanie asked quietly. "How long do the doctors say Grandmere will live?"

Karl sighed and gently told her what Sven had told him. "Maybe as long as fifteen years."

Melanie shuddered. Caroline and Karl both noticed and glanced at each other. "I don't know if it's just because I'm twenty-four, or if I'm just very immature, but I don't think I could live like that."

Caroline reached across the sofa and stroked her daughter's back, much like her daughter stroked the dog. "Mel, life becomes sweeter as you grow older, believe it or not. I think your Grandmere wants to live now as much as she always has. Practicality has nothing to do with it."

"I agree with your mother," Karl said. "This morning Mom told me how comforting and satisfying she found simply having a cup of coffee and a cigarette. I think growing older brings its own particular joys in things we take for granted now."

Melanie simply stroked the dog and said nothing for a while. Finally, she announced, "I'm getting a dog just as soon as I get settled in with Drew."

With that, Rob appeared with a bottle of wine in one hand and a dog cookie held out temptingly in the other. "Gretchen? Wanna cookie? Good girl wants a cookie?"

Gretchen's ears pricked up and she was off the sofa in a long, fluid leap. Rob rewarded her with the treat and a pat on the head in passing before he settled himself in the dog's spot on the sofa and began pouring the wine into their glasses. "I think of her claws on this leather, and it's like nails on a blackboard," he said. He refreshed Sven's waiting glass on the ottoman and set the bottle on the floor. "Sven doesn't give a damn."

Gretchen, realizing she had been displaced, scratched at the old, handsome Oriental rug under the dining table and settled herself into a ball there.

"I didn't know Sven was such a dog lover," Karl admitted.

Rob took a sip of his wine and grinned. "I just thank God he never wanted to adopt a child. He'd begged me for a dog for years, but it never seemed practical, as much as we travel and the hours we were working. But now he's got Gretchen and he spoils her terribly."

"I take it you're not a dog person, then," Caroline asked slyly.

"If it makes Sven happy, I'm happy," Rob generously answered.

"If what makes me happy?" Sven asked as he appeared with a platter of cheeses and crackers, plus bowls of cashews and large green olives. He set the food down on the ottoman and slid onto the sofa next to Rob, nudging his shoulder as he did.

Rob looked at him with a feigned blank expression and said, "Why, I have no idea. What makes you happy?"

Sven retrieved his wineglass from the ottoman and laughed. Then, looking at each face around the ottoman as his guests eagerly helped themselves to the food, he said, "Right now—this minute—makes me inordinately happy."

Rob took a bite of an olive and said, "I'd like to stay tonight, if that's okay."

While neither Caroline, Melanie, or Karl appeared to pay any attention, each tensed as everyone waited for Sven's reply.

"You're home, you know that," Sven said easily. "I'm glad you're staying."

"Cool," Rob told him breezily, but the loving look he gave him escaped no one's attention, least of all Sven's.

"So, what's tomorrow's plan?" Caroline calmly interjected.

"I'm wallpapering my guest bath at the Palm Beach place," Rob volunteered. "And staying out of Frank's line of fire."

Sven laughed and reached for a smear of goat cheese and a water biscuit. "And all of *us* are supposed to show up at Mom and Dad's for brunch by eleven," he said. "Following brunch, we get to pick out what we want from Mom and Dad's stuff. Sorta like Christmas."

"*Anything* we want?" Melanie asked incredulously.

"Pretty much," Sven told her. "The apartment Mom and Dad are moving into is very small. They plan on keeping their bedroom stuff, the breakfast room table and chairs, and their favorite pieces from the sunroom: Dad's recliner and Mom's chair and ottoman, the wicker sofa, and the occasional tables. That's about all they've said they wanted."

Caroline cleared her throat and anxiously took a sip of her wine before she said, "Sven, there's something I want very much, if you don't want it."

"Mom's desk," Sven said, and took a bite of his cracker. Through a mouthful, he said, "It's yours."

Caroline clapped her hands like a little girl. "Oh, Sven! Are you sure? I know how much it's worth. There was a picture of one identical to it in a house in the Hamptons in *Architectural Digest*. I almost died when I saw it in the magazine. I've wanted it for my home office so badly."

Sven smiled at her, and his eyes danced a little. "I knew you would appreciate it and how you've admired it for years. I'd rather you have it. That way, if Mel wants it someday, it'll stay in the family."

"But I want it now," Melanie whined. "I adore all that mid-century modern Scandinavian design. Those are the kinds of pieces I want for my apartment with Drew in Manhattan."

"Sorry, dear," Caroline said smugly. "Age before beauty."

"Melanie, there are several other nice mid-century pieces at Mom and Dad's," Sven offered. "I'll tell you what, you take what you want, and Rob and I will help you pick out paint colors, fabrics, and accessories for your place in New York."

"Really?" Melanie squealed delightedly.

"Absolutely. Once you get moved in we'll start," Rob assured her.

"Oh, God." Karl groaned. "What am I going to do with all the stuff Melanie wants? Where are we going to store it? We downsized to get into our town house and we have no storage at all."

"Let me worry about that," Sven offered. "Besides the store, I have warehouse space. And besides, it'll be cheaper for Mel to use my suppliers and craftsmen down here to get things reupholstered."

Melanie jumped up and hugged her uncles in turn. "Thank you guys so much!"

"I warn you, though," Sven told Melanie. "You'll have to pay for shipping once it's done."

"It's a deal!" Melanie told him before she sat down and helped herself to a handful of cashews.

"Where is your apartment, by the way?" Rob asked her.

"Murray Hill," Melanie told him. "I can't remember exactly which street, but it's between Park and Lexington. Thirty-fifth Street, maybe? Anyway, it's a small two-bedroom in a doorman building."

Rob and Sven looked at each other with raised eyebrows.

"Are you renting or buying?" Sven asked carefully.

Melanie looked guiltily at her parents. "We're buying. Drew's parents gave us the down payment as a pre-wedding gift."

"This is the first I've heard of this," Karl said, not disguising his disapproval.

Caroline placed her hand on his forearm and said gently, "Andrew's parents are in a position to help them out, dear. I think it's a very generous gift."

"Is your name on the mortgage?" Karl asked Melanie directly.

She looked at her father pleadingly and said, "Of course, Dad. It's a gift to both of us."

"She's done very well, Karl," Sven said smoothly. "It's a very good investment."

"I'll say," Rob added.

Nonetheless, Karl considered the amount he had been tucking away against the day he knew Melanie would want a wedding. It was by no means near the amount of a down payment on a Manhattan apartment. Inwardly, it added to his assumption that things came too easily to his future son-in-law, but he knew better than to voice his misgivings. He looked around the circle of eager faces in Sven's living room and smiled. "Congratulations, Mel. It sounds like you're on your way."

Melanie gave him a relieved grin and took a deep breath. "I have some other news as well."

Karl looked at his daughter and felt himself tense as if for a short, sharp blow.

"Good news, I hope," Sven said encouragingly.

"I got a phone call from Sotheby's. They wanted me to come up for an interview within the next ten days. I've got it scheduled for a week from today," Melanie announced triumphantly.

Rob whistled and remarked, "That is a coup!"

"I'm so excited," Melanie declared. "Drew is, too. I called him at work to let him know. I'll fly up early next Friday morning and spend the weekend with him after the interview. Hopefully we'll have something to celebrate."

"What will you do if they want you to start right away?" Caroline asked cautiously. "You're right in the middle of the semester."

"I have a graduate assistant," Melanie reminded her mother. "Up til now, there's not been a lot for him to do, but he's good, and I'm sure there's something we can work out."

"Sotheby's," Karl said to no one in particular. The prospect of Melanie's departure from the town house had always been understood, but now that it was a large step closer to being realized, he felt winded. The image of the USAir flight that had flashed across his window at an impossible speed came to him. After feeling for so long that his life progressed predictably and methodically, it now seemed to accelerate with a force that pushed his back deeper into the sofa's cushion. His parents' preparations for the end, Melanie's race to begin a life of her own, and the anxious stasis of Sven's life all seemed to have accumulated with a force that overwhelmed him for that moment.

Around Karl the conversation moved on with laughter and loving companionability. Karl fell silent and nursed his wine; the flavor remained bright, but his appreciation of it dimmed. He had stalled, and he wasn't quite sure how to continue.

10

AT 2:17 KARL woke with a sense of stark terror. The time floated ghostlike on the ceiling over the bed, swimming before his eyes as he struggled out of sleep. He couldn't remember if he had reminded Sven to call their father at nine to remind him of their mother's medications. His dreams had been complicated scenes of his father's helplessness and anger, Sven's wearied back bent as he scrubbed what looked like bile from his parents' kitchen floor, while out of sight and out of reach, his mother cried softly and begged in Swedish not to be spanked. Helplessly, he'd searched for Caroline while a phone rang repeatedly with a call he knew to be Melanie from New York.

As he tried to separate the dream from the sweaty reality of being knotted in the covers of Sven's guest bed, he became aware of a throb in his head and an urgent need to pee. The ceiling image of the time shifted to 2:18 with a digital blink. It was real, he knew he was seeing it, but it took him a minute to realize the time was being projected overhead by the clock at his beside table. He turned his head and was relieved to find Caroline sleeping on her side next to him. With effort, he unknotted himself from the bedcovers and sat up, trying to remember the way to the bathroom.

At last feeling up to the trip, he stood carefully to accommodate his spinning head and made his way out of the room and down the hall to the bath. After softly closing the door behind him, he braced himself for the pain he knew would come with the flip of the light switch. He closed his eyes against the light in anticipation as he flicked the switch. The light permeated his eyelids with a softer glow than he'd expected, and he opened his eyes. The throbbing in his head didn't worsen, but his headache was real. Self-conscious about making noise in the small house, he pulled down his boxers and sat to pee, feeling immediate relief from that particular item on his list of late-night woes.

He flushed and stood, pulling up his boxers as he got to his feet. A quick search of the medicine cabinet yielded a bottle of Costco aspirin, and he eagerly shook two into his palm and turned on the tap. Not seeing a glass near the sink, he tossed the aspirin into his mouth and dry-swallowed them before he filled his cupped hands with water and drank gratefully. The medicine cabinet's mirror reflected his wet, haggard face, and the light overhead exaggerated the bluish circles under his eyes. For a moment, he found Sven's face superimposed on his own.

Wearily, he turned away from that startling image. He turned off the tap and switched off the light, and thought of returning to bed with dread. Despite Caroline's comforting presence, the bed and unfamiliar room threatened a return of nightmares. He decided instead to go into the kitchen and pour himself a glass of milk to soothe his stomach against the aspirin, and to give himself a few minutes to dispel the dreams that lingered like cobwebs at the edges of his consciousness. As quietly as he could, he made his way to the kitchen.

As he entered, he was startled by a figure sitting at the table in the dark. The kitchen door was open and the cool breeze from outside swept across his bare chest, intensifying his burst of fear.

"Did I wake you?" Sven asked quietly in the dark.

"No, but you scared the hell out of me," Karl admitted in his softest voice. "I had a bad dream, and a headache, and I needed to pee," he said to the form of his brother. As his eyes grew used to the dimness, he could make out Sven's white guinea-T and the brighter parts of his hair. An orange tip moved in the dark and flared briefly. Immediately the smell of cigarette smoke was blown toward him by the incoming breeze. "I thought I'd have a glass of milk," Karl added.

"Help yourself," Sven told him. "The glasses are on the shelf next to the refrigerator—can you see them?"

Reluctant to turn on a light, Karl stepped to the refrigerator and opened the door. Immediately he had enough light to find the glasses and pour his milk. Sven got up and held out his own milky glass to Karl expectantly. Karl obliged him by filling his glass before screwing the lid back on and replacing the milk on its shelf. When he closed the refrigerator door and was pitched back into darkness, he was no longer disoriented. He made his way to the kitchen table and sat down opposite his brother. "What are you doing up in the middle of the night, sitting in the dark?" he asked.

"Rob snores," Sven admitted. "I've gotten used to sleeping alone. I never used to notice it."

Karl heard the clicking of claws move from the dining room into the kitchen and felt Gretchen's wet nose nudge his wrist as she had done earlier. He stroked the back of her head, and she sat next to him. He could feel her warm breath against his side. "Seems like Gretchen's up as well," he told Sven.

Momentarily, a flame lit up Sven's face as he pulled it toward the tip of another cigarette. "She'll leave you alone in a moment," he said and exhaled. "She wants to be near me all the time."

"When did you start smoking again?" Karl asked him. "I haven't seen you with a cigarette since I've been home."

Sven chuckled. "I don't keep them with me. They stay on a shelf here in my kitchen—I hide them from myself like Dad tries to hide Mom's. I only smoke after meals and if I can't sleep. It's very comforting," he admitted.

"Mom told me the same thing when I caught her sneaking cigarettes yesterday morning," Karl said.

"Scary, isn't it?" Sven commented. "We even have the same secret vices. Would you think I was a bitch if I told you I'm glad she's slipping away?"

Karl answered his stomach's rumbling with a deep drink of his milk. Sven's question was more difficult. Finally, he said, "I don't think you're a bitch for wanting some of this responsibility off your shoulders."

Sven sighed and took another hit off his cigarette. "It's more than that, Karl. You're different. You got to grow up and go away. I've been Mom's baby for forty years. You can't imagine what it's like having someone with a claim on you like that."

"No, I can't say that I can," Karl told him gently. "It must be . . ."

"It's terrible," Sven interrupted. "All my allegiances are screwed up. I owe Rob more than that. Hell, I owe *me* more than that."

"Yes, you do, Sven," Frank told him with conviction. "It's time you started putting yourself first. I'm amazed at how much of yourself you give away. I know I'm at the periphery of your life, and I admit I'm pretty self-absorbed—but maybe that gives me some perspective on the situation that you don't have."

"Thanks, brother, I need to hear that right now," Sven said. "It's just that I think of her, not being understood and sort of lost in herself, and it makes me so sad," he admitted bleakly. "Rationally, I know there's nothing I can do anymore, but it's a habit of a lifetime to be Mom's . . ."

"Baby?" Karl finished. "Sven, it's way past time for you to separate yourself from her. I don't mean to sound cold, but it's a little sick, you know? You're a grown man. Your responsibility to our mother ended a long time ago, as far as being the baby is concerned."

Sven nodded in the darkness and took a long draw off his cigarette. Absently, he blew smoke rings off toward the refrigerator. "I know that, Karl," he said finally. "But I'm not so sure that I don't need some time to just figure out who I am, by myself."

"Is that what's keeping you from getting in step with Rob's plans to expand your business up in New York? Is that what's keeping you and him apart?" Karl demanded softly.

"I see you've been talking with Rob," Sven commented dryly, then sighed. "Twenty-six years is a long time to belong to somebody."

"No, it's not," Frank replied, thinking of himself and Caroline. "It's not something you give up at a time like this. It would be like throwing the baby out with the bathwater."

"I know you're right, Karl," Sven admitted. "That's why I've come to the decision I have. Do you want to hear it?"

"Sure."

Sven flicked the ash off the end of his cigarette, and after a final drag, he stubbed it out in the ashtray. "I'm going to let Mom and Dad know that I'm moving with Rob to New York. It's not going to be next week or anything, but definitely within the year. It'll take that long to wrap things up down here and get it together up there. There are all kinds of decisions to make, like whether or not we want to sell both places or keep one as a second home. I could make Johann a partner and keep the store down here open. Johann is capable, if he's ready to commit."

"I think you're making a wise decision, Sven," Karl encouraged him. "But why make a big deal out of it with Mom? In a year, she won't know whether you've gone or not. Why bother her with it now?"

"Because I think it's just as important for her to let go of me as it is for me to be free," Sven said carefully.

"Isn't that the same as asking her permission?" Karl asked skeptically.

"No, it's not," Sven insisted. "It's giving her a chance to feel like she has had a hand in my decision. Do you think she'd let go if she didn't feel as if she were looking out for my best interests?"

"You're giving her a chance to be the adult," Karl reflected.

"Yeah, and I'm giving me the chance to finally grow up," Sven told him.

Karl nodded in the darkness. "I wish it wasn't so hard for either of you."

Sven laughed despite himself. He managed to squelch his amusement to a few quiet chuckles before he said, "It's all a bunch of bullshit. But it's my life, you know? She's been my mom and my best friend for my entire life. There will be so many voids created when she's gone. Mom's a huge part of my life. The only thing I can do is try not to be more neurotic than you already think I am."

"I don't think you're neurotic at all," Karl told him evenly. "I couldn't do everything you've done—looking after Mom and Dad especially."

Sven made a dismissive motion with his hand. "That's part of being the late-in-life baby. And a result of not getting on with my life years ago. It's just that I've always had this close bond with Mom. And then there's the me-and-her-against-Dad dynamic. It is neurotic. But I've been a good son. Now I'm ready to be a good partner to Rob and to be good to myself as well."

"You'll be fine," Karl said confidently.

"Wish me luck, big brother," Sven said, betraying a need for his approval that was very real.

"I do, and I love you, kid," Karl said.

"Thanks," Sven said with a tremble in his voice.

Karl stood. "I'm going back to bed; I think you should, too. Enough deep thinking for one night."

"You go ahead," Sven said and reached for his cigarettes once more. "I want to sit here and enjoy what I'm feeling right now."

Karl nodded and started past him. At the kitchen door he paused for a moment and then took a step back. Moving behind Sven, he wrapped his arms around his shoulders and hugged him tight. Then he kissed the top of his head and moved away.

"What was that for?" Sven asked him.

"For all the times in the past thirty-five years that I wanted to do it and didn't." Without another word, Karl walked out of the kitchen and went back to bed.

SATURDAY

11

KARL WOKE EASILY at the same time he normally did at home. His internal clock was righting itself despite the demands brought of this unexpected holiday with its swift changes of beds and emotional currents. Rolling onto his back, he searched the ceiling over the bed for the projected time from the clock at the bedside. There was still enough dimness in the early March morning to make out that it was six-ten. He lay for a moment and was relieved to find his headache had disappeared. Despite the early-morning interruption of his nightmares and the time spent with Sven in the dark kitchen, he felt rested and relaxed. The aspirin, milk, and conversation with his brother had eased Karl's subconscious demons, and he'd slept the rest of the night peacefully.

Beside him, Caroline breathed deeply, still wound comfortably in sleep. Karl watched her sleeping for a moment. The fatigued sadness that had creased her face the night before had disappeared. Karl admired the familiar contours of her features. She was what nineteenth-century literature would have described as a handsome woman. Hers was not the striking loveliness that his mother had and still possessed. While Annike was pure Nordic, Caroline's own distinctive looks were a hybrid of many streams of genetic confluence. A typical eastern North Carolinian, she came from mainly Anglo-Irish stock with an insistent strain of Choctaw-Cherokee characteristics.

Those very qualities had first attracted Karl, who found her looks exotic. He had been easily captivated by her hazel eyes and prominent cheekbones. As she had matured into the woman who lay beside him now, she had maintained her economical body that had been knit from birth to last near a hundred years. Her multitudinous family was long-lived with no evidence of dementia, even among the aunts, uncles, and cousins who had passed their eightieth year. Karl took particular comfort in that knowledge, watching Caroline in the intimacy of the guest room that morning. While it had been made abundantly clear to him over the past few days that time was indeed rushing along at a speed that confounded him, the stillness of that moment alone with his beloved wife provided him with an opportunity to savor her presence for several serene moments.

Karl pushed back the bedcovers and stood as gently as he could so as not to disturb her. For a few seconds he experienced the familiar head rush of rising. It seemed as if the room continued to move with his momentum, and he waited for the scene before his eyes to still. The increasing regularity of that disorientation on rising was now starting to trouble him. After seeing his parents' sudden spurt of aging, he briefly entertained the thought that his head rushes on rising might be more than simple middle-aged low blood pressure. The sensation passed and he dismissed the thought, ascribing it to an overactive imagination.

He concentrated instead on another familiar morning ritual. He was drawn to the window, and he pulled the shade away from the edge of the window frame to peek out at the new morning in the unfamiliar neighborhood. The guest room faced the street, and Karl looked out on the growing light reflected as an orangey-rose dawn slipping out from the ocean's rim a block away. It was a serene view. An easterly breeze ruffled the fronds of the coconut palms in Sven's front yard, while the sprinkler system hissed and spread arcs of water across the gleaming grass of the lawn.

Other than the sprinkler's wet whispers, Karl heard no sounds. The house was still, and he assumed he was the first one up. He found the idea of being the first one to shower appealing. The thought of washing off the unseen psychological grime he'd accumulated since the morning he'd left home was motivating. As quietly as he could, he left the window and gathered his essentials for bathing and changing clothes. He settled on a clean pair of white corduroy pants and a pale blue long-sleeved Henley from the Gap, given to him by Caroline. Those decisions made, he slipped out of the room and pulled the door closed behind him, turning the knob so it would close silently. Then he made his way through the sleeping house to the bathroom.

Within twenty minutes he was showered, shaved, dressed, and mentally ready for the demands the day would bring. After stashing his dirty underwear and his dop kit back in his suitcase, he left Caroline's sleeping form and started to the kitchen. Gretchen trotted from the kitchen to greet him, her claws and collar tags tapping and jangling loudly in the quiet house. Awkwardly, he patted the dog's head as she twined herself around his legs in an enthusiastic greeting. Together he and the dog proceeded into the kitchen, where he found Sven sitting in the same spot, as if he'd never returned to bed.

"Good morning," Sven told him. "There's coffee ready."

"Have you been up all night?" Karl asked him as he maneuvered around Gretchen's continuing dance by his legs to the coffeepot.

"No," Sven said and yawned. "I thought about what we talked about, and then I went back to bed. I was finally able to sleep like the dead."

"Me, too," Karl told him as he poured a generous amount of half-and-half from the container by the coffeepot. "No more bad dreams."

"I'm glad," Sven told him. "There's yogurt and fresh fruit if you're hungry," he offered.

Karl sat down and shook his head before taking an audible sip of his coffee. "Not yet, thanks," he said. "I need some coffee before anything else. Did I wake you this morning?"

Sven watched him as he set down his coffee mug and stretched out his legs. "Yes, but don't worry about it. I wanted to get coffee started before everyone started getting up." He looked his brother over and said, "You look good. That blue suits you. You don't look a day over thirty-five."

Karl warmed to the unexpected compliment. He looked at Sven, who appeared younger than his years despite the wrinkles crinkling the corners of his eyes—the telltale smoker's squint. Still, Sven looked tired and somewhat strained despite his tousled hair and eager smile. "You look pretty good yourself," Karl returned, "but I've always seen you as a kid. I can't help it. It's hard to believe you've turned forty."

"We have good genes," Sven said and shrugged. "But I've aged, I can tell. Smoking does that to you."

"No cigarettes this morning?" Karl asked offhandedly.

Sven pointed to the open door and said, "I've already had my allotment while you were showering. I don't want my company to gag first thing in the morning."

"Thanks, we'll all appreciate the fresh air, believe me," Karl said and looked down into his coffee mug. They sat in silence awhile, each absorbed in his own thoughts, before Karl cleared his throat and said, "Who's making this brunch at Mom's?"

Sven laughed. "You're looking at the chef. Mom really can't cook anymore. She gets things out of proportion and forgets to turn down the heat, so unless you like the taste of scorch and salt lick, it's better to just do it myself."

"Well, you'll have help. I'm sure Caroline will want to pitch in," Karl promised.

"That'll be fine," Sven said, "but it's really no big deal."

Gretchen, who had sunk with a sigh next to Sven's chair, rose and trotted out of the kitchen. By the sounds of her claws scrabbling on the terrazzo floor, Karl knew someone else had risen. In a moment Rob appeared at the kitchen door, pulling the sweater he'd worn the day before over his muscled torso. Gretchen reared up on her hind legs and placed her paws alarmingly near his crotch. Instinctively,

Rob hunched and backed away before bending slightly and taking the dog's head between his hands and gently shaking it.

"Hey, sweetheart," Rob said as his eyes sought out Sven's. He smiled with a possessiveness that was familiar to Karl yet struck him as almost disturbingly intimate. While he had always known that Rob and his brother were lovers, they had nevertheless seemed to be circumspect around him. They had the banter of familiar intimates but were never demonstrative in his presence. Yet Karl was struck by the carnal interest that flashed in Rob's smile and eyes this morning. He felt a little disconcerted but inwardly kicked himself for being so staid. He was secure enough in his own masculinity that homosexuality in and of itself didn't bother him. Yet when he was presented with its practice, he was always a bit taken aback.

"Hey yourself," Sven said gently and returned Rob's suggestive look. "Your glasses are on top of the refrigerator," he reminded his partner.

Karl caught Sven's look as he returned his partner's greeting and found it to be perfectly natural considering Sven and Rob had been together over half their lives. He thought of how silly his immediate reaction was and dismissed it as out of hand. He was in his brother's house, and this was his brother's life.

Rob gave Gretchen's ears a final shake, inspiring the dog to back away and give herself a more thorough shake on her own. Rob twisted and reached up for his glasses. Once they were in place, he looked at Karl and said, "You're up and dressed early."

"I wanted to beat the women into the bathroom," Karl admitted.

"I hear ya," Rob said as he strode to the coffeepot and busied himself making his own cup.

"It's going to be a beautiful day," Sven reported. "Are you sure you want to be cooped up in that guest bath all day hanging wallpaper?"

Rob made his way to the table and sat down. He blew across the rim of his coffee mug. "I've put it off for three weeks and it really needs to be done," he told Sven. "Are you going to be tied up with Karl, Caroline, and Melanie all day?"

Sven nodded. "I want to spend as much time with Karl's family as I can. God only knows when we'll all be together again. Besides, I'll be the cook all day, brunch and dinner. Mom can't handle it by herself."

Rob took a sip of his coffee and settled back into his chair. "Well, I want to spend some more time with them, too," he said defensively. "How late do you think the day will run?"

Sven reached across the table and sought his partner's hand. He gave it a squeeze and said, "It won't be late. Mom and Dad will want supper by five. I can't imagine us getting back here later than seven." Sven released Rob's hand and settled back into his own chair.

"I've got an idea," Karl said suddenly. "Sven, why don't you get dinner started and leave us to feed ourselves, clean up, and get back here on our own. That way you and Rob could have dinner together and meet us back here."

"That sounds like a plan," Rob agreed eagerly. "We can go to that Italian place we love. I've been dreaming of their yellowtail livornese. I'm sure I could get us reservations at five."

Sven looked at Karl and asked, "You wouldn't feel like I was abandoning you or anything?"

"Hell no," Karl said. "That's why I suggested it. Besides, you'll need to get back here to let Gretchen out and feed her, won't you?"

"I'll come here at three-thirty and take care of Gretchen," Rob promised. "You meet me here by four and you'll have a chance to shower and change before we head out for dinner."

Sven sighed and looked out the kitchen door wistfully. "It sounds wonderful," he admitted. "How long has it been since we ate out on a Saturday night?"

"Too long," Rob replied. "We haven't gone out since we had dinner with Tim and Tricia two months ago."

"Are you sure you don't mind?" Sven asked Karl once more.

"Actually, I'm glad we're here to entertain Mom and Dad and give you a break," Karl told his brother.

Sven smiled gratefully and turned to Rob. "Like a date?"

"Absolutely," Rob told him. "It's a done deal. I'll be waiting for you here."

"Okay!" Sven agreed excitedly. "Damn. This is a real treat."

Karl grinned and nodded at Rob. "That was easy. I do come up with a good idea once in a while."

Rob nodded at him gratefully. "It was inspired. Sven will be able to relax and enjoy himself for once."

"You can say that again," Sven concurred. "I never know when Mom or Dad will call with some small thing that is a huge crisis in their minds. You have no idea . . ."

"No, I don't," Karl interrupted him gently. "I feel bad that I'm so far away and can't be around to give you a hand with all those little things. This trip has really opened my eyes, you know? It's so easy for me to assume everything is perfectly normal from where I sit eight hundred miles away."

"Don't be so hard on yourself, Karl," Sven said consolingly. "Even if you lived across town, I bet Mom and Dad would still call me. And Mom's not the only one to blame, though she always has been a little proprietary over me."

"A little," Rob commented wryly.

"C'mon, Rob, be fair. Dad's just as bad. As far as he's concerned, since I'm not married with two point three kids, my life is somehow not as validly busy as other people's," Sven said.

"That's true," Rob agreed. "Your father still thinks of you as a teenager. He acts like your work is only a hobby, and he discounts your relationship with me entirely."

"I think both of your assessments of how Dad sees you are totally correct," Karl agreed. "Straight people, myself included, I hate to say, tend to see gay people as having way too much fun."

"Well, we can hardly blame you," Rob said jokingly. "We're the ones who picked out *gay* as our adjective. It makes being homosexual sound a little fizzy and empty-headed."

Sven snorted and said, "Like our life is some big disco party orgy, complete with cocktail umbrellas, which we go to after shopping for grooming products."

"We haven't been to a club in years," Rob told Karl with some exasperation. "In fact, we haven't been on a vacation since 1999. Travel for us is always business."

"Do you know what I'd give just to have the time to spend the morning at the beach?" Sven asked tiredly. "It's only a block away, but the only time I see it is when I walk Gretchen."

"Really?" Melanie said as she strode into the kitchen and walked straight to the coffeepot. "Well, Mom and I plan to spend the morning on the beach tomorrow, and I'm going to play my spoiled-niece card and drag you along with us." She reached for a coffee mug and turned to pet Gretchen, who seemed very excited by all the people appearing in her usually quiet home.

Sven chuckled and gave Melanie a fond look. "And good morning to you, too, Miz Melanie."

"Good morning, guys," Melanie replied as she poured her coffee and generously creamed it. "Do you have any Splenda?"

"Look in the drawer under the coffeemaker," Rob told her.

Melanie located the sweetener and emptied the contents of a packet into her coffee. "What are we talking about?" she asked cheerfully as she took the empty place at the table and sat down.

"We're giving your uncles the evening off to go out to dinner alone," Karl informed her. "And we're going to do dinner with your grandparents."

Melanie took a tentative sip of her hot coffee and sighed with contentment. "That sounds nice, but we'll hook up with you guys back here later, right?"

"Absolutely," Rob promised. "I want to spend as much time with you as I can."

"Me, too," Melanie said and gave him a private smile. Then, to Sven, she announced, "I don't expect you to take me shopping while I'm here this time. The Kate Spade bag you sent me for Christmas was more than generous. I have to tell you, I love it. I use it all the time."

"I enjoy spoiling you," Sven said, glowing happily with Melanie's appreciation of his gift, but he added, "I wish I had time to take you to the shop. There's so many things there I think you'd appreciate. I have a set of French porcelain coral branches that make me think of you. I found them at the Clignancourt flea market in Paris."

"They sound lovely," Melanie told him, "but don't hold on to them on my account. I'm looking forward to you and Uncle Rob helping me put the apartment together once I get moved and settled in. I'm going to hold you to your promise."

"Sven and I have a surprise for you," Rob said and glanced at Sven.

Sven caught his glance and shot it back with a nod and a smile. "You can tell her," he offered.

"Sven woke me up at three o'clock this morning and told me he'd decided we were going to move to New York," Rob announced happily. "Or was I dreaming?" he added teasingly.

"No. You weren't dreaming," Sven said decisively and looked at Karl, then at Melanie. "I had a talk with your father here, and he told me he thought it would be a great thing for Rob and me to do. We've been talking about it for a while, and we feel we have the clients and the opportunity to do this. How would you like having us up there near you?"

Melanie clapped her hands together and squealed with excitement. "My two favorite people in the whole world? I'd love it. Are you kidding?"

"No kidding," Rob said seriously. "It won't be for at least a year; we have things to get settled first, but we *are* going to do it." He looked at Sven tenderly and said, "It's like a big adventure, isn't it?"

Karl watched as Sven reached across the table and laid his hand against Rob's cheek in reply. Then Sven looked at him and said, "I got my big brother's take on it, and he thinks it's time."

"Well, I don't know how much I had to do with the decision, Mel, but I think it'll be great for you to have your uncles close by to keep an eye on you for me," Karl teased.

"Hey! Who's to say I won't be there to keep an eye on them?" Melanie replied happily. "They are getting older."

"Who is?" Rob asked and chuckled. "I feel like I'm twenty-five and just starting out again, don't you, Sven?"

Sven stood and took his coffee mug to the counter. "I don't know if I'd go quite that far, but I don't think we need any looking after just yet." With that, he poured himself what was left of the coffee and started to make a fresh pot.

"When are you and Andrew thinking about getting married, Mel?" Rob asked earnestly.

"Oh, God," Melanie said and tapped the table with her fingertips nervously. "Not you, too?"

"I'd be lying if I didn't say I was wondering," Rob answered her honestly. "I mean, you and Andrew share a mortgage—why not go ahead and get marriage out of the way?"

"When are you and Uncle Sven going to get married?" Melanie answered slyly.

"Who says we're not already?" Sven answered as he carefully poured water into the coffeemaker. "After twenty-six years and as many legal documents as we've had drawn up, I already consider myself married, don't you, Rob?"

"Of course," Rob answered. "A ceremony with some tolerant priest or a justice of the peace in Massachusetts is really sort of beside the point by now."

Karl followed this little exchange with interest. Rob and Sven had never discussed their relationship in such a way, and Melanie had avoided the issue of a marriage commitment to Andrew with quiet insistence ever since she had announced her intent to move in with him nearly a year before, when he had taken a job with Credit Suisse. Karl listened intently, hoping Melanie might be more forthcoming with her uncles than she had been with him and Caroline.

"I don't know if it's beside the point or not," Melanie replied. "I, for one, would like being a part of some ceremony for you and Uncle Sven. When I was little, I used to daydream about being your flower girl. I could picture myself in a long white dress, walking up the aisle of our church, dropping rose petals and everything. I still want to do it if you ever decide you want a ceremony."

Sven clicked on the coffeemaker and, after tasting the remains of the earlier pot in his mug, frowned and dumped the contents down the sink. "Mel," he said as he returned to the table and sat down, "the only way I'm going to ever get married is in a Catholic church, with a full mass and everything. And you and I both know that's never going to happen in our lifetime. Instead, I made a promise to God to be true to Rob in the spirit of the Catholic marriage vows, without the ceremony. So far, so good. I'm happy with how things are, and I think Rob is, too."

"Damn right," Rob interrupted. "But if I could walk down the aisle with Sven in his Catholic church and get married with a nuptial mass, I'd do it for him, even though I'm not Catholic. You *can* have all that, Mel. I guess I don't understand why you wouldn't want it."

"Fair enough," Melanie said and sighed. After glancing at her father, she said, "I do want that . . . the mass and everything. I just am not ready for it right now. It doesn't have anything to do with the way I feel about Drew. He's actually ready to get married now. I just can't get my head around it. If I get this new job at Sotheby's, I'll want some time to get settled into meeting their expectations, as well as finding and sorting out my own expectations of myself. If I get pregnant, God forbid, I'll get married immediately. I just don't see the point of it right now." She looked around the table and thoughtfully took a sip of her coffee. She set the mug down decisively and continued. "I want to appreciate the whole process of getting married. I want to enjoy it. Every girl I know who's gotten married has been a raving maniac by the time of the wedding, and I just don't want to be like that. Do you understand?"

"Mel, you know the girls who ended up being raving maniacs about their weddings are raving maniacs to begin with, don't you?" Rob queried astutely.

Melanie laughed. "You're not wrong. But I've been a bridesmaid enough in the past two years to be tired of the whole psychodrama that goes with big wedding plans."

"So it's not that you aren't sure Drew's the one," Sven said, "it's that you want to experience the whole deal in a mature way."

"Something like that. Yes," Melanie said confidently.

"Just out of curiosity, when do you think that might be?" Karl asked gently.

"I don't know, Dad," Melanie responded honestly, "in a couple of years, maybe. But it will definitely happen before we decide to have children."

"I can live with that," Karl said, and he reached across the table to wrap his hand around hers, which was holding her mug.

"I can, too," Caroline announced from the dining room before striding into the kitchen with Gretchen dancing by her side.

"How long have you been standing there spying?" Melanie asked with a laugh.

"I wasn't spying, I was listening. That's the most articulate statement you've ever come up with on the subject, as far as I know," Caroline said as she came to stand behind Karl. Bending down, she kissed the top of his head and put her hands on his shoulders.

"Let me get another chair," Sven said as he started to rise.

"No. Sit," Rob said and looked around the suddenly crowded kitchen. "Now that I can tell Caro good morning, I need to be heading back up to Palm Beach."

"Oh, don't leave," Caroline said with disappointment.

"I really do need to go in order to be back here by three-thirty," Rob said as he made his way toward the dining room. In the doorway, he stopped and turned. "Have a good day with the parents. I'll make us some special drink, kamikazes or cosmopolitans—something festive—when you all get back here."

"I'll be looking forward to that," Karl said wryly. "I'll need a drink by then."

Sven stood up. "I'll walk you out," he said to Rob with a grin.

"Oh, for God's sake," Melanie said in exasperation. "You can kiss him good-bye in front of us."

With that, Rob stooped slightly and kissed Sven on the mouth. "See you back here by four, okay?"

Sven's fair complexion reddened under his light tan. "Drive safe, please."

Rob nodded and lifted his arm to wave to the room. "See you guys back here tonight."

As Rob left to a chorus of good-byes, Sven moved to the coffeepot and checked its progress. Caroline claimed Rob's seat and scooted her chair up to the table. Resting her chin on her upraised hands, she looked at Melanie and said, "I want you to know I'm proud of you."

"Thanks, Mom," Melanie said happily, then added, "But what for?"

Caroline reached across the table to enclose her daughter's hand with her own. "I think you're pretty mature to want to get married when *you* want to. I think I understand you better than these guys do. It used to be that marriage was a means in and of itself for young women. Women used to think, 'I'll get a man, and then my life can begin.' I don't see you prioritizing your life that way. You are thinking like an adult woman and not like a dizzy girl. There will be a time for marriage when you're not trying to get so many things done at once. I'll look forward to sharing that time with you. Okay?"

Melanie looked long into her mother's eyes and sighed. "Mom, you are the best. You really get it, don't you?"

"Yes. I do," Caroline said and gave her daughter a wink. "How long before that coffee's ready, Sven?"

Karl watched the exchange between his wife and daughter with a mixture of wonder and pride. Their relationship had matured into one of mutual respect, and that satisfied him very deeply. Together, they were the real axis his life had turned upon for many years. That orbit remained as fixed and dependable as the seasons and gave his life a great part of the solidity he craved. For a moment, he found himself acutely aware of how blessed he was. Blessings, for Karl, were fortunes to recognize with gratitude, not spiritual capital to accumulate. Nonetheless, for the second time in as many days, he found himself profoundly grateful to a God he still appreciated in the abstract. All the discussion of nuptials and Catholic masses brought to his mind the Latin response that translated as "and brings joy to my youth." Karl had said those words many times as an altar boy before Vatican II, while extending the cruets of wine and water prior to the consecration of the host. Some of those carefully memorized phrases in the holy language popped into his mind at the oddest times. Now, sitting in Sven's sunny kitchen, he recalled how faith had felt to him as a child, when he still believed in such things as a God who kept scores and dealt punishments as well as blessings. When he'd been a kid, it had made sense. Watching his daughter and wife in a nimbus of morning sun, he wondered when God had stopped being relevant.

Karl glanced over his shoulder and found Sven bent slightly, watching the final drips of coffee go into the pot. He had made a difference in his brother's thinking last night. Sven had acknowledged it that morning, and it made Karl feel good. He turned his head and watched as Caroline let go of Melanie's hand and leaned back into her chair with a chuckle at some tidbit he'd missed as his mind tripped on Latin phrases that snuck out of the recesses of his memory. He looked at Melanie as she ran her fingers through her hair, pulling it to the back of her head. The sun picked out its honeyed tones and made them gleam.

Feeling more grounded and less adrift in the world of emotional demands he'd landed into two days before, he drained his coffee mug. "I'm a lucky guy," he said out loud to no one in particular.

12

THE EARLY MORNING continued amiably as Caroline, Melanie, and Sven drifted one by one out of the kitchen to shower, dress, and get on with the day, leaving Karl to snack on yogurt and fruit as he glanced at the morning paper. By ten-fifteen, the group was moving outside to get in their respective cars for the drive back down to Boca Raton. Melanie elected to ride with Sven, leaving Caroline and Karl to follow in the Camry.

As much as Karl wanted to spend time with his mother and father, he was reluctant to leave Sven's bright house at the beach. The morning had been so mellow, he hoped the mood would continue throughout the day, but he had doubts that it would. His mother's mental shifts were like mercury, he had no idea if she would be able to keep it together or if her sense of time and place would shatter into little shimmering balls that slid incongruously across the surface of the day. His father's overbearing behavior gave him some concern as well. Karl hoped he was in a good mood.

Some of this he discussed with Caroline as they made their way south on I-95. For the most part, Caroline did her best to reassure him that everything would be fine. He found her calm presence heartening. Though the early-Saturday-morning traffic was sparse, the distance from Singer Island down to his parents' house was a longer drive than Karl had anticipated.

"Can you believe Sven has been making this drive every day for the past few months?" he asked Caroline with a mixture of disbelief and admiration.

"Well, his shop is about halfway in between, isn't it?" Caroline commented. "At least that breaks it up for him some."

"Be that as it may," Karl insisted, "it's still a hell of a lot of time out of his day. It's no different than if we had to drive to Chapel Hill every day on the way home from work."

"True," Caro obliged. "He's been very diligent in taking care of them. They are lucky to have him close by. Do you think he'll keep it up after they move to Palladian Gardens?"

Karl lifted his eyebrows and shook his head. "I think he'll keep it up as long he thinks Mom needs him, at least for the next year."

"If he and Rob do make this move to New York," said Caroline, "he'll soon have a lot of other things to focus on rather than your parents."

"That's one reason I encouraged him to make the move," Karl asserted. "But I have to tell you, Caro, I still wonder at the rift between him and Rob. I don't think Sven's responsibility to our parents is all there is to it."

Caroline glanced at him, then turned in her seat to look at him. "Karl, you saw them last night, and then again this morning . . . what makes you think there's some other underlying tension? They seemed very happy to me. A little stressed, but beyond that, those two are as perfectly suited for one another as you and I are."

Karl shifted in his seat uncomfortably and switched lanes to pass a landscaper's rig. "They've been together almost as long as you and I have," Karl started cautiously. "But sometime around twenty-five years together, didn't you ever wake up one morning and think, What in the hell am I doing?"

Caroline chuckled and reached over to pat his shoulder. "Of course I did. Didn't you?"

Karl glanced at her briefly as he pulled back into the right lane. "I did, but I wasn't sure if you ever did," he admitted.

"About the time Melanie got her undergrad degree, I spent the summer thinking about what life would be like on my own," Caroline confessed. "It seemed like Mel's milestone was one for me as well. Our life seemed to have stagnated somewhat. We were still in the old house. We were both absorbed in our work and not really communicating very much." Caroline paused and looked out the windshield. "I certainly made a conscious decision then that I wanted to stay with you, but some things had to change."

Karl nodded and sat silent for a moment, absorbing her admission. Finally, he said, "I did the same thing, but a little after you. I think I felt you pulling away somehow. All of the reasons we had spent our lives together revolved around the house, bringing up and educating Melanie. I was craving some change as well."

"It's part of middle age, Karl," Caroline said gently. "I think it says a lot about us and our relationship that we were strong enough as individuals to think things through, and to recommit ourselves to moving ahead together without making a federal case out of it."

"I love you," Karl said simply.

"And I love you," Caroline responded. "Still, we came to the conclusion that we needed to make some personal and professional changes, like moving to the town house. But we did it together. Isn't that what Rob and Sven are going through right now?"

"I guess it is," Karl conceded. "I just wish I had told him about us last night when I was talking with him. But you know, no matter how sophisticated I think I am, I can't get past this fundamental belief that Rob and Sven's relationship is different because they're gay."

"In what way?" Caro asked honestly.

"I don't know," Karl told her as he fumbled for his answer. "It's just that my ideas about being a man don't accommodate giving another man that much say in making decisions about how I run my life."

"I can understand that," Caroline told him. "It's so hard not to think of Sven as the wife and Rob as the husband. I think it's natural for us to try and draw those lines of dominance and submissiveness. It's just the way the paradigm works."

"But you don't feel submissive to me, do you?" Karl asked with concern.

"Frankly, no," Caroline told him. "So, if that way of thinking isn't really true for straight people, why should it be true for gay couples? I feel like I'm an equal partner."

"Sven and Karl have always struck me as being partners," Karl said truthfully. "I mean, when it comes to work, Sven has his sphere and Rob has his, yet the boundaries get blurred when they actually take on a job. They help each other."

"But you are concerned that Sven feels submissive to Rob?" Caroline asked him with interest.

"Sven told me he wanted an opportunity to think for himself," Karl told her. "He said he was tired of trying to make everything right for everybody. I'm not sure that by encouraging him to move to Manhattan with Rob, I was seeing him as the wife. Maybe I would have better served him by encouraging him to go it alone."

"Don't be absurd," Caroline answered with alacrity. "You told him what you honestly thought. And I agree with what you told him. After twenty-six years, Sven knows his part in that relationship, and what's more important, he knows how *he* defines himself. It's obvious he's got the more giving and caring personality. I think that his willingness to be the nurturer is why we see him in a wifely role."

"I think you hit the nail on the head," Karl agreed. "I certainly am not a very nurturing person—you've always held up that end of the relationship for us. Still, I'm not certain that telling him to follow Rob to New York was not discounting him in some way."

"No, you went with telling what you felt was right, all things considered. I would have told him the same thing," she concluded bluntly.

"Well, that's good to hear," Karl said with some relief. "It did seem to me like it would be a waste of twenty-six years to give up on the relationship because of . . ."

"Middle-aged angst," Caroline concluded for him. "That's what people do—they throw everything away because of this chasm you come upon when you're middle-aged, and you think the only way across it is to leave everything behind and jump, free as a bird. Look at all the couples we know who've done that."

Karl nodded and changed lanes again. His exit was coming up. "You're absolutely right, of course," he told his wife.

"I'm glad you think so." Caroline smiled. "You and I just held hands and jumped together. Buying the town house and starting a new phase of our lives in a new place is one of the smartest things we've ever done. I think Sven and Rob moving to New York and beginning again is wise, too. Don't you?"

Karl switched on his turn signal and merged into the exit lane for Glades Road, then said, "I think it will bring them closer together. I really do. Once they get away from all this history down here, they'll need each other in a whole new way."

"Damn straight," Caroline said and laughed. "Straight? Get it?"

Karl snickered and said, "You're a trip, as our daughter says." As he swung onto Glades Road, he caught sight of Sven's Excursion a traffic light ahead. He was glad. He wanted them all to arrive as a group and get in their greetings together. For the rest of the way to his parents' house, he kept an eye on the big back end of Sven's SUV, until he pulled into the drive just after Sven did.

Annike and Frank were waiting for them in the front yard. They stood by a grouping of ixora around a cluster of queen palms on the side of the lot opposite the drive. It looked as if they'd simply been on a stroll in the front yard, with Frank's arm protectively around Annike's waist, but Karl knew they had deliberately come outside to wait for them. Annike's face radiated happiness, and Frank's grin bespoke a pride and longing to welcome his family.

They were smartly dressed and made quite a picture for Karl, Melanie, Caroline, and Sven to hold in their memory as a snapshot of that moment. Karl was deeply touched by their eagerness to see his family, and the care they'd given to making the impression that everything was alright.

As they all spilled from their cars, Annike broke away from Frank's embrace and started toward them. For Karl, so much hung on how she greeted them. Would it be in Swedish or English? Was she as fully there as she seemed to be?

"My whole family!" Annike declared, reaching out her arms as if to embrace them all. Karl felt relief flood him as Melanie stepped into her grandmother's waiting arms and hugged her close. Shyly, Frank stepped up beside them and waited his turn to be embraced by his granddaughter. Karl watched as Melanie released her grandmother and warmly embraced Frank in turn.

Caroline presented herself next to be hugged and exclaimed over, as Sven and Karl hung back. "Oh! It seems like forever since I've seen you," Annike told Caroline.

"And you are as lovely as ever," Frank added as he hugged Caroline.

"Boys!" Annike said and held out her arms. In tandem, Karl and Sven stepped forward to be embraced by their mother. She let them go and stepped back to look them over. "And where is Rob?" she asked Sven.

"He has to work today," Sven told her gently. "But he sends his love."

"*Nonsense!*" Annike said as she drew Sven close to her side, wrapping her arm around his waist. "*Han gjorde icke vilja till ha att göra med din fader,*" she said softly. *He didn't want to deal with your father.*

"*Plundra tanken Pappa skulle hellre njuta av rättvis Karl och hans familj idag. Särskilt sedan dess vi vill bli be om till deras sakerna. Du veta hur Pappa få,*" Sven whispered to his mother. *Rob thought Dad would rather enjoy just Karl and his family today. Especially since we will be asking for your things. You know how Dad gets.* Karl noticed that Sven gave her a secret look and nod.

"*Han er en skarp pojke,*" Annike replied with an understanding nod. *He is a smart boy.*

Karl caught enough of the exchange to get the gist of it.

"Stop it, you two," Frank said irritably. "This is a family day. I don't want you jabbering in private so we can't understand you. It's rude."

"Okay, Dad," Sven answered obediently.

Mollified, Frank gave him a curt nod and reached for Karl's hand. "How much of that crap can you still understand?"

Karl took his father's hand and clasped his upper arm. "Enough to get me in trouble."

His father returned the familiar pressure of Karl's grip and said, "You let me know if they say anything about me, deal?"

"It's a deal, Dad," Karl told him. "Sven was just checking on Mom," he lied gently.

His mother looked at Karl and slyly winked. "Why don't we all go in and have a nice Bloody Mary before brunch?" she suggested brightly.

"Sounds wonderful," Melanie said as she put her arm around her grandmother and turned toward the front door.

"Mom, I don't know if you should," Sven said quietly.

"Get off her back," his father replied just as quietly. "She took her medicine at seven-thirty. She can have one drink. Don't be so bossy for once."

Sven shrugged and laughed. "Okay, Dad. I promise to be easy on you guys today. It's a holiday, right?"

"Yes it is," Frank said as he reached for Caroline's hand. "Now, you'd like a Bloody Mary, wouldn't you, Caroline?"

"I've been looking forward to one all morning," Caroline admitted. "And you make the best ones in the world, so put me at the head of the line."

"I already have a pitcher made and waiting in the refrigerator," Frank told her happily as he led her up the walk. "God, you look good. You look like a girl—how do you do it?"

Caroline flashed her father-in-law a flattered smile and laughed. "Karl keeps me on my toes."

"I bet you need to keep *him* in line," Frank said with his own laugh.

Sven nudged Karl's shoulder and rolled his eyes as they brought up the rear and entered the house. Karl returned his look with a grin as he shut the door behind them and followed the group into the dining room. Like Sven, he scanned the set table to see if there was anything out of place. Both were relieved to find it set perfectly and graced by a bowl of cut flowers. Further surprises awaited them in the breakfast room. The table held a finished casserole that promised to be deliciously eggy and a plate of thinly sliced ham. A tray held croissants wrapped in a white napkin, and various condiments were set out among bowls of fresh fruit cut and ready to be spooned onto the plates stacked off to one side.

"Who made brunch?" Sven asked with a forced note of brightness in his voice.

"Your father and I," Annike said gaily from the counter. "You would be proud of him, Sven. I found a recipe in *Southern Living* for the quiche casserole, and your father insisted on helping me. Doesn't it smell heavenly?"

"Dad!" Karl called across the room, "you've been holding out on us. I didn't know you were a chef."

As his father turned from the refrigerator with the pitcher of Bloody Marys, he gave Karl a grin and said, "Just another talent I've discovered. I hope you can get it down."

"I'm sure it'll be terrific," Sven said as he began filling glasses with ice from a bucket on the counter. "You and Mom have it looking really nice in here."

Frank shot Sven a wary look but then ascertained that he was sincere and gave him a smile. "It's important to your mom that everything be just so."

"You did a great job, Dad. I mean it," Sven said softly but just loud enough for Karl to hear above the chatter generated by Annike, Caroline, and Melanie.

"You've got dinner covered, right?" Frank asked.

"Yes," Sven told him. "But I'd better get the meat out of the freezer."

"I took care of that," Frank said proudly. "It's thawing in the sink."

"Excellent," Sven said as his father began to pour the drinks. "Dad, I'm going to get dinner started and then take off. Rob and I are going out to this Italian place we like. I thought you and Mom might enjoy having Karl's family all to yourself for a while. They'll clean up for you. Is that okay?"

Frank stopped pouring the drinks for a moment and glanced at Sven with a disapproving eye. "Well, I guess it'll have to be, since you've made plans," he said resentfully.

"Dad, it was my suggestion," Karl chimed in easily. "I thought Sven might enjoy a night off with Rob, and we'd get to enjoy you and Mom ourselves."

Frank nodded as he finished pouring the last drink. "So you and Rob are back to being all lovey-dovey, then?"

"Dad, I never said we stopped," Sven answered quietly.

"You're a fool, is what I'm saying," Frank told him angrily. "You make me sick, the way you run after him like a teenaged girl."

The conversation on the other side of the room stopped abruptly, and the silence stung everyone in the room but Frank. He picked up a glass of the cocktail and drank half of it before setting it down on the counter and filling it up once more. "What's everybody waiting for?" he asked irritably. "Come and have a drink. Let's get this party started."

Caroline shot Karl an alarmed, questioning look, which he answered with a grim smile. Melanie looked from her grandfather to her uncle and seemed to comprehend in a flash the nature of the discord. Annike just stood and glared at her husband angrily.

Gracefully, Melanie strode to the counter and waited for her grandfather to hand her a drink, which he did with a set smile. "I can't believe you're old enough to be having a Bloody Mary with us old folks," he told her.

Melanie's laugh seemed a brittle tinkle in the charged room. "You're not old, you're timeless, Grumpy . . . I mean Gramps."

Frank laughed and gave her a genuine smile. "How can I be grumpy when you're so pretty? I'm in a good mood just having you around. Caroline, Annike, come get your drinks. I want to make a toast."

As Karl and Sven took up their glasses, Caroline and Annike each accepted one from Frank. Once everyone held a glass, Frank raised his and said, "To family. To being together, and to the future!"

They each echoed his sentiments and the glasses met in small clinking tones. Then the group broke into various subgroups as everyone chatted amiably and enjoyed their drinks. The ugly cloud of Frank's little outburst dissipated and dispelled as the liquor lulled everyone into a feeling of ease and heightened hunger. Before long, Annike invited each of them to make a plate, and appetite overcame conversation. Frank's cooking was genuinely appreciated and complimented. In the dining room where they had spent festive times together, the little family did come to feel like it was a holiday. As they treated themselves to seconds of food and drinks, the mood grew mellow.

13

AT LAST FRANK, seated at the head of the table, tinkled his fork against his empty water glass and called for everyone's attention. "You all know by now that Annike and I will soon be moving into a small apartment. Besides having a chance to all get together here in this house once more, part of our plan for today is to have you all choose the furniture you want, and divide up the keepsakes. You're welcome to have anything we won't be taking with us, and if you chose something that we are . . . well . . . you'll just have to wait a little longer for it, right, Annike?"

"That's right," Annike said brightly. "But we are sincere in saying we want you to be able to keep something from our many years of homemaking, to remind you of home and of us. I have divided the family pictures into albums, with a set for Sven and a set for Karl. Other than that, please take whatever you want. Whatever is left, we are going to give to charity."

"Oh, yes," Frank added, "I will pay to ship whatever you want. I've already talked to the moving company about it. Now, here's what we're going to do, I have a legal pad to make a list and a roll of masking tape and a Sharpie to label the furniture. So why don't you all sit for a minute and think about it, while I go get my supplies."

"Dad, Mom," Karl said, "on behalf of Caro and Mel and myself, I want to thank you for your generosity. I'm sure there are things that each of us want, and I want you to know we'll cherish whatever we get."

When he'd finished his little speech, Sven, Caroline, and

Melanie applauded. Then they began to murmur amongst themselves excitedly.

"Karl," Frank said as he stood. "Would you come with me for a moment?"

"Sure, Dad," Karl said and stood. He waited until his father made his way to his end of the table, and then followed him as he walked not into the main house but into the foyer. By the front door, his father stopped and took down the crucifix that had hung there for as long as Karl could remember. In fact, Karl remembered the same crucifix hanging by the front door in their house in New Jersey. He remembered that when he was a little boy, his mother would pick him up on her hip to wave good-bye to his father each morning as he left for work, and part of that memory was his mother teaching him to say a Hail Mary for his father's day and his safe return. It had been a regular part of his childhood. And the crucifix was as much a part of the front door as the jamb itself.

Frank looked at the cross in his hand and slowly extended it to Karl. "Son, you don't know this, but I wasn't raised Catholic. I wasn't raised as anything. The most you know about my side of the family is that we didn't get along." The old man stopped and looked again at the crucifix he held out to his son. "I became a Catholic so I could marry your mother. And I was happy to do it. The priest that gave me my instruction, Father Frost . . . I'll never forget him . . . anyway, he gave me this on our wedding day and told me to keep it hung by my front door, so that every time I came in or went out, I would remember what I believed in. It's hung by my front door ever since."

Karl took the cross from his father and was amazed at its heft. It was not a cheap piece of sentimental bric-a-brac, but was freighted with something more substantive, than superstition. The corpus did not possess a contemporary, bland-faced Christ, but the face of agony and redemption in the old style, before the faith had become obtuse and accommodating.

"Karl," his father said softly. "I know you don't believe anymore, and I respect your feelings on the subject. But I ask you, please, take this and hang it by your front door. Make sure Melanie gets it when the time is right. There's an awful lot of answered prayers associated with that piece of wood and metal in your hand. You can say you're doing it just because you're humoring your old man. But hang it up by your front door and let all those prayers I've said for you over the years go home and stay with you, will you?"

"What about Sven?" Karl asked his father. "Sven is still a believer. You should give it to him."

Sadly, his father shook his head. "Karl, no grandchildren are ever going to be passing through his front door. Whatever Sven believes is going to die with him. You're the one that has some effect on the faith of the children that will come."

Karl looked at the crucifix and saw it for what it meant to his father. He remembered what it meant to him once. He realized how churlish it would be to tell his father he didn't want it or what it meant. He nodded at last and said, "Thanks, Dad. I'll hang it up by the front door, I promise."

Frank patted his son on the shoulder. "Don't worry about Sven. I gave him his own crucifix when I helped him buy that little old house on Singer Island. I've never been there, but he told me he'd put it up by his front door."

Karl searched his memory of Sven's house for the image of a crucifix, and did recall seeing one in the living room. It had struck him as incongruous in that stylishly minimalist space. Over the bank of light switches by the front door, the red wood of the cross and ivory-colored corpus looked startlingly out of place. "It's there," he assured his father, "right by the front door."

"Well, this one's yours," his father said. "Keep the family tradition alive, will you?"

Karl looked at the crucifix and saw what it meant to his father.

He remembered what it had meant to him once. He realized how churlish it would be to tell his father he didn't want it. He nodded at last and said, "Thanks, Dad. I'll hang it up by the front door." He turned away before he had to face his father again. He wasn't sure he would keep his promise, but it was a harmless one to make when it seemed to mean so much to the old man.

"I'm going to get my pad and tape," Frank said. "Be thinking of what you want—I'll be right back."

Karl didn't answer, but he nodded his head. Suddenly, he didn't want anything else from his father's home. The weight of the crucifix and what it stood for was almost more than he could bear. He couldn't imagine wanting another thing to bind him to what he had been, and what he still was somewhere inside. He sidled up to Caroline and asked her what she'd done with her purse.

"It's on the chair in the living room," she said. "Why?"

"Dad gave me his crucifix and I don't want to forget it," he said.

"Let me see," she said.

He handed it to her and she looked at it admiringly. "It's very old," she said.

"It was a wedding gift from Frank's priest," Annike said clearly. "It's hung in every place we've ever lived."

"Then we will cherish it," Caroline told her and stood. "I'm going to put it in my purse."

"It has been blessed," Annike said. "It will bless your home."

"Thank you, Mom," Karl said as he resumed his seat and Caroline strode away.

"It's a big deal, Karl," Sven said seriously. "I don't think he could have given you anything that meant more to him."

"I think it was sweet of him," Melanie said. "I'll have to get one for my place with Drew."

"No," Karl said suddenly. "Your mother and I will get one for you and have it blessed. It's a family tradition."

"Okay," Melanie said in surprise. She knew her father was not an overtly religious man. "I didn't know it meant so much to you."

Karl looked at his daughter and told her—as he was telling himself at that moment—"Some traditions are worth keeping."

"I have a request," Annike announced quietly. As everyone turned to her, she placed her hands on the table and folded them together in a gesture that could have meant either pleading or prayer. After a moment, she said, "It would make me very happy if we could all go to mass together tomorrow morning. I know it's very early, but I promise you won't have to dress up. I wear pants myself," she admitted with a nervous chuckle. "But since it's the last time we will all be together, I'd like to have you all in church with me," she concluded humbly.

"Mom, it's not going to be the last time we all get together," Sven said gently.

"It will be the last time I will be aware that we are," Annike said baldly. "It's no good pretending we don't all know that. In a way, I am leaving you all. At least when I lose my mind I get to watch moments of my life again, like reruns on TV. One of the memories I'd like to have is all of us together in church, as a family."

Karl felt blackmailed. His mother's request was certainly not out of character. She had always been the one to get them to church each and every Sunday morning when Karl was a boy. She was the one responsible for the inculcation of the faith in her two sons. It was out of fear of offending her that Karl had insisted that he and Caroline be married in the Catholic Church, despite the fact that Caroline's religious life was spotty at best and she had announced her intention to remain a Protestant. However, at Annike's insistence, she and Karl had raised Melanie as Catholic. Karl felt the maternal steeliness in Annike's attitude toward Catholicism that he had been subjected to all his life. Presented with her request at that moment, part of him wanted to rebel and refuse outright. He had long marginalized religion in his life, and with this request his mother was making a last-ditch effort to bring him back into the fold.

In the silence that followed Annike's request, Karl felt Caroline's knee press his thigh under the table. He knew what she was communicating, but he remained silent despite her insistent urging with her knee.

"I'd love to go with you, Grandmere," Melanie finally said. "The last time I went to church was Ash Wednesday. It'll be nice to go as a family. I remember going to Christmas Eve masses at your church since I was a little girl."

"I didn't know you went to mass on Ash Wednesday," Karl said to his daughter. "You didn't mention it."

"It's no big deal, Dad," Melanie said defensively. "I go on all the holy days. I always have, even in college."

"I had no idea," Karl said honestly. In that moment, he wavered. As he was about to speak, Caroline reached across the table and folded her hand around Annike's clasped ones. "We'll all come," she said, without even glancing at Karl. "We'll pile into Sven's big Excursion and meet you and Dad there."

"It's no big deal to me," Sven said. "I usually meet Mom and Dad there on Sunday mornings anyway. I like going to the 8:00 A.M. mass. That way I have it over and done with."

Karl looked at his brother and nodded. Finally, he turned to his mother and said, "I'll go. But I want you to know I'm doing it for you and nobody else."

Annike looked at him and smiled. "Thank you, Son."

She won, Karl thought bitterly, *but she always does.* Resentfully, he shifted in his seat to move away from the touch of Caroline's knee under the table. For a moment, his resentment rested on an adolescent feeling that his opinions and ideas weren't being considered or respected. That his mother had so shamelessly played her health card on something he considered trivial annoyed him. And the fact that he was so easily and deftly manipulated by her stung.

"You guys ready to divvy up the loot?" Frank asked cheerfully as he laid his legal pad, masking tape, and pens on the table and sat down.

Caroline laughed nervously and looked around the table. "Well, I'm not shy," she said. "Annike, could I please have your desk? I've admired it for so long, and I'm trying to put my office together in the town house. I promise you I'll take good care of it."

"You certainly may have my desk," Annike responded happily. "But I will tell you to get another chair for it. The one I have is not comfortable. Better to let it go to Saint Vincent de Paul."

"Thank you so much," Caroline said and stood. She walked to her mother-in-law's side and hugged her.

"It has so many happy memories for me. Frank and I bought it in a very nice shop in Stockholm, when I went home after my mother died," Annike told her as Caroline patted her shoulder and looked up at her with her still-clear blue eyes. "I am so pleased it will have a new home with you."

"Mom, I want your grandmother's blue-and-white china," Sven said eagerly.

"There's not a great deal of it," Annike told him. "I think there are only five full place settings. It was old when my grandmother was a girl."

"It's genuine Chinese export," Sven told her. "If you let me have it, I won't just put it away. I'll use it every day."

"Oh, I know you will," Annike said with a smile, then she turned to Melanie and said, "Sven used to beg me to use those dishes when he was a little boy. Sometimes he would surprise me by taking them out and setting the table here in the dining room."

"I did," Sven said and grinned. "I used to pretend we were having a big dinner party with all kinds of interesting people. When Dad got home, I'd take him by the hand and drag him in to look at the table, and he'd always ask me if I was having another party—didn't you?" he asked his father.

"Yeah, I played along," Frank admitted grudgingly, "but I always used to wonder why you spent your afternoon planning a dinner party instead of playing outside."

"Old things have always interested Sven," Annike said proudly. "Even when he was little, he used to ask me about the stories behind those dishes and the clocks. Those were really the only old things we had. When I met Frank, he was stationed in Germany and I was still living in Paris, working as a secretary at an engineering firm that had contracts with the army. I had nothing and your grandfather had less. When we married just before he was discharged, I came here with only my two suitcases."

"How did you get the china and clocks here, Grandmere?" Melanie asked. She was genuinely interested. She'd never heard this part of the story before.

"My grandmere shipped them to me," Annike said as her eyes grew misty. "She said I must have something of my homeland, of my past, to make my home in America more familiar."

"I think Melanie or Caroline should have first dibs on the china, Sven," his father said abruptly.

"Uncle Sven is welcome to it, as far as I'm concerned," Melanie told her grandfather. "I already have my wedding china picked out, and I've been buying my everyday dishes and storing them away for the past two years."

"How about you, Caroline?" Frank offered. "Wouldn't you like that antique china? It should stay in the family. You could keep it for Melanie's children."

Caroline shook her head. "No, thank you, Frank. I have tons of china of my own and I really don't have anywhere to store it since we've moved into the town house. I think Sven should take it."

"Dad, I promise you that I'll pass it along to Melanie's kids someday. I think it should stay in the family as well," Sven said earnestly.

Frank gave him a sour look. "Are you sure you won't get sick of it and sell it in that store of yours? You know how much something that old is worth. Who's to say you won't mark it up and move it along?"

Everyone looked away from Frank nervously. Karl finally spoke up and said, "Dad, Sven really appreciates it, and I don't think he'd ever sell it. I think Sven should have it."

Sven looked at his father anxiously but didn't say anything more.

"Take it, then," Frank told him dismissively. "I suppose you have other stuff picked out as well, though I don't know why. It's not like you haven't already gotten your share."

Karl watched Sven's expression drop in defeat, and it seemed as if his shoulders sagged as well. Karl sensed his father's comment was aimed deliberately below the belt, and he wondered why. "Wait a minute, Dad. Why are you being so difficult to Sven? What are you talking about?" Karl said with some annoyance. It seemed to him that his father was just being obnoxious.

"Dad loaned me thirty-five thousand dollars for the down payment on my house," Sven said evenly. "To date, I've only been able to pay him back about seven thousand."

"Six thousand, six hundred and fifty dollars, to be exact," Frank announced.

"That's none of our business," Karl said abruptly. "That's just between you and Dad."

"No," Frank insisted. "It came out of the pot, and turnabout is fair play. You didn't come whining to me for a down payment on your first house. I've never favored one of you over the other, and I think that the way things are going, Sven won't ever pay me back."

"Dad, really . . ." Karl began.

"So what else do you want, Sven?" their father demanded.

"Actually, that was it, Dad," Sven said and stood. "I just wanted the blue-and-white china. That's all. If you guys will excuse me, I'm going to start washing up."

"Sven, wait," Annike said as he began to make his way to the kitchen.

"Let him go," Frank said disgustedly. "You have always been so eager to give him anything he wants. It's always been you two in your own little world. It's always made me wonder."

"Wonder what, dear?" Annike asked placatingly.

"You know what I'm talking about," Frank insisted.

"No, Frank. I have no idea why you're always so hard on Sven," Annike said defensively.

"Well, since you brought it up," Frank said angrily, "I've always had my doubts that he was my son to begin with."

Sven stopped and turned around to glare at his father.

"Frank, no one wants to hear your wild imaginings right now. This is family time. Besides, I have no idea what you're talking about," Annike said confusedly.

"You know damn well what I'm talking about," Frank said dismissively. "Look at him! He's Fredrik Von Schewen's kid, not mine. I've always thought you had an affair with Fredrik. That's why you've been so partial to Sven all these years. He's your lover's son. And I may have forgiven *you*, but I can't ever seem to accept *him*," Frank said, punctuating his remarks by jabbing a finger at Annike and at Sven.

Everyone was dumbfounded by Frank's venomous accusation and outburst. Sven stood frozen in place. Caroline and Melanie looked at each other and then at the tabletop before them. Only Karl looked at his father with openmouthed amazement.

Karl remembered Fredrik Von Schewen. For a period of about eight months when he was eleven years old, the young Swede had been a frequent visitor to their home in New Jersey. Single and alone in the United States after college, he had worked with Frank as a

developmental engineer for the company Frank had been employed by
before IBM. Sensing the young man's loneliness and remembering his
own when he'd been stationed in Germany as an army engineer after
World War II, Frank had taken the young man under his wing and
brought him home to visit with his Swedish wife. Karl had taught
the man how to play softball. They had often played catch in the
backyard before his mother called them in for dinner.

Karl remembered him fondly. To be honest, Karl thought, Sven
did have the look of the man. Compared with Karl's dark hair and
height, which were obviously a result of his father's genes, Sven
looked as if he could be the offspring of the young, blond, compact
Swede Fredrik. Karl searched his mind, trying to remember why
the young man had stopped coming by, but he'd been only a kid, and
the comings and goings of the adult friends of his parents weren't
his main concern at the time. His father's accusation had summoned
the man from nowhere, forty years later, in the dining room of his
parents' house so far from that place and time.

"You are a goddamn jealous fool," Annike said and slammed her
hand down on the table, startling everyone to attention.

Frank eyed his wife with the look of a cur that had been kicked.

"How dare you accuse me of being unfaithful!" Annike said, and
leaned forward across the table as if to slap her husband.

"Convince me I'm wrong," Frank demanded.

"No! You have wasted forty years of our lives with this insane
stupidity," Annike shouted. "This is not the first time you've brought
it up, and I have had enough."

Everyone else in the room did their best to keep their mouths
closed. Annike's forcefulness and anger stunned them like a blow.
She had never been prone to arguments and shouting. Her outburst
was so out of character for her normally placid personality that Karl
and Sven had never witnessed anything remotely like it, even when
they had angered her as children.

"Frank Preston," she spat as she stood to confront him, "I am disgusted with you. I have always wondered why you were so resentful of your own child. I have listened to you as you have belittled him and mocked him his entire life. You! The man I have slept next to nearly all my life, the man I have loved for so long, have been tormenting yourself and Sven over Fredrik, a mere boy, who you *yourself* brought into our home. If you weren't so blindly jealous, you would have seen it was you Fredrik Von Schewen fancied, not me. He was a poor, lonely, confused youth who needed your approval far more than mine." And then Annike began to laugh.

"You're crazy," Frank said, stunned by her counterattack.

"So I've been told," Annike managed to get out as she laughed even harder. Finally, she contained herself enough to say, "I may be crazy, but I am not lying. I confronted Fredrik with what I saw and he admitted he was in love with you. Oh, how he cried. He begged me not to tell you. He was so frightened for his job, his citizenship application. He thought if anyone knew he was a homosexual he would never work in this country again, maybe even be deported. Why do you think he stopped coming to our house? Did you think it was because of me?"

Frank looked as if Annike had hit him. Guiltily, he glanced around the table with obvious embarrassment. "You never told me any of this," he said accusingly. "When you got pregnant after so long, I didn't think I had anything to do with it. I mean, it had been twelve years, for God's sake. I thought something was wrong with me."

"Let me tell you something, husband," Annike said bitterly, "there was nothing wrong with you. You always told me birth control was a woman's business. So I made it my business not to get pregnant again, until the emptiness in my life was unbearable."

"I had no idea you thought your life was empty," Frank managed to utter, raising his hands as if to ward off her words. "You never discussed it with me."

"You were never interested," Annike said and folded her arms across her chest. "I had Sven for me. You had abandoned me emotionally and kept me locked up in this birdcage, refusing to let me work or have any sort of life of my own. It was you that cheated by letting your own jealousy and wild imagination come between us. But Sven is your son just as much as your beloved Karl is. I couldn't be unfaithful to you—I could never let myself do that. But I *could* have another child to fill my life, and I did, and I will not apologize."

"Annike, when did I ever abandon you?" Frank pleaded.

"You must excuse me," Annike said to the room, ignoring her husband. "I am afraid I have wet myself. It is because of all the laughter." With that, she backed out of the room and left them.

Frank dropped his hands and looked up at his youngest son, "Sven . . ."

Sven just looked at him and shook his head before leaving the room and going into the kitchen.

"Karl, Caroline . . . I'm so sorry," Frank said earnestly. "I hate that you had to hear that. But it's been eating away at me for years. I admit I'm a jealous man. And Sven is just so goddamn *not* what I wanted or expected out of a son. Karl, you know I'm not a bad father. But you know you've always been my favorite. Please tell me you understand."

Karl looked at his father for a moment, trying to think of how to respond. Suddenly so much became clear to him. He had always basked in his father's approval, and all his life he'd geared circumstances and made decisions consciously and subconsciously to make his father proud, to keep his father's approval. Then there was the realization of why his father was so vocal in his disapproval of Sven and his homosexuality: not only did this revelation make sense of his father's emotional battering of Sven, it also made Karl realize that his father's long-harbored jealousy was, at least in part, behind Karl's own status as the favored son. It had never occurred to Karl that his father might have been desired by another man. But in the case of Fredrik Von Schewen, Frank had to have been aware of something. And the way he must have dealt with it was by projecting it all onto his wife. The resulting treatment of his son was such a complex puzzle of jealousy and self-doubt that it beggared Karl's reckoning. He didn't know what to say to his father. Forty years of abusive behavior couldn't be excused or pardoned by a simple sentence.

A bitter silence spoiled the air. Finally, Melanie pushed her chair back and stood. As she walked to her grandfather's side, she said, "C'mon, Gramps. Get your tape and Sharpie. Let's me and you go through the house and mark my stuff. That way I can get first dibs on everything."

Gratefully, Frank stood and nodded at his granddaughter. "C'mon," Melanie urged him as she took his hand. Obediently, he allowed himself to be led into the main part of the house. Karl watched them leave the room and then dropped his head and massaged his brows with his hand.

"Wow!" Caroline said finally. "How 'bout them Steelers?"

14

KARL CHUCKLED and looked at his wife. "Who knew?" he asked rhetorically.

Caroline lifted her hand and placed it on the back of his neck and massaged it firmly for a moment. "Why don't you take Sven and I'll take your mother?" she suggested.

Karl nodded and gave her a smile as she dropped her hand from his neck. "That's probably the best way to get past this," he said.

"Poor Sven," she said. "To have all that dumped on his head without warning."

Karl stood and said, "Poor Dad, to have carried all that crap around for so long."

"Promise me that you won't keep something like that bottled up inside you for years," Caroline said anxiously. "I hate to say it, but you're a lot like your father."

"Not like that, I'm not," Karl told her vehemently. "Besides, you and I don't have the kind of relationship Mom and Dad do. When have I ever kept you locked away, or ever not encouraged you to be everything you can be?"

"Never," Caroline told him and smiled. "You're right. Our marriage is nothing like theirs."

"Thank God," Karl said with a sigh.

Caroline stood up. "Why don't you go talk to Sven, and I'll make sure your mother's alright," she suggested.

Karl nodded and gave her a smile as she dropped her hand from his neck. "That's probably the best way to get past this," he said.

Caroline gave him a gentle nudge toward the kitchen and turned toward the foyer to make her way to the master bedroom. Karl watched her leave the room and reluctantly turned toward the kitchen. Just as he'd had no words for his father, he had nothing to give his brother. What could he say?

Karl found Sven in the kitchen loading the last of the breakfast dishes into the dishwasher. Sven looked up at him with a bitter little smile and said, "Welcome to my world." He sighed and closed the dishwasher door with a sudden whump. "Dad has been throwing these little tantrums on a fairly frequent basis for a year or more. Don't let it rankle you. It'll all blow over soon. Mom will pout for a little while, and finally Dad will apologize and things will just go on . . . and on and on," he ended tiredly.

"Can I give you a hand with anything?" Karl asked Sven gently.

Sven clicked the dishwasher on. As it began its high-pitched mechanical whine, he turned to Karl, smiled, and asked, "Can you peel potatoes?"

"Sure," Karl said eagerly. "That's one kitchen chore I'm proficient at."

"Excellent," Sven said as he took two steps and opened the cabinet door under the counter by the sink. He pulled a five-pound bag of potatoes from the bin and swung it onto the counter. "Because I hate peeling potatoes. I got a bag of those little baby carrots, so all we have to do is throw them in. If you'll peel the potatoes, I'll brown the roast."

Karl moved to the counter and opened the bag of potatoes, then began to look for a peeler. Before he could locate one, Sven opened another drawer and handed it to him. "What do you want me to do with them once they're peeled?" Karl asked.

Sven gestured toward the double sink and said, "Just put the peelings in one sink and the potatoes in the other. Then rinse them off before you cut them up to add to the pot."

Karl nodded and began the process. He was glad to have something to do with his hands. He heard Sven behind him rummaging in the refrigerator and placing a pot on the stove. Within a few minutes, he'd peeled half the bag and could hear the hot sizzle of beef hitting the bottom of the pot, followed by the appetizing scent of meat seared in butter. Glancing over his shoulder, he caught sight of Sven as he stood before the stove with a carving fork in his hand. Sven glanced over at him and smiled.

"I think you should take the clocks," he told Karl. "You don't see many short-case Swedish clocks. Mom's are treasures. They're from the early nineteenth century, and they both still work. I had them cleaned and oiled a couple of years ago," he added.

Karl could picture the clocks in his mind. As a child, they had first frightened, then bored him. When he thought of their loud, deliberate ticks and tocks, he thought of time dragging on and on. He thought of having to wind them. To him, they were as demanding as a pet. He couldn't imagine himself taking the time to make them run properly. "Unless Caroline or Melanie wants them, I'll pass," he told Sven. "They used to give me the creeps when I was little."

Sven laughed and turned the meat. As it browned, he opened a bottle of red wine and stood holding it, waiting for the right moment to add it to the pot. "I'll take them, then," he said. "I used to lay awake at night and try to time my breathing to the ticking. I can't tell you how many nights I fell asleep doing that."

Karl turned his attention back to the dwindling bag of potatoes. "You know, Sven . . . it's hard for me to imagine what your life was like after I went to college. You were only six years old. It's like we hardly ever lived in the same house."

"True," Sven said and poured the red wine into the pot. Karl was immediately aware of its scent marrying with the beef. Sven turned the heat down under the pot and walked to the refrigerator and pulled out a container of whole baby mushrooms. After closing the refrigerator door, he made his way to stand next to his brother at the sink. "I remember waiting for you to come home from college. It was a big deal to me. Every time you came home, you made it a point to take me somewhere, to the movies, to the beach mostly. I thought it was so cool having a brother who could drive. All my friends' brothers were just kids. My brother was like a big *cool* kid." Sven removed the plastic wrap from the package of mushrooms and rinsed them in their container, draining the box through his fingers.

"You were a cool little kid yourself," Karl told him. "You didn't act spoiled or bratty. I enjoyed taking you places. But you were so pretty. Everyone used to ask me if you were a boy or a girl."

Sven shook the remaining water from the package into the sink and strode back to the pot to add the mushrooms. "I heard that for years," he admitted. "I caught all kinds of hell because of it." He chuckled and said in an affected black accent, "Is you a boy or a girl, or is you a faggy?"

"Was it rough?" Karl asked as he finished with his task and gathered the peelings in his hands to transfer them back to the bag and into the trash.

"It was interesting," Sven said wryly as he stepped away from the stove to the cabinet and took out a can of golden mushroom soup and a can of beef consommé from the cabinet. As he busied himself opening them and emptying their contents into the blender, he told Karl, "It makes you ask yourself some tough questions. I think it would be the same thing if I had been born really ugly. When you're marked by your looks, you have to figure out who you are on the inside really fast."

Karl rinsed the potatoes under cold water and transferred them by hands full onto the counter by the cutting board. "When did you know you were gay?" he asked Sven cautiously.

"Oh, I pretty much always knew," Sven said as he added the blended soups to the pot of roast and red wine. "At least I had a sense of being inappropriate when I was being myself. I remember

Dad giving me these looks, like I had just stepped off the spaceship, whenever I would say or do things. I learned fast to sort of keep what I thought was perfectly natural about things like china and antiques to myself." He stirred the pot with a wooden spoon and came to stand beside his brother at the cutting board. Taking up a potato and a knife from the block, he expertly halved, then quartered it before cutting it into fork-sized pieces. "Cut them like that, okay?"

Karl nodded at his instruction, then proceeded with the task of reducing the potatoes to bite-sized chunks. "Did all that change when Rob came along?" he asked Sven with unfeigned interest.

Sven turned his back to the counter and leaned against it while Karl cut potatoes and said, "When Rob came along, it was like finding your twin when you didn't know you had one," he explained thoughtfully. Then, with a salacious grin, he added, "Of course, Rob wasn't anything like a brother. He was pretty aggressive."

"Rob told me he promised God that if he could have you, he'd never ask for anything else," Karl said with a smile. "I think it must be pretty special to meet someone that young and never grow apart."

Sven pushed himself away from the counter and returned to the refrigerator for the carrots. "I think it's karma," he said with a laugh. "You know, I can't really explain it. I don't know where he stops and I begin anymore. But I think that's a good thing. Then, when he decided to move to the condo in Palm Beach, I wondered if it wasn't time to look for someone else. You know, I've only ever slept with four guys in my life. But those three others made me realize I'd rather be with Rob."

Sven laid the bag of carrots on the counter and reached for a colander from yet another door under the cabinet. As he rinsed the carrots, he told Karl, "I've had some months living alone, and I've enjoyed them. But it seemed temporary the whole time. Like I knew Rob would be back." Sven tore open the bag and dumped the carrots into the colander. As he rinsed them under the tap, he added, "When he asked if he could stay over the other night, it was the first time in eight months we'd slept together. Other than his snoring, it was like he'd never been away."

"I guess if you guys could survive Dad, you can survive anything," Karl said as he grabbed handfuls of potato pieces and walked them to the pot. "I just dump these in, right?"

"Right," Sven said as he passed him with the dripping colander of baby carrots. As he added the carrots to the pot, he said, "You have no idea what Dad has put me through over Rob all these years. Did you know he threatened to send me to live with you in Raleigh when I was sixteen?"

"I know he went so far as to bring up the idea with me," Karl confided carefully. "He told me it would be for your own good, but Caroline and I weren't convinced. We could have taken you in, but I told Dad to just leave you alone. It was his problem, not yours."

"And what did he say to that?" Sven asked him as he stirred the potatoes and carrots in the thin gravy. "I bet he wasn't happy."

Karl took the knife to the sink and rinsed it before carefully drying it with a dish towel and placing it back into its slot in the block. "I'm guessing from his little outburst today that Dad has never been happy with you," Karl said gently. "I'm so sorry. If he'd been a different man, your life would have been a lot easier."

Sven turned the oven on and continuously pressed its digital pad until it read 375 degrees. Once he'd pressed start, he put the lid on the pot holding the roast and vegetables before he opened the oven door to sit the pot on the lower rack. "There's nothing to be sorry about, Karl. If he'd been a different man, so would I. And I'm pretty happy with myself." Sven closed the oven door and looked at his brother with a smile.

"I'm glad that's the case, Sven," Karl told him affectionately. "You deserve to be happy." He watched as Sven moved across the kitchen and began to wash out the blender. "What do you think of his little outburst just now? I have to tell you, I thought it was pretty fucked up."

Sven looked out the window over the sink thoughtfully as he rinsed the blender. As he began to wipe it dry, he said, "Oh, it's not the first time I've heard it. Dad's told me he didn't believe I was his son lots of times. He's never done it in front of Mom, though, at least not until today. It's just one of the many ways he's tried to fuck with me over the years."

Once again, Karl was surprised by how much his age difference and distance from his brother had isolated him from the emotional wear and tear his family's interaction had placed on Sven. He was smotheringly worshipped and adored by their mother and emotionally abused by their father. Karl wondered how far it had gone. "Did Dad ever whip you?" he asked quietly. "I just ask because I can count on one hand how many times he whipped me with a belt."

Sven turned and leaned against the counter once more. "He never spanked me that much. I caught the odd slap or two, but he never beat me physically. He just made the climate I had to live in torturous. My days were like the seasons; I went from summer in the daytime with Mom to hard winter at night when Dad got home. I got used to it when I was small. By the time I was ten, I figured out how to stay under his radar as best I could."

"That's no way to live," Karl said sadly. "I didn't grow up in such an atmosphere."

"Well, it is what it is, Karl. No way to change all that old history now," Sven commented, and looked toward the breakfast room across the counter. From the hall emerged Caroline and Annike, dressed in a different pair of slacks and sweater.

"Smells good in here, guys!" Caroline announced approvingly as she and Annike sat at the table.

"Is that pot roast I smell?" Annike asked.

"Yes, Mom. And I didn't forget to put in the bay leaves this time," Sven told her with a smile. "Karl helped, too, so it's a joint achievement."

"I peeled potatoes," Karl commented dryly. "Sven did the most work."

"I shall enjoy it more knowing you worked together," Annike said happily.

Without moving from the cabinet where he leaned, Sven said, "Mom, now that I've got dinner started, I'm going to take off. I'll see you at mass tomorrow morning."

"Oh, why leave now?" Annike asked with obvious disappointment. "I am enjoying having us all together."

Karl walked into the breakfast room and sat down across from his mother, saying, "I gave Sven the night off to go out to dinner with Rob. That way, I and my family can enjoy you and Dad all to ourselves."

"But Sven can go out to dinner with Rob anytime," Annike fretted. "You are so seldom home."

"True," Karl said, "but we'll all be together over here tomorrow afternoon to say good-bye before we leave. We'll have to drop off your car before Sven takes us to the airport."

Annike nodded at Karl but turned to Sven and said, "*Är den här på grund av din fader? JAG veta du måste bli vred med honom, utom du måste lov på grund av hans dålig beteende.*" *Is this because of your father? I know you must be angry with him, but you mustn't leave because of his bad behavior.*

"*Nej Pappa har ingenting till gör med den,*" Sven replied calmly. "*Vi bestämd den här i min ålder hus framför vi kom. I'm inte vred på Pappa,*" he said, and he gave his mother a reassuring smile. *No. Dad has nothing to do with it. We decided this at my house before we came. I'm not angry at Dad.*

"*Han vilja tänka du er vred med honom,*" Annike pled as Caro watched Karl try to follow along. *He will think you are angry with him.*

"*Han veta JAG reser vek,*" Sven said evenly. *He knows I am leaving.* "*JAG talat honom när vi fik här. JAG rättvis vilja till glida ute utan talande till honom ackurat nå. JAG er rättvis trött om honom for tiden,"* he added, more insistently this time. *I told him when we got here. I just want to slip out without speaking to him just now. I am just tired of him at the moment.*

Annike nodded sadly and told Caroline, "Please excuse us. I don't mean to exclude you."

"It's no problem," Caroline said consolingly. "I wish I had another language sometimes so I could deal with moments like this in private."

Annike patted her hand, turned to Sven, and said, "Go. Give Rob my love."

Sven made his way across the kitchen and around the counter to his mother's side. He bent and gave her a hug. "Thanks, Mom. There are salad makings in the refrigerator. Caro and Karl will give you a hand getting dinner finished."

Annike patted his back and smiled as he stepped away and looked down at her.

"Caro, Karl, I'll see you back at my house. Thanks for giving me the night off," he said.

"Go have fun," Caroline told him with a small wave.

On a sudden impulse, Karl got to his feet and hugged his brother. "We'll take care of everything here. Don't worry," he said.

Sven gave him a grateful smile and waved before slipping out the kitchen door.

Once the door closed behind him, Annike looked at Karl and said, "He has every reason to be angry with his father. Frank's behavior towards him is abominable. But Sven just lets it roll off his back. I have tried to talk to Frank, but he is so stubborn. I want to spank *him* sometimes."

"Dad is just acting out," Karl told her gently. "He has a lot of misplaced anger about how things are right now, and he takes it out on Sven. I just didn't know he was so cruel," he concluded sadly.

Caroline reached across the table and touched Annike's shoulder.

"I think Sven understands. He's in a tough place. He loves you both very much and he knows his father loves him, no matter how he takes his frustrations out on him."

Annike sighed defeatedly and looked at Caroline. "I wish I believed that. But I don't think Frank has ever loved Sven, for whatever reason. What makes me sad is that he is pushing Sven away, and once I am gone he will be very lonely. Sven only puts up with Frank's meanness because of me."

Caroline and Karl exchanged significant glances over the table. They knew of Sven's plans to move to New York, but apparently Annike didn't. Yet she seemed already to be aware that Sven wouldn't maintain a close relationship with the man who had resented him his entire life.

"I'm sure it will all work out, Mom," Karl said evenly.

"I wonder where your father has taken my granddaughter?" Annike said as she looked around. "Surely they must have had time to go through the entire house by now. Even if Melanie wanted everything, there's not that much."

Caroline stood and looked out the breakfast room door onto the lanai. Something caught her eye, and she opened the door and stepped outside. Annike and Karl heard her call out, "Hey, you two! Melanie can't take the fruit trees!"

Frank called something back that Karl and Annike couldn't make out, and Caroline laughed and returned to the breakfast room. "They'll be back in a minute. Frank is giving her a tour of his garden."

Annike smiled and looked at Karl with mischief in her eyes. "Will you sneak me a cigarette from Frank's hiding place?"

Karl smiled and stood up. Without a word, he went into the kitchen and reached high into the cabinet that held her official pack of cigarettes and lighter. Grabbing the ashtray from the counter, he returned to the table and set the items in front of her. "*Njuta av din cigarette, Mama,*" he said with a smile. *Enjoy your cigarette, Mama.*

Annike lit her cigarette and inhaled with obvious enjoyment. Exhaling, she looked at Caroline and said, "Your husband is sly. He pretends he can't remember his Swedish, but he always knows exactly what to say. Does he ever speak it at home?"

Caroline looked at Karl and smiled. "Sometimes he mutters something when he is frustrated, and very rarely he says some things in his sleep, but he never really speaks Swedish, no."

Annike shook her head and said, "I am sorry that Melanie grew up so far away. I wanted to teach her some of the language. It is part of her heritage. I am lucky Sven has kept it up. It makes me happy to know my children have something of me that is only mine, you know?"

"Melanie's French is very good," Caroline said consolingly. "She calls you Grandmere to this day. You taught her to say that because she could never get the Swedish right when she was small."

"I am losing my French," Annike said sadly. "Though there are times when I am aware I am thinking in it. It happens most often when I am back in the days when I met Frank, or remembering my school years."

"I guess it's like you told me," Karl said gently. "If you don't have a chance to use it, you lose it."

"It's true," Annike said. "You know, when we were in New Jersey, I had many opportunities to use my French. The Girards and Benoits both were from Lyons. They lived down our street, and Jeannette and Alise and I were good friends. They helped me find French shops with the most marvelous things—food especially—and I would shop there just to hear French spoken. When we moved here, there was not so much opportunity. Forty years ago, Boca Raton was very southern. Now there are people from all over. There is even an Alliance Française in North Miami. I wanted to join a few years ago when I discovered it, but Frank was not happy about me driving so far south on I-95. And then there was the expense," she said and flicked her ash into the tray. "You know your father," she said as she glanced toward the door.

"Was he being stingy, or didn't he want you to get out by yourself?" Karl asked astutely.

Annike shrugged eloquently and took a drag from her cigarette.

"Has he always been so jealous?" Caroline asked with gentle interest.

"Always," Annike said immediately. "There is a saying that a man with a beautiful wife has no friends, he always said." She shook her head with annoyance. "I suppose I was attractive in my day, and there was a common stereotype that Swedes are very sexually free. That is a bunch of nonsense, but Frank is a very American man. He pisses around his territory like a dog, and I have lived my whole life with him looking over my shoulder. But I have always loved him dearly," she concluded, and shrugged as if to say that explained it all.

"But Karl has never been possessive of me," Caroline told her. "You'd think some of his father would have rubbed off on him."

"How do you know I'm not jealous?" Karl asked, amused. "I get jealous. I just don't bother you with it."

"Thank God for that," Caroline said, looking at him lovingly. "But I hope I've never given you cause to be jealous. You are a devoted husband."

"He gets that from me," Annike said decisively. "He is my son, too. All of his best traits come from me." She laughed.

As Karl and Caroline joined her laughter, Melanie opened the kitchen door and stepped inside with Frank behind her. "Well, you guys are in a better mood than when we left," she said awkwardly.

Frank looked at the little group around the table expectantly. "I smell dinner. I suppose Sven has flounced off in a huff."

"Hardly," Karl told his father with a directness that made it clear he'd had enough of his father's attitude. "It was actually just time for him to go. What surprises me is that he didn't stick around to tell you to go to hell."

Annike looked at Karl approvingly, then gazed up at her husband.

"You go too far sometimes. I'm not sure I shouldn't tell you to go to hell myself."

Frank rubbed the back of his neck and stared down at his wife for a moment. He started to say something, then hesitated. At last, he moved toward the kitchen and said, "It's three-thirty. Would anyone care for a drink?"

"Actually, I'd prefer a cup of coffee," Karl said as he stood. "Would anyone care to join me?"

"I'd like coffee," Caroline said. "I've hit my midafternoon slump."

"Coffee would be nice, thank you," Annike told him. "There are sweets, if anyone cares for some pastries."

"Gramps, I think I'll have coffee as well," Melanie said as she took her father's seat. "I'll get sleepy if I have a drink right now."

"Suit yourself," Frank said as he filled a highball glass with ice from the refrigerator.

Karl stepped around him and tried to remember where his mother kept her coffee. The maker was near the sink, so he acted on a hunch and opened the cabinet above it, where he discovered both coffee and filters. Smiling, he set to his task of making coffee.

"Grandmere, I chose quite a few things from the house for myself," Melanie told her grandmother. "I love the modern Scandinavian pieces you have in the living room. When did you get them?"

Annike waved her hand dismissively. "They are all from the seventies. That was the last time Frank let me decorate the house. It is surprising they have come back into fashion."

"I looked under the chairs," Melanie confessed. "They are all from Denmark. But the look is very in vogue right now. Uncle Rob and Uncle Sven said they'd store them for me and help me pick out the fabrics to get them recovered for my apartment in Manhattan."

"That's very thoughtful of them," Annike said and smiled. "And when are you planning to move to New York?"

"Within a few months, perhaps sooner," Melanie told her confidently. "I have a job interview next week."

"How is your Drew?" her grandmother asked.

"He's good," Melanie said. "He is doing well with his job, and he's eager for me to move up."

"When do you plan to marry?" Annike pressed.

Melanie laughed and said, "Just as soon as I get settled in my new job. I promise you we will get married, Grandmere."

"I am sorry I will not be there to see you married," Annike said and sighed. "You must promise me you will get married in the church and raise your children as Catholics. This is very important," Annike said imperiously.

"I promise," Melanie said cheerfully. "Drew is very High Church Episcopalian, so he has no real problems with the religious thing. We've discussed it already. He respects my religious upbringing. So don't worry," she said, and nudged her grandmother's foot with her own.

"I do worry," Annike said and scolded, "When you put off your wedding in favor of your job, I think you have your priorities backwards."

"Give the girl a break," Frank said as he brought his drink to the table and sat down. "She has her head screwed on straight. Times have changed, Annike."

"That sounds unusual coming from you," Annike shot back.

"Maybe. But I've talked with her, and she has me convinced she knows what she is doing," Frank said generously.

"Frank, you surprise me," Caroline said cautiously. "I happen to agree with you, but I'm surprised you share my feelings."

"I'm not a bastard all of the time," Frank said. "I read the papers and keep up to date. What worked when I was starting my family doesn't go anymore."

"What do you mean?" Caroline asked curiously.

Frank took a sip of his drink and rattled the ice in the glass contemplatively. "Caroline, when you get to be my age, you realize you can't tell young people anything. Look at Sven. I did everything but chain him in his room to keep him away from Rob and from turning out queer. As hard as I pushed in one direction, he pushed harder back. I'll admit my own mistakes. If I hadn't been so hard on him, it might just have turned out to be a phase. Now if we push Melanie to get married, she's going to push back twice as hard not to. I say give her some room to make her own mistakes and she'll come to the right thing on her own."

"Gee, thanks . . . I guess," Melanie said and rolled her eyes.

"Time will prove me right," Frank asserted.

Listening from the kitchen, Karl was struck by how pompous and arrogant his father sounded. As he stood waiting for the coffee to finish dripping, he counted out four mugs from the cabinet over the dishwasher, and as he took them down from the shelf, he decided to push his father's buttons. "It's a shame you can't feel the same way about Sven," he said shortly. "I think he has his head screwed on straight."

"Sven is different," Frank retorted. "He's my responsibility. I'm the one who had to do my best to rear him the way I thought was right. I've admitted I made some mistakes. But you can hate the sin and love the sinner."

"That is a bunch of bullshit," Karl said angrily.

"You can't stand there and tell me you think Sven's living a decent life," Frank said dismissively. "Even the Pope says he's intrinsically disordered. But that doesn't mean he can't change and put his deviance behind him."

"Could you change being right-handed or having blue eyes?" Karl demanded.

"I could learn to use my left hand if it was God's will," Frank spat back. "I don't know what having blue eyes has to do with anything."

"Dad, it's a widely accepted fact that people are born with their sexual preferences in place. You can't tell *me* that Sven would have put up with you all these years if he could change."

"You're just spouting that liberal line about people being born gay," Frank said angrily. "And Sven has just put his back up like a cat to show me he can. I have to hand it to the little fucker, he's stubborn as hell."

"Sounds like someone else I know," Caroline added sarcastically.

Frank shot her an unpleasant look and said, "If it's genetic like the homosexual agenda says, then why aren't there any gay people on my side of the family?"

"That you know of," Karl said as he handed out mugs of coffee. Turning back to the kitchen for cream and sugar, he added, "In those days things like that weren't discussed, but they still went on."

"Son, I was in the army," Frank declared. "You aren't telling me anything I don't know. But I can safely say no one in my family was gay."

"I think my brother Andreas was gay," Annike announced. "He was very sweet-natured and very artistic, like Sven. I confuse Sven with Andreas sometimes," she admitted.

"I always thought Andreas was a little light in the loafers." Frank snorted. "But he didn't give a damn for me, and the feeling was mutual."

"Andreas and I were close, Frank," Annike said heatedly. "He didn't like the idea of you carrying me so far from home, that's all."

"Well, he never married," Frank countered. "Maybe that's where Sven gets it from. I had nothing to do with it."

As Karl put a container of half-and-half and the sugar bowl on a tray, he thought about his uncle Andreas. While he had only seen him on infrequent visits to Sweden, and once when Andreas had visited them in New Jersey, he did remember him fondly. He looked a lot like Sven in height, build, and hair color. Try as he might, however,

Karl didn't remember him as being effeminate in any way. But he hadn't seen the man since he was seventeen, and at that time he was interested in other things. A lack of language skills on both their parts had kept them from more than cursory interaction, but Andreas had always been unfailingly kind to him as a child.

Karl took four spoons from the cutlery drawer and sighed. There was so much of his life that was a blank when it came to family. Frank had never been close with his own father, mother, or siblings. Karl knew that side of the family even less than he knew his Swedish relatives. He'd gone to his grandparents' funerals in western Pennsylvania, but he couldn't even remember the name of the town where they had lived. In Karl's experience, family was really limited to his father, mother, and brother, and now his own wife and daughter. He had no contact with his aunts, uncles, and cousins. This suited him when he thought of Caroline's relatives and their obligations and internecine spats and grudges.

As Karl carried the try to the table, Melanie piped up. "Gramps, what I don't get is why you can't seem to just accept Uncle Sven for who he is. I mean, why can't you let go and just love him for being himself?"

"Because it's wrong, that's why," her grandfather retorted. "Why am I the bad guy? Why don't all of you get it? I believe homosexuality is wrong. It's been wrong throughout history. Let's leave the Church out of it. If homosexuality has always been around, and it's all la-di-da *cool* all of a sudden, why are there laws against it all over the world? Is it me, or is the whole world crazy?"

Melanie nodded thanks to her father as he handed her a spoon and thoughtfully fell silent as she creamed and sugared her coffee. Finally, she looked up and gently told her grandfather, "Gramps, it used to be against the law for blacks and whites to get married. It used to be against the law for women to vote. But the world changes. And that's a good thing."

"I don't know what's so good about it," Frank said irritably. "Karl, what have you been teaching this girl?"

Caroline reached for the half-and-half and said, "Frank, Karl and I believe that the less we have to say about other people's personal affairs, the better. We reared Melanie to believe it's wrong to condemn people for being different. If you think about it, Melanie grew up having two uncles. Sven and Rob have been together since before she was born. And it's been her experience, and ours, that she couldn't have been blessed with two finer people who have cared about and loved her all her life. That Sven and Rob are gay hasn't marred Melanie in any way. In fact, she's better off knowing, loving, and accepting people for who and what they are. Can't you understand that?"

Frank drained his glass and stood. "I'm nearly eighty years old, and I'm not going to change just because the world has gotten to the point where it tolerates things I feel are abhorrent. I don't think blacks and whites should mix in marriage. And I think giving women the right to vote has probably been the reason this country has had to suffer through Roosevelt, Johnson, Jimmy Carter, and Slick Willie Clinton. I am not ashamed to live what I believe, so you all are going to have to love, respect, and accept me for being who I am, too."

Frank looked at each one at the table in turn and rattled the ice in his glass. "I've told you what I believe, and right now I believe I'll have another drink." With that he left the ensuing silence around the table and went into the kitchen for the scotch.

Karl watched his father as he made himself another drink and returned to the breakfast room, only to go out the door that led to the lanai. Once he'd closed the door behind him, Karl sighed and shook his head.

"Melanie, your mother tells me your French is excellent," Annike said cheerfully. "Would you indulge your grandmother by speaking French with me for a while? I'd love to hear about your trip to Paris and Florence this past summer. *Maintenant, me dire de lui, s'il vous plaît. J'aimerais tout savoir,*" she ended in French. *Now, tell me about it, please. I'd like to know everything.*

Melanie happily obliged her grandmother as Caroline turned to Karl and gave him a wan smile.

"I think I'll go out and join Dad," Karl said quietly. "Would you like to come along?"

"No. I'm going to finish my coffee and make the salad for dinner," Caroline told him. "My French is rusty, but I might be able to enjoy the conversation in here a lot more."

Karl nodded and bent to kiss the top of her head as he passed her on the way to the door. "Wish me luck," he whispered.

Coro smiled and nodded in reply.

15

KARL FOUND HIS FATHER sitting at the small table where he usually breakfasted at the far end of the lanai. He sat hunched over his drink looking round-shouldered and small. Karl felt a stab of pity for the stubborn, lonely presence seated before him. "Want some company?" he asked cheerfully as he made his way to the table, stepping smoothly to avoid sloshing his coffee from his mug.

Frank didn't turn but lifted his hand to wave his son onward toward the table. Once Karl was seated opposite him, Frank studied him searchingly from under his bushy eyebrows. "Have you come out to keep me from being lonesome or to nag me about Sven?" he asked tiredly.

Karl met his eyes and held his gaze openly, without challenge. He took a sip of his coffee before responding. "I just couldn't take the thought of you brooding out here by yourself."

Frank nodded and rolled his highball glass gently between his palms. "Look, Son, I don't need you to feel sorry for me. If you're out here out of pity, you can go back inside with no hard feelings."

"I don't pity you, Dad," Karl said honestly. "I don't understand you sometimes, but pity? Never."

Frank leaned back in his chair and crossed his legs. "I've outlived my relevance," he said with a smile. "That's probably the hardest thing to take. It starts when they force you to retire. Then you get to spend the next twenty years or so realizing that what you have to offer the world isn't worth a dime."

"I don't know about that, Dad," Karl said, then added with

disarming candor, "I think what you have to offer the world has a kind of integrity, even if it does go against the grain."

"Well, you're the only one," Frank said. "You haven't spent your spare time writing any letters to the editor yet. You know the ones, they're the kind of old-fashioned, right-thinking, commonsense ideas that go straight into the Old Fart file."

"Maybe you've just been sending them to the wrong paper," Karl suggested.

His father laughed at that, then took a sip of his scotch. "No, Son, I was born in time to be hungry in the depression, help rebuild Europe after World War II, and even usher in the age of the personal computer. But all that experience is just footnotes now. The world is all about right now, not about back then."

"Tell me about it," Karl said evenly. "I'm at the point in my life where it's all about what can you do for me tomorrow. And there's a long line of bright young men and women on my heels, marking time to get where I'm at."

Frank nodded knowingly. "I've been there, boy. But I'll tell you one thing, it's a hell of a lot more like living than what I'm doing now."

Karl felt the soothing warmth of the coffee mug in his hands and searched for something to counter his father's point of view.

"Karl, I'm sorry you and yours got pulled into all that stuff about Sven," Frank shifted unexpectedly. "But it is what it is. Pretty soon, your mother will be out of it and your brother and I can quit each other. There's not much feeling there on his part, and I accept I'm to blame for that."

"You are hard on him, Dad. Sometimes cruel," Karl said, knowing that what his father said about Sven's feelings was true. "It's just, he's my little brother and I love him. You make it hard not to choose sides."

Frank waved Karl's words off like a bothersome fly. "You're right to take up for your brother. I don't give a damn about that. I just want you to respect my point of view."

Karl took a sip of coffee to stall and craft his answer carefully. "I can understand, given what you feel is right, how you can disapprove of his life. But what I can't respect is how you treat him. And I think the reason you treat him the way you do has more to do with his relationship with Mom than it does with him being gay."

Frank grunted, then said, "You aren't wrong. Ever since he was born, Annike has been totally absorbed with his every burp, fart, and hangnail. She taught him Swedish, and that's all fine, well, and good, I guess. But all that accomplished was building a private world that shut me out. No, Karl, you're right, it is more about their relationship than his gayness. But understanding why I feel the way I do doesn't change anything. I find it very difficult to like my youngest son, and I don't care if he knows it."

"Then there's nothing more to discuss on that subject," Karl told him, consciously giving up. "Next topic of conversation: I need to know how you feel about the end . . . about how you want Mom to go. And how do *you* want to go when the time comes to make the hard decisions?"

Frank nodded. "It's all spelled out in the will and the other papers. I was planning on sending you a copy of all that stuff to keep against the day before we move to Palladian Gardens. You'll be the executor of the will. But since you've asked, both your mother and I want you to pull the plug when the time comes. No extreme measures. Our doctors have copies of our living wills in their files. You need to know we have cemetery plots next to each other at Our Lady Queen of Heaven Cemetery. The funerals are already preplanned and paid for. All you have to do is show up, and you don't even have to do that if I've managed to piss you off even more by then," he concluded with a chuckle.

"Oh, Daddy," Karl said, reverting to the familiar name he'd used before his own burgeoning adolescence had abbreviated his father to just Dad, "you could never piss me off that badly. Don't you know that?"

Frank smiled. "I don't know, boy, I ain't dead yet."

"Let's talk about something a bit more pleasant," Karl said smoothly. "Do you think Mom will be well enough to come for Christmas at our house this year? I know we usually come down here, but with Melanie probably in New York and you guys down here, why don't you come to Cary? Geographically, we're in the middle."

Frank smiled ruefully and shook his head. "Karl, I don't know if I'd be able to deal with your mother in an airport now—and by then, it will be doubtful. And, honestly, when you get to be my age, you really want to be home in your own bed. Let's wait on any talk of Christmas for now. I don't want you beholden one way or another. I can't imagine that fighting the crowds is any picnic for you and Caro, either. Just promise me you'll visit whenever you can. It doesn't have to be a holiday. I'll enjoy seeing you whenever you can spare the time to put up with me."

Karl nodded, accepting the obvious, but said, "I promise I won't abandon you just because you're in that tiny apartment in Palladian Gardens. Okay?"

"Son, by now and for the future, let's just consider any chance we have to get together to be a gift. No promises," Frank told him.

"Okay, Dad," Karl said. Karl understood that his father was, in his own way, telling him he couldn't make any promises and was past needing more requests. Time, in many ways, had run out.

"Just remember the phone rings both ways," Frank added, before he took a sip of his drink and scanned the perimeter of the yard. His eyes rested on something, and he consulted his watch and chuckled. He pointed toward the opposite corner of the backyard, where the dead trunk of a royal palm stood inexplicably in the manicured landscape. "Look," he said with a smile, "Lucy and Ricky have made it home."

Frank followed his father's pointing finger. Sitting side by side on the trunk of the old palm, two brightly colored parrots, each nearly two feet tall, nested together. Karl couldn't believe it. The parrots had been nesting there since they'd moved in forty years earlier. Karl had been the one to name them after the Ricardos, whose television show was a family favorite. Somehow the pair of birds had managed to survive and thrive, after all that time, in the same spot. Karl knew that parrots mated for life in the wild and could live for ninety years or more.

"There's something you can count on never changing," Frank said with satisfaction. "Oh, to be an old parrot and not an old man."

Karl registered the wistfulness in his father's voice and his eyes burned with tears. He found much in his father to disapprove of, but there was much more to him that Karl felt a deep and abiding love for. The world was moving on, but his father was tired of moving with it. Karl knew that at some point in time, his father had decided to plant his feet and resist the momentum that moved events and beliefs beyond his capacity to adapt. In so many ways, his father was simply waiting to die, and there was nothing Karl could do or say to make the wait more bearable.

As Frank watched his parrots fondly and sipped at his scotch, Karl made a mental note to start to resist his own subtle stance against the pull of time. He didn't want to spend his last years as his father had, marking the days by the delivery of the morning paper, and the weeks by doctor's appointments and the occasional haircut. But he knew the comfort in the path his father had taken. Karl already knew the peace of arriving home Friday evenings at six and not leaving the town house again until seven-thirty on Monday morning. He and Caroline had already begun to wrap their evenings and weekends tightly around each other, enjoying in their seclusion the absence of stress that came with their strides through the workday week.

Like his father's table on the lanai, Karl had a table on the second-floor deck off the town house's kitchen. A vivid picture came to his mind: he saw himself sitting, grayed, slump-shouldered, and defeated, drinking there alone in the day's dying light. Rejecting that mental picture fiercely, he almost uttered "No!" aloud. Panicked and heart racing as he sat opposite his father now, he didn't know what he could do to change that predictable picture, but he swore he would.

"Dad," he said softly.

Frank broke his gaze from the parrots, who were garrulously going over their day in a series of squawks and beak nudges, to look at his son.

"Dad," Karl repeated as he searched his father's face, "tell me you're going to be okay."

Frank looked at his son's face with a mixture of love and pride. "I'll be fine, Karl. And so will you."

Curiously comforted by his father's simple assurance, Karl nodded gratefully and finished his coffee before it grew cold.

•

When Frank and Karl returned to the house, they found Melanie still conversing with Annike in French, and Caroline readying dinner. Frank made himself another drink, something Karl noticed he did with eager anticipation of what seemed to have become a pronounced habit. Rather than call him on it, Karl let it slide and joined him in a glass of scotch.

As the evening shadows darkened the house, the lamps were turned on and the roast filled the house with the pleasurable scent of dinner, and everyone relaxed for the first time all day. His mood well lubricated, Frank grew loquacious, but his rambling stories and recollections were happy ones. He cast a spell of nostalgia with stories of the family that Karl, Caroline, and Melanie were hearing for either the first time or the four-hundredth, but their freshness or familiarity neither jarred nor cut. There were even recollections of Sven that revealed a fondness on Frank's part.

As the evening played out, Karl took his father's place as storyteller and deft griot of the family's past. His take on family history as the oldest child brought memories and perspectives that his audience found telling in ways unique to each of them. The texture of the past became more velvet and less burlap. Frank and Annike seemed to draw its familiar surface around themselves as comfortingly as a quilt. Lulled by drink, good food, and fond conversation, both of them began to fade gently. They were happily tired, and their fatigue showed as their movements slowed, their heads and shoulders drooped, and their smiles grew drowsy and light.

Caroline and Melanie took care of the dinner cleanup and left Karl to reminisce with his parents in the living room until, at last, it came time to leave them. As Karl stood, Annike sighed and said, "I wish you didn't have to go."

"Me, too," Frank said sleepily, and made his hesitating way up and out of his chair. Gallantly, he extended his hand to his wife and helped Annike to her feet.

"It has been a wonderful day." Melanie sighed. "I'm so glad I came."

"You should be," Karl said teasingly. "I've seen all the tape tags with your name on them. I believe Mom and Dad have fully furnished your apartment. What is Andrew going to say about all this?"

Melanie laughed happily. "Right now, Drew has a sixty-inch LCD TV, his stereo, a queen bed, and a couple of bar stools, and he's perfectly happy. I think he'll be pleased by how generous Gramps and Grandmere have been."

"Who took the clocks?" Annike asked suddenly.

Caroline, Melanie, and Karl each looked at one another questioningly. Finally, Karl said, "Evidently, Sven will take them. He told me he wanted them if none of us did, and it looks like none of us does."

Frank rubbed his chin thoughtfully and said, "It's probably better that he takes them. He knows how to take care of them, and he does appreciate them."

Even considering the scotch's dulling of Frank's cutting tongue when it came to Sven, Frank's comment surprised them all, considering his outspokenness earlier in the day.

"Are you sure you don't think he will sell them?" Annike asked tartly.

"No. He won't," Frank said evenly. "Anybody who makes a forty-mile round-trip visit once a week to keep them wound wouldn't sell them. He loves those clocks." Frank chuckled and turned to Melanie. "Missy, you have to promise me you'll take them when it's time for Sven to give them to you. It's important they stay in the family, okay?"

In reply, Melanie simply walked over to her grandfather and gave him a peck on the cheek. Awkwardly, Frank put his arms around her shoulders and drew her close. Karl watched as he closed his eyes and held her for a long moment before abruptly letting her go and stepping away from her toward the front door.

"You need to get on the road and let the old folks get some sleep," he said gruffly.

"Dad," Melanie said, holding out her hand, "give me your keys."

Rather than argue, Karl considered the sole drink he'd shared with his father and the glass of wine he'd had with dinner and fished in his front pocket for his keys. Handing them to his daughter, he said, "Thanks, Mel. I don't have my glasses, and I can't see that well at night."

"You're getting old, Son," Frank chuckled.

"So am I," Caroline joined in. "I hate driving at night anymore." With that, she turned to Annike and gave her a warm hug. "Good night, my dear mother-in-law," she said with genuine affection.

"I'll see you all at mass tomorrow morning?" Annike asked commandingly.

"Of course," Karl said as he hugged his mother.

"We'll be here til tomorrow morning if we keep dragging this out," Frank said as he turned once more to the door.

With warm chuckles, they all made their way outside. Frank and Annike waited on the walkway to the house as Caroline, Karl, and Melanie busied themselves getting into the car and buckling up. After another chorus of good-nights, Melanie cranked the engine and backed into the street. Karl watched his parents until they drove away. Then, sighing, he laid his head back against the headrest and said, "I don't know about you guys, but I'm exhausted."

"So am I," Caroline admitted. "When you see family only once a year or so, there's so much emotional freight to collect that it's unbelievable."

From the driver's seat, Melanie chuckled. "I feel like I've been on a roller coaster. I had no idea Gramps was so emotionally labile."

"That's a mighty fine word." Karl snorted. "Pain in the ass is probably more succinct. But I have to admit, once Sven left and he got a little scotch in him, he turned into a different person."

"Something he said really struck me," Melanie said thoughtfully. "When he told us we should love and accept him for who he is, it really made me think. I mean, we're all pretty liberal, and he neatly turned our own attitude back on us. I guess he has a point."

Karl shook his head. "He knew exactly what he was doing. But I do have to say, I think he feels assailed on all sides by the change that's occurred in his lifetime. He made me wonder at what point you get sick of adapting and accommodating your point of view to the world's. He's become an anachronism, and he resents it."

"You're not wrong, Karl," Caroline said from the backseat, "but I think that's a male thing. For all her supposed mental troubles, Annike has the more flexible worldview. I think women tend to be more adaptable to change in general."

"All I have to say is, if I ever get to the point where I start writing letters to the editor and become so rigid in my thinking, I'm giving you the legal right to smother me in my sleep," Karl said determinedly. "I don't want to be like Dad when I get old."

Melanie raced through a yellow light as she neared the on-ramp to I-95. "I don't think you'll ever get to be as bad as Gramps, even though you did vote for Bush," she teased.

"Don't worry, Karl," Caroline consoled him. "I won't let you become rigid and irascible."

"When it comes to Sven," Karl said tiredly, "Dad isn't irascible, he's just plain cruel. It's a combination of jealousy over Mom and his own homophobia, and he admits it. But he also admits he doesn't intend to change."

"Their dynamic was set a long time ago," Melanie said carefully. "I think they're both so used to it that they just follow the script. But I have to say I think Gramps is cutting off his nose to spite his face. Uncle Sven is a wonderful man. My life would be poorer without him."

"Melanie, for God's sake, slow down," Karl said as Melanie gunned through yet another yellow light. "I don't mean to be critical of your driving, but I want to get to Sven's in one piece."

In response, Melanie took her foot off the gas and coasted to a speed nearer the limit before putting her foot back down. "I'm sorry, Dad. Subconsciously, I think I'm just trying to get as far away from what we're discussing as I can. My bad."

"Well, Frank's treatment of Sven aside," Caroline said cheerfully, "all in all, it wasn't a terrible day. Your mother did well. To tell you the truth, I couldn't help but wonder if she would break down in some way, given all the turmoil today. From what you've told me about her little fugues, I didn't know."

"I was a bit on edge about that myself," Karl admitted. "But she held on all day. And did you see her stand her ground when Dad came up with that bizarre accusation about something that happened forty years ago? She didn't give him an inch."

"Good for her," Melanie said. "I'd have slapped the shit out of him."

Caroline laughed from the backseat. "She was fuming when I went back to her while she was changing. She was quite appropriately pissed."

"Oh, she's still in charge," Karl said. "You noticed how she maneuvered us all into going to mass tomorrow morning, at eight o'clock, no less."

"C'mon, Karl," Caroline urged from the backseat. "Going to church isn't going to kill you. Why were you so reluctant to say yes? I thought I was going to have to stomp on your foot to get you to answer her."

Karl sighed. He knew his reluctance was indefensible, but he said, "I just resent being manipulated into it. Mom and Dad made me go the whole route, altar boy and everything. I did enough of it when I was a kid to last me a lifetime. The idea of it just gets my hackles up. I'm not that person anymore, and I resent them for not acknowledging that."

"You're putting too much into it, Dad," Melanie said as she joined the eddies and swells of traffic on I-95. "It's not about you. Offer it up."

Karl snickered at her use of that old phrase. When anything annoyed him, or when he had to do something he didn't want to when he was a child, his mother would always chide him and tell him to offer it up as a sacrifice to the Lord Jesus. He had been unaware that he had passed that particular idea and phrase to his daughter. "Okay. Well said, Mel. I'll offer it up."

After that, they fell silent, lulled by the speed and motion of the car as it headed north. Karl became lost in the view of southern Florida from I-95. Where nothing had been when he'd arrived forty years ago, this sixteen-lane river of traffic wound now. To the east and west, the landscape was filled with the lights of human habitation.

They sparkled, those million streetlights and lit windows, shining on lives and families probably not too different from his own.

As they sped through the early darkness, Karl felt the megalopolis surge all around him. He marveled at the engineering of the road under the wheels. It was his job to design these roadways that spanned long distances and connected with the larger web of roads. With a professional eye, he could imagine the blueprints and bids it must have taken for every overpass and gently banked curve. The brute elegance of it entranced him, and he was happy to let his thoughts slide away to something that had sure meaning and calculated purpose.

The world of emotion he'd been living in for the past few days was too unstable under his feet. His father's moods, his mother's fugues, his brother's changes—none of it was designed. It was all uncontrolled cause and effect, and he wasn't grounded in that sort of reality. He liked concrete solutions, and the authentically messy lives of his family had fatigued him in ways he was unaccustomed to. His spirit was as sore as an unused muscle suddenly called upon to torque and twist to a new task. Karl felt the soreness as sure as the sense of speed that was rushing this trip to its end.

"Well, you two," he said, breaking the silence, "I'm not sorry we came. But I have to tell you, I'm glad we're going home tomorrow."

"You know," Melanie said contemplatively, "I heard this tale of an African chieftain who grew tired of everyone in his village complaining to him about their problems. So he had everyone put their problems in a bag and leave them in one big pile of bags. Then he made them, one by one, go to the pile and pick a bag. Everyone in the village prayed they'd get their own bag back. That's kind of the way I feel," she concluded.

"But these problems belong to all of us," Caroline insisted. "This is our family. I do feel lucky to be able to fly out here to visit and then go back home so easily, but I feel badly that I can't leave having made anything better."

Karl thought about what each of them had said as he continued to watch the city slide past his window. As he turned back to look out the tracery of taillights ahead of them, an essential truth struck him as like one of his frequent flashes of inspiration did. He thought it over in his mind, exploring the texture and edges of what he wanted to say. When he had it firmly in his grasp, he said quietly, "I don't think we came to make anything better here. These aren't *problems* that Mom and Dad and Sven and Rob are facing, it's just life. Some problems don't have solutions. I think they just needed us to participate a little bit in what they're going through."

Caroline reached up from the backseat and put her hand on his shoulder. "I think that's the most emotionally astute thing you've come up with in a long time. Good job, baby. I couldn't agree with you more."

Melanie laughed. "Who says you're bad with feelings, Dad? Though sometimes I think you're borderline Asperger's syndrome, you can be pretty perceptive about emotions when you try."

Karl grinned despite himself and felt warmed by their comments. Though his feelings had been tested and still were sore, he didn't feel like there were any more hurdles his parents and his brother could put in his path that he couldn't clear. He was pretty good at designing bridges, and he was getting better at the ones not made of concrete and steel. Still, he had to admit, he preferred the ones that were built with things he could put his hands on.

SUNDAY

16

WHEN THE FIRST tentative knock came at the bedroom door, Karl was at the bridge in his dream. The dream came often enough that he recognized it each time he found himself there. He'd had versions of this dream for as long as he could remember. Unlike most of his dreams, which were like watching a movie where he could see himself in the dreamscape, he viewed and felt this dream with himself as the camera's lens. His eyes took in the scene, but he was absent from it. In fact, no one populated this dream.

He resisted the second knock on the bedroom door, so reluctant was he to leave the dream. His body felt every sensation of the place. His penis was erect and he was aware of having a powerfulness and tautness to his body that he no longer really possessed. The sun shone, but the view was muted in tonality, as if the light were permeating a damp, warm wind that caressed his skin. He was aware that he stood on a beach, seeing things from just behind a lifeguard's towering chair with a long, low bridge running off to a vanishing point on the water.

Karl was aware of the scene and its every detail. He loved the angular simplicity of the setting. The view was a composition of straight lines, as if it had been created with draftsman's tools. Everything was uniquely defined by certain linearity, like a child's drawing of the beach, the sea, and the unending sky overhead. It appealed to Karl's craving for orderliness and predictability.

What was even more alluring to Karl than the simplicity of the dreamscape was its sense of possibility. As he looked over that dream beach, he was poised eternally at the moment of every imminent action. Everything seemed within his grasp there: sex, success, prowess, and passion. Karl felt that all he need do was climb the lifeguard's towering chair, or follow the bridge's certain path over the water, to find everything the future promised. Yet he was aware that he need do nothing more than be there, on that beach in the thick, humid air, and everything he wanted in the abstract would be his. It was a singular, sensual sensation at the instant before the fulfillment of every aspiration.

"Karl? Caroline? It's six," Sven said quietly from the other side of the door.

Karl turned from his side to his stomach and moved his arms over his head on the pillow. He wanted to stay on that beach, by the bridge over blue water leading to everywhere. He felt so close to every pleasant eventuality. He didn't want to wake up.

"Thanks, Sven," Caroline said clearly, despite the undertone of sleepiness in her voice. "We're awake."

"We have to leave by seven-fifteen to make it to mass," Sven said, more loudly this time. "I've got coffee ready."

"Thanks, dear," Caroline told him. "We'll be right out."

Karl resented being pulled from the dream beach into consciousness. He opened his eyes to the dim light of the guest room and found himself facing the window, away from Caroline. The dream disappeared, and all that was left of his visit there was an erection and a sense of lingering strength and self-assurance. He acutely felt Caroline's hand on his bare shoulder as she gently shook him.

"Wake up, sweetheart," she urged him. "We have to get up."

"Okay," Karl mumbled agreeably. "Just give me a minute more. You go on to the bathroom."

Caroline kissed the bare skin on the top knob of his spine at the base of his neck. Then he felt her weight move the bed as she shifted and rose. He heard the whisper of her robe shifting from the chair at the foot of the bed, and the soft pad of her footsteps as she let herself out of the room.

When she had closed the door behind her, Karl rose slowly to avoid the predictable head rush and adjusted his insistent penis inside his boxer shorts before striding to the window and rolling up the shade. The morning view out the guest room window was more familiar now, as were the pinkish dawn stealing over the sky and the wet whisper of the arcing jets of the sprinkler system on the front lawn. He watched as Rob walked a leashed, sniffing Gretchen up the drive to the front door. Evidently, most of the house was up and preparing for the trip to church.

Karl sighed and left the window with the dream still clinging to the corners of his mind. He knew the place from the dream so well, and it seemed so real, that he thought it must have been an actual place at some point, but he could never find it as fact when he actively searched his memory for beaches he'd been on. Now, as always before, he felt a sense of loss in leaving that dreamscape. The dream had lost its oddness in the many times he'd had it, but its physical and emotional impact was still very real. It left him with a young man's virility and testosterone-fueled confidence that he could conquer his world and take from it all that he desired.

Aware of his lingering erection and his wife's imminent return, he first pulled on a clean pair of jeans. He didn't want to have to explain or discuss this odd gift of his dream. After he zipped up his secret, he slathered on some deodorant and pulled a fresh white T-shirt over his head. As he was searching his dop kit for his electric razor, Caroline returned to the bedroom and gave him a smile.

"You've lost your bathroom spot," she informed him. "Melanie just went in for a quick shower."

"Thank God I don't have to pee right away," Karl said as he shrugged and walked to the small dresser by the window and found his face in the mirror hung on the wall. He turned on his electric razor and, knowing it should have enough charge left in its battery, began to shave, more by feel and familiar habit than by sight in the dim room.

Caroline sat on the side of the bed with one leg tucked under her and watched him as he shaved. He found her face in the mirror and gave her a wink. The surge of virility wrought by the dream's landscape and promise still surged through his subconscious like an insistent electrical current. He felt physically enhanced, and the thought of secret purloined sex tempted him as he stole glances of his wife as she watched him admiringly. "You look adorable sitting there," he told her.

She smiled and stretched in the wake of his compliment, but she said, "I don't feel adorable." She sighed and rubbed her temples. "Ooooooh, I'm feeling those cosmopolitans from last night."

They had returned to Sven's the night before to find him and Rob lounging on the sofa with an empty pizza box on the ottoman. By their minimal dress and languid torpor, they gave an unspoken affirmation to Karl's assumption that they had found something more physically fulfilling to do than go out for dinner. True to his promise, Rob had turned off the television, turned on the stereo, and made the first of several shakers of the strong red cocktail. Karl had faded rather quickly. The day had taxed him to the point that a single cocktail had been enough to send him to bed. He'd left Caroline and Melanie to visit and party with Sven and Rob. Gretchen, however, had decided to keep Karl company. She'd nosed open the guest room door and jumped on the bed, then promptly turned a few times and settled against Karl's thighs with a deep, satisfied sigh. Rather than chase her off the bed, Karl welcomed her warm presence and decided to let Caroline deal with the dog when she came in to go to sleep.

"How did you get Gretchen off the bed?" he asked Caroline as he ran the razor in long, even strokes over his neck.

"Sven bribed her off with a cookie," Caroline said and laughed. "For a while, I thought it was going to be the three of us for the night. She growled at me when I tried to push her off the bed."

Karl finished shaving and ran his fingertips over his face to check his work. Finding himself uniformly smooth, he turned to Caroline and smiled. "Are you going to shower?"

Caroline shook her head. "We're going to the beach after church. I'm just going to get dressed and save my shower for before we have to leave."

"I'm going to do the same," Karl said. "I have one more clean shirt," he said as he strode back to his suitcase, pulled it out, and shook it free of creases.

"Do you think your jeans will be okay for church?" Caroline asked thoughtfully.

Karl pulled the shirt over his head and pulled it down to his hips. "Yeah," he said. "Eight o'clock mass is fairly casual. You get a break for making the effort to get up so early."

Caroline stood and took off her robe. Dressed in a small T-shirt and panties, she opened her own suitcase and thumbed through the few folded outfits she found. "Well, I'm going to wear slacks, but I think I can do better than jeans," she said.

Karl stepped behind her and put his hands on her shoulders. "You'll look great no matter what you wear," he said, and kissed the top of her head.

Caroline turned and put her arms around his waist. "Seems like a waste of a morning at the beach, to be out the door on the way to church," she said as she looked up into his face. "I can think of other things I'd rather be doing."

Karl laughed and took her buttocks in his hands. Squeezing them as he pulled her to him, he said, "It must be something in the salty air. I notice both Rob and Sven had that freshly fucked look on their faces when we got here last night."

"Sssssh," Caroline shushed him as she tried not to laugh. "You noticed that, too, huh?"

Karl laughed and let go of her ass to wrap her in a strong hug. "Can I get a rain check?"

"Absolutely," Caroline said as she moved back out of his arms and turned once more to her suitcase. "We have next weekend home alone, remember?"

"That's right," Karl said and stretched. "Melanie will be in New York, and you and I now have plans."

"Promise?" Caroline asked as she pulled out a pair of dark slacks and held them by the waist to let the legs unfurl.

"Uh-huh," Karl said gutturally.

"For now, you better get yourself some coffee and let me get dressed," Caroline told him.

"Damn," Karl said with heavy disappointment as he turned to leave her.

"See you in a minute," Caroline told him as he closed the door behind him.

Karl found Rob and Sven drinking coffee at the kitchen table while Gretchen noisily finished her bowl of kibble by the back door. "Good morning, guys," Karl said happily, feeling a good mood steal over him. The energy of his dream had spilled into his morning.

"Good morning," Rob echoed.

"Make yourself some coffee," Sven told him.

As Karl fixed his mug the way he liked it, he noticed Rob was rather well dressed, while Sven was dressed much as Karl was, in jeans and a navy sweater. "You look sharp," he commented to Rob as he sat down.

"Thanks," Rob said. "I can't be like you cradle Catholics. If I'm going to church, I feel I should dress up a little."

"So, you're coming to mass?" Karl asked him before he took a sip of coffee.

"I am," Rob replied decisively. "In fact, I'm going to spend the day with you."

"Well, that's cool," Karl said happily. "I didn't know if you had plans today or not."

"I did," Rob confessed. "Then I heard how Frank treated Sven yesterday, and I decided I was going to make a point of being around, so if he shows his ass like he did yesterday, I can punch him in the head."

"My boyfriend the pit bull," Sven joked. "I told him that wouldn't be necessary, but he feels he has to stick up for me."

"You're damn right I do," Rob said seriously. "You may be his son, but you're my partner, and I'm sick and tired of him thinking he can treat you like shit and get away with it."

"Don't make a big deal out of it, Rob," Sven said dismissively. "He's never going to change. It's just how he and I interact. You'd have a better day if you just took off and headed back up to Palm Beach. I'll be okay."

"Shut up, Sven," Rob said evenly. "If you won't take up for yourself, I will. I'm dead serious. Your father will think twice about being such a jerk with me there."

"Suit yourself," Sven said. "But don't be surprised if he says something."

Karl looked at his brother, then his brother's partner. "I'll back Rob up," he said. "I thought Dad's behavior yesterday was inexcusable, and I told him so. You don't deserve to be talked to like I wouldn't talk to Gretchen."

Sven smiled, then chuckled. "Okay. I appreciate it. But remember, his tongue cuts both ways. It's really better if you don't get all up in that. He's just an irritable old man."

"Whatever," Rob said. "We're coming back here and going to the beach after church, right?"

"That's the plan," Karl said. "I can't imagine flying all the way to Florida, staying within spitting distance of the beach, and never setting foot on it while I was here."

"Melanie and Caro are really looking forward to it," Sven told Rob. "We'll have about four hours to hang out together before we'll have to head back over to Mom and Dad's so these guys can drop off Mom's car and say good-bye. Are you sure you're up for all that?"

Rob looked at him and nodded before standing and retrieving the coffeepot. Without a word, he reheated Sven's coffee first, then his own before looking at Karl questioningly.

"No, thanks," Karl said.

"I'll take some of that," Caroline said as she strolled into the kitchen.

"Sit down," Rob said. "I'll make you a mug. Cream and sugar?"

"Just black, please," Caroline told him as she sank to her seat with a sigh. "Rob, your cosmos are talking back to me this morning."

Rob chuckled as he poured coffee into a fresh mug. "Do you need some aspirin, an antacid, or anything?"

"I found aspirin in the medicine cabinet," Caroline said as she finger-combed her hair back from her face. "I think once I get some coffee in me, I'll be up to speed."

"I feel great this morning," Rob told her as he handed her the mug of coffee and sat down. "You're a lightweight," he teased.

"How late did you guys stay up?" Karl asked with a look for each of them. "I was out like a light by ten."

Sven chuckled and said, "It was about midnight when we all stumbled to bed. But you looked shell-shocked when you got here last night, Karl. Yesterday wasn't exactly a restful holiday, was it?"

Karl gave him a level look and said, "It wasn't all that bad, but I'm glad it's not something I have to do every weekend."

"Anyone care for a carton of yogurt?" Sven asked as he stood and made his way to the refrigerator, with Gretchen following him hopefully.

"If you have strawberry or banana, I'll take one," Caroline replied. "Now that I've had some coffee, I need something in my stomach."

Sven tossed Gretchen a cookie from the bowl of dog treats before he shifted some items in the refrigerator and drew out two cartons of yogurt. He opened a drawer and took out two spoons before walking back to the table and handing Caroline a container and her spoon. He elected to eat his own while standing.

"What's going on at church these days?" Rob asked Sven.

"It's Lent," Sven told him. "Other than that, nothing special."

Karl sipped his coffee and thought about the season. The world changed as Lent progressed. Winter turned to spring while the church spent its forty days of fasting and abstinence. Those rituals were something he'd long left behind. In fact, he and his father had both had roast beef for lunch two days before, though Sven had served lobster bisque for dinner on Friday. He chuckled without realizing it.

"What's so funny?" Caroline asked.

"I had roast beef on Friday," Karl told her. "I didn't even consider eating fish. I haven't done any of that stuff for years. You must keep it up, Sven. That's the reason for that nice lobster bisque on Friday night, right?"

"Of course," Sven said with a shrug. "It has meaning to me. I make the conscious decision, but I don't feel self-righteous about it, and I don't fault you for eating meat on Friday. I just believe in the traditions. That's all."

"And I get used to plain cheese pizza on Friday nights," Rob said and laughed.

"What church were you brought up in, Rob?" Caroline asked him with interest.

"When we went, we went to a Presbyterian church," Rob told her. "But basically we went only at Christmas and Easter. My family's not very religious. What about you?"

Caroline finished the last of her yogurt, then said, "Oh, I was brought up as a strict Methodist. No drinking, no dancing, blah, blah, blah. My parents were aghast when I married Karl in the Catholic Church, but they reconciled themselves to me agreeing to bring Melanie up as a Catholic. I think they came to the conclusion that it was better than nothing."

"I take it you're not very religious, either," Rob said.

"Not in the sense of belonging to any church," Caroline said. "I have my spiritual beliefs, but I can't organize my life around any church's schedule. I suppose it's nice for those people who need that sort of thing." She sniffed. "But I prefer making my own decisions about spiritual matters, and I don't need them reinforced by belonging to any sort of *club*, and that's really all church is," she said dismissively. "I think Karl feels the same way."

"We're just very private people," Karl told Rob. "If anyone asks, I tell them I'm Catholic, because that's the belief system I was reared in. I still consider myself Catholic, but I don't go to church anymore."

Sven carefully scraped the inside of his yogurt container and licked the remains off his spoon before holding the cup down for Gretchen to lick clean. "And here I am, forty years old and still watching the clock to make sure it's at least an hour between the time I eat and receive communion." He petted the big dog's head as he smiled at the little group around the table and turned to throw his container away in the trash under the sink.

"I can't keep track of all those rules. I think they're meaningless," Karl said with a snort. "I'm surprised you trouble yourself with all that stuff anymore," he told Sven.

Sven only smiled and said, "Melanie better step it up if she wants any coffee before we leave. We really do have to be on the road by seven-fifteen in order to get there on time."

Karl started to say something else to Sven about the strictness of his exercise of faith but thought better of it. When he considered it, it was really none of his business. He'd made the concession to go to church for his mother's benefit, and he decided to just leave it at that. Karl decided not to feel as if he'd abandoned his own principles. He instead decided he was just making his mother happy. And if that cost him a couple of hours on a beautiful Sunday morning, he'd just offer it up.

17

THE CHURCH PARKING LOT was full, though they had arrived fifteen minutes ahead of schedule. Sven managed to find a parking place at the far end of the lot. Karl let himself out of the back door of the Excursion and waited to offer his hand to Caroline as she slid across the seat and stepped down from the high vehicle. She looked up at him gratefully as she stepped onto the pavement and squeezed his hand with unspoken thanks. Karl smiled at her but held on to her hand as their little group assembled at the rear of the SUV and started toward the church.

Karl looked up at the church's façade as they made their way across the parking lot. He had seen the building being built years ago, as his family had numbered among the first parishioners there. Thinking of all the Sunday mornings he'd come here throughout his adolescence and teen years, he stooped a bit and whispered to Caroline, "Do you feel guilty?"

"Of course not," she replied as she sought his eyes. "Do you?"

"Oh, yeah," he said with a smirk. "I think they put the guilt in with the asphalt."

Caroline smiled at him but shook her head, knowing he was being facetious.

Frank and Annike were waiting for them near the front doors. Karl was expecting an elaborate greeting, but only Frank stepped forward with an extended hand for him and a hug for his daughter-in-law and granddaughter. Annike remained where she stood and waited with a look of shy confusion on her face. As Karl stooped to hug her, she gave him an odd look, almost as if she didn't recognize him, though she returned his hug warmly.

"Rob. I didn't expect you here this morning," Frank said sullenly.

"It's nice to see you," Rob responded noncommittally. "Since this is a family event, I thought I should be here, too," he added with a note of challenge.

"Mom?" Sven said from the side of the group where Annike lingered.

"Hello," she replied automatically.

Frank didn't rise to Rob's bait; instead, he turned his back to him pointedly, stepped to Annike's side, and put his arm around her waist. "Well, here we all are, Annike. One big happy family—aren't you pleased?"

Annike's eyes barely acknowledged him as she scoured the parking lot with a searching look. When she didn't find what she was looking for, she turned worriedly to Frank and said, "Wherever are the children?"

Karl heard her and felt his sense of internal buoyancy deflate.

"They're with us," Frank said carefully. "I think we need to be getting inside," he said to his assembled family helplessly.

Annike looked uncomprehendingly at the circle of adults surrounding her, then turned again to look at Frank with uncertainty.

"Let's go," he said gently to her and steered her toward the front doors.

Karl looked at Sven, who returned his glance and shook his head sadly. As the group walked up the steps to the church's entrance, Karl lingered to bring up the rear. He realized his mother had been waiting for her children, not her adult sons oddly paired and accompanied by an unexplained young woman.

Once inside the church, Karl reverted to habit. He accepted a bulletin from an elderly usher before he dipped his fingers in the holy water font and blessed himself; then he genuflected once his father had led them all to the familiar pew. However, once he'd taken his seat at the end of the pew, he did not kneel for prayer as his mother, father, and brother did. Instead, he sat stiffly next to Caroline and looked around the sanctuary.

The church members were in subdued dress for Lent. The altar projected from the rear wall into the sanctuary, which was arranged like an amphitheater around it on three sides. Their family's pew was located in a wedge-shaped section to the right of the altar. From his vantage point, Karl had a direct view of a tableaux, set up where the choirmaster's lectern usually stood, that held a life-sized crucifix surrounded by pots of dried grasses and cactus. Uncomfortable sitting face-to-face with the crucifix, Karl reached for a missalette from the rack on the back of the pew in front of him and found the readings for that Sunday. He handed it to Caroline so that she could follow along, and Caroline accepted the missalette with a nod, although it was unnecessary, as she knew from many years of bringing Melanie to church how to find the readings on her own and, indeed, when to stand, kneel, and sit.

To keep himself distracted from the crucifix in his direct line of vision, Karl looked out over the church as it filled up. He recognized a few faces, and marveled at how frail and elderly some of them had become. He also noticed the increase in black and brown faces in a church that had been predominantly Irish and Italian in his day. The Caribbean diaspora had reached this parish in Boca Raton. When he realized by the looks of strangers that he was staring, he opened the bulletin in his hand.

He read the usual greeting from the head pastor, a monsignor who had come to the church after Karl had left. He gave the general comments a quick read, then looked at a reprinted letter from the bishops of Virginia that outlined the church's view on same-sex marriages and civil unions. It was restrained in its language, yet it left no room for interpretation. The bishops were strongly discouraging of secular support of such affairs and counseled the dioceses under their jurisdiction to remain firm in the church's rejection of even civil unions for homosexuals. The letter was reprinted under the innocuous heading "Of Interest to Our Parishioners." Disgusted, Karl folded the bulletin and placed it in the tray on the back of the pew in front of him.

At last, the procession of altar servers, the lectors, Eucharistic ministers, and the priest made their way up the center aisle, and Karl stood along with the congregation. There was no music at this early mass, so they all merely stood as the various mass servers took their places and the priest began mass.

For the next thirty minutes, Karl acted appropriately. He stood or knelt as was required by form and habit, but his mind was all over the place. His thoughts ran the gamut from resentment to rebellion to resentment again. He never really heard any of the readings, and during the priest's homily, he silently debated with the tormented crucified Christ on the cross in front of him. He wondered at the distance of years and wrongs that separated the figure on that cross from the church he sat in. He angrily demanded answers to the difficult questions he had about his family's struggles. His internal argument raged while mass continued on around him. The face on the crucifix never changed its serene expression of surrender and peace in the face of its fate. Karl stared at that effigy of Christ and waited for something, anything, to lessen his anger and resentment.

At last, the time came for his pew to file forward for communion. Karl felt his father's eyes boring into him as he got off his knees and sat back down on the pew. Then he changed his mind and stood. He hadn't planned on receiving communion, but he realized that if he sat, everyone in their pew would have to file awkwardly past his knees. At first, he intended to sit back down after his family filed past him, but he didn't. Instead, he folded his hands and led the family to the Eucharistic minister. He made the small bow and extended his hands to receive the host before stepping aside and placing it on his tongue. He regarded the crucifix once more and crossed himself before returning to the pew and kneeling.

Karl was careful not to bite the host as it rested on his tongue, but waited for it to soften until he could swallow it whole. No longer able to confront the face of Christ in front of him, he simply bowed his head to wait for communion to be over. It was then that he felt a curious lightening in his chest. Where he had moments before felt a clenched fist behind his sternum, now he felt instead a spreading warmth that he recognized as something like peace. He fought against trying to define the sensation. He tried to empty his mind of everything but the sense of expansiveness and acceptance in his chest. Then his mind intruded with rationalization, and he was left clutching after that fleeting moment of faith. For an instant, he'd believed that everything was okay, and he'd felt himself let go of his carefully crafted sense of irony and rejection of the whole experience of church. For just that little while, he was simply, profoundly, at peace. And then it was gone.

Karl raised his head and looked around. Everyone watched as the altar servers replaced the bowls of unused hosts back in the tabernacle and the priest closed the door. At that, Karl joined with everyone else as they crossed themselves, got off their knees, and sat back down.

Within a few moments mass was over, and Karl stood, moved to the aisle, and genuflected once more before reaching for Caroline's hand. She surprised him by looking directly at the crucifix before them and making a graceful approximation of his own genuflection before turning with him to lead the others, out of the sanctuary. Outside the church, his family formed a small circle. Annike stood close to Frank's side as if overwhelmed by the others who seemed to tower over her diminutive form. She looked at them curiously but without any real recognition.

"Did you enjoy mass, Mom?" Karl asked her gently.

She smiled at him shyly, and said, "Yes."

"Grandmere, are you looking forward to seeing us this afternoon?" Melanie asked softly.

Annike cocked her head and stared at Melanie before looking at Frank questioningly.

"I think we need to be getting back home," Frank said stiffly. "Thank you for coming all the way down here. I was proud to have all of my family in church."

"Dad, do you need us to follow you home? Will you be alright?" Sven asked anxiously.

"We'll be fine," Frank said without any rancor. Instead, he seemed remarkably resigned to the awkwardness of the situation. "I just need to get her back around familiar things. She'll be fine."

"We'll be back about three," Sven told him. "Do you have anything for lunch?"

"Sure. There are leftovers from last night," Frank told him wearily. "You all take off and enjoy the beach. Hopefully, by the time you come back, your mom will be back to herself again."

"See you soon, Annike," Caroline said gently and waved.

"Good-bye," Annike said, with the same shy smile she had given Karl.

"Come on, dear, let's go home," Frank urged his wife as he guided her with his arm around her waist.

Annike turned to walk away with him but glanced back at her family and waved politely, "Good-bye," she said warmly.

They all stood in front of the church and watched as Frank got Annike to the car and helped her in. When he had her seated and belted inside, Frank closed her door and gave them a wave.

"She had absolutely no idea who we were," Karl said as he waved back.

Caroline took his hand and said, "True, but she looked at us as if she thought we were rather nice people."

"I imagine what I'd feel like if some girl my age came up to me and said 'Hello, Grandmere,'" Caro said and shuddered. "I would think she was crazy. That's how I felt anyway."

"It's okay, Mel." Sven patted Melanie's arm comfortingly as he pulled his keys from his jeans pocket with his other hand. "Once she gets back home and gets reoriented, this shouldn't last very long. She'll probably be fine by the time we come back."

"C'mon. Let's head home," Rob said as he stepped away. Slowly, the others followed his broad shoulders to the car, dodging traffic across the long expanse of the rapidly emptying parking lot.

Once they got in the car and under way, the mood seemed to lighten a bit. Caroline nudged Karl's shoulder and said, "Now, that wasn't so bad, was it? You were dreading going to mass like you would a whipping. I thought it was nice."

Karl was about to respond that if he'd known his mother was not going to recognize them, he'd have skipped it altogether. But remembering the transcendent moment he'd had after communion, he decided against it. While it wasn't a miraculous conversion, it was something, and far more than he would have expected. He thought perhaps for all he'd given the church in the past ten years or so, it was all he could expect. But the undeniable fact was that he did feel something still. It was too private to be flippant about or even try to explain, so he settled on nudging Caroline's shoulder in reply and giving her a smile.

"Did you read that homophobic letter in the bulletin?" Melanie demanded.

Rob looked across the front seat at Sven, who was steering them north. When Sven didn't reply, he said, "Frankly, I thought it was unnecessary and just plain wrong."

Caroline sighed and said, "At least it wasn't a letter from the archbishop of West Palm Beach. Those bishops were from Virginia, and you know what a conservative stronghold that state is."

"Yes, but whoever puts the bulletin together here decided to reprint it," Melanie fumed. "I think it's so un-Christian and bigoted. I don't need that kind of crap put in my face at church, of all places. They should save their moralistic ranting for the pedophile priests they've shielded and protected for years."

"Sven," Karl added, "I read that letter, and I wondered how you could sit in that church knowing how those people feel about you, your life, and your partnership with Rob. I frankly can't see why you stay in the Catholic Church. How do you live with it?"

"I've asked him the same thing," Rob said. "I mean, okay, I understand they don't approve, but why make such a big deal out of it? Even if being gay were a sin, it would be just one of many. They let all kinds of sinners in their doors. I don't know why all the organized religions are making such a big deal out of gay marriage."

"Seriously, Sven," Karl pressed. "How do you reconcile being gay with being a practicing Catholic?"

Sven drove on in silence for a moment, letting the air get back in the car after being forced out by all the large questions and opinions it had been filled with. Finally, he said, "You know, you guys all have these really strong opinions about religion, and rejecting Catholicism, and being gay, and whatever, but none of you have suggested anything meaningful to replace it with."

No one in the car said anything in reply. When no one countered his statement, Sven continued confidently, "I believe in Jesus, the Blessed Mother, the angels and saints. I believe in the Eucharist. Those things make me a Catholic. Not one of you has offered me anything to replace that with if I take my big gay ass out of the Church in protest. If I did that, what would I be left with? What you guys have? You don't even go to church. What do you believe in? I'm sorry if I seem like some wimpy, no-balls faggot for taking the Church's shit about being gay. But, it seems to me that all of you have dumped the church and replaced it with nothing but irony and smugness. Don't worry about me. I'm fine with being a Catholic."

The car was silent for a long time before Caroline finally muttered, "Well, I guess you told us."

Sven laughed. "Look. I admit seeing that letter about civil unions in the church bulletin got under my skin, too. But I'm able to separate the Church from God, and the dogma from what God's really all about. All I know is I go looking for God and I always find him at mass. Where do you all find God?"

"I don't usually go looking for him," Rob quipped.

Sven said adamantly, "I'm not joking."

"Sven," Karl offered after a moment, "if being a practicing Catholic is meaningful to you, I'm happy for you. I just don't look for it anymore. I got out of the habit."

"Sven, I have to agree with Karl," Caroline said. "I guess that's why they say people *practice* religion. I'm terribly out of practice myself. I'm sorry if we seemed condescending."

"And I'm sorry if I seemed smug, Uncle Sven," Melanie offered. "I just can't reconcile the hypocrisy with the essential message. There's no evidence Jesus ever said one word about homosexuality. The church expects us to believe it's Christ's voice on earth, but what I hear it saying about gay people doesn't seem charitable, loving, or forgiving. That's what Christ was all about."

Sven sighed audibly and paused, obviously thinking of how to respond. Finally, he said, "Melanie, no priest has ever attacked me personally for being gay. And I don't make a point of bringing a rainbow flag to mass."

"Isn't that just being accommodating?" Melanie demanded. "Aren't you just partitioning your conscience?"

"That's not what it's about," Sven explained patiently. "Members of any faith make their own decisions about its particular rules and regulations. If they didn't, you wouldn't see any Baptists or Arabs in the liquor store."

"True," Melanie conceded, "but it shouldn't have to be that way."

"In a perfect world, no," Sven countered, "but I don't live in a perfect world."

"This is an unwinnable, endless discussion," Karl said calmly. "I will say, I went to mass this morning for the first time in years, and I have to tell you I did feel something . . . something good and positive . . . profound, even. Why don't we all agree that religion is a personal thing and leave it at that? Sven?"

"What?" he replied.

"I respect you. I wish I had your faith," Karl said honestly. "Now, let's talk about something else."

"So what are you going to do with Dad's crucifix?" Sven asked gently.

Karl thought a moment, and looked at Caroline. She returned his look with a questioning one of her own. "I'm going to hang it by my front door," he said finally. "Out of respect, for one thing, and maybe because I believe in my own way I'm still a Catholic, too."

"That's good enough for me," Sven said with finality, then, with a purposeful brightening of his voice, he asked, "Now, are we going to take a picnic to the beach, or are we just going to hang out there for a while and then grab a bite back at the house?"

"I don't know about you guys," Rob said. "But I'm going to make a gallon of screwdrivers and take it out with us. Anybody who wants one is free to join me."

"Count me in," Caroline said cheerfully.

"Me, too," Melanie added. "I want to just lie in the sun and enjoy a little bitty buzz until it's time to head back in."

"Sounds good to me," Sven agreed.

Karl thought about the tension that held all of his joints tightly screwed into their sockets at the moment. There had been so many times over the past few days that he'd felt like he was holding together too many fiercely struggling personalities and demands. A couple of hours in the warm sun with the ease of a drink loosening his tightly wound nerves sounded truly appealing. For a moment, he considered the driving he still had to do, then he thought of Melanie's insistence that she drive. He decided to hell with it. In a four-day weekend, he deserved to unwind a little. He turned to Caroline and put his hand on her knee. "Don't let me get drunk," he instructed her.

"Don't worry," she said with a smile. "I'll keep an eye on you."

With that, he felt some of the anxiousness drain from his body. Karl surrendered to the momentum of the big SUV as it carried him north, closer to the beach and nearer to letting go.

18

BACK AT SVEN'S HOUSE, an eager gaiety took over the small group as they prepared for the beach. Karl noticed it as they all retreated to their bedrooms to change. The coming few hours promised to be relaxing, and all they expected of each other was an amiable good time. For the time being, all the weighty topics that defined the boundaries of his family were well marked, acknowledged, and taken care of. All he wanted to do now was withdraw from the tension on those borders and find some contentment.

When Karl closed the guest room door behind Caroline, he pulled his shirt over his head and spread it carefully over the back of the chair at the foot of the bed. "Are you going for the full-bathing-suit routine, or are you just going to wear something cool?" he asked.

Caroline stepped out of her pants and folded them carefully before laying them on the bed. "I think you're asking me if I plan to go in the ocean, is that it?"

"Well, yeah," Karl answered as he pulled off his jeans. "I don't think I want to go swimming. The water's probably only about seventy degrees, and the wind is probably cool off the water."

Caroline pulled a strappy undershirt from her suitcase and a pair of shorts that came well above her knees. As she unhooked her bra, she said, "That's what I was thinking. I don't think I'll be swimming."

Karl stole an admiring glance at her bare breasts before she pulled the shirt over her head. He pulled down his boxer shorts and kicked them toward his suitcase before he stooped to pick them up. Caroline pinched his bare ass hard and giggled. "You are in rare form today," Karl said as he gave her a smile over his shoulder.

"You have the cutest butt in the world," she said teasingly. "There's not a hair on it."

"That's what you get for marrying a Swede," Karl said as he stepped into his trunks and pulled them up. "But I have hair on my chest," he said.

"Yeah, but just the right amount," Caroline purred. "I don't think I could stand being married to a gorilla."

Karl carefully adjusted himself in his trunks and sealed the Velcro fly before snapping them closed. He tugged his T-shirt over his head and held it as he flexed a bit to tease Caroline's admiring eye. When she rolled her eyes at his preening and snapped her own shorts, Karl turned and took out a less-fresh T-shirt from his suitcase and pulled it on.

"Where are your Tevas?" Caroline asked him. "I reminded you to bring them."

"And I remembered them," Karl said, "but I think I'm just going to go barefooted. It's not hot enough to turn the streets or sand to molten lava."

"Suit yourself," Caroline said as she pulled a pair of flip-flops from her suitcase and dropped them to the floor. As she stepped into them, she glanced at the closed door and whispered, "You don't think we offended Sven about the whole religion thing, do you?"

"No," Karl whispered back. "I think he stated his position rather well. I don't think he's mad. Don't worry about it."

Caroline nodded her head. "We didn't mean to be condescending. It's just gotten to the point that no one we know believes in anything, or at least doesn't talk about it."

"Excluding your family," Karl said back.

Caroline rolled her eyes and nodded. "Are you ready?" she asked in a louder voice.

"Yep," Karl said happily. "I'm starting to feel like a Florida boy again." With that he opened the door, and they made their way into the living room.

Sven stood at the sofa folding beach towels. He, too, was bare-footed and dressed in only a longish pair of board shorts that hung low on his narrow hips. Karl noticed that Sven was slick as a seal, with no trace of hair on his chest or belly. He looked like a teenager with his long, raggedly cut hair and slender form. "I thought we'd each take a beach towel," he said to Karl and Caroline, "but I have some beach chairs if you want to schlep them for two blocks."

Karl looked at Caroline and said, "A towel's fine for me, but I'll carry a chair for you if you'd like one."

"No," Caro said agreeably. "A towel is all I need."

"Do you guys need another towel to dry off with?" Sven offered.

"We decided not to go swimming," Caroline replied. "I think we just want to enjoy the sun."

Sven nodded, then moved past them toward the kitchen. "I'm going to check on Rob. He insisted on packing a cooler."

As he spoke, Rob emerged from the kitchen carrying the cooler with one hand. He was dressed as Sven was, in only a pair of board shorts. Unlike Sven's skinny form, Rob's was stocky and well muscled. His chest was well developed, and he boasted a set of solid abs.

Caroline nodded at him appreciatively as he made his way into the living room. "Speak of the devil," she said.

Bashfully, Rob ducked his head and looked at the cooler in his hands. "I have drinks and snacks packed," he admitted shyly. "I believe screwdrivers are healthier than Valium or Prozac."

"I'll second that, Uncle Rob," Melanie said as she strode from the hall into the living room to join them. She had on a black tank swimsuit, which she filled nicely. "Drew got on Prozac during the last year of his MBA, and it was hell on our love life. But he got through it and stopped taking the meds."

"I think that qualifies as too much information, Mel," Sven said as her gave her a once-over. "That swimsuit fits like a glove. God, I remember you when you were nothing but elbows and knees. It's hard to think of you being an adult, much less having a love life."

Melanie laughed and preened a little. "Okay, prude," she said. "If it makes you feel better, you can pretend I'm still ten. By the way, I have sunscreen," Melanie announced as she held up a small bag that contained a variety of beach items. "I'll share."

"Oh, good!" Caroline said, relieved. "I didn't even think to bring any or consider needing it until this minute. You need some as well," she said to Karl, calling attention to his fair skin.

"It looks like we're ready," Rob announced. "Let's go."

"Can Gretchen come?" Melanie asked as she looked around for the dog.

"Not today," Sven said firmly. "She's a lot of work on the beach. She's a scent hound and naturally wants to follow all those delicious beach smells. She won't stay still. Right now, she's taking her morning nap in her kennel."

"Okay, then," Rob said impatiently, "let's go."

The walk to the beach wasn't far. From where Sven's street intersected with the beach road, it was only a little over two blocks to the public beach access that ran along the extreme edge of the island. There was a concrete sidewalk poured alongside the massive boulders that formed a breakwater for the inlet that lead to the port of West Palm Beach. As they walked along the sidewalk, Karl looked across to the island of Palm Beach just across the inlet. In the distance, he could make out the pink bulk of the Breakers Hotel. Singer Island lay immediately to the north of its expensive, privileged neighbor, while between the two islands the inlet teemed with jet skis and pleasure boats of many sizes, both sail and motor craft.

The weather was wonderful. Nearly eighty degrees, with a slight but steady onshore breeze that protected them from the sun's heat, it promised to be a postcard-perfect morning. The little group made their way east to the beach, leaving the concrete walkway before it dead-ended at the old and ugly sand-pumping station at the inlet's intersection with the sea. Today, as it had for years, Karl noted, the sand-pumping station served as a diving platform for teenagers who ignored the posted signage warning them off the structure. As a teen, Karl had jumped off the building's projecting framework himself. That unique diving platform and a different variety of cute young women had lured him as a youth to Singer Island from the familiar beach a few blocks from his parents' house.

Karl smiled to himself, recalling some of those teenage adventures, as he walked along the beach to a spot Rob decided was perfect for them to set up residence. As the others unfurled their towels into the breeze and stooped to settle them on the sand, Karl caught Caroline's eye and said, "Watch this." He knelt in the sand and proceeded to dig out a shallow hole with sides that sloped at comfortable angles both toward the sea and the island behind them. He smoothed the spoil from his small dig into two hillocks on the sides of the hole, and then carefully spread his towel over the void. After brushing off his knees and shins, he sat into what was now a comfortable chair of sand.

"Oooh, that's nice," Caroline said, looking over at him from her flat towel. "Make me one. Please?"

Smiling, Karl got to his feet and offered her his hand to help her stand. Once she was up and out of the way, he made quick work out of creating a sand chair for her as well. "There," Karl said triumphantly as he finished arranging her towel over the hole and its sides for her.

Karl returned to his own improvised beach chair, and Caroline sank into hers with a satisfied sigh. "This is amazingly comfortable," she said luxuriously. "My back and legs are completely supported. The only thing is; I can't turn over."

"Why would you want to?" Karl asked. "Look at that view of the water! And we won't be out here long enough for you to be worried about tanning evenly."

She sighed happily, leaned across the short distance between them, and gave him a kiss on the cheek. "Thanks!"

As Karl wriggled his hips to enlarge the hole his butt rested in, Rob appeared in front of them, extending two large plastic cups, each with a generous offering of iced vodka and orange juice. "If you get munchy," he said as they took their drinks from him, "I've got some peanuts, cashews, and packages of peanut butter and crackers in the cooler. Just let me know," he said as they took their drinks from him.

Karl took a sip of the drink and found it stronger than he'd antici-pated. "Rob, are you trying to get us drunk fast?" he asked with a laugh.

Rob sat cross-legged on his own blanket between Caroline and Melanie and iced two more cups before filling them with the screw-driver mixture from a plastic milk jug. "They may seem strong now, but the ice will melt quickly out here and dilute it for you," he said.

"You sound like you have experience doing this," Caroline told him.

"Oh, I've lived in Florida all my life," Rob told her. "When I was a kid, my family spent nearly every weekend on the beach. My dad liked surf-cast fishing, and my mom loved the sun. It's a habit we're all paying for now with regular trips to the dermatologist."

"Have you had problems with skin cancer?" Caroline asked him with concern.

"Oh, yeah," Rob told her. "I lathered up in SPF 60 before we left the house."

"Me, too," Sven ventured from his blanket next to Melanie at the end of their row. "While we tan beautifully, people from northern Europe were never meant to live this close to the equator."

Karl scanned his own chest, belly, and legs. While he did have an occasional freckle on his thighs, he was mostly free of moles and dark spots. However, he could feel the southern sun's intensity through the onshore breeze. It was intense despite the fact it was still technically winter. Spring officially remained a couple of weeks away. "Mel, you'd better pass me that sunscreen when you're done," he said. "I don't want to spend the next week with a burn and peeling skin."

Melanie smoothed the lotion over her shins, taking care to cover the tops of her feet, before she passed the bottle to her mother. Caroline, who had naturally darker skin thanks to her Native-American heritage, rubbed only a little lotion onto her face, shoulders, décolletage, and thighs. "I don't burn," she said. "I turn red, then brown. I've always been lucky that way, thanks to some distant relatives who were Cherokee."

Karl took the bottle and applied the lotion generously over himself. Thinking how miserable a sunburn would make him in a buttoned shirt and tie in the coming week, he didn't neglect his neck.

At last, everyone was lubricated inside and out with the aid of Rob's strong drinks and Melanie's sunscreen. Conversation hit a lull as each became absorbed in their own thoughts. The only sounds were the persistent lapping of the shore break, the gulls passing overhead with their harsh laughter and calls, the shrill laughter and happy shrieks of small children, and snatches of songs from a hundred different radios and portable stereos. Offshore, a few brave souls chanced the chilly surf in the turquoise sea.

Karl sighed in contentment and reached for Caroline's hand, lightly lacing his fingers with hers on the warm sand between them. He felt his mind slowly empty under the warm sun. Images of his father and mother chased themselves behind his closed lids. Whenever thoughts of them turned troubling, he consciously replaced them with pleasant memories of them when they had been much younger.

Karl's memories took him to the beaches in New Jersey, where his father had driven them for Saturday or Sunday outings from Wildwood all the way down to Cape May. He thought of playing Skee-Ball and the rides on the boardwalk. He remembered the icy-cold, dark blue water of the northern ocean and the way his mother would brood over his blue lips when he'd run from the water's edge back to the blanket they all shared. His father would take him out beyond the breakers to wave-jump, encouraging him to swim as he himself strode along the bottom until they reached the sandbar. There his father would hold his hands and encourage him to jump up into the uplift of the swells. Karl remembered how safe he had felt as his father would gather him to his chest while Karl clenched his waist with his knees and they rose with the waves, bobbing in the water like happy seals.

"Hey," Sven said, rousing Karl from his drowsiness as he squatted beside him.

Karl opened his eyes and looked at his brother's smiling face. "Hey yourself," he said with a returning smile.

"Did I wake you?" Sven asked.

"No," Karl told him. "I was just far away, thinking about being a little kid up in Jersey."

Sven admitted, "So was I, but I was remembering being down here on the beach with you."

"We did spend a lot of time together on the beach in the neighborhood, didn't we?" Karl reminisced.

"You taught me how to swim in the ocean," Sven reminded him. "It's funny. Because of you, I've never been frightened of swimming in the sea."

"I did that?" Karl asked him doubtfully.

"Oh, yeah, it was you," Sven said without hesitating. "You used to take me wave-jumping when I was small. Don't you remember?"

"I can't believe you were thinking of that," Karl said with a chuckle. "I was just remembering Dad doing the same thing with me."

"Dad did?" Sven said doubtfully. "I thought it was a game you made up."

"No," Karl said gently. "Dad used to take me wave-jumping up until I was about ten years old. He used to hold me and throw me up in the air sometimes. Or let me stand on his thighs and dive into the swells."

"That's what you did with me," Sven told him. "Dad never went swimming with me. It was you who taught me all of that stuff."

Karl did remember playing with Sven in the ocean when his brother was small. He marveled at the idea that his parents allowed him such responsibility for Sven when he was so little. "I guess I did. I must have been pretty sure of myself, to take you out so far when you were that little."

"I never thought anything about it," Sven said. "I trusted you completely in the deep water. You used to hold me and hug me and wipe my face when I breathed in seawater and got choked," Sven said admiringly. "I remember how safe I felt with you holding on to me. I felt like I could do anything. No, I felt like *you* could do anything."

"How old do you suppose you were?" Karl wondered.

"Maybe about six, seven, tops," Sven said. "But I can remember being younger than that and you taking me out in the water. You were so much bigger than I was. You were a great brother."

In his mind's eye, Karl found a younger Sven's blue eyes and towheaded delight at being out with his big brother. It all seemed so long ago, but now it seemed only a heartbeat away. Sven now sat on the sand beside him, his hair shining in the sun, and those same blue eyes gathered in a shallow fan of wrinkles at their corners as he squinted in the strong sunlight.

"I missed you so much when you went away to school," Sven continued. "I used to go sit in your room. When it didn't smell like you anymore, then I knew you were really gone and you wouldn't be coming back to stay, at least not like before."

"I had no idea you missed me so much," Karl said, touched deeply by Sven's recollection.

"Oh, yeah, you were a big deal for me." Sven smiled. "Our family was so small—once you were gone, it was just me and Mom and Dad. Things changed once you left. Dad was really working hard and he was remote and irritable when he was home. Mom was pretty cool; still, it wasn't ever the same without you."

"I was just so much older," Karl offered by way of an explanation. "I was just doing what I was supposed to, I guess."

"Oh, I know that. Your life took you so far away is all." Sven paused then asked, "What made you choose to go to NC State?"

Karl smiled. "I wanted to go to their engineering school, for one. Also, I didn't get accepted at Georgia Tech. But I guess the truth of it is I wanted to go *away* to school. I wanted to go back to where there were seasons. Hell, I don't know . . . it just worked out that my life took me away from home. I'm not unusual in that respect."

"Yes, of course," Sven said. "I just wanted you to know I missed you, that's all. You shouldn't ever think you don't matter just because you live so far away."

"Thanks, Sven,"

"Um, before the day gets busy and gone," Sven continued, "I want to thank you for dropping everything to come down this weekend. Speaking for all of us, we needed you."

"It's not a big deal to come for a visit, Sven," Karl said. "I would have come sooner if I'd known things were so out of hand. I don't know that I've managed to make any of it better, but I'm glad I came."

"Well, you have made it better," Sven said emphatically. "It's not that you did anything big. But it's been good to have you to talk it all out with. You've helped me see some things that were right in front of my face but that I couldn't seem to recognize on my own."

"Really?" Karl asked. "What? I haven't been much help."

Sven glanced across at Rob lying on his stomach with his arms over his head. Sven lowered his voice and said, "Talking with you about me and Rob making some changes was a big help. I just want you to know I'm not going to get all clingy and needy or anything, but I would like to continue talking with you, get together more in the future. I'm embarrassed to admit it, but I still miss you, you know?"

"And I miss you," Karl said, realizing how much he meant it. "I'll admit it's easy to get caught up in the day-to-day stuff at home, and to make other things in my life a priority, but I promise you, we'll try to stay in touch better, okay?"

"That's what I'm talking about," Sven said. "I'm just going to call more and let you know what's going on. Maybe fly up some weekend. I'd love to see your and Caro's new town house."

"I have an idea," Karl said impulsively. "Why don't you and Rob plan to come for Christmas this year? I know it's early to be thinking about the holidays, but they'll be here before we know it. I mentioned the idea to Dad and he wasn't eager about it at all. He thinks traveling with Mom will be impossible by then, and to tell you the truth, I think he'd rather be home in his own bed. But there's no reason you and Rob couldn't come. We could start a new family tradition. If Melanie's in New York, we're halfway between you and her. Why don't you think about it and talk it over with Rob?"

Sven looked at him like a happy child and said, "You don't know how much I'd like that, Karl. Pretty soon Mom's going to be gone. Dad and I aren't ever going to be close, so you're my family," he ended simply.

"Yes, it's true. You're my family, too, remember. We'll work at it, okay?" Karl said with a catch in his throat. As he nervously drank his now watery screwdriver, Sven touched his shoulder briefly and stood. As he did, his knees cracked loudly.

Sven laughed at the sound of his own creaks and said, "I'm getting old."

"No, you're not." Karl laughed. "Because that would mean I'm getting *really* old, and I've decided I'm not going to get old—not like Dad is, at least."

"God forbid," Sven said with a chuckle. "We'll let him be one of a kind. Deal?"

"Deal," Karl said as he shielded his eyes and looked up at his little brother.

Sven nodded and stepped away toward his place at the other end of the group.

Karl felt Caroline's fingers tighten around his own and he looked at her questioningly.

"Thank you," she whispered.

Karl understood that her thanks were on Sven's behalf, not her own. In reply, he lifted their hands from the sand and kissed the back of hers lightly before untwining their fingers and letting go. He closed his eyes, and immediately an old forgotten image appeared in his mind. He was standing chest-deep in the ocean, with Sven's skinny little-boy knees digging into his belly and back. He held him easily on his hip and watched as his teeth chattered against the cool wind rushing over them. Sven looked out to the horizon and turned his head, suddenly flinging stinging seawater from the tips of his wet, matted hair. He looked Karl in the eye and laughed as the oncoming swells approached. Karl bent his knees, submerging them both to the level of Sven's chin, and jumped as the swell hit them and carried them high. Sven laughed with joy and Karl smiled and smiled.

Lulled by the liquor, the sun's languor, and the susurrous crash of the waves, Karl soon dozed off. There was too much of the experience of this beach he wanted to enjoy to trade for the possibility of the beach of his early-morning dreams. If the entire weekend had been spent under such a generous sun and peaceful, ambient sounds that surrounded him on this Sunday mid-afternoon, he would not have been so tired. As it was, both his body and his spirit were fatigued by the demands his family had placed on him. However, the fatigue was gentle, not bitter. He had grown to expect this unfamiliar weight. Karl realized how much family weight he had been free of for so long, living hundreds of miles away. He had surprised himself by how easily he had taken on the burden. Before this weekend, he would not have thought himself capable of so much empathy.

"Guys," Sven said loudly. "It's quarter of one. I hate to be the head dyke and get you marching, but if you want showers and any lunch, we need to be getting back to the house."

Rob sat up and rubbed his eyes like a little boy. "I'll shower outside and let the family use the bath in the house," he offered.

"I'm going to do the same," Sven said.

"Oh, I hate the thought of chasing you out of your bathroom," Caroline worried.

"Don't," Melanie said with a laugh. "You haven't seen the outdoor shower. Can you say 'Zen-like retreat'?"

"It's that nice, huh?" Caroline replied dubiously.

"Girl," Rob said, "you don't think two gay guys are going to shower under a garden hose, do you? Sven and I built an outdoor spa."

Karl roused himself from his silent torpor and looked at Caroline. "Why don't we be adventurous and claim the outdoor shower for ourselves?"

"You are a wickedly interesting husband, you know that," Caroline said, rising to the bait. "I just might take you up on that. Is it big enough for two?" she asked Rob.

Rob grinned at her and nodded. "Private enough, too."

Caroline stood up effortlessly and said, "Okay, Karl, you're on. We have first dibs," she announced.

"You *go*, Mom," Melanie cheered, and stood as well. "I'll use the bath, then."

Karl stood a little unsteadily and was once again beset by a head rush. It was starting to annoy him—this constant disorienting sensation on rising. Without saying anything to anyone, he made a mental note to give his doctor a call. He doubted it was anything dire, but he wanted to be sure of it. He was, after all, getting old, he thought. He shook his head to dismiss that thought and replaced it with the novel idea of sharing the outdoor shower with his wife. "You're on," he said to Caroline with a smile.

Caro had noticed his momentary unsteadiness, and concern crossed her face like the shadow of a gull. Wordlessly, she stooped and retrieved Karl's and her own beach towel, and walked a few paces away to shake them free of sand. The others followed suit, and soon they were padding across the notably warmer sand to the concrete walk along the inlet.

Karl felt sorry to be leaving the beach. As the midday light spread lovingly over the long stretch of sand and surf, he felt cheated, envying the people there who continued their beach day uninterrupted by imminent demands and flight schedules. He took a moment to absorb the sounds and smells and sights all around him, breathing in a deep appreciation of the place. Warmed by his time in the sun and mellowed by the drink and the comfort of the company, he felt some of the sense of well-being from his morning dream return to him. He hung back a bit to wait for Sven, and as his brother caught up with him he told him, "This really is a remarkable place you live in."

"I know," Sven said with a grin. "Eight years ago, I found this place and thought I'd better grab on to it while I could still afford it. You would not believe the rate at which it's appreciated."

"Oh, yes, I would," Karl said ruefully. "Do you think you'll have to sell it to make the move to New York?"

Sven sighed. "That's something Rob and I will have to discuss. Actually, his condo will bring a lot more just because it's on the ocean in Palm Beach. But getting a place in Manhattan big enough for the both of us is a forbidding prospect. Real estate prices there are insane."

"Wouldn't you be better off getting a pied-à-terre in Manhattan and keeping your place here?" Karl asked. "I'm kicking myself for never visiting you before. I had no idea what I was missing."

"Well, you're welcome anytime," Sven said eagerly. "It's not that expensive to fly down for a long weekend, you know. I'd love to have you whenever you can come."

Karl looked around and smiled. "I hope you mean that, because I intend to come back. And consider this: I've got a little money stashed away. I'd have to talk to Caroline, of course, but maybe—if you can't afford to keep this place on your own—maybe we could discuss the possibility of buying a share of your house. That would give you some cash to work with and also help you keep the house. Just file the idea away for future thought, okay?"

Sven gave him a loving smile and a vigorous nod of his head in reply.

As they walked back to Sven's house, Karl considered his impromptu suggestion. The more he thought about investing in a share of Sven's beach house, the more he liked the idea. Every year, he had lost his vacation time because he never took it. If he could coordinate leave with any of Sven's frequent buying trips to Europe, he and Caroline could easily come down several times a year, whether Sven and Rob were there or not. In many ways, the idea made a lot of sense.

Once they returned to the house, Sven volunteered to make sandwiches while Caroline, Karl, and Melanie showered. Giggling like children, Karl and Caroline gathered clean towels, a change of clothes, and their bath items before making their way to the outdoor shower, adjacent to the rear of the house on the end opposite the kitchen. There, Rob and Sven had extended the patio and enclosed two sides with a six-foot stucco wall. Just off the patio was a small dressing area, with low benches along each side and hooks set into the wall for clothes and towels. Beyond the dressing room was the shower itself, featuring a large overhead spray and a showerhead on either wall. Brightly colored tiles were set into the stucco, and the concrete floor was covered with a mosaic tile in yellow and blue.

With suddenly shy smiles, Caroline and Karl stripped and stepped into the shower. Blessedly, there was both hot and cold water. Caroline waited in a corner until Karl had adjusted the temperature of the over-head shower and stepped under its rainfall. Blissfully, he turned his hot face up into the warm water and rinsed away the sweat and sunscreen before reaching to pull Caroline under the water. For a moment they simply clung to each other, enjoying the rush of the water and the beaming of the sun overhead as well. Caroline turned Karl as gently as she would a child and picked up the bar of soap to lather him all over. Once she'd accomplished that to his obvious pleasure, he returned the favor. Again they came together in an embrace as they rinsed off under the generous showerhead. They took turns shampooing each other's hair and rinsing again until they were clean and dripping. Finally, they took turns drying each other off. While there was every opportunity for the experience to turn erotic, Karl felt deeply satisfied and nurtured by the simple intimacy of the shared shower.

As they dressed together in the area off the shower, Caroline traded a relaxed, happy smile with Karl and said, "I could get used to living like this."

"Sven's told me we can come back whenever we want. Could you picture us staying here, just the two of us, while he and Rob are off on one of their trips?" Karl ventured happily.

Caroline sighed with pleasure as she pulled her blouse on over her head. "That would be heavenly."

As she turned to the mirror over the low bench and combed her wet hair, Karl said, "We just have to make it happen."

Caroline found his face in her mirror and said emphatically, "We will."

At last, dressed and hungry, they left the outdoor shower and went into the kitchen. Rob and Sven were finishing their sandwiches and smiled and nodded as they came in. Sven swallowed and said, "So, how do you like our outdoor spa?"

"I'd shower out there every day," Caroline said as she pulled out a chair from the table and sat down.

"Your sandwiches are on the counter." Sven pointed. "Rob, looks like we're up next."

Rob swallowed the last of a glass of milk and stood, taking Sven's paper plate and used napkin to the trash along with his own. "I'll get the towels and shampoo," he said as he made his way toward the rear of the house.

Karl picked up two paper plates holding chicken sandwiches with lettuce and tomato on the side. He carried them to the table and sat one plate before Caroline before taking a seat himself.

"What can I get you to drink?" Sven asked as he stood.

"Just water, please, for both of us," Caroline told him.

Sven walked to the refrigerator and pulled out two bottles of water. As he put them on the table, Rob reappeared with their towels and a bottle of shampoo. "Melanie's plate is ready, too, whenever she gets in," Sven told them. "I hope the sandwiches are okay."

Both chewing with obvious relish, Karl and Caroline nodded.

"We'll be back in a few minutes," Rob said as he stepped past the table and opened the door for Sven. Together, they went outside to shower.

Karl looked at Caroline and raised his eyebrows knowingly as he chewed.

Caroline managed a sly smile in return.

"What are you two smirking about?" Melanie asked as she strode into the kitchen, fully dressed, with carefully dried hair.

"I was just thinking today was the first time I've washed someone else's hair since you learned to bathe yourself," Karl told his daughter and laughed. "Your sandwich is on the counter and there are drinks in the refrigerator," he added.

Caroline took the last bite of her sandwich and chewed thoughtfully for a moment before she swallowed and said, "Mel, now I know why you were always so eager to come visit your uncles. This little house is wonderful, and the town is like something out of the 1950s. I love it here."

Melanie picked up her sandwich plate and joined her parents at the table. "I love it, too."

"Don't you want something to drink?" her mother asked her.

"Not right now," Melanie answered around a mouthful of her sandwich. "I'm starved."

"I wish we could just stay here until we have to go to the airport," Karl said wistfully. "I really dread going back over to Mom and Dad's."

"Why is that?" Caroline asked him carefully.

Karl sighed. "It's all just so final, in a way. This will be the last time I can ever go *home*."

Caroline reached across the table and touched his hand. "Knowing that must be difficult. But if you think about it, that house hasn't been your home for a long time."

"I know," Karl said. "But somewhere, deep inside, when you say *home*, you automatically think of the place your mother and father live."

"That's true," Melanie said. "I think of home as being where you two are."

"That's funny," Caroline said thoughtfully. "I don't feel that way at all. When I think of home, I think of where you two are."

"Maybe that's a Mom thing," Melanie said.

"Well, they had to leave the house sooner or later," Karl said sadly. "But there's more to it than that. I just hate the idea of going back and facing the fact that they are both so frail and so close to being gone. I just don't want to say good-bye."

Caroline nodded sympathetically but said nothing. Melanie

looked at him, but she had nothing to say, either. Karl took a sip of water and looked at the clock on the stove. The day was slipping away fast. The momentum of the visit had swept him to this point of stillness, and that soon would be gone as well.

They wouldn't have more than an hour at his parents' house before it would be time to leave for the airport. An hour was not such a long time to endure, nor was it sufficient time to try and convey what he was feeling. And what Karl was feeling at the moment was inchoate and unformed. He pictured his mother and father curled together in the golden light of their afternoon nap, as he had left them on Friday. At the time he had thought his heart would break at the knowledge that they were so utterly alone in that quiet house. Soon he would be leaving them there again.

But they wouldn't be there for long. Their imminent move to Palladian Gardens was heartening to him. Somehow, he thought they must be looking forward to it with some degree of excitement and pleasure. His father had spoken of the pending move as if he would be on permanent vacation. His mother spoke of it not at all. She knew which wing of the building would be her final home, and there was nothing to look forward to there. While Frank planned to spend his remaining years in front of a sixty-inch LCD TV, Annike faced years of wandering in the past, if she was aware of anything at all. Karl felt he couldn't leave them, but he knew there was no way he could stay. In the truest sense of it, they were leaving him, and about that he had no say.

"We'd better finish getting dressed and get our bags zipped up," Caroline suggested.

Karl nodded and stood. Like Rob, he gathered his lunch things and dumped them in the trash. "I'm ready to go home," he said. They all knew which home he meant at that moment. It sat waiting, a two-hour flight away.

19

WHEN SVEN PULLED his SUV up to Frank and Annike's drive, Melanie had to brake sharply to keep from running Annike's car into the back of it. Karl instinctively threw out an arm to brace himself against the dash as the car lurched with its own momentum before it came to a full hard stop. Before Karl could ask Melanie what was going on, a Range Rover with a realtor's magnetic sign backed leisurely into the street from the drive alongside Sven's car. Karl caught a glimpse of a young woman and two small boys before their curious faces pulled away.

Sven turned his big vehicle into the drive and Melanie cut her wheels hard to the left in order to swing wide and pull up on the drive beside the SUV. Annike and Frank stood on the front porch, waving at them as they all unbuckled themselves and got out of the two cars.

"Your timing is perfect," Frank called out as they closed their doors.

"That was the Lawrences," Annike explained. "This is the third time they've come to look at the house."

"Maybe this time they'll make an offer," Frank said as his family joined them on the porch.

"They have two small boys," Annike said wistfully. "It would be so nice to sell this house to another young family just starting out like we were."

"We weren't just starting out," Frank said truculently. "We'd been married for fourteen years when we moved into this house."

"Yes, but with Sven just an infant, and you starting a new job, in a whole new state, it was like starting over," Annike replied firmly.

"Hello, you two," Sven said with a smile. "Mom, are you feeling better?"

"Yes, dear," she replied sweetly. "I was a little foggy this morning, but I'm feeling better now. Come in. All of you."

"Why don't we sit in the sunroom?" Frank said as he led them through the house. Once they walked into the bright room, he went straight to claim his favorite chair and sat down.

"Can I get anyone anything to drink?" Annike offered.

Karl looked around the room and watched as Rob, Sven, Caroline, and Melanie found places to sit. In turn, each of them declined Annike's offer. "We just ate lunch a little while ago," Karl said as he waited for his mother to sit.

Annike looked at her oldest son fondly and said, "Karl, would you come with me for a little while?"

Karl cocked his head and looked at his mother curiously but said, "Sure. Where are we going?"

Annike addressed the room, saying, "You won't mind if I steal a few minutes alone with Karl, will you?"

"Where are you going?" Frank demanded.

"For a walk around the block," Annike said evenly. In reply to her husband's concerned look, she said, "We won't be gone long."

Frank nodded and turned to Melanie. "So, how did you enjoy church this morning? Father Raul is pretty good, isn't he?"

Before Karl could hear Melanie's response, his mother was by his side and taking his hand. "Come," she said. Karl obliged her with a smile and allowed himself to be led back through the house to the front door. As he opened the door and stepped back to let his mother pass, she let go of his hand and said, "Your father told me all of you came to church this morning, even Rob. I'm sorry I wasn't quite all there. I really appreciate you coming."

Karl stepped through the door and closed it behind them. "I actually went for your benefit, but it turned out I was glad I did. I guess if you're brought up in the church, you miss it as an adult if you get out of the habit of going."

Annike walked down the narrow path to the drive with Karl following behind her. Once they reached the street and Karl joined her at her side, she said, "I'm pleased you got something out of mass for your own sake."

"It was an odd feeling," he told her honestly. "But I felt some of the comfort you promised."

Annike looked up at him and nodded her head. As she began to stroll down the street, she said, "Thank you for accompanying me on this little walk. I wanted to have some time alone with you to say good-bye."

"I'll see you again, Mom," Karl promised. "I'm already thinking about coming back as soon as you and Dad get settled in your apart-ment."

"Don't," Annike said calmly. "I'd rather you remember me as you've seen me today, right now, not when I've become an animated doll."

"Mom, I'd never see you that way," Karl protested.

"Yes, you would," Annike said plainly. "I won't be myself soon. And I want to save you from going through that grim period. Look around now. It's a lovely afternoon with flowers and sunshine. Please remember me here. Don't visit me when I'm drooling and vacant."

"I am so frightened for you," Karl managed to say. "I'll have to know you're okay. I'll need to know you are not frightened or sad or . . ."

"Karl," Annike said sharply. "It won't be like that for me. If it's going to be anything like what I've been experiencing, it's quite peaceful. It's not unpleasant. What is unpleasant is the struggle to stay, to make myself understand or to be understood. I'll be okay, I promise you."

"You have no idea how much I want to believe that," Karl said. He stared down the sleepy Sunday-afternoon street and sighed.

"You can believe it, my dear. It's true," Annike told him. "All I have to do is let go. Your father will make sure they give me the best care available, and he won't be satisfied until he sees it for himself. He'll only be a building away. I know he'll care for me as he always has."

"But what about me?" Karl demanded. "You are still my mother, even after you're unaware that I'm even there."

"Son, you've more than met my expectations of you all your life," Annike said soothingly. "You are and have always been a wonderful son. I know that as long as I live and after I'm gone, you'll think of me and love me, but your responsibility for me has come to an end."

"I'm not ready to hear that," Karl said miserably. "I can't pretend you're dead. That's too much for you to ask. Never to see you again, or hug you? No, Mama. You can't ask that of me."

Annike turned the corner of the street and made her way on alone as Karl's steps faltered and he fell behind. He watched her walking away, her back held ramrod straight and her shoulders back. "Mom," he called out.

Annike continued walking but motioned for him to catch up.

Karl quickened his pace and caught up to her in three long strides. "Mom, slow down," he said earnestly.

Annike laughed and turned her head to look up at him. "No, Karl, you must keep up. Life goes by so quickly, and if you stop to linger or regret, it goes on without you. I don't want to leave you with any regrets, do you understand? You have nothing to regret as far as I am concerned. You have been a joy to me all of your life. You've given me a wonderful granddaughter and you've kept all of your promises to me. Please, Karl, let me go on now without any regrets of my own."

"I'm not ready to tell you good-bye," Karl said honestly. "As long as I can still see you, and hope that you'll know me, it won't be like you're gone."

Annike kept her even pace along the street, not saying anything for a while as she looked at the familiar houses along the way. Finally, she stopped in front of a house rather like her own. The garage door was open to reveal a cheerful mess of Jet Skis, bicycles, tools, and an inflated boat. In the front yard were abandoned brightly colored toys and a cheerful banner showing an Easter bunny with pastel-colored eggs. "Do you remember the Mazzatellis? There was Tony and Lois. They had their four kids; I think Scotty was your age."

It took Karl a moment, but he did recall the family. Scotty Mazzatelli had been someone he played basketball with, just another kid from the neighborhood, but he did remember him. "Yes, I knew Scotty, they lived here, didn't they?"

"Yes," his mother said as she studied the house. "Tony died six years ago. Liver cancer. The kids are scattered all over the country. Lois lived here after Tony passed away. I used to see her working in her yard when I went for my walks. We talked. We knew each other from church. Lois was in the choir at ten-thirty mass; she had a wonderful voice."

"And what happened? Did she move?" Karl asked with minimal interest. He had no idea why his mother had picked out this house to reminisce about the neighbors, but he decided to humor her.

"Well, like I said, I was used to seeing her out in the yard—then I didn't anymore. We started going to eight o'clock mass, so I didn't see her in church. I didn't think anything about it until about six months ago, when I heard what happened to her." Annike paused and looked Karl in the face before she continued. "One of her kids, the older boy, I think, came home to see her and found her living in filth. She had been smearing her own feces on the walls. God only knows what she'd been eating or how she'd been functioning. It turns out Lois had dementia, too. Her son put her in a nursing home, but she didn't live long after that," Annike concluded.

"Why are you telling me this, Mom?" Karl asked sadly.

Slowly, Annike began to walk again, and Karl followed along beside her. "You want to keep things as they were. That's not going to happen. Who's to say I won't become as bad as Lois, playing with my own shit. Do you think I want you to see that? Do you think I want you to see me that way?"

"No, Mama. I know you don't want that," Karl answered her, frustrated. "But it doesn't have to be that way. No matter what, I'll still see you as my mom. I'll still love you as much and need you as much, no matter what."

Annike swept her arm in front of her and said, "You walk down these streets in the old neighborhood and you say, look at how it's changed. The young people are moving in. I walk these blocks and I see ghosts. Bob and Kathy DeSantos were killed by a burglar. Cancer. Strokes. Suicide. They've all come through here. Frank and I are among the last ones left who moved here in the beginning," Annike said unwaveringly.

"So are you glad you're moving to Palladian Gardens, then? Away from all these ghosts?" Karl asked her gently.

"No," Annike said firmly. "I'm telling you I'm glad I'm losing my mind. I am tired, Karl. I am ready to die," she said simply.

"Oh, Mama," Karl pleaded, "don't give up on us yet."

Annike laughed. "I'm not giving up on *you*," she said firmly. "I'm just giving up on myself. Now, listen to me carefully, Son. I am lucky to have the chance to tell you the things I want to tell you. Many of these other people never got the chance to say good-bye to their loved ones. I want you to know I love you very much, but I don't want you to worry or grieve for me. Everything is going to be alright. Do you hear me?"

"I hear you, Mama," he said. "But I can't say good-bye, not today," his voice quivered and he found himself slipping into a comfortless feeling of abandonment and fear. Unapologetically, he felt himself begin to cry as he said, "Don't leave me, Mama."

They turned another gentle loop that brought them back to Annike's street and within sight of the house. Annike stopped and reached out her arms to her son. Karl stepped into his mother's embrace, unembarrassed by the emotion they displayed on the street. "I love you so much, Mama," he whispered. "You have been a wonderful mother and a friend. Can't you understand that I can't just hug you good-bye now and act like you've died? There are so many more things to tell you, to share with you. Don't push me away."

In reply, she held him tighter against her small frame, and then at last she did push him away and stood, smiling up at him. "I thank you for everything you've said, Karl. But where I'm going, you can't come. I let you go so you could become a man. Now you must learn to let me go so I can be free to slip away. Everything will be okay. Don't worry," she said again. "Promise me?"

"I promise you, Mama," Karl told her as he wiped his eyes awkwardly with the back of his hand. "But you know I'm lying, don't you?"

"Only time will tell," Annike said, "but I will never know, will I? Please be the man I know you are and keep your promise," she said and turned to walk the rest of the way home, knowing Karl was following along just behind.

Karl let her lead the way back to the house. He tried to find the wisdom in his mother's fiercely independent strides to the end of her consciousness and her life. He thought it would be more painful to cling to her once she became a shell of the woman she had been. The final good-bye could be years away, and the thought of all the good-byes in between was like the fraying of a rope that held them together. He watched her straight, resolved back as she walked up the pathway to the front porch, and he found it in himself to appreciate her attempt to sever the tie cleanly to spare them both the abrasion of living on and on without any resolution. But he knew he would not be able to let go so simply. For all that he liked the elegant, concrete solutions to complex questions, life didn't always accommodate his inclination.

As Annike reached the front door, she stopped and stood, waiting for him with a smile. He marveled at her understanding of him. In her own way, she had freed him from the years of regret he would have experienced otherwise. In this way, he understood where he got his own desire for the simple but apt answer. She had handed him his future, free and clear of emotional debt. Karl found himself taking the final steps to her side with self-assurance. He understood. In reply, he placed his hand on the doorknob and bent swiftly to kiss her cheek. He then said in his long, unspoken first tongue, "*Tack själv, Mama. Du veta hur mycket JAG älska du. Minas så pass.*" *Thanks, Mama. You know how much I love you. Remember that.* Then he opened the door for her and watched as she passed him.

Once inside the house, it was easy to find the others by the loud discussion raging in the sunroom. As they drew closer, they heard Melanie say, "Gramps, you can't deny this is a manufactured war. Bush and his cronies had every intention of going to war with Iraq when he entered office. He simply lied to the nation about why."

"Melanie, it doesn't matter whether there were weapons of mass destruction or not. Saddam Hussein is a friend of terrorists and he maintained a terrorist regime. The end justifies the means. We freed the Iraqi people, and I believe with all my heart that all men yearn to be free," Frank countered.

"But you're looking at the Iraqis like they have American concepts of personal freedom, and they don't," Melanie replied heatedly. "Americans can't just go over there and go, 'Poof! You're free! Now you can be like us.' It doesn't work that way, Gramps."

"Well, now at least they have that chance," Frank retorted.

"Yes, but how many American lives is it going to cost to help them keep that chance?" Melanie asked.

"That's why we have to stay the course and get the job done," Frank said doggedly.

Sven looked at Karl beseechingly. "I have a headache," he said quietly.

Caroline stood and stretched. She looked at Annike and Karl and said, "This is like watching Fox News on cable. You haven't missed a thing."

"No! It's important," Melanie said firmly. "Not talking about issues like this is what's led the American people into another Vietnam."

"Iraq is nothing like Vietnam," Frank insisted.

Annike strolled into the room and looked at Melanie and Frank in turn. "Let's agree to disagree, okay? Soon it will be time to say good-bye, and I don't want this ugliness to spoil what time we have left."

"I agree," Rob said quietly from his place on the sofa beside Sven. "I think the American people will have their say about all this in November. Until then, we're stuck with what we have in Washington. The best we can do is hope for common sense to prevail."

Frank snorted and started to say something, but Karl broke in, saying, "I think both Melanie and Dad are very well read on the issues. I see some validity in both arguments. But I agree with Mom. I think you guys should settle down."

"You're always the rational one," Frank said. "Your grades and your draft lottery number kept you out of Vietnam; otherwise, I think you'd be more inclined to my point of view."

"Oh, Dad's always in the middle of the road," Melanie said dismissively.

"Speaking of the road," Sven said, and glanced at his watch. "We need to be heading out pretty soon."

Frank lowered his feet from his recliner and pushed himself up. "Melanie, young lady, you're young, and that makes you liberal. But I have to hand it to you, you can hold your own in a political discussion." He stepped over to his granddaughter and stooped to give her a kiss on the cheek.

Melanie lifted her arms and draped them around her grandfather's shoulders after accepting his kiss. "And you're old and make Rush Limbaugh look like a lightweight, but I still love you."

Frank grunted in reply and rose from her embrace with a look of affection. Turning to Karl, he said, "You think you could give me a few minutes like you did your mother?"

"Sure, Dad," Karl said. "Do you feel like a walk around the block, too?"

"No, a turn around the backyard is good enough for me," Frank said as he walked to the back door of the sunroom. "All of you excuse us, will you?"

"Sure thing, Frank," Caroline told him. "Talk him into another visit soon, will you?"

Frank gave Caroline a nod and waited as Karl strode across the sunroom to join him. Once he met him at the door, Frank opened it and gently urged his son outdoors with a firm hand at the small of his back. Following Karl to the orange trees, Frank said, "You had a chance to talk to your mother?"

Karl stopped in the shade of the elderly trees and watched as his father joined him there, his face dappled with sunlight and shadow as the warm afternoon sun filtered down on them through the dark green leaves. "Yes, Dad. We had a good talk."

"I assume she told you she didn't want you to visit her once she's completely gone," Frank said calmly.

"Among other things, yes," Karl told him resignedly.

"Your mother has a lot of pride, Son," Frank said. "You know I'll want you to respect her wishes."

"And I won't give you a fight about it," Karl said evenly. "It's like she said, I'll prefer to remember her as she was today. Happy and in charge of things. She's something else."

"It's not just you," Frank said quietly. "She's thinking about the right time to tell Sven good-bye as well. And you know how hard that must be for her. The thing is, when you are on the edge of losing control, you get pretty set ideas about the things you still can make clear."

"The only way I can agree to not see her anymore is in knowing you'll make sure she's taken care of," Karl told him. "But if you go before she does, all bets are off. You know I can't just abandon her to that wing at Palladian Gardens and not be sure she's okay," Karl insisted.

Frank nodded and said, "I wouldn't expect any less of you. Like I've told you, you've got the powers of attorney. Don't be afraid to use them if you have to."

"I'll do what's right, Dad," Karl assured him.

"I don't do needy real well, Karl. I'm saying that straight up, I just want you to know I still want to see you once in a while, whenever you can make it. It doesn't have to be any special occasion," Frank said beseechingly.

"Dad, the comfortable years of going about my own business and neglecting my family except for once a year at Christmas are over now," Karl assured him. "I want to spend more time with you and with Sven. We're a small family. Losing Mom is going to knock us down to three quarters of what we have now. Just know I love you, and I won't abandon you."

"Thanks, Karl," Frank said humbly. "I'm resigned to how things are going to be. It'll be good to see you while the end creeps up on me. You don't know how I wish it would just all be over with sometimes."

"No, Dad," Karl said firmly. "I can't feel the way you're feeling, but I want you to know you don't have to go through it alone. I could throttle you for letting things get to this point before you called me down here. Don't do that to me again. Do you hear me?"

"Yeah," Frank said and chuckled. "I hear you."

"You're going to be okay until you move to Palladian Gardens, right?" Karl asked quietly.

"Oh, yeah," Frank said. "I might be able to get us in a little sooner if the house sells before June first."

"If you need any help, just let me know and I'll fly down," Karl told him.

"I promise I will, but I think we'll be just fine. Sven does a good job of looking out for us," Frank said.

"Ease up on him a little, Dad," Karl told him firmly. "It's not fair for you to take all your frustrations out on him. I know you don't care for how he lives his life, but he's accommodated you in it and he's a good son."

Frank looked toward the house and put his hands in his pockets. "All I can tell you is I'll try," he admitted honestly. "But we'll never be close. It's too late for that. And I don't want you to think that's ever going to be any different than what it is. I don't like how Sven lives his life—I never have—but he has been good to your mother and me. I can find it in myself to respect him."

Karl sighed and nodded his head. "Okay, Dad, at least that's something."

"It's you I loved," Frank admitted openly. "I am so proud of you."

"You know, Dad, this morning at the beach, I remembered you taking me wave-jumping at the shore way back when I was a little boy. I remember how safe I felt with you holding on to me. You taught me not to be afraid. I love you, old man. You were one hell of a good father to me."

Karl watched as his father's eyes filled with tears, but Frank turned his back to him before he wiped them away. "You need to be getting to the airport," Frank told him gruffly. "It's funny, but this time I don't want to let you go."

Karl took the two steps to his father, wrapped his arms around his shoulders, and held him close for a moment. "I'm glad I came, Dad. It's been a good weekend."

Frank patted his son's back awkwardly and simply said, "Thanks, boy."

With that, Karl dropped his arm and walked his father back to the house to begin the final farewells. For Karl, every step was fraught with meaning. It was the last time for so many things, from being in his old backyard to leaving his old home. But Karl's need and his nature wouldn't allow him to invest so much feeling in so much minutiae. He braced himself for the necessity of leaving and the hugs and lingering touches along the way. It was part of the process. But it wasn't the end by any means. Nothing ever ended without cutting marks that scarred though they were meant to heal with time and perspective.

20

ON THE WAY to the airport, wedged in the backseat of Sven's SUV along with Caroline and Melanie, Karl remained quiet. The highway provided him with the solace of motion. He was beginning to feel that if he lingered here under the southern Florida sun a moment longer, he would be trapped like a fly in a spiderweb, wound tightly in the past and waiting to be drained of life. The big vehicle carried him along, and he watched as the palm trees and subdivisions flowed past. The towering buildings along the coast looked like a bunch of shoeboxes upended to resemble a cityscape. Now that Karl was heading home, the whole place assumed the aura of a dream. And despite the friendly chatter in the car along the way, it was a dream he was ready to wake from.

Nearing the airport, Sven said, "Did you speak with Dad about when you thought you might be coming down again?"

Karl suppressed a sigh and replied, "We left it open. Dad was clear that it didn't have to be attached to any holiday. He just wants me to visit when I can."

"Well, we do, too," Rob said from the front seat. "You don't need a reason, and you know you always have a place to stay."

"Your home is so lovely," Caroline said, "I want to come back next week. You must be careful about offering an open invitation."

"You haven't even seen my place on Palm Beach," Rob replied slyly. "Next time you can stay there and soak up some of that social élan and experience my interior-design style. Sven's house is all him."

Melanie said, "Does that go for me and Drew? I'd love to get him to fly down with me. He needs a break from that Manhattan winter."

"Of course, darling," Rob said encouragingly. "But hopefully we'll be visiting you in your new place in Manhattan soon. We should plan to get together there so Sven and I can get some measurements and start work on turning Drew's bachelor pad into your first home."

"I'll email you as soon as I hear back about my interview," Melanie said. "But whether I get the job at Sotheby's or not, I'm planning to move up as soon as this semester is over."

"Rob, there's something else," Karl interrupted suddenly. "Talking to Sven this morning, I invited you and him to come to us for Christmas this year. I think it's time we started some new traditions. Caro and I would love to have you visit and to spoil you, as you've done us. I can't promise snow, but I can promise you a more seasonal Christmas up in Cary."

"That sounds good to me," Rob agreed.

"I think Johann could handle the shop for a few days by himself around Christmas," Sven said thoughtfully. "I don't see any reason why we shouldn't go ahead and commit. Then we can begin to schedule around it."

"Okay! Let's do it," Rob said as he turned in his seat to look back at Caroline. "Are you sure this is good for you?"

"Absolutely," Caroline said. "I really enjoyed staying home for Christmas last year rather than spending it in the airport. But it would be so nice to share it with you and Sven. If you'll come to our house, I promise you you'll enjoy yourselves."

"Oh, that works great for me as well," Melanie said. "If I've started a new job, I might have to stay in Manhattan, and I'll feel better knowing you all are being together for the holiday."

Karl settled back into his seat feeling satisfied. For all the airy promises to stay in touch and to keep the fraying ends of his family together, he felt like he had offered a positive, well-received solution—an event they could all look forward to, knowing that their lives and demands on their time in reality would work against all the other, less concrete promises he'd made. As for his father and mother, well, there was the long summer and fall ahead to find time for a visit. But in the hopeful enthusiasm of a family weekend, many plans seemed practical and workable that later dimmed to mere wishful thinking. At least their Christmas plans were a certainty, and that was a start.

As Sven pulled up to the departures curb at the airport, everyone spilled from the car with the rushed determination to be on their way. Sven opened the back door of the SUV and handed down their luggage quickly to Karl, leaving Rob to hug Caroline and Melanie good-bye. Sven turned to close the SUV as Rob dropped his arm over Karl's shoulder and squeezed his triceps. Karl turned to look at his brother's partner and found Rob looking at him with genuine affection.

"Thanks for talking some sense into Sven, Karl," Rob said quietly. "You've made a huge difference to us just by being here this weekend."

"I'm the older brother," Karl said. "It's my job to knock some sense into my two little brothers," he told Rob, making his status of being at once loved and accepted perfectly clear.

Rob laughed and, after another firm squeeze, dropped his arm and stepped away to allow Sven to embrace his brother. "Thanks for everything, Karl," Sven said with his familiar happy smile. "Give us a call to let us know you made it home safe and sound," he added before letting Karl go and stepping away.

"I will. You take care of yourself, kid," Karl told him.

Sven nodded and then glanced at Rob. "We better get out of the way," he said.

Rob waved to them all as he got into the car.

"I love you," Sven told Karl quietly, and then he, too, waved good-bye and got in the car.

Karl joined Caroline and Melanie on the sidewalk and watched as Sven put the big vehicle in gear and pulled away from the curb. In just a moment, he had merged into the steady stream of traffic and was gone.

"Dad," Melanie said carefully, "why don't we just check in curbside and let them take your bag along with ours?"

Karl turned to look at his daughter and was prepared to object, much preferring the easy-on, easy-off approach to flying, but he held his tongue. Instead, he nodded and followed along behind Caroline and Melanie as they stepped up to the curbside check-in. "Where's Dad's crucifix?" he asked Caroline suddenly.

"Still in my purse, Karl. We didn't forget it," she told him calmly as she patted her large shoulder bag.

Karl nodded and murmured thanks. As she looked at him worriedly, he gave her a smile and patted her shoulder. "The idea we'd forgotten it hit me like a jolt," he admitted.

"It's okay, dear," she reassured him. "We haven't forgotten anything."

Soon, all three of them stood as a group and brandished their IDs as the airline agent ran through the list of preflight questions. After ascertaining that they had packed their own bags, were carrying nothing prohibited, and were not carrying anything for anyone else, the attendant handed them back their IDs along with their boarding passes. "Well, here we go," Karl said as they waited for the automatic doors of the terminal to open in front of them.

As they stepped through, Melanie groused, "This is the part of flying I hate. Getting through security is its own little trip to hell, but waiting at the gate to board is the worst. You're neither here nor there."

"Oh, dear, let's hope the flight isn't delayed, in that event," Caro said evenly.

Karl stepped up to the departures board and confirmed the gate number and time of departure. "Looks like we're okay," he told Caro.

"We won't have that long a wait," he assured Melanie. "I don't imagine we'll have to sit long before they begin boarding. We've cut our timing a little thin."

Melanie gave him a smile and then led the way to security. As they followed along behind her, Karl noted that she had not lost all of the coltishness she had possessed as a teenager. She had inherited his long legs, and as she strode purposefully to the long security lines ahead of them, Karl imagined that she shared his long-legged dread at being corralled when he was ready to move, move, move. Now that the weekend had drawn to an end and his family was in the process of reclaiming their own routines, he wanted nothing more than to be moving toward home.

They passed through security slowly but without a hitch. Each of them surrendered their shoes and bags and miscellaneous accoutrements to the gray bins with the complacency of sheep. Only Karl had to find a bench to become properly shod once they'd reclaimed their belongings. Melanie announced that she wanted a magazine and left them to find a news shop on the concourse. Karl sat on a bench to coax his feet back into his sneakers as Caroline waited patiently. As he stood, Karl again experienced the familiar head rush, which made him pause momentarily and clutch at Caroline's arm.

"Are you okay?" she asked him quietly as his head stopped spinning and the walls became still.

"Lately I've been getting light-headed if I stand too quickly," Karl told her. "I'll call Dr. Harraksingh about it next week. My blood pressure must be low or something."

"That's probably all it is," Caroline said comfortingly. "But it wouldn't be a bad idea to get yourself checked out. How long has it been since your last physical?"

Karl made an annoyed gesture with his free hand and began to walk down the concourse. "Don't start," he warned her.

"I have some other questions I want to ask him, too. Like what the chances are that Mom's dementia is genetic. It wouldn't hurt to find out, for Melanie's sake as well as my own. I forgot to ask Sven about it. But he didn't bring it up, either, so I'm hoping it's not a high probability for us."

Caro nodded but looked determinedly ahead. "I'm not going to be slack about this," she warned.

Karl accepted that with a nod of his head and merged into the concourse traffic with other hurried passengers. When they reached the restrooms, Karl stopped and looked down at Caro. "Do you need a pit stop?"

She looked up at him gratefully and said, "It wouldn't be a bad idea, for both of us."

Karl nodded and said, "I'll meet you back out here."

With that, they separated and Karl made the quick turns into the restroom and to the wall banked with urinals. Once Karl was in place at the urinal and unzipped, his prostate decided to thwart his attempt to urinate. He closed his eyes and tried to picture rushing waterfalls, the sound of a fully opened tap, until finally he was rewarded with a result. Mentally, he added another question for Dr. Harraksingh. He thought of the gloved, probing finger with some dread, but it was a demand of middle age. Finally relieved, he quickly zipped up again and washed his hands. Finding the paper towel holder empty, he rubbed his hands on his jeans and then made his way back out to the throng.

As he stood waiting for Caroline, he watched the people as they passed by. Everyone wore an expression of tension and eager determination; even the children, dragging their own small carry-ons behind them, already wore the heavy concentration of their elders as they made their way to and from the surrounding gates. Only the babies in the strollers seemed to be enjoying themselves, glancing with interest at their surroundings as they rolled serenely along. Karl marveled at the number of people making their way out of southern Florida on a late winter Sunday evening. Everyone had somewhere else they wanted and needed to be. He lived in a nation in constant motion. If anything distinguished Americans, he thought to himself, it was their capacity for restlessness and movement.

"Are you ready?" Caroline asked him, interrupting his reverie.

"Where do you suppose all these people are going?" he asked rhetorically.

Caroline placed her hand on his arm and guided him back into the flow of travelers. "Everywhere and nowhere, sweetheart. Just like us."

They found Melanie waiting for them at the gate, holding two additional seats on the row facing the gate. "Here, Dad," she said as Karl sat next to her. "Switch boarding passes with me so you can sit with Mom. I don't care where I sit."

Karl obliged and eyed her boarding pass. "Do you prefer the window?" he asked Caroline.

"No," she said, drawing a medicine bottle out of her purse. "I'm going to take an Ativan and hopefully sleep all the way home. Would you like one?" Karl thought about it briefly, then held out his palm to receive the tiny white pill. As he popped it in his mouth and dry-swallowed it, he watched as Melanie declined the same offer. "When did you get a prescription for tranquilizers?" Melanie asked her mother.

Caroline laughed as she screwed the lid on the medicine bottle and slipped it back into her purse. "You get one automatically when you are diagnosed with menopause. Believe me, sweetheart, they come in handy, and I'm not ashamed of taking one if I need it."

"No wonder you always seem to have it so together," Melanie teased. "You're high as a kite."

"Not always," Caroline assured her, "but keeping order over a bunch of hormone-crazed teenagers in English class does have its challenges."

"What do you have them reading now?" Karl asked.

"Well, besides the approved survey textbooks, I've got them reading Ian McEwan's *Saturday*," Caroline told him. "It's amazing how seriously they're taking it. The class discussions are very lively."

"That's an interesting choice," Melanie said approvingly. "I wish my high school English teacher had been as challenging."

"I think they like being challenged," Caroline said. "But more than that, I think they like the way I listen to their opinions. It's exciting to watch them open up and articulate what they're getting from the book."

A gate agent stepped to the counter and called for passengers needing special assistance and travelers with small children to begin boarding. Karl glanced at his boarding pass and wistfully recalled his first-class seat on the way down. He was consoled by the Ativan already stealing into his system. In a way, that would be better than a free drink in first class. He realized he'd drunk more in the past few days than he had in months. He wasn't sure he approved of his increased level of alcohol intake as he recalled his father downing shots of scotch.

When their seats were called, Caroline and Karl stood and gave Melanie a sympathetic look. "We'll meet you at the gate at RDU," Karl told her.

Melanie held up her copy of *People* magazine and said, "I'll have all the news about the beautiful people to keep me company. I can't believe I've been so neglectful in keeping up with the state of Jessica Simpson and Nick Lachey's marriage."

Caroline and Karl stepped up to the kiosk and surrendered their boarding passes to be scanned before making their way quickly down the jet ramp and onto the plane. Seated in row nine, they were well forward, and Karl found himself pleased he didn't have to lift his and Caro's bags into the overhead bin. He ducked and got into his seat by the window, and Caro squeezed in next to him. Immediately after buckling up, Caroline looked at him and asked, "Would it annoy you if I put my head on your shoulder when I get sleepy?"

"Of course not," Karl told her with a smile. "What good is a husband without a shoulder to sleep on?"

Caroline gave him a smile before leaning her head back against the headrest and closing her eyes. "I'm afraid I won't be much company on the flight," she said. "I just all of a sudden I feel talked out. I feel like I've been *on* for three days."

"Tell me about it," Karl said sympathetically. "I'm just waiting for the Ativan to kick in so I can let go myself."

Caroline opened her eyes and looked at him lovingly. "You did good, Karl. I've never seen you so empathetic and engaged with your family. But now we can get back to being our normal self-absorbed selves."

"Thanks for noticing, Caroline. I really surprised myself," Karl said quietly. "I admit there were times when I wanted to hold up my hands and say, 'Boundaries, people. Boundaries!' But this wasn't a weekend to hold any of them at arm's length. I think they really needed me this weekend. I hope I was there for them."

"You were, and more," Caroline assured him. "But I have to admit, it was intense."

Karl chuckled in agreement and turned to look out his window. The rampers busily went about their purposeful tasks as the last of the sunshine turned the airport's landscape vividly pink and orange in the level light. Karl turned from the scene in time to see Melanie making her way past, heading to the rear of the plane. They exchanged little waves before she moved on.

Karl closed his eyes and laid his head back against the headrest. The tiny white pill was potent and fast. Karl could feel himself relaxing all over. It was not unlike the sensation he'd felt after communion that morning at mass, but the pill promised a deeper and longer-lasting cessation from his tension and anxiety. Karl kept his eyes closed as the flight attendant made her way down the aisle, loudly closing the overhead bins. Not long after that, he felt the jolt and slow movement backwards as the big plane was pushed away from the gate. Karl heard the engines rev up and pull the jet forward toward the runway, but he elected to keep his eyes closed and ignore the flight attendants' pantomime of seat belt fastening and oxygen mask adjustment. The captain's voice penetrated Karl's dwindling consciousness with a cheerful welcome and announcement of weather and anticipated arrival times.

Karl had made this flight many times in years past. Now, more than ever before, he was aware of exactly what he was leaving behind as the plane accelerated and lifted him back toward home. His southern Florida role of son and brother had been only a small part of his life. The fact that the role he had relegated to Boca Raton had now burgeoned and would require more consideration in his life in Cary was bearable under the pill's spell. How it would be twisted and adapted to in reality remained to be seen, but Karl was relieved to feel he had the capacity to adjust.

He thought of his mother, bravely walking the streets of the old neighborhood as it changed, with new faces and stories that no longer captivated her or held her interest. She had seen out the lives of the original residents of those homes, and she didn't have the capacity to absorb the lives of their replacements. What she had remaining from forty years of living in Boca Raton was only herself. Annike was determined to remain herself, though soon her self would be a reduction—a distillation, really—of who she had been before. Without much fuss, his mother had hugged him good-bye and left him with a no-nonsense answer to his questions of how he was supposed to act. It was no different than when she had packed him off to kindergarten or college. He knew he was loved, but he also knew what was expected of him. While his mother might be leaving him before she was really gone, she had made it alright, just as she'd kissed his skinned knees, and later soothed his abraded heart when early crushes had instructed him in the first lessons of love lost. Reflecting on her last good-bye now, he could not fault her for anything she'd said in freeing him from responsibility and guilt.

Karl's thoughts turned to his father. Like Annike, Frank had made it easy for Karl to walk away and reclaim his own life, despite the diminution of his father's vitality. Karl saw him in his beloved backyard, mourning the debilitation of his friendly orange trees. They had outlived their fruitfulness, yet Frank couldn't have them cut down and hauled away. He still tended them as if they were at the height of vigor, though they needed little more than rain and sunshine. Likewise, his father had asked him for nothing more than the occasional pleasure of his company.

By moving himself and Annike to Palladian Gardens, Frank had provided for them as he always had, making even the end as practically deliberate and efficient as his life had always been. Frank promised no unseemliness of need or emotion. He would die as self-contained as he'd lived. It was just a matter of Karl providing a comforting bit of company along the wait. All Frank required from Karl was a dependable reflection of his own former strength.

Karl's thoughts turned to Sven. The grown man remained in many ways the skinny little boy Karl had held and tossed like a golden dolphin to flash in the sunshine before diving into the sea. Karl realized that no matter how old they became, he would always remain Sven's big brother. It had been a pleasure to discover Sven still held him in the esteem and with the love he'd had as a child. Karl had never recognized Sven's loss as he'd left him behind to stride into his larger world. Sven had missed him as the years went by, and Karl had relegated him to the status of a fond plaything left on a shelf as the teenager became a man. It was only now that Karl realized his honest tolerance and mild interest in his brother had managed to sustain a love forged much earlier, when he'd played a larger role in his brother's life. He'd never given any thought to the notion that his opinions still had the power to inspire and guide his little brother. Yet over the weekend, Sven had managed to move from the periphery of Karl's concern to a closer state of connection. While he naturally loved the brother, it felt to Karl like an unexpected gift to find he liked the man his brother had become.

As the jet cruised along, Karl dozed, thinking of these things. While he had flown down anticipating his family as a set of obligations, he had found them to be more obliged to him than the other way around. He was, as Sven pointed out, the one who got to grow up and go away. Karl had lived extricated from the daily routine familiarity with his parents and brother. They had no chance to make demands of him when he was physically and emotionally distant enough to preclude any expectations.

Yet the bonds between them all were real. Karl realized he had done them a disservice by expecting them to be like the hastily dressed mother and son that shouted in the street under his window on Thursday morning. Frank, Annike, and Sven were knit of the same stuff that made Karl, he realized now. In the emotional hothouse of his four days at home, with its disturbing revelations and comforting connections, Karl found himself enhanced by their interaction, not diminished, as he'd fully expected to be. As he flew home, he carried them still. There was no sense of letting them go, only the recognition that they were a part of the warp and weft of his life. While the future would require his attention to each of them in different ways, it wasn't a future that seemed weighty and hard to carry. His family was all of a piece with who he was.

In his deeply relaxed state, Karl's thoughts turned to revisit the landscape of his early-morning dream. He wondered if such a beach really existed. He had no immediate recollection of a bridge that led out over the ocean so clearly leaving a beach. Certainly not one that required a lifeguard's chair to watch over swimmers. Though his chosen profession had made him familiar with many bridges, most took their departure from land in isolated places, not beaches, and certainly not a beach with a lifeguard tower. No, his dreamscape must have its place in reality on some island, but he had no island ready on which to locate it.

But now, seeing once more that humid light as he remembered the dream scene, Karl was again aware of the possibilities of the place. It was a young man's beach. That he found himself there at fifty-two, renewed in vigor and vitality, with every assurance of physical and intellectual fulfillment, represented his own resistance to growing older. While he was realistic about his age and its wear and tear on his body and spirit, that he could still find that beach in his dream and stand on it with a younger man's enthusiasms and desires was his assurance that he would not face his father's future. Karl felt like he would never come to believe he was irrelevant. Instead, he felt the fulfillment of his mother's promise in his name. Karl felt strong, and he felt up to the challenges of growing older. In the course of four days he had both regained and lost some of his most closely held beliefs about family. The weekend in Boca Raton had left him with family relationships he knew he could sustain. It was beyond any doubt. He still had the fulfillment of many possibilities to look forward to. He needn't go looking for the dream; the dream found him and sustained him with a growing sense of who he was.

Karl was smiling to himself when the plane's wheels skidded along the runway at RDU. He eagerly looked out the window as the lights of the runway and terminal flew past. He was almost home. Caroline lifted her head from his shoulder, and he looked into her drowsy, questioning eyes. "We've landed," he said gently.

Caroline smiled and reached to brush away at the dampness she'd left on his shoulder. "That went fast," she said as she stretched within the confines of her seat.

"I think you slept all the way," Karl told her. "Now I'm dying for a cup of coffee."

"Oh, that sounds good," she said as she bent to look out the window. "Are you hungry at all?"

"Not really," Karl told her as the plane began a slow, sharp turn back toward the terminal. "I'd be happy with a scrambled-egg sandwich later on."

"I can do that," Caroline said evenly. "Now I'm just ready to be home."

"Me, too," Karl told her honestly.

•

Within the hour, Melanie turned the car onto Belgravia Street and drove much faster than Karl would have preferred. He didn't say anything to his daughter, however, because he could sense in her speed the urge to be back at the town house, which he felt, too. In the early evening, the street was deserted. All of the neighbors had withdrawn into their houses, and lights filled the second-floor living rooms in a line of warmth and welcome. When they pulled into their own drive, Karl noted that the lamp in their own living room window, set on a timer, was lit and waiting for them. It was warming to find the town house ready for their return.

Melanie left the car in the drive, and they all stepped out into the streetlight's glow. With choreographed efficiency, Melanie marched to the trunk of the car and pulled out their carry-on bags while Caroline walked up the steps and unlocked and opened the front door. Karl carried Caroline's bag and his own up the steps and over the spill of mail waiting on the foyer floor. He walked past Caroline and climbed the stairs to their bedroom. The familiar squeaky step made Karl smile. Surrounded by his own walls and the scents of home, he laid the suitcases on the bed and unzipped his own. He wanted the Tynnigo candle.

After a quick search through his clothes, Karl found the box holding the candle. He tore off the plastic sheathing and opened the box to pull the candle out. It rested heavily in his hand, and he held it to his nose and breathed in deeply. The scent was even more pronounced here at home than it had been in Sven's store. He left the wrapping where it fell along with the box and walked back downstairs to show Caroline.

She wasn't in the living room or the kitchen. "Caro!" he called. "Come here, I want to show you something. Where are you?"

"I'm in here," Caroline said from the foyer.

Karl stepped from the living room into the foyer and watched as Caroline took down a small, framed watercolor that hung by the front door and placed it carefully on top of the foyer table. Without looking at Karl, she picked up her purse from the table and drew out his father's crucifix. She took a moment to dust it with a Kleenex from her purse before she hung the crucifix from the nail. Once she had it hung and straightened with a gentle nudge of her finger, she looked back at Karl and smiled. "It fits perfectly," she said.

Karl looked at the crucifix hanging there, and an image of his father's foyer filled his mind briefly. The crucifix did indeed look as if it had been meant to hang by his own front door. "Thanks, Caro," he said.

Unexpectedly, Caroline crossed herself and stepped away. She came to stand by Karl's side and said, "I'll take all the blessings I can get."

Hesitantly, Karl switched the candle in his right hand to his left and crossed himself as well. Then he looked at Caroline and held out the candle. "Smell this," he said.

Caroline took the candle and sniffed it, then followed with a strong inhalation of its scent. "It's lovely," she told him before she looked at the label. "Tynnigo?" she asked.

Karl took the candle from her hand and said, "It's the name of the island my grandmother retired to. It also happens to be the name of

Sven's store. He has these made by some old guy outside Paris. It smells exactly like the island," Karl told her excitedly. "He gave it to me."

"Well, let's bring it into the kitchen and light it while I make some coffee," Caroline said as she took his free hand to lead him from the foyer.

Karl followed along with her to the kitchen and placed the candle on the table. As Caroline made coffee, he searched the junk drawer for a book of matches, then he lit the candle and moved it to the center of the table. "Sven's shop is pretty amazing," he told Caroline, "but I'm glad you didn't go. I saw a settee there that you would have loved for your office, but it was nearly five thousand dollars."

"Oh, my God," Caroline said as she carefully measured coffee. "Was everything so expensive?"

"Proportionately, I'd say yes. This candle was marked fifty-two dollars," Karl told her.

"I can't believe you paid that much for a candle," Caro said as she switched on the coffeemaker and joined him at the kitchen table. Before she sat down, she leaned over the candle and took another deep smell of its unique scent. "But if you did, I think it's worth it."

"No, Sven gave it to me," Karl told her again. "Sven told me to let him know when it burns down, and he'll ship me more. He was so pleased I recognized the scent and appreciated what it meant."

"He really craves your approval, you know that?" Caroline asked him.

"Yes," Karl admitted, "and I'm going to make it a point to start letting him know he has it."

"He and Rob are pretty special," Caroline said. "I wish they lived closer by. I think they'd make great friends."

"I do, too," Karl told her. "But no matter where they live, I want to make them a larger part of our lives," he added with conviction.

"I'm glad," Caroline told him. "It seems like you found your family again."

Karl sighed and watched the candle flame. "I never really lost them—it's just that this weekend reminded me I do have a family, and they're pretty wonderful people."

"Are you reconciled to what's happening to your mom?" Caroline asked gently.

Karl looked at her a moment before he said, "That's going to take some getting used to, but she did her best to free me from worry and grief. My mom is pretty remarkable."

"And what about your father?"

"Oh, Dad and I are going to be fine," Karl told her. "We're enough alike that I can trust my instincts on how to take care of him to the extent he needs to be taken care of," Karl said confidently.

"This visit home wasn't what you expected at all, was it?" Caroline pressed.

"No," Karl admitted. "But I wasn't who I expected myself to be, either."

"In what way?"

"I came home feeling better about a lot of things, including myself," Karl answered. "Sometimes the answers are just inspired in unexpected ways. Don't ask me to explain it—I can't. It's like waking up with the solution to a design issue clear in my mind. Sometimes, I just have to reach for it and it's there."

"That's what I love about you." Caroline smiled as she stood. "Your inexplicable Apollonian moments of inspiration. Your *coup de foudre*. I've learned to trust it over the years. It's good to know you trust yourself."

"Where are you going?" Karl asked as she moved away from the table.

"To tell Melanie there's coffee," Caroline answered. "And to get my chocolate that Sven gave me."

"I need to call Dad and Sven to let them know we're home safe," Karl said.

"You do that, and I'll be back shortly," Caroline told him as she strode away.

Karl stood, meaning to walk to the wall phone in the kitchen, but instead he opened the back door and walked out onto the deck in the chilly, dark night. He felt a deep happiness at being back home, as well as an unexpected eagerness to get back to work the following day. It was either a result of having been away or a gift of his dream beachscape, but he felt there was nothing he couldn't do. Some night bird tittered in the darkness, and Karl looked up past the row of town houses across the common area to gaze at the sky. The stars suspended overhead sharply glinted in the cold air. He noticed that two were moving toward each other. As he stared, he could make out wing lights on each bright point of light—it was two planes flying in opposite directions. He watched as they passed each other. Everything was moving, he thought. He felt lucky he'd had a chance to see just how unimaginably fast everyone he loved was moving as well.